The Last Enemy

The Last Enemy

GRACE BROPHY

Published by
Soho Press, Inc.
853 Broadway
New York, NY 10003

Library of Congress Cataloging-in-Publication Data

Brophy, Grace,
The Last Enemy/ Grace Brophy
p.cm.–(Soho Crime)
ISBN-13: 978-1-56947-496-9
1. Americans–Italy–Fiction. I. Title

PS3602.R6463L37 2007   2006052206
813'.6–dc22

10   9   8   7   6   5   4   3   2   1

For my husband Miguel Peraza
Poeta che mi guidi

And in loving memory of my parents,
William and Mary Brophy

Author's Note

THE CITY OF Assisi, the birthplace of St. Francis and a sanctuary of love, peace, and spirituality, is the least likely setting for
a story of betrayal and murder that begins on Good Friday, the
holiest day in the Christian calendar. But as Dorothy Sayers
wrote in her disclaimer to *Gaudy Night*, writers of murder mysteries "are obliged by their disagreeable profession to invent
startling and unpleasant incidents and people." It is important, therefore, that I affirm that all events and characters in this
story, unpleasant, startling, or otherwise, are entirely my own
invention. As well, some of the history and dates, institutions,
and place names, including Baranj in Bosnia, St. Andrew's in
Newfoundland, and the count's language school in Assisi, were
created out of whole cloth or reshuffled for dramatic purposes.

The last enemy that shall be destroyed is death.
Novissima autem inimica detruetur mors.
1 Corinthians 15:26.

Contents

Prologue

RITA MINELLI WAS devoted to Saint Rita. When she was a very young child, she'd prayed to Saint Rita to make her mother love her. In high school, she prayed that she would be asked to join a sorority. When those prayers weren't answered, she prayed for Michael O'Brien to invite her to the senior prom. He didn't, but Rita doubted that her mother would have let her go anyway. Her mother didn't like the Irish. "They drink," she said.

Not all of Rita's prayers went unanswered. She was accepted to Barnard College, an answer to one of her more fervent prayers, but her father died the summer that she graduated from high school and her mother said there was little enough money to pay for household expenses, let alone to send Rita to an expensive private college. Rita thought that if her mother gave up smoking four packages of cigarettes a day, the savings, together with her Regent's Scholarship, would go a long way toward paying the tuition, but she was ashamed of her rebellious thought and it went unuttered. She attended Brooklyn College, more devoted than ever to Saint Rita.

She was twenty-two when she graduated from Brooklyn College in 1979. Between graduation and the age of forty-four, when her mother died of lung cancer, Rita's life was uneventful. She taught English at Erasmus, a Brooklyn high school, went to the occasional movie with one of her unmarried women friends, and very infrequently went into Manhattan for dinner and a show. She was asked out a few times by a fellow teacher. He seemed interested, but her mother didn't like him, even though he wasn't Irish. It came to nothing in the end, and he married the Spanish teacher whose homeroom was across from his.

When her mother died, Rita called her father's only living relative, a married sister living in Vineland, New Jersey. Her Aunt Marie said traveling to Brooklyn for the funeral was too long a trip. She sent a mass card instead, a large one with gold engraving and her mother's name written in script. Rita also called her mother's younger brother, Umberto, in Italy. He told her it was a bad time of year for an academic; he had lectures and exams scheduled for the coming week. He held the Chair of Modern Languages at the University of Perugia, and Rita had to acknowledge that his work in promoting the Italian language was too important to drop at a moment's notice. Umberto didn't send a fancy mass card, but he did agree to let Rita bury her mother in the family vault in Assisi after Rita told him that this had been her mother's dying wish. Her father, Salvatore, had been buried with his parents in St. Anne's cemetery in Brooklyn. Livia, her mother, had rarely slept with Salvatore in life. It made no sense to change this arrangement in death.

Rita's parents had met in Assisi in 1946, at the end of World War II. Salvatore, a first lieutenant in the American Army, was employed by the American occupation forces to monitor the referendum that was to decide Italy's future. He noticed Livia Casati as soon as she had joined the voting line. It was the first time that Italian women could vote, and only a small number had showed up at the polls. She stuck out from the rest, not only because she was taller, but because of her bearing. Like a queen, he thought. Her clothes were newer than those of the other women in line, and although it was a warm spring day, she wore a fur jacket. He could tell that she was a snob from her carriage and by the way she avoided physical contact with the others. But he didn't mind. He enjoyed looking at her. Once he caught her eye and winked, but she looked away.

Until she joined the line, the voting had been peaceful. Then an old woman, shabbily dressed in a man's oversized wool coat, started talking in a loud voice, "It's time for them to go, them that think they're better than the rest of us."

Some women in the line nodded in agreement but most stared straight ahead.

The old woman spoke even louder the second time, "We'll take care of the Mussolini lovers." She looked straight at the woman in fur and told her, "There's plenty of rope left for the likes of you."

The newcomer flushed a deep crimson and her posture became even more rigid. At first the soldier thought she would reply, but she broke from the line and hurried away. On impulse, he ran after her. When he caught up with her, her eyes were bright with tears.

He grabbed her hand. "Don't mind her; she's an old fool. Please come back. I'll put you at the head of the line."

"I don't care who wins! I hate them all!" she replied. Two large tears rolled down her cheeks but she left her hand in his.

They were married three months later. They would have wed sooner but she had to be vetted by the American Army. His commanding officer was reluctant to approve the marriage. He told Salvatore of Livia's father's prominence in the Fascist party, that the man had been killed by a bomb meant for Mussolini. And because he liked the young lieutenant, he pointed out with some delicacy the differences in their social class. Livia Casati's young brother was a count; her family were members of the Italian aristocracy. Did he think that the daughter of a count could be happy in Brooklyn married to a high school mathematics teacher? But Salvatore refused to take *no* for an answer. He loved Livia and knew that he would make her happy.

The Casati family were more adamant than the American army. Livia's mother and brother refused to attend the wedding. Her brother Umberto, only fifteen at the time, tried to forbid the reading of the banns, but Livia was twenty-two and there were no impediments beyond the family's outrage. It was ten years before Livia and her mother were reconciled. The birth of Rita, and time and distance, effected the reconciliation.

Livia returned to Assisi only once after that, when Rita was five years old. They stayed for a year and Livia hoped it would be forever. Although Rita missed her father, it was the happiest year of her life. Her grandmother gave her the affection she had always craved from her mother. But hers was a short-lived happiness. Her cousin Camillo was born at the end of the year, and her grandmother transferred her affections to her grandson, the future Count Casati. She no longer had time for little Rita. Shortly afterward, Rita's father arrived in Assisi to reclaim his wife and daughter. They returned to Brooklyn, Livia more bitter than ever, and Rita with a new prayer to St. Rita: that one day she would return to Assisi.

Livia's wake, held in Brooklyn, lasted for two days and two nights. A few of Rita's friends and colleagues attended, as well as the new neighbors from next door. The other neighbors, the ones who had known Livia, stayed away. It took twelve days to make the arrangements for shipping her mother's body to Assisi, and Rita was very busy during that time. She put the house up for sale, at a bargain price, closed her savings account at Brooklyn Dime, and had the bank manager issue her a certified check. She notified Social Security of her mother's death, called her high school to say she would not return in September, and sold all the household furniture and knickknacks, including her mother's collection of majolica and Venetian glass, to Harry, the antique dealer on Ocean Parkway. He gave her $3,500 for the lot. A week before she was to fly to Assisi, she visited Manhattan for the first time in four years. She spent all but three hundred dollars of Harry's money on new clothes. With what was left, she had dinner in a Spanish restaurant on Eighth Avenue. She took a taxi home to Canarsie later that night, something she had never done before.

Rita's new life started the day they interred her mother in the family vault in Assisi. She had no intention of returning to Brooklyn, although she had neglected to mention this to her uncle or to his wife. In addition to his teaching position at the University of Perugia, the count headed a language school in Assisi that catered primarily to the priests and nuns who came to Italy to study and pray. When one of his English teachers, a woman from Liverpool, gave notice the day before the summer session was to start, Rita volunteered to teach the course in her stead. When it turned out that someone was needed to organize a school trip to Florence, she volunteered for that as well. One night when the family was attending an art exhibit in Perugia, Rita moved her clothes from the small maid's room in the attics to her grandmother's bedroom, which was still empty two years after her death. She explained to her family when they returned later that evening that she had spent many happy hours there as a child. In early September, the countess casually inquired when classes would begin at Erasmus. The count was more direct. He asked when exactly she was going home. "I'm not returning to Brooklyn," Rita announced defiantly. "Assisi is my home."

The Last Enemy

Book One

Waiting for Rita

I

A ROUGH WIND lifted the decaying leaves that lay in front of the burial chamber and sent them swirling through the iron gates that separate the living from the dead. Two figures occupied the chamber's narrow inner space. The first, a woman, lay face up, her head resting on a stone altar step. One of the leaves had lodged in her hair. The second figure, enveloped in the cloak and hood of a pilgrim, bent and reverently removed the leaf. The woman gazed upward at the intruder, as though pleading for mercy or forgiveness, and the figure knelt and applied a firm pressure to the woman's open lids, sealing her eyes in the first ritual of death. A sudden noise disturbed the stillness of the night, causing the cloaked figure to look up, but it was only the cooing of a pigeon. The figure then made the sign of the cross over the woman and whispered a benediction in Latin before proceeding to raise her skirt. The woman was dressed for enticement and her stockings, of black lace, had etched a deep red welt in her firm white thighs. The cloaked figure unhooked the garters and gently eased the stockings down the still-warm legs, exposing the woman's dead flesh to the frigid night air. The pigeon, nesting for the night, cooed again, but the intruder was too intent to hear.

2

IT WAS LATE March, crisp and cold, with the smell of snow in
the night air. Those who stood on the steps of the Bar Sensi
waiting for the procession of the cross to pass were shivering
with cold. Some had ordered red wine or grappa to warm
them. But the Casatis were traditionalists. They would wait to
have their wine—a good French Chardonnay—and mandatory
fish dinner later in the evening.

Viewing the Good Friday procession together as a family was
a Casati ritual. For the first few hundred years, they had viewed
it from the portico of their home on via San Francisco. (The
family had been resident in Assisi since the Fourth Crusade.)
For the past thirty years, they had viewed it in the Piazza del
Comune and from there gone to dine with family and friends
at a local restaurant. Five of them were gathered together that
evening: Count Umberto Casati, Amelia Casati, his English-
born wife, their daughter Artemisia, their son's daughter Paola,
and John Williams, a Canadian cartographer. They were waiting for a sixth. Rita Minelli, the count's niece, was missing.

"Perhaps we should go back to the house to see if she's all
right? You know how devout she is," the countess whispered to
her husband. "She won't want to miss this."

"Leave well enough alone," the count replied sharply. "Let's
have at least one evening free of her simpering platitudes."

He spoke louder than he'd intended and Amelia quickly
glanced around, hoping that John Williams hadn't overheard. "He's right behind us. He may have heard you," she
murmured.

"Good," the count responded. "Perhaps he'll get the hint and
leave. Who gave her permission to invite him, anyway?" He
looked at his wife accusingly.

"I couldn't refuse when she asked. If I had, she would have

come alone and made it evident to everyone that she's the despised relative. I did my best in a difficult situation."

The count was only half-listening to his wife's excuse. He'd just heard the distant drumroll from below, an indication that the procession was fast approaching the Piazza. Two men moved quickly through the Piazza, filling and lighting the cressets that adorned every public building in Assisi. Soon the electric lights in the Piazza would be extinguished. The evening stars and the flicker of flames from the cressets would serve as the only guides to those carrying the crosses symbolizing the passion and death of Christ.

Umberto had carried one of those crosses when he was only twelve. The Franciscans had wanted to cancel the procession that year. "The war has caused enough suffering," they'd told his father. "The people don't need further reminders. And where will we find the young men to carry the crosses?"

His father, who was head of the Fascist party in Assisi, viewed the procession as emblematic of Italy's great strength, its ability to observe its rituals despite the hardships of war. He volunteered his son. Although still too young to wear the black shirt, Umberto could don the white robe of a cross-bearer.

Most of the other processionists that year were elderly, former cross-bearers who had volunteered to replace the young men who'd been sent to war. One of them, a pensioner of his father's, had offered Umberto a folded towel as padding for his shoulder while they were dressing. "The cross bites into your skin," he said. Umberto had rejected the offering.

When they'd first exited the Basilica, the drumroll, one long beat and two short, had invigorated young Umberto. He had fasted all day and his dinner was waiting; he was impatient to get to the bottom of via San Francisco to begin the ascent to via Portica and the Cathedral of San Rufino. He soon realized how foolish he'd been to reject Pietro's towel and the reason for the other processionists' deliberate pace. The cross, a minor burden when he had first assumed it in the Basilica, grew in size and weight with each step. He could feel the rough wood biting through the cheap cotton of his robe; he was sure he had a splinter in his shoulder. He had tripped twice on the long robe, the hood obscured his vision, and his feet were raw from the cobblestones that bruised his tender unshod flesh. The unvarying drumroll was maddening.

He never again participated in the Good Friday procession. The memory of that night in 1943 would suffice him for eternity.

His wife could tell by the frozen look on Umberto's face that he was not listening to her. He rarely did. Good Friday was always difficult. She couldn't understand why he insisted on punishing himself by watching the procession each year. She knew he had dropped out once when he was only a boy, before the procession had reached the cathedral. For most people this would have been a minor failure; for Umberto it had assumed the proportions of a tragedy.

Looking at her husband by the light of the cressets, she could see how little he had changed in the years since they'd married. He was still strikingly handsome. His black hair, once worn long in the fashion popular at the University of Perugia, was now gray and cut close to his head, but it was still ample for a man of seventy-one. He stooped a little now, but other women still looked at her with envy when they appeared together in public.

I still love him, she thought with some surprise. He's demanding, arrogant, and most of the time not very likeable, but when has love been rational? She'd blamed her husband for alienating Camillo, their only son, and when Camillo died, she'd blamed him for his death. But despite his own loss, and Amelia knew it was great—the title would now die with him and family name and honor were paramount to Umberto—he had held her in his arms every night for five months, sometimes through the night, when she was in despair and spoke of killing herself. I love him, Amelia acknowledged to herself. And now more than ever, he needs me.

Artemisia Casati watched her mother watching her father. I'm still outside their circle, she thought, and blamed her mother for excluding her. She couldn't remember ever having loved her mother, not even when she was a young child. Marie, their maid, had fed, washed, dressed, and loved her, had supplied all her physical and emotional needs for the first ten years of her life. She supposed that she had loved Marie in return. She had certainly cried when Marie left, the day after her tenth birthday, to return to Sicily. Her father's response to Artemisia's tears was that she was too old for pampering, but Artemisia knew it was her mother's decision that had sent Marie to Sicily and her to boarding school in England.

She leaned against one of the portico's pillars, the darkness creating a wall of privacy between herself and the others. The muffled drum acted as a prompt to her memory. She remembered exactly the day and hour when her father had first really noticed her. It had been the Good Friday after her brother's death. Artemisia had volunteered that year to carry the cross that Camillo had carried in previous processions—begged, in fact, since no woman had yet carried one of the crosses. It wasn't until Good Friday morning that Artemisia told her parents that she would be one of the processionists that year. When she took the cross in her grasp, the look of pride on her father's face provided her first moment's assurance that she was loved, perhaps had been loved all along.

Artemisia did not repeat her father's failure. Tall, athletic, and a Jesuit in temperament, she'd planned with care to

ensure her success. She had practiced carrying the cross in
the cloisters during those long winter twilight hours when
only the Franciscans had access to the Basilica. The robe,
made especially for her, had shoulder and torso padding
built in.

She had grown close to her father since that day seventeen
years ago. He had helped with her career, discussed art with
her, and introduced her to the right people in the Italian art
world. Her first job, as an assistant curator at the National
Gallery of Umbria, had come through his influence. Last week,
the count had called her into his library to tell her the news:
She was front-runner to become the new director of the
Umbrian National Gallery.

Her recently published book, *A Woman's Art*, had received
international acclaim. Without this achievement, she wouldn't
even be a candidate. But Artemisia also knew the Italian art
world and acknowledged to herself that her father's influence
had made the difference. She smiled with some satisfaction at
the thought that not only would she be the Gallery's first
woman director but, at thirty-seven, the youngest director of a
regional art museum in Italy.

Her mother's overloud whisper directed at Artemisia, but
probably overheard by everyone on the steps, brought her
out of her reverie.

"Do you have any idea where Rita is?" Amelia asked. "When
we left the house, I thought she was in her room dressing and
was going to come later with you and Paola."

Artemisia shrugged her shoulders. "No idea. I walked here
by myself. Ask Paola," she responded, showing no particular
concern. She hadn't told anyone about Rita's visit to her room
earlier that day, certainly not her mother.

It was too late, however, for further questions. The lone
drummer had reached the crescent of via Portica and could

be seen entering the Piazza. A drumbeat reverberated through the Piazza and through history. The drummer passed the Piazza del Populo, where noblemen from the upper town had fed pork stuffed with human remains to their enemies in the lower town. He passed the Torre del Populo, where an Assisi barber was rumored to have murdered his cuckolding wife by throwing her from the tower. He passed the Temple of Minerva, whose steps had been consecrated first by Roman and then by Christian zealots with the blood of their enemies.

The mournful beat of the drum moving ever closer had also reminded Paola of previous Good Fridays. She hated the ritual of the Good Friday procession, and for most of her teen years she had managed to avoid it by sneaking out of the house to meet her friends. But no matter where they went in Assisi, they could still hear the lamentations of the drum. Her high school boyfriend had devised a contest: See who can inhale and hold it for the full drumroll. They were smoking pot, and it was no small feat to keep the smoke down for the full ten seconds. She usually arrived home and was in bed, feigning sleep, before her grandparents returned from their precious dinner and their pretentious friends.

This year Paola was in Assisi on sufferance and had decided that accommodation might be the wiser course of action. Orlando, the bar's manager and an old friend, had found her a spot in the corner of the portico, immediately outside and to the left of the bar door. He'd even found her a chair so that she—a slight five-foot-two-inches tall—was well hidden seated among a standing crowd of German and English tourists. In the twenty minutes that they had been waiting for the procession to reach the Piazza, she had smoked a half package of cigarettes, nervously lighting each new cigarette from the previous one before stamping it out on the cement floor.

She'd always found it hard to concentrate when she had an important decision to make. In the past, she had let the decisions make themselves, generally following whatever person or idea seemed strongest at the moment. It was different this time. She knew that whatever decision she reached, its consequences would affect her for the rest of her life. She had desperately needed someone to turn to. God help me, she thought, why did I choose Rita?

It was John Williams's first Good Friday in Assisi, yet perhaps more than other onlookers, he understood the need of the cross-bearers to lessen their future purgatorial torment through an imaginative recreation of the torment of Jesus. Rita had repeatedly urged him to join the processionists this year and had even asked permission on his behalf, but in that, at least, he had resisted. He and Paola were both suffering from the effects of too much Rita.

He had arrived in Assisi in early December and had met Rita as their fingers touched in the holy water font after mass at San Stefano's, on the Sunday before Christmas. She had approached him outside, smiling, hand extended. "You're new here," she said in English. "I saw you a few days ago buying meat at the butcher; you left your guidebook on the counter. I called after you, but I don't think you heard me! How is your Italian coming? Please don't think I'm meddling, but I'd noticed that you had trouble ordering your groceries. I teach at a language school here in Assisi. Most of our students leave after three months speaking basic Italian. I teach English there. It's obvious you don't need my course. You're Canadian, aren't you? I could tell by your accent."

She was right about his need to learn Italian. He had always been a loner and had believed himself to be self-sufficient. He hadn't realized until he arrived in Assisi how much comfort and human interaction there is in the simple act of buying groceries or of ordering a meal in a restaurant. In Assisi, he was cut off from the comfort of shared language. The tradespeople smiled politely when he tried talking to them. At least Rita talked back.

They met the next day for coffee and every day after that. She became his guide and interpreter. She told him where to buy groceries, which restaurants offered good value, which coffee bars to frequent. She had even helped him to find an inexpensive apartment. He had complained of the cold, and for Christmas she had given him a cashmere scarf. She had hinted that they should spend New Year's Eve together. When he didn't respond, she had asked directly. "I won't take no for an answer," she had said.

His headaches had grown more frequent since the New Year. The nightmare that had haunted him since adolescence had assumed a different, more menacing shape. The hooded figure that lurked in every dark corner of his sleep had turned into a woman. She loomed over him, her breasts foul with the smell of fetid milk, urging him to drink. The nightmare had become even more persistent in the last week, the hour after waking more terrifying. He thought often of Addison's dying words, "See in what peace a Christian can die." If he could choose death he would, but without redemption, dying would bring no peace. He knew better than most that for those who shed innocent blood, there is no redemption.

They were still waiting for Rita, but the procession moved inexorably on, pausing for no one, through the Piazza del Comune and up via San Rufino, each drumroll a call to those seeking salvation to remember the passion of Christ, to seek forgiveness in his death. In their demonstration of faith, the processionists were indistinguishable from one another. They had shed the outward signs of age, wealth, and gender when they donned their robes in the Basilica and took up their crosses. Some of the onlookers would later claim that Rita had been among them, that she was the one who had stumbled as they climbed toward San Rufino.

Book Two

O death, where is thy sting?

I

IT WAS EARLY morning and Sergeant Genine Antolini was thinking about chocolate while waiting for her replacement to appear. Genine was always thinking about chocolate—éclairs, cornetti with dark chocolate filling, and her favorite, Baci creams. Just thinking about the moist fudge center of a Baci with its nut topping had her salivating. Like most people, Genine had a number of bad habits but she publicly acknowledged only one, an incessant craving for chocolate. It was Lent and Genine had restricted her chocolate intake to one café marocchino a day. But tomorrow was Easter Sunday, Lent would be over, and Chocolate Heaven awaited. As soon as her replacement signed in (Franco was late as usual), Genine would stop at the Bar Sensi for a café marocchino and then catch the bus to Santa Maria degli Angeli and home.

It had been a long night. Only two tourists from New York, lost and looking for their hotel, had set foot in the station. And one telephone call, a complaint from the Sisters of the Redemption that Giuseppe Guido, drunk as usual, was camped out in front of San Ruffino, cadging contributions from the tourists leaving Good Friday services. Giuseppe had been delivered to his mother's house on via Metastasio and the New Yorkers had been sent on their way with a map of Assisi, their hotel clearly marked in red. Genine wondered how any one could get lost in Assisi, a town of fewer than twenty main streets. But with its warren of winding alleys, hidden squares, and steep cobbled stairways, Assisi was a world away from the straightforward grid of Manhattan streets.

Good Friday is always slow in Assisi. The citizens of Assisi, if one excepts the nuns and priests living there, are no more religious than most Italians; the men and younger women leave churchgoing and godly intercession to their mothers and grandmothers. They prefer the footballs fields or the Collestrada mall, with its boutiques and fast food shops, for hanging out. But Good Friday is the most sacred of holy days in Catholicism, particularly in Assisi, rooted as it is in the legend of Saint Francis, *il piu santo dei santi*. The teenagers from Santa Maria degli Angeli, who normally liked to congregate in the Piazza Santa Chiara on Friday night, boisterous and happy, playing their boomboxes way too loud for Assisi's more sedate residents, were at home with their families. The Irish pub in Piazza Matteotti at the top of the town, generally good for a few disturbances on a Friday night, was closed, its owner back in Dublin for the holidays.

The noise of the outer door opening stopped Genine's musings. Franco had finally arrived, no doubt direct from a night of salsa dancing in Perugia. She was surprised when instead of Franco, she saw two women, both laden with baskets of flowers, standing in the doorway. She recognized the older woman at once: Sophie Orlic, a Croatian and something of a troublemaker. She knew the other woman too: a girl actually, of about nineteen, though not by name. She had passed her many times on Corso Mazzini wheeling her newborn—a sweet doe-eyed infant daughter—Genine recalled. She knew from their faces that this was serious. The younger woman had been crying and her legs were buckling as she approached the desk. The Croatian was also visibly upset, her face flushed, her breathing heavy, as though she had been running. Genine motioned them both to a bench along the wall and hurried from behind the desk.

The older woman spoke in concise, stilted Italian. "We were arranging flowers in the cemetery for Easter. We found a dead woman in one of the vaults."

"Was it someone you recognized?" Genine asked.

"It's the American." Sophie paused a moment before speaking again. "Rita Minelli."

The younger woman started to cry, and her tears spilled down unrestrained onto her coat and into the basket of flowers at her feet. Orlic, who in their previous encounters had struck Genine as a woman of little feeling, surprised her by taking the younger woman into her arms. She cradled her gently, speaking her name in tender whispers. Genine thought she'd called her Christina but couldn't be sure.

2

COMMISSARIO ALESSANDRO CENNI, Alex to his friends, had just won the football match for Perugia with a free kick directly into the upper right corner of the goal when Inspector Piero Tonni, the game referee approached. "Beautiful goal, Alex. We've got the championship locked up this year, for sure."

Cenni laughed, "*Grazie*, Piero. For sure, your neutrality is appreciated by the Foligno team. What's up?"

"The questore called. Trouble in Assisi. An American, niece of a friend of the PM's, was murdered last night. Looks like she was raped. He wants us there as soon as possible."

"Give me ten minutes to shower. And call Elena. We'll need a woman with us if it's rape. Tell her to meet us at Assisi head-quarters in thirty minutes."

Acknowledged by his colleagues to be the best midfielder in the Poliza di Stato football league, Cenni was currently assigned to a special task force established by the prime minister to deal with international terrorism and politically sensitive domestic crimes. The murder of the niece of a friend of the PM is hardly a sensitive domestic issue, Cenni thought as he soaped himself. But if she's an American, then of course the questore will insist that we take over.

All Italy was on terrorist alert that week. Since 9/11 all of Europe had been on terrorist alert all of the time. But Easter was a particularly difficult period with a few million tourists in Italy, a good many of them American, to celebrate Holy Week. The American authorities had issued an advisory a few days earlier warning its citizens to stay away from Rome, Florence, and Venice. The mayors of Florence and Venice were livid. Tourism was their main source of income and Americans were their biggest spenders. The mayor of Rome was too busy looking after his political career to care one way or the other. Cenni was sure the PM had agreed to the warnings, probably even encouraged them. He was anxious to play with the big guys and he finally had his chance.

The threat of terrorism was nothing new to the Italian police. They had been living with domestic terrorism, right and left, for more than a hundred years. Cenni's colleagues had been none too happy when they were forced to attend a lecture on terrorism given by the Americans. He could still hear Piero's grumbles. "A whole lot they can teach us about terrorism. How many of their prime ministers and judges have been kidnapped and murdered?" Cenni had responded with gentle irony. "Perhaps that's why!"

Piero Tonni was a complainer by nature. He complained when they had too much work and when they had too little. He didn't like the food they served in the cafeteria—the pasta was from a box, the sauce too spicy, the cheese too old. When Cenni suggested that he go home for lunch, he complained that his mother's cooking was too rich, it was making him fat. Only Piero, Cenni thought, would break the Italian code of silence on mamma's cooking to serve a higher god, his need to complain. Cenni was sure that the entire ride to Assisi would be one long litany of complaints and was surprised when he got into the car to find Piero singing *Volare* off key. He was even more surprised when Piero pulled into one of the larger Ponte San Giovanni gas stations and instead of filling up with gas, ran inside the coffee shop. He returned with a roll of Baci chocolates.

"I thought you were on a diet?"

"They're not for me," Piero answered, his face pink with embarrassment. "You remember Sergeant Antolini. You know, the blonde who helped us when that painting was stolen from the Basilica museum. She loves chocolates."

"The blonde!" Cenni responded laughing. "You're very delicate. Isn't she the one with the huge breasts? If I remember correctly, you couldn't take your eyes off them. I'm surprised you even noticed the color of her hair."

Piero flushed even darker. *"Dottore!"*

Whenever Piero addressed him by his title, Cenni knew to tread lightly. "Sorry, Piero. Is there something I should know?"

"Not really. I took her to dinner a month ago. That new trattoria in Piazza Dante. I haven't called her since."

"If you're not interested, why the chocolates?"

"Who says I'm not interested? I figure if I don't call for a few weeks, she won't get the wrong idea. I'm not sure I'm ready to get serious."

"You don't have to get serious with every woman you take to dinner, even if it's more than once. In my experience, if a man takes a woman to dinner and he doesn't call back within a week, she writes him off. You'll need a lot more than a five pack of chocolates if you want to relight that fire."

Their conversation came to an end as Piero maneuvered the car around the barrier at the Porta Nuova to show his identification to the officer on duty. Cenni thought it just as well. They were in new territory and he wasn't sure if either of them wanted to stay there. In the four years that he had worked with Piero their talks, when they went beyond the details of a case, had focused on football or food.

When they pulled up next to the newsstand in Piazza Santa Chiara, they could see that Elena had arrived before them. Her yellow Volkswagen was blocking the entrance to police headquarters. The relationship between Fulvio Russo, Assisi's Commissario, and his counterparts in Perugia was generally acrimonious. Cenni was sure he'd hear tomorrow about his officer's lack of courtesy.

Inspector Elena Ottaviani was one of the new issue of woman officers who had come into police work within the last ten years. Cenni had worked closely with a number of EU police organizations in the fifteen years since he had joined the Polizi di Stato, and he inevitably made comparisons. He was impressed with the way Italy had accommodated its women officers without turning them into shorter versions of their male counterparts. They patroled the streets, manned the computers in the back room, answered questions at the front desk, took their places in the front lines of the riot police, and did so in long hair, short hair, painted nails and lips, even occasionally doused in perfume, and generally they performed their duties well and without complaint. Piero could take a leaf from their book, he reflected.

As he started to get out of the car, Elena emerged at the top of the stairway. She noticed at once the glance Cenni gave to her Volkswagen. "*Mi dispiace, capo.* I only intended to be there a minute. I'll move it." Elena was the only one of his officers who didn't address him by his first name. He assumed it was a piece of her generally complicated nonconformist attitude.

"I'll re-park the car and ride with you to the cemetery. The body's already there. Convenient, don't you think?" After re-parking her car, she slid into the back seat, still talking. "They found her shortly after seven-thirty AM. The police surgeon was called almost immediately, and he's there too. Appears they don't read directives very well," Elena opined, a reference to the bulletin that had been issued nationwide at the beginning of the year.

Cenni needed no reminders. The wording of the directive had been unambiguous. *All police organizations will immediately report any serious crime involving Americans to the Polizi di Stato Task Force on Terrorism.* A regional phone number and name had been appended and Cenni's name was listed for the Perugia Questura. He wondered why Fulvio Russo had waited so long to call, and why he had called Carlo Togni and not him directly. No doubt, it will come out during the investigation, Cenni thought. Whether it would have serious repercussions was another matter, one he preferred not to think about at the moment.

"Do you think we should go inside first, to introduce our-selves?" Piero inquired anxiously.

"The sergeant's up at the cemetery," Elena replied, nudging Cenni in the back. "You can introduce yourself up there. I'll fill you in on the details before we get there. I have a copy of the murdered woman's application for a *soggiorno*. They gave it to me—after some arm-twisting," she appended, this time direct-ing her words to Cenni.

On the short drive to the cemetery, Elena filled them in on what she had just learned. "The victim's American. One Rita Minelli, niece of Umberto Casati. Old Assisi family, friends in high places. Oh, and he still refers to himself as *Count Casati*. Guess he was out to lunch when they passed the Act of 1947," she added, referring to the law enacted at the end of the war abolishing Italian titles. A fervent anti-monarchist, Elena had been raging for the past two weeks. A member of the PM's party had suggested in Parliament that the time was ripe to bring back the monarchy. Cenni had ducked into the men's room at least twice in the past week to avoid one of her tirades.

Elena ignored the pained look that passed between the two men and continued her recital. "Minelli was forty-five, if we're to believe what she wrote on her application," she tacked on needlessly. Cenni reflected that Rita Minelli would have had to submit some evidence of her age when she applied for a *permesso di soggiorno*, probably her U.S. passport. Elena knows this, he thought, but he also recognized that they each had their own way of dealing with violent death. Elena's was to establish an immediate distance between herself and the victim. It was one of the few criticisms he had of her police work.

"She arrived in Assisi last June to bring her mother's body home for burial and never left. She's been teaching English since July at her uncle's language school here in Assisi. Lives with him and his family. Two of the ladies who arrange flowers at the cemetery found the body shortly after seven-thirty AM, in the Casati family vault. Her head was bashed in, probably with a statue from the altar. Looks like rape! That's sum total of what I got from the officer on desk duty. Sergeant Antolini will be our liaison on the case. She can fill us in on the rest."

An aficionado of American culture, she finished by humming "Love Is in the Air," a deceptively benevolent look on her face. Piero grinned but said nothing. Cenni was still struck by the amount of teasing Piero accepted from Elena. She needled him constantly, yet they remained friends. It appeared that she was also his confidante on the subject of Sergeant Antolini. But Piero was not the only one to get the needle.

"Say, *capo*, you travel in exalted circles, perhaps you've met this woman?"

"Perhaps," he replied, not responding to Elena's teasing. But it had been with something of a start that he'd heard the Casati name when he'd spoken to the questore earlier that morning. He had met Artemisia Casati at an art reception in Perugia a few months back. Under the circumstances of that first meeting, it might be a bit awkward to meet her again, but that was a problem to be dealt with only if it arose. The commissario was not one of those people who embrace trouble before it arrives.

3

THE ASSISI CEMETERY is located immediately below Rocca Maggiore off the back road that leads to Gualdo Tadino. Cenni knew the cemetery well although he had never been there on police business. Hanna Falkenberg, his Swedish grandmother, had an affinity for Italian cemeteries. He could still hear her. "Alex, *caro mio*, if you want to understand the national character of a people, visit their cemeteries." When he was still too young to understand the nature of blackmail or to withstand the force of his grandmother's personality, she had often lured him and his twin brother Renato on her cemetery jaunts with the promise of chocolates and Coca-Cola. He would sit next to her while she drove her red Bugatti, a large box of handmade chocolate truffles on his lap, listening in wide-eyed gluttony while she instructed him and his brother on life, love, and the pursuit of the Etruscans.

They didn't find any Etruscans in the Assisi cemetery. It hadn't been opened until the 1700s, so was too recent to house any of Umbria's earlier inhabitants, but it was there that Hanna Falkenberg had met Renato Cenni in 1931. Shortly thereafter, his grandparents had merged their interests, first in the bedroom and later in a chocolate factory. After his grandfather's death, Hanna (she refused to answer to "Nonna") liked to walk through the cemetery grounds, her grandsons by her side, and reminisce about that day long ago when their grandfather had watched her pluck four long-stemmed red roses from a large bouquet decorating one of the more elaborate mausoleums and place them on one of the simpler flat stones. "Taking from the haves to give to the have-nots," she had said, when he had protested. "Petty theft!" was his response. They had quarreled good-naturedly about it until his death in 1961.

Cenni stopped his reminiscing when Piero parked their car near the cemetery's main entrance, next to an ambulance from the Assisi Hospital. Apparently, it doubles as a mortuary van, he thought, noting the two attendants in white coats sitting inside. As they walked toward the cemetery gates, they could see three police officers surrounded by a small crowd of women, all carrying some type of flower arrangement and all talking at once. He was too distant to hear what they were saying but could guess. They had come to the cemetery to decorate the graves of their loved ones for Easter, and a dead American, whatever the circumstances, was no excuse for keeping them from their familial duties. One of the officers, a woman, approached.

"We've been wondering when you'd arrive," Sergeant Antolini said brusquely, looking at her wristwatch. "The medical

examiner is waiting at the mausoleum. He's been there since
shortly before ten. The mortuary van has been here even
longer. And we can't let any visitors into the cemetery until you
give the okay." Cenni noted that she had directed her comments to him and Elena without once acknowledging Piero.

"*Mi dispiace*, Sergeant," Cenni said, smiling deferentially. "Lots
of traffic on Easter weekend between Perugia and Assisi." It had
taken him only forty minutes to get to Assisi from the time he'd
received the first call from the questore, but he would need all
the help that the Assisi police could provide. He also surmised
that at least some of her hostility was directed at Piero.

"Why don't we walk there together, Sergeant? You can fill
me in on the details. Your knowledge of the people involved
will be very helpful. Inspector Tonni can stay here and assist
your officers in calming the ladies," he said, motioning to one
of the women who appeared particularly agitated. "Inspector
Ottaviani will accompany us to the mausoleum." He avoided
looking at Piero while he gave his orders.

The apology and accompanying smile worked. Sergeant
Antolini's rancor receded. "Perhaps we should walk around the
walls and go through the side gate," she suggested. "It's faster
that way and we can avoid the crowd at the front."

"*Grazie*, Sergeant. What can you tell us about the murder victim? Did you know her?"

"I knew her as well as I know most people in Assisi; better
actually. She's been into the station five or six times since she
arrived in June, the first time to apply for a *soggiorno*. There
were no problems there—her mother was Italian, the uncle is
prominent in Assisi, and from what I remember, she had a
substantial bank balance. The second time was in August.
She filed a complaint against one of the ladies who arranges
flowers in the cemetery." She paused for dramatic effect
before continuing.

"I think you'll find this interesting, Commissario! One of the two women who found the body this morning, Sophie Orlic—well, she's the flower lady that Minelli complained about in August. Minelli accused Orlic of blackmailing one of the other flower ladies, a woman from Orlic's own country."

"Which is . . . ?" Cenni inquired.

"Croatia," the sergeant responded. "Minelli had gone to the family vault to see if the engraver had completed the inscription on her mother's sarcophagus and found this other woman—an Irene Rapaic—sitting on the portico crying."

"Was it?" Cenni interrupted.

"Was what?"

"The sarcophagus, was it engraved?"

"Of course not," the sergeant replied matter-of-factly before continuing. "I was surprised that she was able to get a coherent story out of Rapaic. Minelli's Italian is—*scusi*—was quite good. Rapaic's is terrible! We had to hire an interpreter when we conducted our investigation."

"Was it blackmail?" Cenni asked.

"Technically! Orlic was holding Rapaic's passport. They're from the same village. But Orlic hired herself a lawyer, one of the good ones," she added flippantly, "who said that Orlic had paid the other woman's travel expenses to Italy and was paying her living expenses in Assisi. The lawyer argued that his client was only holding the passport as security until the debt was repaid. Orlic agreed to return the passport, which we made sure she did. Rapaic left Assisi after that; she's now working in Foligno."

"You said she came to the station five or six times. A bit often to be visiting the police I should think."

"The third time was right after the New Year. Minelli came in to complain that Orlic had followed her home one evening. They had words in the street. Orlic called Minelli an interfering American *putana*. After that, whenever Minelli came in, she'd ask to speak directly to Commissario Russo. You'll have to ask him why she was there so often," she said, avoiding Cenni's eyes.

"What happened after Orlic threatened Minelli?"

"Nothing. I told Minelli I'd have a word with Orlic, that she should go home and forget about it."

"Did anything come of it?"

"No, and that was almost three month's ago. *È vero*, I can understand Orlic's anger. From what she'd told me, Rapaic never repaid the travel money. On top of that, Orlic had to pay her lawyer's fee. She was out at least a thousand euros, probably more."

"Tell me what Minelli was like. Did you like her? I sense from what you've told me so far that you had at least some sympathy for the Croatian."

"Vivi e lascia vivere!" she replied to Cenni's question.

"Live and let live!" Cenni repeated, his tone puzzled.

She explained: "I don't think Minelli understood the concept. What happened between the two Croatians goes on all the time. Orlic made some sacrifices to get here. She works hard, does okay, then sends money home to a relative or neighbor to bring them here. Like everyone else, she wants a return on her money."

"So you agree then, Minelli was an interfering American *putana*," he stated provocatively.

Antolini laughed. "Interfering anyway. She liked to get involved in other people's business. The first time Minelli came into the station, one of our clerks was having some trouble at the computer. Minelli walks over, uninvited, and starts explaining the ins and outs of Microsoft Word. Lucille was embarrassed. She didn't want the rest of us thinking that she couldn't do her job."

"And the two women who found the body. Where are they now?"

"Orlic's back at the station. Been there since nine this morning when we brought her there from the cemetery," she
replied, looking at her watch again. "We told her she'd have to
wait to talk to you."

"And the other one?"

"I sent her home. She's just a kid, really; she was very upset.
She's Albanian, married to a local from Bastia. They have a six-
month-old baby. I didn't think it would serve any useful purpose to hold her at the station. She didn't even know Minelli."
The defensive tone of Sergeant Antolini's reply suggested that
she was expecting a reprimand for not following procedures
strictly.

Cenni smiled affably as he held open the side gate for her
to enter. "Very kind, Sergeant, just what I expect from all our
officers. We can take her statement later today, or tomorrow,
when she's up to it."

"Grazie, Commissario. Sei molto gentile," the sergeant said. She
looked up at him and smiled. Ah Piero, Cenni thought, catching his breath. Your days of eating mamma's rich food are
surely numbered!

4

THE ASSISI CEMETERY is built in the form of an amphithe-
ater. The highest tier, guarded at its back by a stone wall, provides an unimpeded view of the small towns and checkered
farms that lie between Perugia and Assisi. The rich always get
the best views, Cenni groused to himself as they approached
the vault. Located at the far end of the top tier and separated
from its nearest neighbor by a row of towering cypress, the
vault was a smaller version of the Temple of Minerva in the
Piazza del Comune. Its entrance porch, built of Assisi pink
stone, was fronted by four Corinthian columns surmounted by

a pediment inscribed in Latin: *Novissima autem inimica detrue-*
tur mors. The last enemy that shall be destroyed is death, he translated
to himself. Safe and unimaginative, he thought, recognizing it
as New Testament, probably Corinthians.

A reception committee of three waited on the porch. Cenni
recognized the medical examiner at once. They had worked
together on previous cases, not always with success. Marcello
Batori had been in the civil service for more than thirty years.
Early in his career, he had established a reputation as a creative
forensic pathologist but also as one who too often jumped to
premature conclusions. In the last few years, he had become
forgetful, he had always been slow. Some of Cenni's colleagues
had recently circulated a petition asking that Batori be
replaced by someone younger. Cenni hadn't expected the petition to be successful, wasn't even sure that he wanted it to be,
and had refused to sign. Article Eighteen was sacrosanct in
Italy, unless the PM's party had its way. It protected the employ-
ment rights of the weak and vulnerable as well as the incompetent. Cenni could only hope that Minelli's autopsy would
pose no unusual problems for Batori and so no regrets for him.

From the photography and equipment cases sitting on the
portico floor and the plastic sheathing on their shoes, Cenni
recognized the two younger men as forensic science police.
Their happiness at seeing him was evident from their chorus
of enthusiastic *buongiornos.* Cenni nodded in return. The number of cigarette butts on the portico floor indicated to him that
they'd already swept the place clean of fingerprints and were
waiting for permission to leave. Batori advanced to meet
Cenni, a wide smile on his face, his hand extended.

"Alex, *come stai,* it's been a long time! The Ronchitti murders, wasn't it? We did a good job there. Put him away for life.
Ah, but this one! Sad, very sad. A young woman, still in the
prime of life. But you'll want to see for yourself."

The burial chamber was long, narrow, and dark. The only natural light came from the midday sun that filtered through the decorative grilles, splashing a lacy pattern on everything in its path. The outer walls were lined with sarcophagi, the dates and names of those who had died engraved in simple script. In the center was a stone altar, its only ornamentation two vases of the same stone flanking an altarpiece of surpassing beauty, a copy of Cimabue's Crucifixion from the upper Basilica. The artist had not just copied the original, he had recreated it, adjusting for the size of the vault. The kneeling figure of St. Francis in the original had been painted out, giving greater emphasis to the contorted figure of the dying Christ and the pleading gestures of those who waited below to receive his body. The sepia figures in Cimabue's masterpiece, the result of centuries of oxidation, had served the imitator well. In a space that received little natural light, the faded browns and ochres provided quiet relief for those who came to pray.

Below, Rita Minelli lay supine on the stone floor, her head pillowed on the first step, her eyes closed, the body recumbent as though already laid to rest. Her flared black wool skirt, which had been pushed up to mid-thigh, modestly covered her genitals. Black stockings and lace panties were pulled down about her ankles, emphasizing the winter whiteness of her calves and thighs. A pair of black, spike-heeled pumps was solidly attached to her feet, the needlelike toes pointing upward as if in supplication. Her upper garment, a black wool cape, was still buttoned at the neck and showed no sign of disturbance. However she had died, there had been little bleeding. Only a small smear of dried blood, no more than three inches in diameter, was evident on the outer edge of the bottom altar step. "A tableau vivant," Cenni uttered, more to himself than to Batori, who was standing behind him.

"D'accordo!" Batori replied as though Cenni had been speaking to him. "The murderer certainly tried to create the appearance of rape, but not very successfully."

"Is her position and clothing exactly as you found them?"

"No one told me it was your case, Alex, or I would have followed standard procedure," Batori responded defensively, picking up the implied criticism in Cenni's question. "The call came from Fulvio Russo's office. But she's as close as possible to the way I found her," he said, finally answering the question. "Forensics took pictures before I got here."

"How did she die?" Cenni asked, this time less aggressively.

"Until I do the autopsy it's just conjecture. Right now, I would say a sharp blow to the back of the cranium, just above the right ear. Not much doubt of it! There was no external bleeding, but when I get her on the table I'm sure I'll find extensive intercranial injury."

Cenni interrupted. "No external bleeding! Isn't *that* blood?" he asked, pointing to the brown stain on the edge of the step.

"I found a small cut on her right temple, Alex, and a slight bruising of the forehead, hidden by her hair. Probably incurred when she fell. The cut bled only slightly. No, I'm sure the blow to the back of her head killed her. Perhaps not immediately, but it definitely rendered her unconscious. I can give you more positive answers after the autopsy."

"Am I to assume then, that the murderer hit her on the back of the head, rolled her over, and raped her while she was unconscious, possibly dead? And where's the murder weapon?" he asked, not waiting for a response to his first question.

"We have it here, Dottore," the more assured of the two forensic investigators replied, holding up an object that was packaged and sealed in clear plastic.

Cenni frowned. "I would have preferred it if you had left

the crime scene as you found it until I arrived. But no matter," he said, shaking off his irritation. "Tell me about the weapon." He extended his hand to receive the package.

He could see through the wrapping that he'd been handed a statue of the Virgin, some eighteen inches high, mounted on a heavy base. The electric blue of the robe and the garishly painted face showed through the plastic. The newspapers will have a field day with this one, he thought. AMERICANA ASSASSI-NATA DALLA VERGINE was sure to be one of the headlines.

"How do you know it's the murder weapon?"

"The base is white plaster. It's cracked, recently from the look of it. And Dottor Batori found a paint chip in the victim's hair," he added defensively, nodding toward the pathologist. "He also told us that the base is heavy enough to have caused the damage to the cranium. We found the statue lying two feet from the body. It's the weapon."

"That's correct, Alex," chimed in Batori. "But I'll compare the bruising on the cranium to the size of the base for confir-mation. It'll be in the postmortem report."

Cenni realized from the resentful expressions on their faces that he was out of order. He had some sympathy for the three civil servants. They had been called in by Fulvio Russo, Assisi's commissario, to do a job and had followed his instructions. It's not their responsibility to figure out territorial politics, Cenni acknowledged to himself.

"*Mi dispiace,* a few more questions and I can get you all out of here," he said civilly. "You have a lot of follow-up work to do today and tomorrow's Easter. You'll want to get home to your families."

Inspector Ottaviani watched in admiration as the tension dissolved. A *mi dispiace* here, a few smiles there, and we're all friends again, she thought. The commissario had a reputation in police circles for charming his subordinates into line and his superiors into agreement. Some of her fellow officers, all women, claimed that a single Cenni smile could elicit a confession of homicide from a purse-snatcher. What mattered to those who worked for him though, was that the apologies and the smiles were sincere. Viewing an uncontaminated crime scene before the medical examiner and the forensic investigators went to work was an article of faith for Cenni, but his reputation for fairness was well founded. He would hold his fire for the person responsible. God help that ass, Russo! Elena thought with some pleasure.

Cenni said, "Marcello, what can you tell me about the time of death? It would appear that rigor is established."

"When I arrived at a little after nine, rigor had completely set in. Death occurred at least twelve to fourteen hours before then, I'd say, probably earlier. Estimating time of death from body temperature and degree of rigor is always tricky, you know that, Alex. It's always best to have other evidence for corroboration. Sergeant Antolini tells us that the victim was first missed at seven last night. There's a sign posted out front that the cemetery gates are locked at five in the winter, so we can probably assume she was dead before five. And if not before five, then definitely before seven, when her family reported her missing."

Cenni groaned inwardly. Typical Batori! Estimating time of death from a sign on the cemetery gates and an unsubstantiated comment from an unidentified witness. He said aloud, to no one in particular, and again sharply, "Is this true? Had Minelli been missing since seven last night?"

Sergeant Antolini grimaced, glancing over at Batori with some grievance, before breaking the silence. "Not exactly, Commissario. No one in her family reported her missing. They didn't even know she was dead until Commissario Russo telephoned them shortly after the body was found. What I *actually* said to Dottor Batori was that Count Casati told Commissario Russo that the family had expected Signora Minelli to accompany them to the Good Friday procession at seven and to join them later for dinner. She never showed up, but they *said* they weren't concerned." Cenni noticed the emphasis on *said*. "They'd heard she was one of the processionists, so the family wasn't surprised when she didn't join them." *So there!* was written all over her face.

"The family knows then that she's dead and how she died?" Cenni asked.

"I believe that Commissario Russo informed the family of the circumstances of her death," Antolini replied.

Another of his rules broken, Elena thought to herself. The family will be well supplied with alibis before we get to them.

"What about a handbag? I don't see one."

The technicians and Batori turned in tandem to look at the sergeant. Her turn again!

"The woman who found the body—Signora Orlic—she brought it back to the station with her. Said she was afraid someone would take it and she'd get the blame. Commissario Russo locked it in his desk."

"I think we can wrap up here," Cenni announced gruffly. "When can I have the exhibits and forensic report?"

"On Monday," the senior technician replied. "Late Monday," he amended, looking at the other technician to be sure they were in agreement.

"I'll do the autopsy Monday morning. You can have my report by the end of the day," Batori piped up, not waiting to be asked. Worried that I might ask him to work on Easter, Cenni surmised.

"Good. I'll see your reports on Monday, no later than five," Cenni emphasized, dismissing the technicians with a nod.

He turned to the sergeant, his demeanor and voice noticeably softening, or so it seemed to Elena.

"Sergeant Antolini, you can send the attendants up to remove the body. Let's section off this area of the cemetery, this tier and the one below. If any of the families want to leave flowers they can give them to your officers. If they have complaints, they can call my office. I'd like a key to the side gate and to the vault if you have an extra," he said, still addressing the sergeant. "If not please have them made."

And then to Batori, "*Scusi*, Marcello, I cut you off earlier. You were saying that appearance and reality might be at odds here. I tend to agree. Is there any evidence beyond the disarrangement of her clothing to suggest rape? Bruising of the genitalia, body fluids?"

"Nothing from a cursory examination, but that doesn't mean it wasn't rape or intended rape. The rapist may have been scared off. Again, the postmortem will tell us more." Batori lowered his voice, either in respect for the dead or because he didn't want the others to hear. "One thing for sure, Alex. She's pregnant. Two months, possibly more."

5

CENNI TOOK A deep breath and then exhaled, releasing some of the tension that had been building since he'd first received the questore's call. The others had gone below to make arrangements for removal of the body and he was alone. Even the sun had retreated, taking with it its little bit of warmth. He shivered, more from the austere beauty of the crypt than from the cold. It had none of the baroque ornamentation that decorated many Umbrian gravesites, no little tokens of family affection: pictures of the deceased covered with heavy plastic to protect them from the elements, statuettes of patron saints, terra cotta figurines of the Virgin holding the baby Jesus. There were no amulets warding off Satan and no flowers, wilted or fresh, filling the exquisitely carved stone vases.

He had a policeman's superstitious belief, borne out in recent years by forensic science, that the murderer invariably leaves his signature at the crime scene. But apart from the body of Rita Minelli, the *prima facie* evidence of murder, there was little in the Casati vault to identify her killer. Rough impregnable stone, the sole building element of the vault, was not likely to yield clear fingerprints. Until a few days ago, the weather had been unseasonably warm; then the temperature had dipped to below zero Celsius, and the crusted earth surrounding the vault was too hard for footsteps to make an imprint. A light dusting of snow had covered Assisi in the early morning hours, but the snow had not begun to fall until after midnight, long after Rita Minelli had died, and it had melted quickly. The vault itself was surprisingly clean of debris, only a few decayed leaves and the omnipresent blessings of pigeon droppings. He surmised that the vault was swept regularly, and he made a note to find out when it had been cleaned last. He looked down, finally, at the dead body, drawing a second deep breath.

The fastidious disarrangement of the clothing was an artifice. Batori had found no bruising of the external genitalia or semen in the vestibule of the vagina in his preliminary examination, and in Cenni's view, it was doubtful that the medical examiner would find anything additional to establish rape when he had Minelli on the table. Victims of rape do not go silently to their graves. Their last moments of suffering and fear are imprinted on their faces. Rita Minelli's face reflected quiet repose.

He thought of his father, who had died in his sleep of a stroke without uttering a sigh. His was the peaceful death that people pray for, yet his mother had found him at seven in the morning lying next to her in bed, his face frozen into a grimace of pain.

The undertaker had tried unsuccessfully to rearrange the twisted features into the gentle lines they had loved.

The blinds were drawn and three candles were burning on the library table set against the wall when he and Renato had gone into their parents' bedroom to view their father's body. Alex had trouble adjusting his eyes to the dim light, and as he left the room he tripped on a footstool that his mother kept near the bed. He giggled and his brother, who always had a sense of occasion, kicked him in the shins to keep him quiet. He didn't feel any guilt, however. The person lying there, dressed in his father's best gray suit, face contorted by suffering, bore no resemblance to the man who had kissed and hugged him the previous evening.

However Rita Minelli had died, it had been with neither fear nor suffering, of that Alex was certain. It was possible, of course, that she had been struck down from behind and then raped while unconscious or dead. Necrophilia was not unheard of in Italy and Minelli had died in a cemetery. The case most often cited in police circles was that of the gravedigger who had begun by touching corpses to achieve sexual arousal and had ended by having sex with hundreds of women before he buried them. The most recent case had occurred more than fifteen years earlier, somewhere in the Veneto, and had involved necrophilia after disinterment. The corpse of a fifteen-year-old girl had been dug up and violated just a few days after her burial. Neither culprit had engaged in necrophilic homicide, however, which as Cenni knew from the literature was rare, despite the attention given to it by the press and to its notorious practitioners, Ted Bundy, Jeffrey Dahmer, and Citizen X, all of whom had achieved sexual satisfaction by mutilating their victims after killing them. At the least, if sexual sadism were involved in Minelli's death, Cenni would have expected to see bite marks on the body.

He put on a pair of gloves before kneeling to examine the corpse. Batori could be careless and might have missed something. He checked the upper torso and neck for signs of bruising or bite marks. There were none, but there was a long black strand of hair or fiber caught in her left earring. He removed it gently, taking care not to tear it. It was black like Minelli's hair, and perhaps Batori had thought it was just that, but the texture, even to the naked eye, was closer to animal hair. There was a small knot at the end of the fiber, possibly a piece of fringe from a scarf, Cenni thought, as he placed it carefully in one of the small envelopes that he carried. He'd have to warn Batori to look for similar fibers when he did the postmortem.

He examined her clothes carefully, hoping to find more of the same fibers. Under her cape she was dressed for a liaison. Ecru lace see-through blouse, matching camisole, scanty silk panties, and garter belt, all designed for enticement, hardly appropriate for visiting a cemetery on a cold March day, particularly on Good Friday, he thought. Had she planned to meet her lover in the vault? Possibly he was a married man? It was a gruesome and uncomfortable place for a sexual encounter, but late on a winter's evening they would have found privacy. Assisi was the proverbial small town despite the millions of tourists who visited it annually. The permanent residents were few and they knew each other's secrets, and they talked. He suspected that in Assisi the cemetery was one of the few places where a couple could meet clandestinely.

The tidiness of it all was baffling. The skirt pushed up to the hips, yet carefully arranged to cover the dead woman's genitals. Minelli had been wearing a garter belt underneath her panties. If rape were intended, why had the rapist taken the time to roll down Minelli's stockings. A leg fetish, perhaps, yet nothing else at the crime scene suggested a sexual ritual. The choice of murder weapon was likewise baffling. It was doubtful that the murderer would have brought such a weapon with him. The idea was outlandish and the statue of the Virgin would have been difficult to conceal. Looking around him at the Cimabue reproduction and the pristine and expensive stone vases, Cenni wondered how anything so commonplace could have found its way into this memorial to taste and money.

After fifteen years with the police, he'd learned to trust his instincts. He was sure that the rape scene was a staged diversion to mislead the police and was just as sure that a woman had created it. Just then he heard the voices of Elena and the mortuary attendants in the background. They were returning to remove the body. He took one more look at Rita Minelli before standing. Was Batori right, he wondered? Had she known about the baby? Had she been happy? He hoped so.

Alex Cenni was different from many of his colleagues and, at times, regretted it. The years of viewing battered and mutilated bodies had dulled his colleagues' stolid imaginations and, in some cases, their souls, allowing them to view murder victims with detachment. The worst of them, those he actively avoided, treated the dead with disdain, even with brutality. But after fifteen years with the Polizia di Stato, thirteen of them investigating homicides, Cenni still felt the burden of recognition of the dead. They were his teammates from the football fields, the waiters who brought him coffee in the cafés, the neighbors who greeted him on the streets. And because he still harbored a residue of Italian chauvinism, women and children created the greatest burden. Five years ago, he had done what few Italian men do voluntarily: He had gone to see a psychiatrist, a friend from his university years in Bologna. He was concerned about the personal attachment he felt to each new victim. His friend, the Freudian, had focused on Chiara.

Alex had met Chiara in his first year at the University of Bologna, in the registrar's office. They were each heading for the same line at the same time. He'd jumped over a trashcan trying to get there first and had landed on his knees. She had laughed uproariously, peals of delight that invited everyone within hearing distance to join in.

"Perhaps you should add Western Civility to your roster," she'd said jokingly, offering him a hand to help him stand. After that they became inseparable. At the end of their first year of law school, they'd shocked their parents and even some of their friends by living together. They'd planned to marry after receiving their law degrees.

But those years of happiness also coincided with the era of kidnappings. Everyone who was anyone in Italy had been vulnerable. On the right or left, it didn't seem to matter. Sometimes the kidnappers wanted money, sometimes they wanted to draw attention to their causes, and sometimes they weren't sure what they wanted. Some of the victims survived and returned home, some came home minus body parts, and some never came home. Chiara was one of the latter. Her kidnappers were never caught nor was her body recovered. Her parents both died within a few months of her disappearance. Her father, a judge sitting on Italy's highest court, had died from the effects of the heart attack he'd suffered after opening a package containing his only child's right index finger, her mother, by suicide, a few months later.

Alex was also a victim, an outcast from love, an encyclopedia of neuroses, if he were to believe the incantations of his friend. Psychic trauma, self-inflicted pain, repetition of unpleasure, death instinct, post-traumatic stress syndrome were some of the terms Sandro had used. Alex had quit after four sessions, feeling sane enough if he reflected on those of his colleagues who were not suffering from repetition of unpleasure. One thing that Sandro had said was true, however: that his job as a policeman was the cause of his pain. "Quit, do something else," Sandro had also said. "I'll think about it," Alex had replied—adding to himself, but not until I've found Chiara.

6

CENNI WAS ABSORBED on the drive back to Assisi, Piero was sulky, and Elena, talkative. "It's too peculiar," she said. "That's the strangest rape case I've ever seen. She looks like she died in her sleep. I was talking to Batori on the way down to the ambulance. He thinks it was staged. What do you think, Commissario?" she asked, glancing back at Cenni over her shoulder.

"I think Batori should keep his opinions to himself until he's completed the postmortem," he responded. He noticed the blush rising on the back of Elena's neck and realized that he'd spoken too roughly. "Sorry, Elena, but I'd prefer to wait for the postmortem before jumping to conclusions. But, yes, I too think the rape was staged," he added, his tone of impatience a clear signal to his subordinates that he was thinking and didn't want to talk. Elena and Piero exchanged knowing looks, and Piero used the opportunity to go through a stop sign.

"What was the exact time that the Assisi police identified the body?" Cenni asked a minute later, addressing his question to Elena, adding rhetorically, to Piero, "Was that a stop sign back there?"

"Around eight o'clock," Elena answered, turning to address him directly. "Sergeant Antolini said she was supposed to end her tour of duty at eight but when she called *il lupino* at home . . . Commissario Russo," Elena amended, noticing Cenni's raised eyebrow, "he told her to stay with the two flower ladies until he got there. He then insisted that Antolini accompany him and the two flower ladies back to the cemetery. That was just after eight o'clock."

"The questore called me at the stadium close to eleven!" Cenni said aloud. A three-hour lapse of time, he thought. Plenty of opportunity for Russo to make mischief.

Fulvio Russo, *il lupo* to his friends, of whom he had none, had now been commissario of the Assisi station for twelve months. Assisi is one of those backwater towns where the commissario is either on his way up or on his way down, or as in the case of Assisi's previous commissario, on *her* way up. Anna Duccio was now in Rome enjoying a spectacular career, a rising star, whereas Russo, as everyone in police circles knew, was destined for obscurity, although he himself was not yet convinced that his time had passed. He was still young, not yet forty, and until a year ago, had enjoyed a career of firsts: the youngest officer in Perugia to be promoted to commissario, the best-looking (if one admires Nordic muscularity), the one with the richest wife. Even his flaws were excessive. His disposition for cupidity and backstabbing was unequalled, but if one is rich and good looking in Italy, such flaws are generally overlooked.

It was the cupidity that finally sank Russo, and the questore had done the sinking. Russo had been caught suppressing evidence of fraud by his brother-in-law, a parliamentarian, who had devised a scheme to buy two thousand hectares of Umbrian land that had been secretly earmarked by the government to become a national wildlife sanctuary. This type of land grab is not unusual in Italy—it happens every day, in fact—but Russo had acted imperiously when the papers had first stumbled upon it. He had huffed and puffed, cajoled and threatened, and in the end had tried to bribe one of *L'Unità*'s more intrepid reporters who, as it happened, had come to their interview wired for sound. That Russo was still on the police force was a testament to his brother-in-law's millions. That he was no longer stationed in Perugia, and unlikely to return, was partly due to *L'Unità*, but mainly to the questore, who also had a rich wife. The questore had his own talent for backstabbing and very much disliked competition.

Russo had been given his nickname by a subordinate some ten years earlier. An attractive woman, she'd found it necessary to ward off Russo's advances whenever they were together. The name caught on rapidly, helped no doubt by his almond-shaped eyes of that curious shade of green that turns to a dirty yellow in certain lights. The nickname (amended to *il lupo* when repeated to Russo by one of his minions) had delighted him at first. He reveled in the image of himself as a rapacious preda-tor. What he didn't find out until much later was that the woman had used the diminutive, *il lupino*.

Cenni had worked with Russo for five years in Perugia. He had learned to work around him, by flattering him or whatever else was necessary. He was prepared to do the same again, but he was beginning to suspect that Russo had his own plans, none of which included being worked with. He had already vio-lated the rules of engagement twice, the first time by not call-ing Cenni or the questore immediately after the body was found, and the second by speaking to the Casati family directly to inform them of the American's death.

It's a high-profile investigation, Cenni reflected. A clever man could rise by it. Perhaps Russo thinks it's his opportunity to climb back up. Cenni knew that would never happen. *Il lupino* was a backroom joke in police circles, and a dirty one at that, but he was still in a position to throw a spanner into the inves-tigation. "Tread lightly, Alex," the questore had warned him. "The count has lots of high-placed friends, and he's rumored to be Opus Dei."

Fulvio Russo had now been commissario in Assisi for a year. Plenty of time to worm his way into the count's social circle. He and his new-money wife Grazia had been notorious in Perugia for name-dropping and self-promotion. When they'd first started working together, Russo had treated Cenni in the same way that he'd treated most of his colleagues, and all of his subordinates—with contempt—until the questore had mentioned that Cenni's mother was a Baglioni, one of *the* Baglioni's. After that, every time that Russo threw a climbing party, Cenni had to find a new excuse to stay away. It had gotten close to the point of direct rudeness when Russo was exiled to Assisi. Did the banished Russo now hope to find Minelli's killer himself, thereby acquiring her uncle's gratitude and, with that, access to his high-powered friends? Russo was a barbarian from the north and given half a chance, he would screw up the Minelli investigation for his own purposes, of that Cenni was convinced.

Il lupino was waiting for his counterpart inside the front door when Cenni arrived at the Assisi barracks. Given Russo's history of skipping out of the office early on weekends, and of never showing up on holidays, Cenni found this unnerving.

"Alex, *Come ste?*" Russo said, using the familiar Umbrian *ste*, suspicious in itself since Russo was from Valle d'Aosta and in the past had always made fun of the Umbrian dialect. "Come into my office where we can talk in private," he urged. "Your people can wait out here," he said, slamming the door in Piero's face. As soon as they were alone, Russo confirmed Cenni's suspicions. *Il lupino* had an agenda.

"We have an airtight case here, Alex. You need to know that, so you don't waste your time talking to the family. They want their privacy. I have the murderer right here in the station, Sophie Orlic, the woman who found the body. She threatened the American a few months ago, and more than once. I have it on record," he said triumphantly. "She's a Croatian, a *straniera*," he added. A stranger, the clincher!

"How did you arrive at that conclusion, Fulvio? Has Orlic confessed? I wasn't aware that we'd established that Minelli *was* murdered. There's no evidence of injury beyond a small bruise to her temple and a bump on the back of her head. Both could easily have resulted naturally, a fall after a heart attack, for example. Batori hasn't done a postmortem yet."

Russo sneered: "After she had a heart attack, she staged her own rape! Come on, Alex. We both know *this* is no rape, and Batori confirms it. It points to a woman, to Orlic directly. But it's your turf, Alex. Just trying to help!"

"It's not a matter of turf, Fulvio. We need to work together here. I've already spoken to Sergeant Antolini about working with us directly, and I can use anyone else you can spare." Cenni had full authority to requisition whatever personnel and resources he needed, those of Assisi included, and they both knew it, but he viewed unnecessary displays of authority as counterproductive.

"What about Minelli's handbag?" he asked, not waiting for Russo to accede openly to his earlier request. That too would have been counterproductive.

"It's here," Russo said, retrieving the bag from the bottom drawer of his desk, placing it on top. It was not plastic wrapped and Russo had handled it without putting on gloves. Cenni groaned inwardly.

"Another reason why we should focus on Orlic!" Russo insisted. "A convenient way for her to account for her prints being all over Minelli's bag, carrying it away from the crime scene like that. I checked the bag's contents myself and made a list. There were only six euros in her bag, all in coins, and

Minelli usually carried large sums of money on her person."
Noting the surprised look on Cenni's face, he added quickly,
"Information from her family."

"If you can wrap that, Fulvio," Cenni said, nodding to the
bag, "I'd like to take it with me. Include the list of contents as
well. Perhaps I should talk to Orlic now." He looked at his
watch. "It's after one. Has she eaten?"

"My budget doesn't extend to feeding suspects. When
she's under arrest, we'll be happy to feed her," Russo replied.
"She's right next door, primed and ready," he added with disdain, swinging the door open between his office and the
interrogation room.

7

SOPHIE ORLIC HAD been sitting on the wooden bench in
the police interview room for more than four hours. It was
the first time in years that she'd been alone with her thoughts
for so long a period, without an invalid to feed or dress, flowers to arrange, or deadening sleep to repulse memory. She'd
found early on that it was impossible to keep the dark memories at bay through all her waking hours, so she'd devised
ways to keep them in check. She would remember only those
that gave her pleasure. And even then she had certain rules:
No reminiscences after the age of fourteen, the year that
she'd met Sergio at the lycée.

Too often, however, she was caught unaware, betrayed by
her senses. Just yesterday while working in the cemetery, a
large black bee with blue-violet wings, its body shiny like patent
leather, had lighted on one of her flowers. Startled by its
beauty, she had looked up and caught her breath at the sweep
of countryside below, so like the countryside where she and
Sergio had spent their summers. The memories flooded in of

the long hot days when they were fifteen. They would escape from pulling weeds in her grandparents' kitchen garden and hide behind the tall ears of ripening corn. When she managed to steal some of her grandfather's tobacco, they would roll it in the yellowing corn leaves and assault their lungs with the pleasures of illicit smoke. It was there, hidden behind the tall rows of corn, that they had first kissed.

When they'd turned sixteen, it was spring and the corn was still in seed, so they sought privacy further afield, by the river that ran below her grandparents' farm. Sophie had spotted wildflowers growing amid the meadow grass on the other side of the river, and they had waded through the cool muddy waters, holding hands and laughing as they stumbled on the smooth rocks that lined the riverbed. On the other side, they'd climbed the steep bank until they reached the elusive flowers. Their petals, the color of crushed strawberries, curved inward to cup golden yellow stamen. The flowers reminded Sophie of the magenta goblets flecked with bits of gold that her parents had brought back from their honeymoon in Venice.

That day she and Sergio made love for the first time. He had picked one of the flowers and drawn it softly across her neck and, later, when she had asked, between her breasts and thighs. Afterward, they lay on their backs, the flower filling the air with its delicate perfume, and talked of their future, the children they would have, and the work they would do. They were young, idealistic, and gloriously in love with each other and a world that had not yet betrayed them. Sophie kept the wildflower to show her grandmother. It was she who gave it a name—*peony peregrina*—the rarest of wildflowers and the most protected. For Sophie, it was the most beautiful flower in the world.

"Signora Orlic?" she heard a voice say, drawing her back to the present. She looked up to see a man standing directly in front of her. He was tall, two or three inches over six feet, of medium build, and casually dressed in a brown leather jacket and faded jeans. Perhaps because she was still caught up in her memories, she noticed the color of his eyes first. They were a translucent blue-violet, the color of lapis lazuli, a sharp contrast to his jet-black hair. Like the bee, she thought, and just as likely to sting.

She nodded in assent, looking down at the baskets of flowers at her feet, avoiding his eyes. She had done more than daydream in those four hours of waiting; she had also planned. She would say nothing beyond what they asked. *Yes, No, I don't know*, she had chanted to herself, creating a mantra that would protect her and Christina.

"I'm Commissario Cenni," he responded to her nod. "This is Inspector Tonni," he added, introducing a shorter, slightly rotund man, with ginger hair, light green eyes, freckled skin, and a glum expression. "Officer Tonni is ordering lunch. Which will you have, pizza or panini?" Cenni asked, smiling.

8

ALEX CENNI WAS a modest man but within the bounds of reason. His grandmother, an addict of Bogart films, often teased him, "Kid, you're tall, dark, and handsome with a six-figure bank balance. What's not to like?" He also knew that he had charm, whatever that meant. It seemed to work on most people when he turned it on. But not this day, at least not on Sophie Orlic.

From the sergeant's description, he had expected a countrywoman, large, broad-boned, ruddy complexioned, and stolid. The woman who gazed back at him before lowering her eyes could have stepped out of any of the Annunciation masterpieces in the Uffizi museum: da Vinci, Botticelli, di Credi. It didn't matter. The youthful Virgins were all alike, with their delicate pointed chins, short upper lips curved into a cupid's bow, pencil thin brows emphasizing the heavy-lidded eyes, translucent fair skin with just the faintest blush of rose on the rounded cheeks. Her nose was less perfect than those of her predecessors; it had a slight bump, and she was certainly older than they, in her mid-thirties he guessed, but her expression of impassivity was the same as theirs.

She had refused his offer of food, her manner of refusal suggesting that to eat with the police was a compromise from which she would never recover. Cenni had told Piero to buy extra, just in case, but Orlic had watched in freezing silence as they ate their pizzas. Forgetting his diet, Piero had eaten the extra pizza, whether frustrated because he was still smarting from Sergeant Antolini's cold shoulder or because Orlic's fixed stare made him nervous. Cenni asked if she would like an interpreter, but she responded, *No*, that she understood Italian well enough. And she didn't want a lawyer either, not unless the police were paying. Not that she needed either, he acknowledged to himself later that day. Her answers to his questions were a series of *si's*, *no's*, and an occasional *non lo so*. When she couldn't provide a monosyllabic answer, her response was brief and unelaborated. A defense lawyer's dream, he thought.

From what he was able to piece together from her reluctant responses, she had spent all Friday evening in her apartment near Porta San Giacomo arranging flowers for the next day. And, *no*, she hadn't gone near the cemetery. On Saturday morning, she'd left her apartment at ten minutes to seven to walk to the cemetery with two large baskets of flowers. Orlic had expected her assistant to meet her at the side gate at seven but she was late. "I left the side gate unlocked so my assistant could get in and went ahead to begin the day's work."

"How did you come by a key to the side gate?"

"The cemetery gave it to me."

"Why did the cemetery give it to you?"

"I asked."

"I doubt that everyone who asks for a key gets one. Let's try again, Signora Orlic. What reason did you give for needing a key?"

"I have twenty-three customers and I need to get in before the gates are opened to the general public."

"Does anyone else have a key?"

"I don't know . . . maybe."

"Does your assistant have a key?"

"No."

"Does she have a name?"

"Who?"

"Your assistant. And please don't answer *yes*. I'd like her name!"

"Alba Luchetti."

It took another series of questions to elicit that Orlic normally started her work at the Casati mausoleum, as it was the closest to the side gate. It was right after entering the side gate that she realized the key to the Casati vault was missing.

"Was that when you were at the vault or before you reached the vault?" he asked, wondering why she hadn't seen the body through the grilles.

"Yes."

"Yes, what?" he asked sharply, losing patience.

"Yes, before I reached the vault."

"Isn't it a bit unusual to check for the key only when you get to the cemetery?" Cenni asked. "Why didn't you check for it before leaving your apartment?"

"No, it's not unusual."

Another series of questions before she gave a fuller explanation.

She kept the keys in order on a large rectangular key ring. The Casati key was nearest the catch as it was the first vault that she visited every Saturday. "And I always check my keys before leaving the apartment," she added matter-of-factly, responding to Cenni's earlier question. It wasn't until she was walking toward the vault, just after she had entered the side gate, that she realized that the key she needed first was gone.

"The key ring is old, it has a faulty catch," she added by way of explanation.

"Why don't you buy a new one?" the commissario asked with a half-smile.

"Key rings cost money," she replied.

"And just that key was missing? No others had dropped off?"

"Yes. No others," she replied, ignoring the implication of his question.

After another three questions, she acknowledged that she had walked back along the path to look for the key. When she didn't find it, she started to look in the bushes along the side of the path.

"How long did that take?"

"Ten minutes."

While Orlic was still looking, Alba came down the path. Alba had a copy of all the vault keys, and Orlic suggested that they use her key to open the Casati vault. At that point, with some urging from Cenni, Orlic described her normal routine. For the first time she responded with some enthusiasm, pride in her work overcoming her obvious dislike of the police.

She worked in two cemeteries, Assisi and Santa Maria degli Angeli. For the Assisi cemetery, she purchased all the flowers from a wholesaler in Rivotorto on Friday mornings and did all the arrangements in her apartment on Friday evenings. On Saturday mornings, she left for the Assisi cemetery before 7:00, carrying half the flowers in two large baskets. She usually met Alba at the side gate. She removed the dead flowers from seven of the vaults, replaced the water, and then arranged the new flowers in their containers. Alba did the same for five of the vaults. When they finished the first set of flowers, they would walk back together to her apartment to pick up the remaining flowers, a five-minute walk. Sometimes they would have a coffee in her apartment. She generally finished her arrangements by 11:00 and then checked on Alba's.

"Why, don't you trust her?" Cenni asked, amused.

"You don't just plunk flowers into a container. You have to know how to arrange them. Some flowers in a mixed arrangement need to be positioned so they're more prominent than others. Most of my customers want the more expensive flowers to be more visible, roses before carnations. And the foliage needs to be arranged correctly. It's not that easy and Alba is still learning!" She responded at length and with spirit, irritated by his question.

"So you and Alba went to the Casati vault together. Why didn't you just take her key and let Alba get on with her work?" Cenni asked, watching her face carefully. She took more than the usual time to reply.

"The key ring is large and the catch is difficult to open. Besides Alba had to pass by the vault anyway," she replied in the indifferent tone that she'd used for most of her answers, but a barely perceptible twitch at the side of her mouth told Cenni that she was pleased with her response. It's her first unrehearsed answer, he thought.

The gate to the Casati vault was shut. It was only when she inserted the key and tried to turn it that she realized the gate wasn't locked. She'd even remarked on this to Alba. They had both seen the body even before they entered the vault. But it wasn't until they were inside that she knew it was the American.

She also agreed with Sergeant Antolini's earlier statement that
Alba probably hadn't known Minelli.

"Did you or Alba touch anything in the vault while you
were there? The body?"

"No."

"Why not? Weren't you concerned that she might need
help?"

"I knew she was dead as soon as we entered the vault." For
the first time that day, she volunteered some information without being asked. "I trained as a physician's assistant. I was married to a doctor. I know a dead body when I see one," she
stated, haughtily. The carrot or the stick, Cenni thought. One
of them usually works.

"The statue. Where was it when you entered the vault?"

"It was lying a few feet from the dead woman," she replied.

"Did you touch it?"

"No."

"Where was it normally located?"

She shrugged before answering. "It was the first time I'd
seen it."

"What about the murdered woman's handbag? I understand from Sergeant Antolini that you brought it back to the
station. Surely you know from all the police dramas you've seen
on TV that you're not supposed to touch anything at the crime
scene."

"I don't watch television," she replied.

At that moment Piero looked up from his note-taking,
pleased that the interview was finally going their way. The suspect was getting less cautious. A half-smile flitted across his
face, but not quickly enough. Orlic met Cenni's eyes for a
brief moment before she looked away. Cenni knew immediately that she wouldn't be making any more flippant remarks
that day nor any mistakes.

"I thought I was doing the right thing," she said, responding a second time to the previous question, this time without being asked.

"I don't understand? Why should you think that?"

"The bag was open. I thought someone had tried to rob her. I was worried he might return before the police arrived?"

"Why he?"

"It was obvious from her clothing that she'd been . . ." She stopped in mid-sentence and breathed deeply. "Raped," she finished abruptly and looked down at the basket of flowers at her feet.

"You didn't consider that the murderer might have made it look like rape, that it might not have been a man?" he asked, scrutinizing her face.

"No," she replied, looking directly into his eyes. If she'd been injected with botox, he thought, her face couldn't have been less expressive.

Cenni had questioned many murder suspects in his years of police work, and Sophie Orlic was certainly a suspect in the murder of Rita Minelli, with motive, means, and opportunity. None, except those with their lawyers present, had kept their composure half so well. He reflected that Sophie Orlic was either a complete innocent, just dull-witted and distrustful of the police, or a highly intelligent adversary. From the flashes of intelligence she had displayed in the last hour, he was inclined toward the latter opinion. He thought of the poster that he had hung on his bedroom wall when he was fourteen, the *Annunciation* by da Vinci. Too bad for Sophie Orlic that he was no longer susceptible to Renaissance Madonnas.

9

IF, AS RECENTLY rumored, the party of the prime minister was planning to sell Italy's public monuments and buildings to lower the national debt, then via San Francisco would be a good place to start, Cenni reflected, as he and Piero approached the Casati home on foot. Bordered on the west by the Basilica of St. Francis and on the east by the Piazza del Comune, it was a street lined with civic and religious buildings of both historical and architectural significance. Located across from the Oratorio dei Pellegrini, built during the Renaissance to house and comfort pilgrims, a few doors down from the medieval Casa Comacini, headquarters to the masons who had come to Assisi to build its many shrines, the Casati home was the last fully private residence on via San Francisco. The others had all been sold to religious foundations, turned over to the government to pay taxes, or subdivided into apartments or into stores selling religious kitsch.

"The family had either great wealth or even greater determination, to hold on to this place through greed, famine, pestilence, and taxes," Cenni remarked idly to Piero as they waited for someone to answer the door. It was, he also noted to himself, a rare example of a medieval townhouse that had not been tortured in later centuries to conform to more elaborate architectural fads. He was curious to see the inside.

The young woman who answered the door, a servant judging from her demeanor, was dressed in street clothes rather than a uniform. A good sign, Cenni thought, that the family might not be as pompous as the questore had suggested. Cenni showed her his credentials and smiled. That appeared to fluster her for the moment, but she gathered her forces admirably and asked them to follow her.

The entrance hall to which they had been admitted cut through the center of the house, from front to back. A series of vaulted arches suggested to Cenni that the hall had been carved out of multiple smaller rooms. The walls, painted a Tuscan yellow, were hung with family portraits—some of them quite good, he thought from his quick appraisal as he walked down the hall. At the end, she opened a door into what appeared to be the family sitting room.

"The count will be with you in a moment. He asked that you make yourself at home," the servant said, smiling faintly. She left by a different door.

Piero accepted the invitation to make himself at home by sitting on the largest, most comfortable-looking chair in the room. Cenni wondered if *Better sit than stand* was the Tonni family motto. He walked about the room slowly, using this opportunity to get to know its inhabitants before he met them in person.

It was a room he liked. It was at the back of the house and he could see a large stone terrace through the French doors that stretched across the south end of the room. The ceiling was high and vaulted, yet the room seemed intimate and informal. Various-sized oriental rugs, mainly tribal, covered the highly polished chestnut wood floors, and one prayer-sized Persian lay in front of the fireplace. Painted a warm white, the walls were covered with family photographs and a few amateurish-looking watercolors. The only important work of art in the room was an Impressionist painting hanging over the fireplace mantle, a Sisley he found upon examining the signature.

Built-in shelves on each side of the fireplace held a stereo, an old-fashioned record player, a small portable television, a VCR, and lots of books, about half of them with English titles. He smiled, noting the number of murder mysteries shoved in among the Dickens, Thackeray, and Austen novels. There were two full shelves of works on and by feminists— Italian, French, and English authors mixed together—and a number of books on the occult; surprisingly, three of them written by Aleister Crowley, the Englishman who had been expelled from Sicily in the 1920s for scandalous acts of black magic and for trafficking in heroin and cocaine. Some Sicilians had even accused Crowley of human sacrifice. Umberto Casati's father had been a close friend of Mussolini, and as Cenni recalled from his studies of drug use in Italy, it was Mussolini's followers who had driven Crowley from the island. He wondered if there was a connection?

The record, tape, and CD collections were diverse, suggesting an eclectic taste for rock, blues, jazz, and opera. The furniture was chintz-covered, overstuffed, and worn, and a small fire burned behind the grate. It was a room in which people could put their feet on the coffee table, he thought with envy, remembering the rigid enforcement of his mother's rules: *Shoes off in the house, feet off the furniture.* He was examining the photo of a good-looking young man prominently displayed on a large refectory table when he heard the door opening and looked about.

The man who entered the room was in his late sixties or early seventies, tall, thin and slightly stooped, well over six feet tall, about his own height, Cenni thought. He had gray hair, cut close, and was wearing thin wire glasses. He was dressed informally but with elegance, in an English tweed jacket, open-necked dark gray knit shirt, and black wool slacks, Italian cut: all expensive. He must have been quite good looking when he was young, Cenni thought. He's still handsome and certainly distinguished, a man who knows his own importance. The count extended his hand in greeting.

"Dottore, I was told you'd be paying us a visit. Please have a seat," he said, motioning to a sofa adjacent to the chair that Piero had already taken. Without waiting for Cenni to comply, the count seated himself directly across from Piero, in a straight-backed wing chair. He eased himself slowly into the chair, holding on to the arms for support. "Arthritis of the back," he said unapologetically, in response to the surprised look on Piero's face.

"A terrible tragedy!" the count began, not waiting for Cenni to introduce himself, Piero, or the subject of their visit. "For something like this to happen on Good Friday and in Assisi, makes it that much more heinous. You can be fully assured that I will do whatever is necessary to assist the police. Assisi doesn't need this type of publicity! A reward, perhaps," he mused.

"And your niece, it's certainly tragic for her as well as for Assisi. She was still a young woman, forty-five I understand," Cenni interjected, then stopped, annoyed at himself for reacting so openly to the count's detachment.

"Well, of course, uh . . . Inspector. That goes without saying," the count responded dryly, demoting him for insubordination, Cenni assumed. "As I said, I'll do all I can to help. Please tell me what that might be."

"I'd like to know as much as possible about your niece, what she was like, who her friends were, why she was here in Italy. But before that, I understand that Dottor Russo called you this morning and that he also sent over one of his own men, Inspector Staccioli, to secure the house. I'd like to speak to Inspector Staccioli before I begin interviewing your family and your household staff, and I would also like to visit your niece's living quarters. I asked one of my own staff, Inspector Ottaviani, to meet me here with the forensic police. Assuming they're somewhere in the house, I'd like to speak to them as well."

"Surely it's not necessary to interview my family," the count rejoined sharply, focusing on only one of Cenni's requests. "My wife, daughter, and granddaughter are all distraught over this brutal murder. My wife is in bed under a doctor's care. We haven't yet told her that my niece was raped. I prefer that you not disturb my family with unnecessary and frivolous questions. Whatever you need to know about my niece, I can tell you. I discussed this very point with Dottor Russo this morning, and he understood my position perfectly."

Piero had followed their exchange as a disinterested observer might watch a tennis rally, waiting patiently for one of the players to hit the ball over the line. He finally had his patience rewarded. Now he's done it! he thought.

"I do understand your position, Signor Casati, perhaps even better than Dottor Russo," Cenni responded, his tone dangerously deferential. "I must point out to you, however, that this is a police investigation into, as you yourself stated very precisely, a brutal murder. No one who knew the victim or saw her on the day of her death is exempt from questioning. That includes all the members of your household: your wife, daughter, and granddaughter. If you prefer we can question your wife in her room with her doctor present." He checked his wristwatch. "I would like to meet with the household in thirty minutes—in this room, or in another if you prefer. And now, with your permission, I would like to speak to officers Staccioli and Ottaviani."

10

PIERO HAD BEEN disappointed when the count had acceded so easily to Cenni's demand to interview the family with a simple *certo*. He had been hoping for some entertainment to cheer him up after Sergeant Antolini's brush-off. It would have been an interesting battle. Cenni was well known for his skill in handling the rich and famous, the principal reason the questore assigned him to so many high profile police investigations. But Piero had been working with Cenni now for more than four years and knew that every now and then he got his back up. As Elena would say when that happened, using an expression she had heard in one of those women's flicks she was always watching, *Fasten your seatbelts, it's going to be a bumpy night.* Very bumpy, Piero thought, as they followed the count below stairs to the kitchen.

The kitchen was the kind of room Piero liked. He loved to eat and the Casati kitchen was just the place in which to do it. It was located immediately below the family room but was at least twice its size. When the house was originally built, it had probably served as both kitchen and storerooms for root vegetables, barrels of wine, flour, salt, and other provisions the family would have needed to get through the cold Umbrian winters. The ceilings were at least fifteen feet high, and supported by massive oak beams blackened with the smoke of centuries. A large alcove on the east wall, carved out of stone, was now used to cure meats and age cheeses. It was also lined with wine and port barrels, although he doubted that a count would drink wine from a barrel. Probably for the servants, he thought. He counted four large oak presses, similar to the one that his *nonna* had in her kitchen when he was growing up. She'd kept biscotti in a jar on the top shelf. He remembered climbing up to the top by pulling out the bottom drawers and using them as steps. He still had a scar on his elbow from one of his falls. He had no regrets, though. That day she had let him finish the whole jar.

There was a huge fireplace on the west wall, large enough for a grown man to enter without stooping. It reminded him of a fireplace he'd once seen in Toledo the year that he and his mother had visited Spain. It had stone benches inside, covered on top with tiles. The guide had told them that the family would sit inside the fireplace in the winter to stay warm. At some point the Casati family had installed a modern gas

stove, stainless steel sink, and large refrigerator in the back of
the kitchen, but the original stone sink and wood-burning
stove were still the centerpieces of the cooking area. In the center of the room stood a large refectory table, at least twelve feet
long. One side held baskets of fresh vegetables, two large
loaves of bread—just out of the oven he surmised from the
warm smell of yeast that filled the air—and what looked to be
the beginnings of a *torta di pasqua*. At the other side were four
police officers, all comfortably ensconced drinking coffee and
eating biscotti. *Fasten your seatbelts*, Piero said to himself when
he spied Elena among them.

The commissario was close to the boiling point. From what
he had observed since entering the house, it appeared that
nothing had been done to secure it or Rita Minelli's living
quarters. If Staccioli was not able to produce the only existing
key to Rita Minelli's room, it meant that any member of the
family or their servants had had plenty of time to search her
room and remove anything that might embarrass or incrimi-
nate them, he reflected. He acknowledged to himself that the
murderer, if actually living in the Casati house, would have had
ample opportunity the previous night to search Minelli's room
before the body was discovered. But the real irritant was that
one of his own officers was relaxing with Russo's lazy bastard!

Elena looked uncomfortable when the commissario entered
the kitchen. She put her cup down and jumped up, a slight
flush rising on her checks. The two forensic technicians also
stood, but Staccioli, an older man of high complexion and
inordinate bulk, remained quite at ease. He nodded to Cenni
but made no effort to acknowledge that a senior officer had
entered the room.

The commissario was the first to break the silence:

"Inspector Staccioli, I understand from Dottor Russo that
you were sent here to secure the house and the murder victim's

living quarters. I would like you to show me her rooms, but first may I have the key?" he said, extending his hand, palm upward.

The confused look on Staccioli's face confirmed what Cenni had already guessed, that he didn't have the key, had probably not asked for it, and in all likelihood had not even visited Minelli's rooms since entering the house. The count intervened before Staccioli could respond.

"There are only two keys to my niece's rooms. One she had. I assume that she carried it on her. The second is with the other household keys in the library, which also serves as my office. One of the conditions of my insurance policy is that I keep the library locked when I'm not using it. It contains some very valuable manuscripts; three are *incunabula*. The library is also equipped with a highly sophisticated alarm system," he added self-importantly. He paused for a moment and then continued, anticipating Cenni's next question. "The key is still there."

"Grazie a Lei," Cenni responded, his tone warmer than it had been in the sitting room. "I would like to talk to you further about your household arrangements. But before that, I wonder if you'd give me a few minutes alone with my staff. I need to review some aspects of the investigation with them. After that, I would like Inspector Ottaviani and our lab technicians to visit your niece's rooms, let's say in five minutes."

As soon as the count had exited the kitchen, closing the large oak door that separated it from the hall, Cenni upbraided Staccioli, his controlled anger evident to both Elena and Piero, but apparently not to Staccioli, who not only remained seated but also began immediately to make excuses.

Cenni interrupted him after the second excuse, which, although rambling, had something to do with counts being different from regular people.

"Inspector, you were sent here to secure the rooms of the murder victim, not to enjoy coffee and biscotti at the expense of Signor Casati. And please, stand when I address you!"

Staccioli shuffled slowly to his feet and brushed the crumbs from the front of his jacket with studied nonchalance. Cenni observed this dissension in the ranks with mild amusement. Due for his pension soon . . . knows he'd have to murder a senior officer, at the very least a vice questore, before he'd lose it. Still, for the sake of the children, . . . he thought, looking at Elena.

He continued, "Don't bank on that pension quite yet, Staccioli! There are ways and ways, and I know them all! When you work on one of my cases, you follow the book, to the letter." He surveyed the three remaining officers who, together, had inched sway from Staccioli. "I shouldn't have to remind any of you that this is a murder investigation for which there are clearly established procedures, none of which you appear to have followed. It doesn't matter to the police if the victim is the niece of a count or a day laborer, the procedures are the same. Perhaps you should all review the Act of 1947," he added, ending his lecture with a conciliatory smile.

Piero decided it was a very mild lecture, indeed. He's given me worse for running a stop sign, he thought, although he had enjoyed that last bit about the Act of 1947. Maybe now Elena will lay off lecturing the rest of us on the blood-sucking aristocracy, had been his first thought. Fat chance, his second.

Cenni said nothing further in condemnation of anyone else in the room, but Elena knew that her time was coming.

II

RITA MINELLI'S BEDROOM and bathroom were on the second floor of the house, in the back, with a view overlooking the garden and the church of San Pietro. The rooms were en suite with access through a single door into the sleeping area. Elena saw immediately that both bedroom and bathroom were equipped for someone with a handicap. They had constructed something similar in their own small apartment in Perugia for her father who had fallen from scaffolding some five years before and was now confined to a wheelchair, widening the doors to his bedroom and to the bathroom that they all shared and installing steel bars so he could lift himself onto the toilet without help. But anything beyond these simple measures was too expensive and too difficult to get approved by their landlord. She looked around the rooms, noting the ample space for maneuvering a wheelchair, the large open shower with safety seat, the furniture designed to be easily opened and closed by someone sitting down, admiring them for their potential to make life easier for the handicapped, but also resenting the privileges of the rich.

"These rooms belonged to the count's mother when she was alive. She was in a wheelchair for three years before she died two years ago," volunteered Lucia, the Casatis' maid, who had escorted Elena and the two technicians up to the rooms.

The maid seemed curiously unaffected by the murder although she obviously wanted to gossip about it and, after unlocking the bedroom door and handing Elena the key, she waited rather conspicuously in the hallway. Elena was aware that most women were more relaxed around women officers and so more likely to provide information that they'd normally withhold from the police. She also knew that the commissario recognized this and used it—and her—by placing her in situations where she was likely to gain their trust. The feminist in her rebelled at this tactic, but the police officer used it to advantage. Although Elena knew she was rationalizing, she soothed her conscience by telling herself that the same women who revealed more than what was good for them did so only because they really didn't respect women as police officers.

The forensic technicians had started dusting the room for prints when Lucia, peering into the room, interrupted. "What are they doing with that black powder?" she asked.

"They're dusting for fingerprints to see who else has been in the room," Elena answered, smiling warmly to suggest that she was open to further talk.

"Oh, they won't find anything. She locked her door whenever she left the house. I never clean in there, not since Christmas anyway, when she asked the countess for the key."

"She cleaned the rooms herself!" Elena responded, feigning disapproval. "How strange! But Americans are strange. They're always afraid people are trying to rob them. We found that out last year when we were investigating some hotel robberies in Perugia. Many Americans won't leave their keys at the front desk."

"I don't know what she thought I'd want that belonged to her. My clothes and jewelry are a lot better than anything she has," Lucia responded indignantly. "When she first came here in June she dressed like an old lady. *Brutta!* She always wore sneakers when she left the house, even with her mink jacket! I'd be ashamed to go out looking that way." She glanced furtively at the technicians and then lowered her voice. "In January, right after the New Year, she started dressing better, a lot like Signora Artemisia, even had her hair cut like hers and had her eyebrows tweezed. They were like bushes before. My friend Romina—she waits tables at Il Duomo—said that the *americana* used to come in there with a man. Romina said she treated him like a boyfriend. He's a lot younger," she added triumphantly, providing this last bit of gossip as conclusive proof of Minelli's execrably bad taste.

"But I'm sure the family is devastated. It's obvious they thought a lot of her. Look at the rooms they gave her, with such beautiful views," Elena said admiringly, hoping to draw the maid out further.

Lucia lowered her voice even more, looking around before speaking. "The count hated her! He was furious when she took over his mother's rooms, but the countess said they should let her be, that she'd be leaving soon. And Signora Artemisia, she hated her, too. She was always making fun of the way she dressed. We used to laugh together."

"I guess that stopped in January when Signora Minelli started dressing like her?"

"Oh, no! Yesterday, they had a big row. I was cleaning the stairs and heard them talking very loud from Signora Artemisia's room. *Bada ai fatti tuoi!* I heard Signora Artemisia say to the Americana."

"Mind your own business. That's pretty brutal. I wonder why?"

"Something about a book, I think. When I passed the room, the *Americana* was holding this large book, like one of those moldy books in the count's library. I dust in there every Tuesday and Saturday," she added, wrinkling her nose in disgust. "Signora Artemisia started talking in English when she saw me, so I don't know what she said after that, but I could tell she was very angry."

"And the countess! She liked her niece?"

"*Non lo so.* But she's a very nice lady, very kind to everyone. She used to sit with the count's mother for hours talking to her and holding her hand, even when the old lady was gaga. She was very sick, you know, had that disease where you shake all over. I had to help Sophie put her into the shower."

"The information you just gave me about the quarrel between the Signora and the *Americana,* you must tell that to the commissario when he interviews you."

"Oh, I can't!" Lucia responded, apparently forgetting that Elena was the police. "She'll kill . . . be angry with me!" Lucia amended with a suppressed giggle, realizing the significance of her first choice of words.

"You needn't worry. Your interview with the commissario and Inspector Tonni is private. They won't repeat anything you tell them unless it's absolutely necessary."

The mention of the commissario redirected Lucia to warmer thoughts. "*Il commissario è molto bello.* Is he married?"

Elena smiled, but before she could respond, one of the forensic technicians interrupted to tell her they were finished. He was carrying a large see-through plastic folder containing loose papers, and a sealed manila envelope. "We found these hidden under the mattress," he said, handing them over to Elena. "We're finished dusting them for prints. These, too," he added, and handed her two small diaries, bound in black leather.

"So that's where she hid them!" Lucia exclaimed. "Oops," she added, and giggled again at her blunder.

12

WHILE INSPECTOR OTTAVIANI and the two technicians were in Rita Minelli's rooms finally performing the search and secure operation so necessary to a murder investigation, the count gave the commissario and Piero the grand tour. They moved first to the outside of the house, to the area directly beyond the kitchen door. A neatly arranged vegetable garden was located to the right of the door, and it appeared that someone had recently been cleaning out the winter debris; a hoe had been left standing upright in one of the raised beds. A large merry-go-round of a clothesline was located to the left. Toward the front hung two pairs of women's panties (red with black lace edging) while further back a few bedraggled dishtowels flapped in the wind. Cenni suppressed a smile when the count, who had also spied the skimpy undergarments, pushed the line vigorously until the dishtowels came to the front.

The kitchen garden was enclosed on all sides, in part by a brick wall some five feet high and in part by a small stone structure located at the bottom of the garden. From where Cenni stood, the structure appeared to be in use as a gardening shed. He wondered if in less grand times it might have been a pigsty and walked down the gravel path to take a closer look. He circled the pighouse, and at the back came upon a very steep stone stairway without a handrail. It was in considerable disrepair. The count, who was highly proprietary, followed Cenni to see what he was looking at.

"Nobody uses that stairway any more, too dangerous. It leads to a *vicolo* below the house, which connects directly to via Fontebella. Our old gardener tried to keep the steps in repair, but he died a few years back. The new man can't be bothered," he added, in disdain. "You'd take your life in your hands trying to get down those steps." The count then agreed with the commissario's supposition that the garden stairway was the only exit from the house that did not lead directly to via San Francesco.

From the servants' floor, Umberto Casati's term for the kitchen area, they returned to the street floor, the main living area of the house. The floor contained four large rooms: the family sitting room; a dining room directly across from the sitting room, heavily formal and filled with antiques; a drawing room, also formal, and used only when the family held parties and receptions, as well as a small bathroom whose door was discreetly hidden behind a velvet curtain. The fourth room, the library, which fronted via San Francisco, appeared to be the most important room in the house, if Cenni were to judge by the highly sophisticated alarm system that the count had to deactivate before they could gain entry.

It was an impressive room, perhaps the most impressive that Cenni had yet seen in a private dwelling. Octagonal in shape, the room was lined with ceiling-to-floor cabinets with doors of hand-blown glass. The cabinets were filled to capacity with morocco-bound manuscripts, the bindings on most suggesting great age. But the real beauty of the room was its vaulted ceiling, which was frescoed with motifs in the grotesque style of painting that had been common in the late 1500s. The ceiling was a profusion of exotic birds, flowers, and forest animals, all intertwined in rich dazzling color. The count told them with great pride that the ceiling was attributed to the Florentine, Alessandro Allori, who had also worked for the Medici on the Uffizi ceiling.

The few pieces of furniture—the count's desk, which was placed directly in front of the windows to capture the little natural light that entered the room, and four display cases—were antiques, seventeenth-century, according to the count, and irreplaceable. The single touch of modernity in the room was the count's chair, which although disguised in cracked leather, was of an ergonomic design, no doubt a concession to his arthritis. The reasons, however, for the elaborate alarm system and the expensive insurance policy were the books and a curious display of Venetian daggers.

Cenni stopped to admire one of the daggers. Its placard described it as a *misericorde*, circa 1560, the blade forged in Damascus. It was a straight, very narrow dagger with a deadly edge. The hilt, which was out of proportion to the blade, was unusual: an elaborate twisting of silver and gold wire in the shape of a mermaid, its pommel a gold ball inset with a large blood-red ruby. The count leaned over Cenni to see what was attracting his attention.

"It's called a *misericorde*," the count explained, "because it was used to give the final mercy cut to one mortally wounded." He mimed a cutting action across the throat. "It would kill instantly, although it's not a fine example of that particular weapon," he added derisively. "Its proportions are all wrong, but the ruby is rare, a star ruby of unusual size and quality and quite valuable. But I think you'll find that the books are of more interest, Dottore." He went on to tell Cenni—and Piero when he acknowledged his presence—that the majority of books were legal documents: "One of the finest libraries of its kind in Italy," he said with great pride. "Three of the books are *incunabula*, printed before 1501," he explained, for the benefit of Piero. Cenni lingered over one of the three manuscripts, admiring its binding, which appeared to be original, until rather vigorously nudged by the count toward a different display case.

"As a jurist, I'm sure you'll find these books of more interest, Dottore," he said in a surprisingly affable tone, even including Piero in its circle of warmth. "They're the original case histories of the Venetian schism. They were presented to Umberto Casati, my ancestor, when he was made Count Palantine in October 1607 by Pope Paul V—Camillo Borghese—in gratitude for legal services rendered to the Roman Curia. I'm a descendent of the Borghese family on both sides of my family," he added proudly. "The Pope and the first Count Casati, my namesake, were second cousins. They studied jurisprudence together in Perugia, even played together as children," he said, unable to contain his enthusiasm for family name-dropping. "It's not widely acknowledged by historians, but the first Count Casati effected the compromise between Rome and the Venetian Republic, saving Venice from the grip of Protestantism."

"Helped, no doubt, by the good offices of the other principals, France and Spain," Cenni said with gentle asperity.

Not bothered by the suggestion that his eminent ancestor may have had substantial help in bringing Venice back into the Catholic fold, the count responded in kind. "With the *terribile frate*, Paolo Sarpi, as one's adversary, even the help of France and Spain would not always have been sufficient."

Cenni laughed at the reference to the friar who had defied Rome and the Borghese Pope and, recalling to mind the wording of the self-serving non-compromise, said, "The Republic agrees *to conduct itself with its accustomed piety.*"

"As the Republic is still doing," the count rejoined.

When they'd stopped laughing at the allusion to the luxurious, licentious, and always refractory Venetian Republic, the count remarked on the commissario's obvious knowledge of church law.

"I studied church law at the University of Bologna," Cenni replied, which drew them deeper into a discussion of the relative merits of the combatants of 1600, with Cenni arguing the case of the Venetian Republic, that the clergy were not exempt from the jurisdiction of the civil courts, which position, as he reminded the count, was now codified in Italian law.

Their lively but friendly discussion helped to blunt some of the antagonism that had been building between them, and Cenni hoped the uneasy peace would last, at least until the family interviews were over. Somehow he doubted it. The noticeable absence of a computer in the library, which also served as the count's office, coupled with the count's fixation on his family's history and eminence, suggested a man who, if given the choice, would have preferred to live in a less democratic age, one in which policemen lacked the temerity to come calling on counts with warrants in hand.

It crossed Cenni's mind that Umberto Casati might be heir to more than Borghese manuscripts. In October 1607, the same year and month that Camillo Borghese, the then Pope, had deeded the Venetian manuscripts to his first cousin, five assailants from Rome had attacked Friar Sarpi at dusk along a Venetian canal for his temerity in challenging the Pope's interdict—and winning. As Umberto Casati, the seventeenth Count, had just assiduously pointed out, he was heir to a double-dose of Borghese genes.

The count, who was not privy to Cenni's thoughts on his ancestor's illustrious bad temper, proceeded with the tour. The layout of the upstairs, which was reached by a different staircase from the one that they had descended earlier to reach the kitchen, was identical to the rooms below, the hall also running front to back with two rooms on either side, each with its own bathroom. The count explained that they had added the bathrooms back in the 1970s when their children were approaching adolescence. The rooms—with the exception of the one that had been used by Rita Minelli and which was still occupied by the forensic police—were empty, their occupants presumably waiting below to be interviewed. Cenni was surprised, as he had been when he'd entered the family sitting room, to find that all the chambers, including the count's, were furnished for comfort rather than elegance: carpeted floors, large modern beds, good-looking wardrobes, and chests that were certainly not antiques. After looking at his wristwatch, Cenni declined the count's invitation to visit the attic rooms, which the count explained "are used by the family as storerooms and in the past housed servants," adding with a slight frown that "servants in these days make their own hours and usually elect to live out."

Cenni had just turned to descend the stairs to begin his questioning of the family when he was stopped by Elena. "Commissario, a minute please?" She pulled him aside to show him the diary and file folder and to tell him the gist of Lucia's gossip: the existence of the boyfriend, the overheard argument between Rita Minelli and Artemisia Casati, the count's open dislike of his niece. She smiled when she told him of Lucia's gaffe about the diaries. "Probably the reason Minelli locked her door and made her own bed!"

Cenni responded absentmindedly, still thinking about the count's fixation on his Borghese ancestors. A good dose of insanity there as well, Cenni recollected.

"*Certo*, Elena. Piero and I will be busy here for another two hours questioning the family. Call Perugia to see if they've received any responses to my earlier inquiries regarding the family's finances, and see if you can locate the boyfriend. I'd like to get his statement today, as soon as we're finished here." When he'd issued his orders, he realized from the strained look on Elena's face that she was waiting for a sign that he'd forgiven her earlier lapse. He knew how much she disliked using her sex to gain the confidence of other women, yet she'd done so with Lucia, and very successfully too. He said, this time with considerably more warmth, "I'd like you to peruse Minelli's diary and her other papers. Call me at home tonight or tomorrow if you find anything crucial; otherwise write down the salient points so I can review them on Monday morning." He hesitated for a moment. "And see what she has to say about the men in her life. Batori claims she was pregnant. Two months, maybe more."

She responded plaintively, "But what about tomorrow! Don't you want me to help Piero?"

"I don't think so, Elena. We'll manage. No point in ruining everyone's Easter."

Elena watched as he descended the stairs and wondered why men are always nice to women in just the wrong way.

13

AMELIA CASATI WAS at a disadvantage whenever there was a major crisis in her household. Her passport identified her as Italian but in all other respects, root and branch, she was thoroughly English. Whatever the circumstances—illness, death, or a fallen soufflé—she maintained an outward demeanor of calm and civility. When her only son and the person she had loved most in the world died at nineteen, she had retired to her bedroom to mourn in private. That need for privacy had greatly disconcerted Anna, her mother-in-law, who had expected some outward show of the grief that they all shared. Anna, with eyes swollen and red behind black veil and dark glasses, was the one who had fainted on the day of the funeral, falling on Camillo's coffin; Amelia was the one who had revived her. So, it came as a surprise to them all, herself included, when she completely fell apart after hearing the news of her niece's murder.

The news had come that morning, shortly after 8:30, in a telephone call from Fulvio Russo of the Assisi police. Amelia was sleeping in after a late and tedious dinner with family and close friends at one of Assisi's notable restaurants. All except Amelia were smokers, and the private room they had reserved was close and airless. They had arrived home shortly after midnight, she with a splitting headache and Umberto still complaining of Rita's lack of courtesy in missing the dinner without a word to anyone. It was not that he regretted her absence—quite the contrary. But his dislike of Rita took the form of petty indictments of whatever she did or said: She spoke English with a Brooklyn accent, she used Neapolitan slang when speaking Italian (it had happened only once), she had taken over his mother's rooms without asking, and so forth.

Amelia had finally snapped as they were getting ready for bed. "You never consider anyone but yourself," she'd thrown at him. "I'm the one who has to act as peacemaker between the two of you. And in this family, peacemakers are not blessed! It's constant tension, waiting to see what she'll do to annoy you and then what you'll do to retaliate. Can't you let anything go? She told me only yesterday that she's planning to marry John Williams. When that happens she'll have to find another place to live. Please try to keep the peace until then."

He had brightened up considerably after that. She could hear him singing show tunes in the bathroom and when they turned the lights out, he'd kissed her firmly on the mouth and immediately fallen asleep. She lay awake for another hour, listening to him snore.

After Amelia's collapse, Umberto had called their doctor, who had come immediately and given her a sedative, with the promise that she'd feel better in a short while. But she didn't feel better. She was consumed by guilt. From the day that Rita had arrived in Assisi, Umberto and Artemisia, even the servants, had treated her niece as an outsider, a scavenging bird pecking off scraps from the Casati name. When Rita was not around—and sometimes even when she was—Artemisia ridiculed her. She laughed at Rita's hair, her clothes, her thick eyebrows, and even her piety. When Rita started dressing and wearing her hair like Artemisia, Artemisia had grown crueler, calling her *la americana grottesca*.

Amelia blamed herself. She had not been a perfect mother. Camillo had been such a beautiful child, with flaxen curls and large blue eyes—so like her own dear father, always kind to everyone. And when he laughed, it was infectious. They all laughed with him. He was her golden child, filling those parts of her that until his birth had been empty. She would have been content with Camillo, but Umberto had wanted two children. Artemisia had been born three years later. It had been a difficult pregnancy and Artemisia proved to be a difficult child. Amelia had been sick the full nine months that she carried Artemisia, and Artemisia had been sick another nine months with colic. Where Camillo had taken after Amelia's English family in looks, Artemisia was wholly Italian. As an adult, she had an arresting, almost disturbing beauty. As a child, she had looked and acted like a gnome. Possessive and greedy, she'd had temper tantrums whenever Amelia had denied her anything. Only Marie, their housekeeper, could manage Artemisia and, as Amelia now acknowledged to herself, love her.

Rita had also grown up without a mother's love. Amelia had met Umberto's sister only once, forty years earlier, when she had returned to Italy with the five-year-old Rita in tow. Newly married and passionately in love with Umberto, Amelia had wanted very much to be friends with her husband's only sister, but try as she might she had found Livia impossible to like. Her sister-in-law had all of her brother's faults and none of his virtues. She was arrogant, inconsiderate, physically vain, and to the distress of the entire household, a hypochondriac. Livia and Rita lived with them for one year, and during most of that time, Livia fancied herself ill with whatever disease was prominent at the time. She'd lain in bed until noon, smoked incessantly, and alienated the servants with her relentless demands. During that year she'd left the care of Rita to Amelia and Anna.

Little Rita was always underfoot, though what in later life would be considered officious, in childhood was endearing. She followed the housekeeper about with a duster in hand, offering to clean the bric-a-brac. She sat with her grandmother for hours holding her wool while Anna knitted, chattering

away about her dolls. If permitted, she would fetch and carry
for hours without complaint: Umberto's glasses, Amelia's book,
her grandmother's rosary beads. At the end of a year, Salvatore
Minelli arrived in Italy to take Livia and Rita home to Brooklyn.
What Amelia didn't find out until much later was that Umberto
had paid for the trip.

And now Rita was dead, murdered, and Amelia felt a profound sadness, in some ways even beyond what she'd felt when
Camillo had died. He had been only nineteen, but he had lived
as though there were no tomorrows—five broken bones before
he was fifteen! He had skied in Cortina, hang glided off Mount
Subasio, driven cars with abandon, had a child when he was
eighteen, defying his father and everyone else to practice his
own beliefs. But Rita was just beginning. . . .

A soft knock on the door roused her to control herself—
for Umberto's sake, she thought. It was Lucia, who looked
guiltily around the door. "*Scusi*, Countess, but the police have
arrived. The count asks if you're feeling any better. The
police want to talk to everyone in the house. The count asks
if you'll come down, or should he bring them up?" she asked,
her barely repressed excitement apparent from the high
pitch of her voice.

"No, I'll come down, Lucia. Please tell the count that I'll be
with him in fifteen minutes."

14

WHEN CENNI OPENED the sitting room door, five women
looked up expectantly, each as different in appearance as
possible in a country as homogeneous as Italy. The count, who
followed immediately behind him, made the introductions:
his wife Amelia, his daughter Artemisia—who acknowledged
their previous meeting with a slight nod of recognition—his

granddaughter Paola, their maid Lucia Stampoli, and their cook Concetta Di Gennari—the last a jolly-looking fat woman and the only one to smile. And such a smile! Wide and happy, it gleamed with gold.

At Amelia Casati's request, Cenni interviewed the cook first. It seemed that Concetta had made special arrangements so that she could come in to prepare their Easter dinner. Normally she had Saturdays off and worked Sundays, but tomorrow was Easter. It was now almost three, and she had two young children at home who needed her attention. At the count's insistence, the interviews took place in the library, with two additional chairs brought in to accommodate Piero and the person to be interviewed, although as Cenni later conceded to Piero, with Concetta he did more listening than interviewing.

Cenni had concluded years earlier that people's dispositions, like most things in life, exist in a continuum. A small number of people by nature are always unhappy; an even smaller number are always happy; and the rest occupy the great in between—with some tears, some laughter, and much tedium. Concetta was on the extreme edge of the continuum. From the moment she sat down, she radiated happiness, her gold tooth always on display. The dead American, God rest her soul, was a wonderful woman; the Casatis were wonderful employers; her Tony was a wonderful husband; their two little girls were gifts from God. Even Lucia was wonderful, although it would be better if she rinsed the dishes before putting them into the dishwasher. Somehow, in among the wonderfuls, she revealed that she rarely ventured out of the Casati kitchen into other parts of the house. She worked six days a week, from ten to four, and had little contact with the family beyond the countess who paid her salary every week. She prepared their midday meal, three courses and a sweet, which was served by

Lucia in the dining room at one o'clock. She also prepared dinner, which was usually something light, cold meat and a salad or a casserole. Lucia or the countess would heat what she'd prepared in the microwave. The family usually dined at seven, eating in the kitchen. As Lucia finished at seven, the countess would put the dirty dishes in the dishwasher. If there were any heavy pots to clean, Concetta did them when she came to work the next day. She never cooked for them on Good Friday—they always ate out.

Signora Minelli had eaten with the family when she'd first come to Assisi but had stopped some time ago. Concetta couldn't remember exactly when and didn't know why. The countess would probably know. The *Americana* was very health-conscious and ate lots of fruit and yogurt, which she kept in the refrigerator. Sometimes they would talk together when she came into the kitchen. They were both devoted to St. Rita. She explained, "Giulia, she's my baby. She's two now and very healthy." She beamed: "And very beautiful! But when she was born, we thought we'd lose her—four months premature and so tiny, less than four pounds. Tony—he's my husband—and me, we made a pilgrimage to Cascia, to pray to St. Rita. Now we go regularly, to say thank you, the last Saturday in every month. We made a sacred promise!

"The last time, two Saturdays ago, we saw Signora Minelli and Signorina Paola sitting together in a café near St. Rita's Basilica. I wanted to stop and talk, but Tony said they looked very serious. He said I shouldn't bother them. We both thought that Signorina Paola had been crying."

She paused, and Cenni thought she wanted to say something more. "Is there something else?"

"I was surprised to see Signorina Paola there. Lucia says the Signorina's a communist, and everyone knows that communists don't believe in saints." She sighed. "Lucia is a terrible gossip and doesn't always tell the truth." Cenni suspected that if Concetta's happiness had an Achilles heel, it might well be Lucia.

15

AMELIA CASATI WAS so different from her husband in manner and appearance that they could have been the poster couple for the questionable truism that opposites attract. Where he was tall and distinguished, she was short and plain; where he bullied, she acquiesced; his arrogance was countered by her diffidence. Unlike the count, who had managed for the most part to ignore Piero and his substantial presence, she acknowledged both detectives with a weak smile before taking her seat. Her blotched face and pink-rimmed eyes suggested to Cenni that at least one person in the Casati family had experienced some pain at the news of Rita Minelli's murder.

Cenni began by offering his condolences on the death of her niece. "I understand from your husband that you're under the care of your doctor. Inspector Tonni and I will have you out of here in no time. Just a few routine questions." At his last statement, she looked down at her fingers, still noticeably ink-stained from recent fingerprinting, her gesture a silent reproach.

Cenni responded by explaining that the police needed to distinguish between prints expected to be found in the burial vault—those of the Casati family—and prints of people who could not be accounted for. He then asked her to describe her previous day's activities with an approximate timetable.

She told him that she'd been to her doctor in Perugia in the morning—a routine checkup—and had returned a few minutes before one o'clock. She had lunch with the family in the dining room, finishing at 1:45. Immediately after that, she had gone to the garden room, located at the back of the family sitting room, where she had arranged some flowers that had been delivered while they were eating. At around two o'clock, she'd carried the arrangement, a bowl of yellow roses, into the hall and had seen Rita letting herself out the front door. For the remainder of the day, until six o'clock, when she retired to her room to bathe and dress for the evening, she had been in the sitting room, writing letters and reading. The doors had been closed to retain the heat and no one had come in during that time. She also told Cenni that she had not been near the cemetery since the previous Sunday, her usual day to visit, and that she had no idea who could have murdered her niece, although she did suggest that the motive may have been robbery. When he'd questioned her further in this regard, she indicated that her niece frequently carried large sums of money on her, a habit she'd tried to discourage but without success.

Cenni found her surprisingly unemotional in recounting her activities on the day of the murder. Umberto Casati had said that his wife was crushed by the news of her niece's death, that she had been so traumatized, her doctor had given her a sedative and had suggested that they not tell her of the rape. Yet, in reciting her timetable, she was composed, articulate, and precise. Rehearsed, he wondered, or just a reflection of the punctilio that Italians find so irritating in the English. If her account was rehearsed, it didn't unduly concern him. Most people have an atavistic fear of the police—the innocent as well as the guilty—and most people, if handed the gift of time, which Russo had allowed the Casati family, are likely to prepare their statements in advance.

Early in his career, Cenni had learned the hard way that the successful interrogation of suspects is a balance of thesis and antithesis. You ask the expected questions to gain their confidence, then

counter with the unexpected to confound and intimidate. In
one of his early murder investigations more than twelve years
earlier—the brutal maiming and killing of a five-year-old child—
one of the suspects, a gentle motherly woman in her late sixties,
had answered all of his questions with assurance, prefacing each
response with a gentle smile and a *mio figlio*. He couldn't believe
that she might be the killer and had shown great sensitivity in framing his questions. She had gone on to kill again, another child,
even younger than the first. The face of the second child, slashed
beyond recognition, had haunted him for years. He still lived
with that failure and the knowledge that no one is exempt from
suspicion.

Cenni said, "Some of our questions may be painful, and for
that I apologize, but the answers are important. They could
help us find your niece's murderer. We've been told that she
was an American, that she came to Assisi in June to bury her
mother, but that's all we know. It would be helpful if you could
tell us more—why did she stay on in Assisi, what was she like.
I would like to understand her better." She surprised him by
responding immediately, without further prompting and in
some detail. Like day and night, he thought, remembering
Sophie Orlic's minimal responses.

"She was the daughter of the count's sister, Livia, who died
in June. Livia was seven years older than Umberto. They were
never close," she added, stressing this point. "After the war
Livia married an American soldier who had been stationed in
Perugia. They went to live in the United States, in Brooklyn.
When Livia died in June, Rita called to ask if she could bury
her mother in the family vault. She said her mother's last wish
was to return to Assisi." She hesitated for a moment before continuing. "I don't believe Livia ever adjusted to living in the
United States or to her lack of social status there. Her husband's grandparents were immigrants from Naples," she added

with a wry smile. A snob but a gracious one, Cenni thought, as Amelia continued.

"The Casati family was of some importance in Umbria before the war and Livia was overindulged by her father until his death—at least that's my husband's perception," she added, smiling shyly. "I only got to know Livia when she returned to Assisi with Rita and stayed with us for a year. Rita was five at the time." She hesitated for a moment as though weighing what to say next, her eyes meeting his gaze with a surprising steadiness

"In Italy it's considered bad luck to speak ill of the dead; in England we're less superstitious," she said apologetically before continuing. "Livia was a bad mother. I can't remember her ever hugging or kissing Rita or acknowledging the child in any way, beyond using her to run errands: 'Rita, *cara mia*, run upstairs and get my cigarettes,' was her usual request. I can imagine if she used a five-year-old that way, how she must have used Rita as she grew older and became less endearing. We all do grow less endearing," she added somewhat sadly.

"You're probably wondering why I'm telling you all this about Livia, but I think it's important if you're to understand what Rita was like." She paused for a brief moment, unwinding the lace-edged handkerchief that she had twisted into a ball so she could blow her nose, an action that Cenni found both surprising and appealing from a woman of such dignity.

"My niece spent most of her life caring for her mother. From what Rita told me, she had no life beyond her mother after her father died. She was eighteen at the time. She taught English in a secondary school in Brooklyn, returning home in the evenings to get her mother's dinner and to clean house. Livia didn't trust anyone and refused to hire anyone to help in the house. To Livia, all outsiders were *stranieri*.

"We each have different ways of reacting to rejection and abuse. Rita's reaction was probably the healthiest for society, although perhaps not for herself. She tried harder to be loved, assuming, as most children do, that it was her fault that she was not. She was always offering help and advice—often to complete strangers—unfortunately, even when the help was clearly not needed . . . or wanted." She stopped and looked at him directly.

She hesitated a moment before going on. "I think, Dottore, that you should know this, since you'll probably hear it from others. . . . The count didn't like Rita. It was her officiousness that irritated him the most. He's a very private man and he doesn't understand people who infringe on the privacy of others. I'm not making excuses for him. At times he was very unkind to Rita, but I do understand why—she was something of a busybody—always, of course, with the best intentions!" Her last remark, ironic and resentful, surprised Cenni. Until then he would have said that Amelia Casati had both liked and felt sorry for her niece. Now he was not so sure.

"You said she arrived in June to bury her mother but this is now March. Why was she still here?"

"Well, when Rita called to ask if she could bring her mother to Assisi to be buried, Umberto agreed immediately. But he assumed—actually, we both assumed—that she would stay a few weeks, then return to Brooklyn and her job. In August, she told us that she had resigned her teaching position before she'd even left Brooklyn. She said she had retired, that she was planning to settle in Assisi!"

"Retired?" Cenni interrupted. "She was young to be thinking of retirement. What was she planning to live on? Did she have money?"

"Under normal circumstances I would never inquire about someone's finances, but I did ask Rita. Needless to say, we were all very surprised by her announcement."

"And her response?" Cenni asked.

"She said there was a pension which she was entitled to claim in a few years. She had also sold the house in Brooklyn for close to a quarter of a million dollars. When Umberto's mother died a few years ago, Livia inherited half her estate. I assume, although I can't say for sure, that Livia left that money to her daughter, a considerable sum. Since July, Rita's been teaching at our school, though only two classes a week. We pay . . . paid her what we pay our other teachers—thirteen euros an hour—but I doubt that even a month's salary would buy one of the outfits I've seen her wearing lately."

"This money—her money—do you have any idea who she's left it to?"

"That's hardly something I could . . . or would ask. She had an Aunt Marie, her father's sister, and a younger cousin. She mentioned them both once or twice but not with affection. I know she had an attorney in New York. She spoke of him when she discussed the sale of the house." She hesitated with a derisive smile on her face. "You probably know more about that than I do, Dottore!—Lucia told me that your officers found some papers in my niece's room and took them away." *And without my permission* was left unspoken but clearly intended.

"Her teaching job at the *Accademia*? How did that come about?" Cenni asked, ignoring the barely disguised rebuke.

"As it happened, one of our teachers, a woman from Liverpool, decided to return home in July without giving notice. We had an intensive English class scheduled to start in mid-July with ten students already signed up. Rita volunteered to teach it, and I suggested to Umberto that we let her. That was before we knew that she had no intention of returning to the States. Rita had great staying power!" The last, uttered more to herself than to him, held an undertone of bitterness beyond the ordinary displeasure a host feels when a guest overstays her leave. Cenni decided to probe further.

"Am I correct in understanding that the school is owned and run by your husband?"

"After the war Umberto and his mother had a very difficult time; Anna had no money. Her husband had foolishly invested all their fluid assets in state bonds. And then, shortly afterward, in 1943, he was killed by a bomb. My husband's father had been a prominent member of the Fascist party and a great friend of *Il Duce*, a matter of public record," she added in explanation, when Inspector Tonni looked up in surprise from his note taking.

"After the war Anna was ostracized by the very people who had asked the count for endless favors when the *fascista* were in power. She discovered, as we all do in the end, that loyalty is a virtue of self-interest. Unfortunately, this was true of her daughter as well as her friends. As soon as Livia saw the hard times coming, she managed to get out by marrying an American. Anna was left with the house, a few antiques, a fifteen-year-old son to be educated, and the manuscripts: of great value now; back then, most people would have sold them to buy food or burned them for fuel. But Anna was an extraordinary woman. She sold the antiques—to Argentine bargain hunters—but figured out a way to hold on to the house and the manuscripts by starting the *Accademia*. Most people think Umberto established it, but the credit really goes to Anna. There were very few women in postwar Italy who could have or would have done what she did. She saw immediately the importance that English would assume in the postwar world. It was a language that she spoke quite well; her governess had been English. She started the school in 1948 and ran it with our help until 1992, when she was diagnosed with Parkinson's disease. Umberto has run it since."

She paused for a moment and Cenni could see tears welling in her eyes. He waited patiently for her to continue.

"After Anna's death, we found that she had left the school to Umberto and Livia jointly. Umberto offered to give Livia half the yearly profits, but she insisted that we pay her half its market value, the equivalent of 500,000 euros. We did, but we had to mortgage the house. Anna was not herself at the end," she said, her voice beginning to quiver. "At one point, she made a will leaving everything to Camillo, my son, who had already been dead some fifteen years. She was always scribbling wills before she died. Most of them were barely legible and none of them were legal. Of course, in the case of the school, Livia was her daughter and the will was properly executed under Italian law . . . but she'd told me so often that I was her true daughter." Her voice faded on her last words and Piero had to learn forward to hear.

She sat silent for a full minute, looking at Cenni without seeing him. Then like a scratched record that's moved beyond its imperfection, she continued as before, her voice measured and clear. "Perhaps now you can appreciate that Umberto's dislike of his niece was not just willful and unkind. It was a natural progression of his feelings for a sister who had deserted him and his mother when she was needed most." She stopped abruptly, and Cenni suspected that she had just now realized that she'd said more than he'd asked for—perhaps more than was prudent. He decided not to push her further on the question of Anna and the school.

"And your daughter Artemisia . . . how did she get along with her cousin? We understand from your maid that she and Rita had an argument just yesterday concerning one of your husband's manuscripts."

Her response was immediate and electric, "Sheer nonsense! Why should Artemisia and Rita have a discussion regarding one of Umberto's manuscripts? Neither of them had anything to do with the library. I doubt that Rita ever entered the library since her arrival in June. It's kept locked except when Umberto is working in there. He and I are the only ones with the combination. I find it somewhat naive, Dottore, that you would credit anything Lucia tells you about us. She's an inveterate gossip, and a malicious one." The latter comment, so out of character with her previous gentle ironies, elicited a surprised look from Cenni and a shrug and a wan smile from the countess in return. "Servants are so difficult to find these days."

"That would appear to be true, that she's a gossip," Cenni responded uncritically, sensing that he still had her confidence, not wanting to lose it. "To my original question then, your daughter and Rita, were they friends?"

"No, not friends exactly. There's an eight-year difference in age. I doubt Artemisia even remembered Rita, who visited us last when she was sixteen. Her mother sent her for the summer so she could improve her Italian. There's certainly no doubt that Rita admired my daughter. She'd even started to dress like her. She's been buying her clothes in Florence and Rome, from the same boutiques where Artemisia shops. She actually purchased the same cape and in the same color," she added caustically.

"And your granddaughter?"

"Paola lives in Rome. She's studying to be an art restorer. She was home briefly at Christmas and is staying at home now for a few weeks to rest. She had a very bad case of influenza this winter, and her doctor suggested that she take it easy for a bit. But there's more than twenty years difference in age between Rita and Paola, hardly the basis for a friendship, Dottore! But since you plan to speak to my daughter and granddaughter yourself, perhaps you should address your questions to them, directly," she responded, this time openly checking her wristwatch.

"Only one or two more questions and we're finished. I understand from your cook that your niece stopped eating with the family a while ago. Was there an argument between your niece and any member of the family?"

"No, certainly not! She stopped eating with us right after the New Year at about the same time she asked for the key to her room. Apparently, she'd discovered that Lucia was reading her diary. I told her to write in English instead of Italian, and not make such a fuss, but she was adamant, insisting that she'd clean her own room. As for taking her meals separately, I had no objection. In truth, I welcomed it. I knew Umberto would prefer it. She had started seeing a man who lives in Assisi, an American, I believe. His name is John Williams. Lucia told me—and anyone else who would listen—that Rita had dinner with him almost every night in Il Duomo. One of Lucia's friends is a waitress there. I met him only once, so there's really nothing further I can tell you. Are we getting to the last question?" she asked anxiously, clearly intent on finishing the interview.

"The last few! I'm intrigued by certain information given to me by the Assisi police concerning the woman who provides flowers for the family vault, a Signora Orlic. I was told that she's had some differences with your niece, that Signora Orlic was blackmailing a woman who'd worked for her and that your niece found this out and reported it to the police. Yet, I was also told that Signora Orlic still works for you. That's rather curious don't you think!"

"No, I don't! Really, Dottore, you should stop accepting gossip as gospel! My husband and I were extraordinarily displeased by what Rita did to Sophie. It's just one more example of her propensity to meddle and cause trouble. Sophie Orlic took care of my mother during the last year of her life. She had been a physician's assistant in Croatia but didn't have a license to work here. We needed full-time care for Anna, and Sophie seemed to be the right person. We sponsored her for a *soggiorno*, gave her a place to live, paid her a salary. In return, she took exceptional care of my mother-in-law and helped around the house. She still comes in twice a month to help with the rough cleaning. When Anna died, Umberto and I were both concerned about Sophie. Sophie told me of an idea that she had to start a flower business. I gave her a small loan, which she repaid, on time and with interest!

"Of course, we knew about Rita's interference and our sympathies were entirely with Sophie. I don't believe it's blackmail to pay someone's travel expenses to Italy, house and feed the person, and then expect a return on one's money. We have complete confidence in Sophie. A good many of her clients were recommended by me. I sincerely hope you're not going to bother her with this business," she added, breathless and flushed. She rose from her chair, saying, "If you're finished with me, I really have a great deal to do. I need to arrange for my niece's funeral, including a mass and a priest to say it." She started to move toward the door without waiting for his acknowledgment that the interview was over.

"Just one clarification and Inspector Tonni will escort you back to the sitting room."

She turned and looked at him impatiently.

"I'm sorry to have to tell you this, but I understand from your husband that you have not been informed. It seems that your niece was raped before . . ."

Her reaction was painful to watch.

"Raped! But . . . it's not possi . . ." She gasped tremulously, the blood rapidly draining from her face as she slid silently to the floor.

It took five minutes to revive Amelia Casati and another ten minutes to calm her husband. Cenni resisted the urge to apologize, which he knew was born of an innate courtesy that had nothing to do with any regrets he might have had over his decision to tell Amelia Casati about the possibility of her niece's rape. He had wanted to see her reaction. He had, and was satisfied that if someone had faked the rape of Rita Minelli, it had not been Amelia Casati.

He had also learned something of the family dynamic. Piero had gone to the sitting room to enlist the aid of Umberto Casati in reviving his wife. The count, who had returned with his granddaughter and Lucia trailing close behind, had spent the next ten minutes railing at Cenni and Piero over their gross mistreatment of his wife. Paola had spent that same ten minutes chafing her grandmother's wrists and making soothing sounds of comfort while Lucia had looked on, interested, but providing no help whatsoever. Artemisia Casati had remained in the sitting room.

16

ARTEMISIA CASATI HAD achieved a certain stature within the Italian art world. The commissario, who had been in charge of a number of investigations into art theft, was only too aware of the eternal intrigues that consume those who dare venture into the science of art in Italy: Historians, museum directors, gallery owners, art critics are all fed into the grinding machine. A year ago Artemisia Casati had published her first book, *A Woman's Art*, on Artemisia Gentileschi, the seventeenth-century Baroque artist, for whom Artemisia had been named and who had also achieved a certain stature—and a certain notoriety—in her own age. The monograph was a feminist-inspired work of stunning scholarship and audacious attributions, overturning quite a number of art historical assumptions. She had asserted, unapologetically, what other feminists before her had only dared to hint, that many of the works of other more famous Baroque artists were actually the

work of the young Gentileschi—indeed, that quite a few of
the paintings previously attributed to Orazio Gentileschi,
her father and teacher, were clearly painted by the daughter.
Artemisia Casati had done more than just tweak some
cognoscenti noses. She had done the unthinkable: She had
written in English and published in America. By all reckoning,
she should have been banished to the back pages of some sec-
ond-rate art magazine, but the book had been a great success
in New York and that, as always, was sufficient for the Italians
who loved anything branded USA.

She was now the darling of the Italian art world and had
been toasted with champagne at numerous receptions, one a
few months ago in Perugia, at the Galleria Nazionale, where it
was rumored she was to be its next director. Cenni's grandmother—a devoted gossip—kept up on these things. His
mother and grandmother, who were both lifelong patrons of
the museum, had in one of their rare moments of unanimity
dragged him along to the reception, insisting that they had to
have a male escort. His mother had gone because she always did
if the event were likely to make the society pages. And besides,
as she told her son, Giovanni Baglione had written Orazio Gentileschi's biography in 1642. A Baglioni before her marriage,
Cenni's mother always claimed kinship with any other Baglioni
so long as he was notable. Alex knew it would serve no purpose
to point out the difference in spelling, so he didn't.

His grandmother had gone for other reasons. She was a
champion of feminist causes and a great admirer of Gentileschi's painting, *Judith Slaying Holofernes*, which was on tem-
porary display at the Galleria. But he knew it was also for the
champagne. Her doctor had restricted her to one bottle a
week. "A mere thimbleful for a woman with my thirst for the
bubbly," his grandmother had said.

Cenni and his grandmother had skipped the reception line. He had no desire to see or be seen and she preferred to enjoy the parade of the beau monde from a comfortable seat, her shoes kicked discreetly out of sight. The Galleria Nazionale, although it lacked the cachet of the Borghese in Rome or the Uffizi in Florence, was his favorite museum. Despite its impressive collection of Sienese and Umbrian Old Masters, it still had the charm and pace of a provincial museum. Visitors could wander through its many rooms, in any order they wished, or revisit the same painting time and again without a guard urging them ever onward. And Cenni had yet to encounter one of those seemingly ubiquitous art tours permitted at the Uffizi, where an overloud and rushed guide focused on a single painting, or a detail of a painting, in a room filled with art treasures:

> "This room, as you can see, is dominated by Caravaggio. Please note the painting on your right, *The Adolescent Bacchus*. Excuse me, sir, can you step aside so my group can view the painting. It's generally believed that the young Sicilian who posed for this highly sensual work was Caravaggio's live-in lover. If you will kindly focus your attention on the bottom right of the painting you can see the subject's dirty fingernails and the worm-eaten rotten fruit. This is an excellent example of the naturalism favored by the artist. Now, in the next room, we will focus on Rembrandt's *Self-Portrait as a Young Man*. But if any of you wish to look at the other paintings in this room, you may take a minute to do so. There's an interesting Venus by Carracci on the opposite wall, but please don't tarry. Our appointment to visit Michelangelo's *David at the Accademia* is in ten minutes."

And the group would sweep out behind their guide, knocking down the old and infirm in their hurry not to miss the next view of dirty fingernails.

At Artemisia Casati's reception four months ago, Cenni had tarried in front of the Uffizi *Judith*, one of the more violent interpretations of the biblical Judith decapitating the Assyrian general Holofernes. Too much blood, he'd thought. He was wondering what Batori would make of the bloodstains on the left side of the sheet. Surely they were too far in front for a neck wound of that type? He had laughed aloud when he realized that he was conducting a postmortem on Holofernes. A voice behind him, cool and detached, had interrupted his forensic musings. "That's an unusual reaction to that painting. Most men turn away in horror." When he looked to see who had spoken, he was disconcerted to find the guest of honor, Artemisia Casati, standing directly behind him. He had confessed sheepishly to his thoughts on bloodstains and they had laughed together.

She had talked of Artemisia Gentileschi as a feminist icon while he had silently admired her namesake's dramatic good looks. She had a long-limbed, loose-jointed body of the type one usually associates with Americans fed on whole grains and hormone-laden beef, but the face and style were definitely Italian. Prominent cheekbones, strong almost masculine jaw, wide-spaced black eyes set beneath dramatically arched brows, a long Roman nose, full sensual lips painted a glistening crimson, and all enhanced by a marmoreal complexion and cropped raven-black hair, which looked, he thought, as though it had been cut with nail scissors, no doubt by the best hairdresser in Rome. He was no expert on women's clothing either, but he was sure that her ankle-length gunmetal gray dress, of soft clingy wool, was a designer's model and had cost a fortune. When she had finished discussing Gentileschi, he had confessed that he had not yet read her book but promised that he would as soon as his grandmother had finished it. They had parted on friendly terms with a promise by him to attend a private reception in Assisi the following week. He had forgotten all about it, perhaps deliberately! She was a study in artifice, somewhat intimidating in her cool detachment, and not really his type. But he had read her book.

Cenni needn't have worried about any awkwardness between them, at least not on her part. She was perfectly composed when she entered the library, extending her hand in greeting as though theirs were a business meeting between equals. As her father had done before her, she ignored Piero.

"Dottore, what a shame to meet again under such tragic circumstances. What can we do to help?" she offered, taking her seat across from him while at the same time reaching for the cigarette box on the count's desk. After taking a cigarette from the box, she hesitated a moment, waiting for one of them to light it. What surprised Cenni was her complete lack of embarrassment when neither of them did. She looked directly at him and reached for the lighter. *"Posso,"* she said rhetorically, before lighting her own cigarette.

He found her apparent self-possession irritating as well as false. Whether Artemisia Casati had liked or disliked her cousin—and on the surface, at least, she was not grieving—Rita Minelli had met a violent and premature death, and the Casati family were deeply involved until proven otherwise. Cenni concluded that father and daughter resembled each other in more than just physical appearance; they had both adopted an attitude of noblesse oblige. They would fulfill their civic duty to help the police, even where they found such duty inconvenient and distasteful and the police vulgarly intrusive. Cenni didn't believe this pose for a second.

His first question was direct and open-ended. He asked if she knew of any reason why someone would want to kill her cousin. Her response was equally direct and needlessly personal.

"I should think that's self-evident, Dottore." She paused, wrinkling her brow. "It is *Dottore*, isn't it? I'm never quite sure how one should address the police," she said before continuing. "A man capable of raping a woman in a cemetery, or anywhere else for that matter, would hardly stick at murder. I'm surprised that you're spending so much time with us instead of looking for her killer. Rapists don't usually stop at one, as I'm sure you must know. Easter week attracts an unusual number of visitors to Assisi. If this were my case, I would start there, as I doubt that any of our local citizens are capable of such vulgarity."

That's all I need, he thought. A detective manqué! But he continued undeterred by the implied criticism. "Why do you assume that your cousin was raped? I never mentioned rape."

"È vero," she acknowledged blowing a stream of smoke his way. "But Dottor Russo did. He told my father this morning that to all appearances Rita had been raped. You haven't given us any reason to think otherwise."

He had no desire to spar with her and responded bluntly:

"Nor will I! Until the postmortem is concluded and we know otherwise, we'll assume she was *not* raped. So again, signora, do you know of any reason why someone would want to kill your cousin?"

"No, certainly not," she replied but the air of ironic detachment that she had shown in her previous responses was less evident. "Rita could be quite irritating at times, and she was certainly a busybody, but that's hardly reason for anyone to kill her—anyone sane, that is. I don't know who her friends were, or if she had any, although I did see her more than once walking with a man in the Piazza del Comune, one of those hermit types that flock to Assisi. You know the ones

I mean: sandals in the dead of winter, no socks, scruffy beards, holes in their clothing—and just as often in their heads. Perhaps my mother knows his name." She had made her position clear. No member of the Casati family was involved in her cousin's death; focus on the crazy hermit!

He then asked Artemesia to describe her activities on the day of the murder—specifically, if she'd spoken to or had seen her cousin that day. She responded that she had left the house a little after 10:00 to get a manicure and had returned at 11:00 when she went to her room to work on an article that she was writing for *Arte*. Some time after—she didn't know the exact time—Rita had come into her room to make a suggestion about the forthcoming publication of the paperback version of *A Woman's Art*.

"You might ask Lucia the exact time," she said, a slight edge to her voice. "I saw her lurking outside in the hall. That's standard Lucia, always listening at keyholes."

She paused, grinding her cigarette into the ashtray—waiting, he was certain, for him to question her further concerning Rita's visit to her bedroom. She's nervous, he decided. She had changed her position in the last minute, crossing her legs, one of which he noticed with some interest had an ace bandage wrapped around the ankle. She's remembered Lucia's presence in the hallway yesterday when she and Rita had words and is ready with a plausible story, but she's too clever to introduce the subject herself. I'll let her stew a little longer, he thought, and waited for her to continue. She lighted another cigarette, this time directing the smoke in Piero's direction.

"At one o'clock I joined my parents and Paola for lunch. When we'd finished—about one-forty-five—my father and I retired to his library to discuss some aspects of an article I'm writing. I was with him until two-thirty, when I went upstairs to my room, where I continued working. At six-fifteen, I shut down my computer and started to get ready for the evening. At exactly seven-fifteen I left the house alone, by the front door, and walked to the Piazza del Comune."

When he asked Artemisia how she knew it was exactly 7:15, she replied that she had been a bit anxious that she might be late, as her parents had already left for the Piazza. She had looked at the clock in the downstairs hallway before leaving the house. "The clock keeps excellent time. It was exactly seven-fifteen."

When he probed further, she added that other than Rita's earlier visit to her room, which had lasted no more than ten or fifteen minutes, she'd not seen her cousin again that day and had no idea when she'd left the house or where she'd gone. She also told him that she'd not seen any other members of the family after returning to her room at 2:30. She might have heard her parents moving about in their room some time after 6:00 but couldn't say for sure. When she'd left the house, the door to their room was open but the room was empty. She hadn't seen her niece after lunch. As Paola's room was the closest to the back stairway, Paola could have come in or gone out at any time without anyone seeing her. She acknowledged the same of herself, finishing with a flourish of self-righteousness, "We don't live in one another's pockets!"

"That's obvious! Your cousin was noticeably missing for more than twelve hours, yet no one in the family reported it to the police," he responded sharply, not trying to blunt his outrage. "The lack of concern about Signora Minelli's whereabouts arises, *apparently*, from the notion that she had decided, and at the last hour, to become a processionist. Yet neither of your parents can recall who provided this information, although they're both under the impression that it may have been you." A small lie, he thought, as he waited for her reaction.

"Well, it certainly wasn't me," she responded indignantly. "I don't monitor anyone's comings and goings, certainly not hers. Believe me, Dottore, my cousin was not capable of carrying one of those crosses. She was far too small and lacked stamina. She could barely get up the hill from our house to the Piazza without huffing and puffing," she added with contempt. "Talk to the boyfriend. He'll probably know."

She was more relaxed now, giving full vent to her prickliness. Cenni thought it a good time to bring up her quarrel with Rita.

"Let's go back for a minute to your cousin's visit to your room yesterday. You said earlier that she'd visited your room to give you a suggestion about the coming publication of your book in paperback. What suggestion was that?" he asked.

She took a long drag on her cigarette, exhaling slowly. Buying time, he thought.

"The dust jacket for the clothbound copy of my book is a reproduction of the Uffizi *Judith*. Rita didn't like any of the Gentileschi *Judiths*, but she hated the Uffizi *Judith*. As I remember, you had a problem with it yourself," she said, before taking another drag on her cigarette. "Rita thought the image too bloody awful, said it was off-putting. She suggested I use a picture of the Spada *Madonna* for the paperback edition. You may remember the Spada, Dottore. It was also on display at the Galleria Nazionale. The child is particularly charming and natural, especially when viewed against other paintings of the same genre and period, but it's hardly equal to the *Judith*. I rejected her suggestion. We may have had a few words about it. I don't remember exactly what was said."

"Bada ai fatti tuoi!" Cenni replied coolly, then waited for her to respond.

She laughed in genuine delight. "Leave it to Lucia to remember the exact words. That one—she's definitely wasted cleaning houses. Such a nose for intrigue! You should hire her!" It was the first time since entering the room that she'd let down her guard. She had a deep, spontaneous laugh, the kind that overheard in a crowded room makes one regret what he's missing. Had he judged her too quickly? he wondered.

"*È vero*, Dottore, I probably did tell Rita to mind her own business. She really was a meddler, you know! From what she'd told me, she had come into my room a few days earlier—uninvited!—to find out which brand of lipstick I use. Lately, she's been copying me in just about everything. She saw the proofs for the book, which were lying open on the top of my desk, and decided that I should change the cover. Rita had no respect for privacy, other than her own, of course. She kept the door to her own room locked. Under the circumstances, *Bada ai fatti tuoi!* was less than she deserved to hear."

Cenni acknowledged to himself that it was a reasonable story and one that would be difficult to disprove. She had added enough detail—but not too much—to make it plausible. But from what the maid had told Elena, she had omitted one detail of significance.

"I understand that your cousin was holding one of the manuscripts from your father's library. What had that manuscript to do with your book?" he asked, observing her closely, looking for any flicker of surprise. He saw none and concluded that she had expected his question or might even be telling the truth.

"Lucia is incorrigible. Rita has never had access to the library. As I'm sure my father has already informed you, the library is kept locked at all times except when he's using it. Even I don't have the combination. She's mistaken! Rita was holding the clothbound copy of my book. I gave her an autographed copy in the summer, shortly after she'd arrived in Assisi. If you look in her room, you'll probably find it there."

"The size and shape of your book are very different from any of the manuscripts in your father's office. It's hard to imagine that Lucia could mistake one for the other," he responded, hoping to goad her further.

Instead she turned his comment on its side. "May I take it then, Dottore, that you've read my book? Have you changed your mind about the *Judith*? It's a wonderful painting. I hope I've convinced you of that at least," she responded, her cold anger banked under an equally cold smile.

For the moment Cenni was content. There's always Lucia, he thought.

17

THE CASATIS' MAID had achieved something of a reputation with the commissario even before she took her seat in the library. From all accounts, including that of Elena, she was a habitual eavesdropper and gossip, and if Concetta were to be believed, a liar as well. Cenni found another unfortunate trait to add to the list. She was a practiced flirt, which he quickly surmised from the many sidelong glances she threw at him and at Piero each time she flipped her long frizzed hair over her shoulder. Piero, who normally was highly susceptible, didn't seem to notice. That says a lot, Cenni thought, about his earlier declaration of indifference to Sergeant Antolini.

Lucia Stampoli was in her late twenties, an inch or two above five feet if one subtracted the stiletto heels, and painfully thin but with Barbie doll curves. She was dressed conservatively, in navy blue wool pants, white shirt, and a navy jacket, but that, he supposed, was a requirement of the job. Her hair, makeup, and jewelry were not conservative and neither were her lips, her most distinctive feature. They were unnaturally full—silicone, he decided—and painted an intense red. Cenni disliked the recent phenomenon that had captured the Italian imagination of filling every fillable erogenous zone with silicone, but what he disliked even more was that he reacted this way. Just last week, Elena had accused him of showing his age when he had complained about noisy teenagers. He had laughed but later had to acknowledge to himself that she might have a point.

After Lucia had settled herself—which had taken some time as she first had to line up her cigarettes, lighter, package of tissues, and *telefonino* on the desktop, cross her legs left to right, and arrange the bracelets on both arms so that they appeared to advantage—she indicated her readiness to begin with a mournful nod. She's decided on a show of grief, but she's actually enjoying herself, Cenni thought, observing the telltale signs of excitement in her flushed skin and glittering eyes. As he had with Concetta, he asked her to tell him about her job. Her response was a pleasant surprise after Concetta's meandering. It was short and factual, with only the occasional digression.

She had started working for the Casati family ten years earlier, immediately after finishing secondary school. The countess paid her eight euros an hour—"Only five euros less than the teachers at the Academy," she added proudly, "and she also gives me paid time off, which is a lot better than any of my friends who work in stores get," she added defensively. Cenni imagined that some of her friends gave her a hard time for being in service.

Her workday started at 10:00 and ended at 7:00, with an hour off for lunch, usually 2:30 to 3:30, after she'd finished clearing the family's luncheon dishes. She did basic cleaning and waited at table Monday to Saturday. She had Sunday off and a half-day on Saturday, when she finished at 2:00. "The countess said she'd pay me for the extra time today," she added, looking at the desk clock. She then described her daily routine. She changed the bed linens twice a week, on Monday and Friday, and did at least one load of wash every day. She'd normally hang the laundry out to dry on the back line in the kitchen garden, unless it was raining or particularly cold. "The countess prefers the smell of clothes that are dried outdoors," she explained. "Oh, and I dust every other day," she concluded, making a face. "Except the library. I dust in there on Tuesday and Saturday."

Cenni interrupted. "Who lets you into the library to dust?"

"Who do you think? I let myself in, of course!" she responded smartly.

"*You* know the combination?"

"Everyone in Assisi knows the combination. Maybe even Concetta!" Lucia said, laughing. "It's written right there on the count's blotter," she said pointing to the desk. "Nine, eight, six, three. The ninth of August, 1963. Camillo Casati's birthday."

When he asked her to describe Rita Minelli, her description was similar to what she had told Elena, although more circumspect. Lucia managed to look sad when she remembered why they were there, and occasionally glanced over at Piero to gauge his reaction. Cenni decided, at least for the moment, not to probe about the diary—since he would read it for himself. If it appeared later that any pages had been removed or altered, he could question her again. He was more interested in knowing Rita Minelli's movements on the day of her death and in resolving the discrepancy concerning the book that Minelli had been holding when she'd had words with her cousin.

Lucia stated that she had seen the American twice on Good Friday. The first time—she was upstairs changing the bed linen—she'd seen Rita Minelli go into Signora Artemisia's room; the second time was at two o'clock. She was just finishing in the dining room and was on her way downstairs to have her own lunch when she saw the American let herself out the front door. It was exactly two o'clock by the hall clock. Lucia added that she'd spent the remainder of the day below stairs, washing and hanging out two loads of laundry. She had finished exactly at 5:00 and left shortly after by the alleyway door. "The countess said I could leave at five to go to confession."

When she had finished, Cenni said, "You're an excellent witness, signora . . . signorina," he amended, noting the distress on her face at the aging title. "Intelligent and precise in all that you've told us. I only wish half the people that we interview were as clear."

She purred in response. Cenni suspected that not many people complimented her intelligence, possibly the reason for the silicone lips.

He said, "I wonder if you can clarify one point for us concerning the discussion Signora Casati had with her cousin yesterday. You told Inspector Ottaviani that the American was holding a book from the count's library, similar in size and shape to one of those," he said, pointing to the books that lined the room. "You're absolutely sure it was from the count's library and not an ordinary book—one, let's say, similar to the Signora's book?" He asked the question with that irritating kind of smile that says *We all make mistakes from time to time.*

"I just told you that I dust in here twice a week. I'd know if it was a book from here," she responded.

"I don't doubt what you're telling me for a moment. It's just that the Signora says you don't know anyth . . . that you're mistaken. She said it was her book that Rita Minelli was holding." He waited for Lucia's reaction. First her throat and then her face became mottled with patches of red, but she didn't respond immediately. Cenni guessed that she was weighing her relationship with the daughter of the house against the defense of her ego. He decided to help.

"You can speak freely. What you say here is confidential and won't be repeated." And because he was a man of some conscience, he added. "Unless, of course, it becomes absolutely necessary." To his surprise, she jumped up from her chair and walked over to one of the cabinets. She opened the glass door.

"Here it is!" she said triumphantly, pointing to a manuscript. "On Tuesday when I dusted this shelf it had only nine books. Now it has ten. They may look alike, but I can tell the difference! This one has a small stain on the back cover," she said, pulling the manuscript from the shelf and pointing to the stain. "What's more, it's the exact same book that's been in the Signora's room for more than two years. She kept it on the top shelf of her bookcase, shoved to the back. I clean her room daily, and I know what's there and what's not there," she exclaimed, exulting. Ego had trumped job security.

18

CENNI HAD DEVELOPED a curious liking for the maid despite her flaws, or perhaps because of them. She wasn't that dissimilar to his grandmother, who also loved to gossip. And at least in what she'd told him during the interview, she appeared to be telling the truth. She'll hold up well before the investigating judge, he decided, if it should come to that. He had asked Piero to make sure that Lucia left the house immediately after her interview; he didn't want her talking to Artemisia before he did a little research of his own. He had also instructed Piero to inform the count that he needed fifteen minutes alone in the library to accept an important call from the questore. A little quiet reading time courtesy of Signor Casati, he thought, opening the book that Lucia had identified.

He was sure that Umberto Casati would never willingly permit the police to remove or examine the book, and he was equally sure that he'd have great difficulty getting Antonio Priuli, the investigating judge in the Minelli case, to agree to an order for its removal. He was working on instinct. On this one, he'd have to work extralegally—*creatively*—if he had to explain his action to the questore. He had fifteen minutes to examine the manuscript for whatever it was Artemisia was hiding, and he had no idea what exactly he was looking for.

He moaned to himself when he found that the frontispiece was in Latin. Beyond the occasional inscription on public monuments, he hadn't translated anything from Latin in more than fifteen years. But as he turned the pages, his luck also turned. The manuscript was a miscellany of documents with different dates and imprimatur, but all the documents appeared to be itemizations of some type and easily understood even by someone whose Latin was rusty. He checked the first and last pages and found that the dates ranged from 1609 to 1614. He turned the pages quickly, aware that the minutes were passing, that the count might come in at any moment. He noticed that some of the leaves were already starting to deteriorate; he could clearly see signs of powder in the folds and he had to turn them carefully.

"*Mannaggia!* Not another list of household goods," he grumbled aloud about halfway through the manuscript. It was the tenth inventory of tables and chairs that he had come across, and he was starting to doubt himself. Perhaps his instincts were off or Lucia had lied. "*O Dio!*" he cried as soon as he turned the page. The words jumped off the page:

Rome　　　　　　*1612*　　　　　*Rapes and Procurements*

Index of Paintings Artimitia Gentileschi

"Mi dispiace, little Lucia!" He offered a contrite apology for his early doubts. How fortunate that he'd kept his promise to read Artemisia Casati's monograph. He knew immediately what he was looking at. He checked the desk clock noting that he had only four of his fifteen minutes left. He'd have to trust to Piero to keep Umberto Casati out of the library. The inventory contained the names of twelve paintings, but he knew the names of most of them already. He scribbled quickly, smiling.

19

"PAOLA, THAT'S THE tenth cigarette you've smoked in the last thirty minutes. You'll have lung cancer before you reach forty. And the room reeks of cigarette smoke!" These dire words, spoken by Artemisia Casati to her niece Paola just seconds before she lit her own cigarette, had some effect on Paola, although possibly not the one Artemisia had expected. After flipping her lit cigarette over the grate and into the open fire, Paola proceeded to crack her knuckles, a habit that she had recently acquired while living in Rome and one that she found surprisingly relaxing.

"For God's sake, Paola, you're acting as though the KGB were in the house and we had something to hide. Why are you so nervous?" Artemisia asked. Paola realized that the question was rhetorical. She's having trouble dealing with her own nerves, Paola thought, watching the rapid up-and-down movement of her aunt's crossed leg. She doesn't want to know about mine.

Her grandparents had left the room a few minutes ago. Her grandmother had gone to her room to make arrangements for Rita's funeral and her grandfather had gone to check on the police. He's in one of his snitty moods, Paola thought.

She'd been on the wrong end of his moods often enough lately to feel almost sorry for the police, although she dearly wished they'd go away. Her turn was next, as soon as the commissario finished his telephone call, and she still hadn't decided on her tactics. How much did they know? How much should she conceal? They were the police, after all. From what Giulio had told her, they seemed to know everything. Giulio was sure the police had planted an informer in their group. Paola sank back into the soft cushions, reached for another cigarette, and ruminated on the mess that she was in.

She had spent the first seventeen years of her life honoring her parents and the last three imitating them. They had been killed in 1984, before she was two, when a homemade bomb they were wiring detonated accidentally. She had no memories of them beyond the ones that had been superimposed by others and a few pictures. Her only photograph of them taken together was on the day they were married in the summer of 1982. In the picture, her father, Camillo, who was a good head taller than her mother, is smiling down at his bride. Her mother is looking directly into the camera with great seriousness. Paola often wondered if her mother knew, even then, how things would end. They had exchanged vows in a small park in Perugia with a few of their friends bearing witness. She had been born two months later. They weren't wed under the laws of Italy or Rome, so Paola knew that made her a bastard.

Paola had been left in Assisi with her maternal grandmother on the day they blew themselves up. When the bomb detonated, it also blew a hole in the kitchen floor, killing an old woman who lived in the apartment below. If Paola had been in the kitchen that day, in her highchair as she usually was, she too would have died. She often thought about the significance of that. For the next three years, she lived with her maternal grandmother, Luciana Stefanak, until her paternal grandparents adopted her after a long custody fight. Luciana, who cleaned the houses of the rich, lived in a small cold water flat consisting of two rooms and a toilet. In the winter she heated the apartment with a portable gas stove.

Paola had read the transcript of the custody trial when she was sixteen. A young lawyer from Todi, paid by some of Camillo Casati's leftist friends, had represented her grandmother. He had done his best, but the count had retained the finest lawyer in Perugia. The custody trial had been described by some of the papers as the powerful against the weak, the rich against the poor, but in the end, the final decision of the court had turned on her grandmother's antiquated plumbing and the gas stove, which was viewed as dangerous. In King David fashion, the court permitted the count and the countess to adopt Paola, but it also ruled that she must spend every Sunday with her maternal grandmother. Paola wondered why the court thought the gas stove was safe on Sundays. So shortly after her fifth birthday, Paola Stefanak, who had taken her nightly bath for three years in a tub that sat in her grandmother's kitchen, became Paola Casati, adopted daughter of the Count and Countess Casati, with an en suite bedroom and bathroom and a maid to pick up after her.

In the beginning, she missed her grandmother terribly and began to wet her bed. But she also started school that year, and she enjoyed the games they played at recess and her friendships with the other children. She loved to draw pictures of cats and dogs; her new parents, who had two cats and a dog, gave her sketchpads and pencils and a place for her to hang her drawings. She stopped wetting her bed shortly afterward. She saw Luciana—she still called her *nonna*—every week as the court had ordered. The countess—she was now *mamma*—took her to Luciana's every Sunday at 9:00 in the morning and picked her up at 7:00 in the evening. In the end, Paola never adjusted well to the notion of either Luciana or the countess as her mother. It was all too confusing to a five-year-old.

When she was seven, she made her First Holy Communion at the Basilica and discovered the frescos in the lower church, which covered every wall and most of the ceilings. She loved them all, but she particularly loved the one of St. Francis preaching to the birds. She identified with one of the small brown birds—the one in the back behind the tree, which over the centuries had faded into the deteriorating paint and was almost invisible. You really had to care about that bird to find it, she thought.

When she was fourteen, Francesca Munzi moved to Assisi from Florence. Her father was the new director of the Assisi Hospital, and Francesca joined their class in the middle of the year. She was tall, had silky blonde hair, green eyes, and breasts, and was immediately popular, especially with the boys. Paola, who was timid and a daydreamer, had spent her free afternoons until then drawing, visiting the Basilica, or doing her homework, but with the arrival of Francesca all that changed. Francesca chose Paola, along with three other girls, to be her best friend.

After classes let out, Francesca would lead the four of them around Assisi—by their noses, Artemisia said caustically. Some times they would drag soap along the windows of the local merchants on Corso Mazzini; other times they would steal doormats and throw them into the closest dumpster. Another of their games, and the one Francesca enjoyed the most, was for the five of them to swoop down on an elderly woman and scare her into dropping her packages. One afternoon, when they were walking down Via Metastasio toward Porta San Giacomo, Francesca spotted a gray-haired woman with a mop and bucket walking in front of them. Paola recognized her immediately. It was her grandmother Luciana.

Andiamo! Francesca cried, grabbing Paola's arm and pulling her along.

Paola wanted to run the other way but she couldn't. The momentum of Francesca and the others carried her with them. She was too ashamed to stop Francesca, to confess that the old lady with the mop and the bucket was her grandmother. Francesca and the others ran off laughing after Luciana had dropped her bucket and its contents had rolled on to the street, but Paola stayed for just a moment, to look back. That insubstantial moment in time, a millisecond in her life, when granddaughter and grandmother looked at each other without acknowledgment, almost without recognition, before Paola turned and ran off with the others, was, as she would realize years later, the most substantial moment of her life. It would change her forever.

"Paola, stop daydreaming! They're ready for you." Paola looked up to see her aunt standing over her. "Stop worrying, the commissario's not an ogre," Artemisia added, half-smiling. "Remember, you're a Casati!"

20

ARTEMESIA LISTENED INTENTLY at the open grate, catching odd snatches of meaning in the swirling wisps of sound wafting upward from the floor below until, finally, she heard the loud bang of the front door. He had left the house. She peered through the slats in the shutter and watched the commissario and the other policeman, the fat one, walk in the direction of the Piazza del Comune. The interview with Paola had been brief. Why, was she no longer a suspect? Her niece often played the fool around men. Perhaps she had done so with Cenni. No matter, though. He was no ordinary policeman, to be taken in by that act.

She had made inquiries about Cenni months ago, after the Gentileschi exhibit. Brilliant, a mutual acquaintance had said, first in his law class. Joined the Polizia di Stato for personal reasons: his *fidanzata* had been kidnapped by the *Brigate Rosse*. Fulvio Russo had offered a different view. Fanatic about social causes, probably votes Communist, thinks he's God gift! Artemisia knew where that was coming from! The Cenni family was distinguished, and rich by all accounts; Fulvio's father worked on the Fiat assembly line.

Fulvio's jealousy soared even further! Cenni's money came from selling chocolates . . . cocoa . . . coca . . . he had sneered. Artemisia had smiled back, remembering the gossip about Giorgio Zangarelli, Fulvio's brother-in-law—new money, distinguished member of the *Camorra*—and discounted most of the jibes. But whatever Cenni's background, his family was not noble. That was Artemisia's rationalization for not minding when he'd missed her reception. No extant titles in his family! On the other hand, there was money there. Others had said the same, not just Fulvio. *Chocolate bars to the stars!*

Artemesia had heard other rumors. Cenni was assigned to a special task force on terrorism, an assignment straight from the prime minister. It made no sense that someone of his stature would investigate the murder of someone of absolutely no importance, someone like Rita. Unless he had requested the assignment? Men like Cenni could do what they wanted. Fulvio had complained that Cenni always got the plum assignments. And the questions that he had asked, with that ridiculous redheaded policeman taking notes, they made no sense. Why should he want to know about her book on Gentileschi?

When he hadn't showed up at her reception, particularly after she had followed up her verbal invitation with a written note, his message was pointed—not interested—or so she'd thought at the time. It was obvious now that she'd been wrong.

She observed herself in the full-length mirror, turning to view herself from all angles. Black set off her dramatic coloring to perfection. She ran her hand across her stomach, still flat and firm. She was in her prime, and very soon she'd be director of a regional museum. Was he aware of her family's Borghese connection? He must know, she reasoned; he had been with her father for more than an hour. She smiled secretly. He could do a lot worse than to align himself with a descendant of Camillo Borghese.

21

"TOO BAD THEY don't have a butler," Piero said, as he and Cenni walked toward the Piazza del Comune. "Then we could pin it on him, and we wouldn't have to worry about checking alibis."

Cenni laughed, remembering Piero's addiction to TV police dramas, which no doubt had prompted his use of the American jargon. His favorite show was *Hawaii Five-O*, with its sugarcane plantation murders and beach bum hangouts, a show that Cenni had seen only once, at Piero's urging. It had absolutely no connection to police work—probably why Piero likes it so much, Cenni had concluded.

"Did any of them have an alibi that we can check?" Cenni responded. "If so, it slipped past me." As Cenni knew, the perfect alibi, substantiated by ten unimpeachable witnesses, is a staple of murder mystery novels but rarely of investigative use. He had learned from experience that perfect alibis are extremely rare and usually suspect. But in Rita Minelli's murder, he was faced with a first. He had five possible suspects—six, if he counted Lucia—and probably more to come, and so far not one of them had produced an alibi that could be substantiated.

The count was in the library between 3:00 and 6:00 and no one had seen him.

The countess was in the parlor—no doubt eating bread and honey, he thought—and no one had seen her.

The maid was in the garden hanging out the clothes and had seen no one.

Artemisia was in her room—perhaps the maid had seen her, perhaps not.

Paola had taken a walk between 4:00 and 7:00 on one of the country lanes that surround Assisi. She had seen no one and assumed, therefore, that no one had seen her.

Sophie Orlic was at home the afternoon and evening of Good Friday—alone and unobserved.

Only Concetta, who was at home with her husband, two children, his mother, and her father, had offered an alibi that could be substantiated. Which makes perfect sense, Cenni thought, since she's not a suspect.

John Williams, the alleged boyfriend and the person Cenni was on his way to interview, lived in an apartment on Via San Gabriele, a few hundred yards above the Piazza del Comune. It was the warmest day that they'd had in a week, and even though it was now close to 5:00, the Piazza was still crowded with Easter Week tourists enjoying the last rays of the dying sun. Those who had plenty of euros in their pockets or were too proper to relax on public monuments sat at tables drinking their coffees or glasses of wine. The college students, surrounded by their ubiquitous backpacks, congregated on the fountain steps, competing for space with the pilgrims who had come to Assisi to observe Easter Week. The fountain crowd was mainly drinking bottled water, but a small group of students was sharing a bottle of wine, trying to appear inconspicuous but without great success. They're quiet enough, Cenni thought. They have nothing to worry about. He knew many of the Polizia Municipale in Assisi by name and found them to be an amiable group, practicing sound police policy. Don't bother the tourists unless they bother you!

"I'll buy you a coffee," Piero said, interrupting Cenni's thoughts, steering him by the elbow into the Bar Sensi, assuming, as he always did, that the invitation was accepted. Cenni took his coffee and Piero an apple tart to the back where they could have some privacy.

Cenni, who always appreciated good coffee, savored his caffè macchiato before speaking:

"With luck, the American boyfriend will confess as soon as we read him his rights, and we can all enjoy our Easter dinner tomorrow, but I'm not counting on it. I'd be surprised if Batori finds evidence of rape when he does the postmortem on Monday. I doubt that a man, particularly a boyfriend, would fake a rape. Why draw attention to himself?"

"It could be someone with a Machiavellian mind, someone who hopes we'd think it wasn't a man," Piero said. "But for my money, it's the bitch," he added, referring to Artemisia. "What did you find in that book while I was outside playing sweeper?" he asked.

"Inspector, you flatter yourself," Cenni responded laughing. "You don't have the timing or the speed to be a sweeper. And if you keep eating those apple tarts, you never will. But you did a great job keeping Casati out of the library. I'd just replaced the manuscript when he walked in. As to what I found, I need to check further to confirm my suspicions, but it looks as though the future director of the Galleria Nazionale may have neglected to credit some of her sources when she published her book on Artemisia Gentileschi."

"Credit her sources!" Piero responded incredulously. "Probably all the university students in this country do the same. It's not even a crime, is it?"

"No . . . at least I don't think so. But it would be viewed that way by the art crowd. Worse, in light of the noses that were put out of joint when her book was first published. That manuscript contains inventory lists connected to various court trials that were held in Rome between 1609 and 1614. If the inventory of paintings that I found is authentic—and I believe it is—then it's a list of the paintings that were submitted as exhibits at the Tassi rape trial in 1612 . . ."

"Rape!" Piero cried, turning a number of heads his way. He lowered his voice. "Rape? I thought we were talking about a catalogue of paintings."

"Agostino Tassi was a Florentine artist, a friend of Orazio Gentileschi—who was Artemisia Gentileschi's father and a painter himself—her teacher in fact. Orazio charged Tassi with raping his daughter and then refusing to marry her. Tassi denied the charge, and it went to trial. During the trial, Tassi challenged Artemisia's abilities as a painter; even swore under oath that he'd been teaching her the rules of perspective on the day he was said to have raped her. The list of paintings that I found in the manuscript—the one that the maid claims Minelli and her cousin were arguing over yesterday—is an inventory of paintings provided by Artemisia Gentileschi to the Roman Court in 1612—I can only assume, to substantiate her knowledge of perspective. Three of the six paintings were later attributed to Orazio, the father, sometime after his death, or perhaps after the daughter's death. The record wasn't set straight for centuries, not until our own Artemisia published her monograph, *A Woman's Art.*"

"So what's wrong with that?"

"Nothing, if the Signora had stated where the information came from, but she didn't. In her book, she demonstrates through painterly technique—style, treatment of subject, use of color—accompanied by a good dose of hubris, that the three paintings were executed by Artemisia Gentileschi. She does this without a single mention of her lucky find. In no place does she acknowledge that she became aware of the incorrectly attributed works because she'd stumbled upon the inventory from the rape trial. If the existence of that inventory got out, particularly after her self-aggrandizement, it would ruin her chances for that directorship."

"I still think that's a ridiculous motive for murder," Piero responded, "but I'd like to read about this rape. Where can I get the book, Alex?"

Cenni laughed. "Collecting clues, Piero? I'll ask my grandmother if you can borrow it—in the interests of justice, of course. And on Monday, I'll ask some sources in Rome to check the archives. Even if I'm right, it's going to be damned near impossible to prove if the document I found in the count's library is the only one in existence. But if Artemisia Casati murdered her cousin, then someone must have seen her outside the house yesterday evening. That's where you come in. I want you to obtain a picture of her. You'll find one in the archives of *Il Giornale dell' Umbria;* one of their photographers was at her reception four months ago. Get it today, and if they give you any trouble, tell them to call me. Show it around in the stores and restaurants that line the streets that go to the cemetery. The locals probably know all the family on sight, but very few locals work in Assisi these days, not since the earthquake. Make sure that you show it to the same people who were working yesterday. In fact, while you're at it, get pictures of the entire family. They were all at the reception that night and I'm sure they were all photographed. You can get Orlic's and Minelli's pictures from their *soggiorno* applications. And assuming Minelli's boyfriend applied for a *soggiorno*, you can get his picture the same way. Otherwise, we'll confiscate his passport. I'd tell you to be discreet, but that's going to be difficult in a town where the family is so prominent."

"Have you any idea how many streets in Assisi lead to the cemetery?" Piero asked plaintively.

"A half dozen, maybe more," Cenni answered dryly. "Start with the most likely ones first, those that connect directly to Porta San Giacomo and Porta Perlici. And if you have no luck at the restaurants, start canvassing the neighbors. There's always someone hanging out a window. Get whatever help you need, but I want this inquiry finished as soon as possible, by end of day tomorrow. People forget quickly. If you need help, ask Sergeant Antolini. She knows Assisi very well," Cenni added, straightfaced.

"I'll do that," Piero responded, equally straightfaced. "But what about Minelli's papers? Did you find anything there?"

"I think so! Her will was in a sealed envelope that the forensic detail found in her room. The wax seal was unbroken. I suppose that could have been faked, but I don't think it was. The name of her attorney was printed on the outside of the envelope, and the initials on the wax seal match his. I called his office in Brooklyn from the library—on Casati's dime but all I got was a message that he'll return on Monday. If the will is the last one she executed, then except for a small bequest to a cousin in the United States and a somewhat larger one to some Italian priest—oddly enough, there's no last name or direction for the priest—she's left everything to her uncle. The will was dated and executed on the third of June, probably right before Minelli left the United States."

"How much?" Piero asked.

"It doesn't list her assets. But if what Amelia Casati tells us is true, it's a hefty sum. Remember, she said they had to mortgage the house when her mother-in-law died, to pay off Livia Casati. That was only a few years ago. So the family must have been hard up for money then. If Umberto Casati knew what was in his niece's will, that definitely makes him a suspect, particularly if he needed money. When we get back to Perugia, you can run a check on his finances."

"What about the granddaughter? She was more nervous than the rest of them put together. And she admits that she was out of the house from four o'clock on. Do you think she's hiding something?"

"Everyone's hiding something. But we're looking for a murderer, and we don't really care if a suspect is cheating on his taxes or his wife so long as the cheating has nothing to do with the murder. The first we leave to the finance police, the second to the wife (or the brothers if she's from Sicily) . . . but try to convince a suspect of that. Maybe the granddaughter is dating a married man and doesn't want *nonno* to know, maybe she's on drugs, who knows? But you're right, she was nervous. Ask Rome to run a check on her. That's where she's been living for the last two years."

"What did you think of the story she came up with when you asked about her meeting with Minelli in Cascia? It doesn't make sense," Piero added, anxious to keep the commissario talking while he finished his second pastry.

"It makes sense to me. She meets her cousin accidentally in the Basilica and they have a coffee together. She votes Communist and prays to Saint Rita, not a contradiction in this country! I'd wager half the people who vote Communist light candles to their favorite saints the night before an election. Finish up, Piero," Cenni added, standing up. "We've kept the American waiting long enough. I can't give you a butler, but perhaps the boyfriend will do."

22

THE AMERICAN BOYFRIEND, as the police referred to him, lived above a shop that sold fruits and vegetables. The proprietor, who rushed to the door as soon as he saw them pass, greeted them with a *"Buona sera"* and the news that the American was upstairs with the police. He then walked out of the shop, leaving his three customers to weigh their own produce, anxious to get some news about the murder to share with his neighbors. Cenni was afraid that he'd follow them up the three flights of stairs to Williams's apartment, all the time murmuring platitudes, some deploring the terrible tragedy that had visited Assisi, others offering assistance to the police, and the remainder a string of apologies if by some ill-luck he'd rented his apartment to a murderer. "Not that Signor Williams would hurt a fly," he added. He finally stopped at the first landing, although Cenni could still hear him talking from below as they buzzed for entrance to the American's flat.

Inspector Staccioli, who had been sent to act as dogsbody until Cenni arrived, admitted them to the apartment. He motioned to a man sitting on a chartreuse flowered couch and then returned to his chair by the door and to his newspaper without saying a word. Still sulking, Cenni thought. Williams looked up when they entered the room and gave them a tremulous smile, a wavering mix of anxiety and sorrow, the latter reflected in the pallid skin and bloodshot eyes of someone who'd recently been crying. He was something of a surprise to Cenni, perhaps because he knew Rita Minelli's age and had expected a man in his forties. He's no more than thirty, Cenni thought, probably younger. He had the thin, almost translucent, skin of the Irish, sand-colored hair, light blue eyes, and delicate but nondescript features, the kind of face one sits across from in an airport or a doctor's office for thirty minutes or more, yet can't remember ten minutes later.

Cenni introduced himself and Piero, and for the second time that day, offered his condolences. From the blank response in Williams's eyes, he concluded that the man spoke very little Italian. The commissario had learned English as a child from his grandmother and decided to forgo the use of a translator. He began, as he usually did, with preliminary questions, asking the who, what, where, and whys of Williams's life and, finally, for a description of his friendship with Rita Minelli. The answers surprised him, considering what had been previously said or implied by the Casati family.

Williams told them that he was Canadian, "Not American, as everyone in Assisi insists on calling me. Italians seem to think Canada is the fifty-first state. Some Americans do, too " he added with a rueful smile. He said he was in Assisi doing research on a group of ecclesiastic maps in the Basilica library. He explained that in the Middle Ages European maps were more ecclesiastic than cartographic, adding that he was writing a book on the influence of the Catholic Church on cartography. He said he had a small fixed income—15,000 Canadian dollars a year—but it was more than adequate for his needs. He had met Rita when he first came to Assisi in December. She was a good friend, and he'd miss her a great deal. "She'd helped me in just about everything," he added. "She even found me this apartment."

Cenni looked about him. Two tiny rooms, an open galley kitchen and the slightly larger space they were in, one small curtainless window looking out on a narrow alley, and the only decorative item, a bad reproduction of Saint Francis preaching to the birds. The furniture, typical of what landlords think suitable for tourists, was cheap and barely serviceable. The only upholstered piece in the room was the flowered sofabed on which he and John Williams had been sitting for the last fifteen minutes. It was, Cenni decided, not only the ugliest couch in memory but surely the most uncomfortable. Out of curiosity, he asked Williams what he was paying by the month.

"Five hundred euros," he replied, "not including electricity."

No wonder the landlord was so quick to reassure me that *Signor Williams wouldn't hurt a fly*, Cenni thought. Tenants who open their pockets for picking don't arrive on one's doorstep every day, although, in Cenni's experience, Americans with easy money were the exception to this rule. He supposed he'd now have to add Canadians to the list.

When Cenni broached the subject of sex, Williams blushed a violent red. "Rita was forty-five, I'm twenty-six," he said, insisting that they'd been good friends only. "Rita may have had other male friends," he added, turning red on red. "I can't say for sure. If she did, I don't know who they were . . . are," he amended, in confusion.

Asked about his whereabouts on Good Friday, he told Cenni that Rita had visited him for two hours in the afternoon and had left shortly after 4:00.

"Two hours is a long time for an afternoon chat," Cenni said. "What did you talk about?"

"Just things," Williams responded, a slight tic pulsing below his left eye. "You know the things friends talk about. We usually went together to Sunday mass at San Stefano's, but Rita thought maybe for Easter we should go to the Basilica. And she was nervous about the Good Friday dinner with her family. Her uncle is . . . was always picking on her. She was worried that he might be rude to us if we chose the wrong fish for dinner. Things like that," he finished lamely.

Tics can be as reliable as lie detectors—more reliable, Cenni thought. He's telling half-truths. They talked about more than just their choice of church on Easter or the correct fish to eat on Good Friday.

Williams concluded his statement by accounting for his time the whole of Friday evening. He'd left his apartment immediately after Rita to attend confession at San Stefano at 4:30—"I was first in line"—and, later, to hear five o'clock mass. When he exited his apartment building, about 4:20, he saw Rita at the top of the street walking toward San Ruffino. "It was the last time that I saw her alive," he said, and his voice shook. Cenni nodded in awkward sympathy.

After mass, he went to Il Duomo for a pizza—"I'm hypoglycemic," he offered in explanation, "so I have to eat often. I couldn't wait until nine or ten at night for my dinner. Rita and I agreed to meet there at six-thirty."

"When she didn't show up, why didn't you notify her family or the police?" Cenni asked.

"At first I was worried," he acknowledged, pausing to run his tongue over his upper lip. "But Rita was really uncomfortable about the dinner with her family. That's why she'd invited me along, as a bodyguard," he added with a self-deprecating smile. "I figured she'd decided to skip the dinner and was taking the easy way out by not showing up."

"Then it wasn't you who told her family that she was one of the processionists?"

"Little Rita, in the procession! Who told you that?" The image of the diminutive Rita carrying a heavy cross up the steep incline to San Ruffino appeared to amuse him, and for the first time since they'd arrived at the apartment Cenni saw him relax.

"And after the procession, what did you do?"

"I followed the processionists up toward San Ruffino. I had planned to attend the service but the church was too crowded, so I went home. I didn't go out again that evening.

I heard about her death the next morning from my land-lord, a little before ten, when I went out for a coffee."

Cenni threw his head back and laughed, causing the timid Canadian to wince. The grocer had known about the murder before the questore. *"Che Paese!"* What a country, Cenni uttered aloud and laughed again.

When he'd stopped laughing, he asked to see Williams's *soggiorno*.

"I didn't know I needed one," Williams stammered and pointed to the passport that was displayed prominently on the plastic coffee table. Cenni picked it up and began flipping through its pages.

"I thought your name was John Williams?" Cenni said impa-tiently. "It says here John Williams Campbell."

"My mother's maiden name was Williams. I never got along with my father and I decided to stop using his name when he died. That was five years ago." Again the tic!

Cenni thanked him for his help, told him not to leave Assisi without permission, and to secure his last request, pock-eted Williams's passport. At the door, he turned unexpect-edly, "Signor Williams, were you aware that Rita Minelli was pregnant?"

"No . . . I don't . . . didn't . . ." he replied, stumbling over his words.

Cenni had known the Canadian's answer even before he'd asked the question. He'd just wanted to see if the tic would return. It had!

So, Batori was right. Rita Minelli was pregnant. Now to find the father, he said to himself.

The Canadian boyfriend, as he was now known to the police, waited five minutes after they'd left before getting up from the couch, waiting to be sure that the fat policeman wasn't coming back.

He'd hidden his nerves rather well, he thought, although he'd been afraid that his legs would collapse under him if he stood to say goodbye. He hadn't offered to shake hands either, afraid his hand might tremble. He was pleased that he'd thought about the passport in advance and had had it ready for them, but not so pleased that they had taken it away with them. All in all, though, he thought he had performed rather well. He deserved a coffee, perhaps at the Bar Sensi. Matteo was in at 5:00.

23

IT WAS AFTER 11:00 when Cenni walked through his front door, nearly twelve hours after he'd received the questore's first call about the murdered American. He was tired, hungry, and frustrated, but mostly frustrated. Even before removing his jacket, he cut himself a long chunk of salami and carried it, a paring knife, and a corkscrew into the sitting room, where he opened a bottle of Sagrantino—the strongest wine he could find—and poured the deep garnet-colored liquid into his largest glass, a beer mug decorated with harp and leprechaun that Piero had purchased in Ireland on his last holiday. It's probably a misdemeanor in France to drink wine from a beer mug, he mused, particularly if it's the quality of a Rosso d'Arquata, but he was less interested in capturing the wine experience than in drowning his frustrations. "The hell with the French!" he said out loud before taking a large swig of wine. It had been a lousy day.

The questore, Carlo Togni, who was often reasonable about the demands he made on those who worked for him, and more so with Cenni, his senior commissario, whom he regarded as something of a prodigy, was the source of Cenni's frustrations. They got on reasonably well so long as they kept their discussions focused on policing and away from politics. Togni had great ambitions, and in Italy the single most effective way to achieve great ambitions is through relationships, so he spent the better part of his days cultivating relationships and left the legwork to his subordinates. But in the murder investigation of Rita Minelli, Togni was afraid that the relationships might be getting away from him.

In his first call to Cenni, shortly before 11:00 in the morning, when he was still concerned that the American's murder might have some connection to terrorism, he'd offered his favorite commissario whatever assistance he would need to find the murderer at once. In the second call, at 2:00 in the afternoon, after Cenni had convinced him that Minelli's murder had nothing to do with the *Brigate Rosse*, Al Qaeda, ETA, or the IRA, the questore had suggested that perhaps Cenni should tread lightly with the count. "Remember, he's a friend of the PM." The third call, at 4:00, was a gentle but firm reminder that the Casatis "are the victims here." The last call, which came sometime after 8:00, to his office, and which Cenni surmised was in response to pressure from higher up, was an ungentle demand that the commissario meet him at 10:00 the following morning. "I want to know more about this Croatian woman," he'd said. And in case Cenni hadn't got the message, he added, "You know who I mean, the woman who found the body, the same woman who'd threatened the victim."

The day that his twin brother lost an election in secondary school to the very unpopular son of the school's principal, Cenni had learned that justice in any society is subordinate to the vicissitudes of politics. He had applied that lesson when he'd first joined the Polizia di Stato by putting aside his personal sense of justice and adopting Cicero's less perfect but more workable one, "Justice consists in doing injury to no man." Umberto Casati had important friends, and Cenni lacked the power to indict any member of the Casati family for Rita Minelli's murder if a decision had already been made higher up that *they're the victims here.* But before he'd agree to arrest someone whom he thought to be innocent, he'd resign. It needn't come to that, though; it never had before. He had his own ways of applying political pressure to the questore. He poured the last of the Sagrantino into his mug and remembering the Irish toast that Piero had taught him, raised his glass in salute. *"Slainte!"* he said, to no one in particular.

A bottle of Sagrantino should put an elephant to sleep, Cenni thought, after he had showered and gone to bed. Instead, he found himself restlessly plumping up his pillow every few minutes. The overloud ticking of the alarm clock, the streetlights that filtered through the shutters, and, finally, his cat Rachel, jumping on his chest without warning, were all working to keep him awake. He had adopted Rachel two years ago after one of his murder investigations. An old woman who'd lived alone in the countryside near Gubbio had been stabbed to death by two boys, nineteen and twenty, who'd been looking for money to buy drugs. The yield from their brutal murder had been ten euros and a black-and-white television set that they couldn't sell. They'd been convicted and sentenced to twenty years in prison, the old woman—who had no family—had been cremated, and Cenni had adopted Rachel. According to the veterinarian who'd subdued Rachel so the police could remove the woman's body, the cat was at least ten years old. If Cenni hadn't adopted her, the animal shelter would have put her to sleep. He still wasn't sure why he'd felt such a strong need to keep the old woman's cat alive: perhaps because it was the only creature left to remember and mourn her passing. After a few months together, they'd come to a reasonable understanding: Rachel bothered him whenever she wanted to; he respected her privacy. Fortunately, though, for his chances of getting to sleep this night, Rachel was a teetotaler. As soon as she'd gotten a whiff of the blackberry smell of Sagrantino on his breath, she'd decided to find another place to sleep.

After Rachel had jumped from the bed, Cenni turned on his side, closed his eyes once more, and tried to sleep. But the thought of the old woman in Gubbio had evoked other memories. The thugs who had murdered the old woman had done more than just steal her money. They had robbed her of dignity at the moment of her dying. With a piece of coal from her fireplace, they had drawn a handlebar mustache on her upper lip and large clown freckles on her cheeks. He felt the same hot anger now as he had then: an irrational anger perhaps, but it had kept him going day and night for three weeks until he'd found her killers.

He was standing once again in the Casati mausoleum looking down at Rita Minelli's body, the shiny white legs with the coarse dark hairs on the upper thighs in stark contrast to the elegantly clothed upper body, her pants and stockings bunched up together at her ankles. The grandmother of a friend of his had worn her stockings in just such a way, rolled down around her ankles. He remembered his friend's mortification whenever she'd come shuffling out of her room at the back of the house, an old woman without elegance or shame, too lazy to roll up her stockings. A cold hard anger had been growing within him all day at the Casati family for their complete disregard of Rita, first in life and then in death, and at the smug righteousness even Amelia Casati exuded that Rita had been nothing more than a nuisance, a family inconvenience.

In her last moment of life, the murderer (and Cenni was sure that the rape had been staged) had robbed Rita Minelli of grace and dignity. His last thought as he drifted off to sleep was sure to give him fitful dreams: For Rita Minelli, he would seek perfect justice.

Book Three

Easter Sunday

I

HE WOKE AT 6:00 on Easter Sunday, the same time he awoke every morning, to the insistent buzzing of his clock radio and to an even more insistent dream of Sophie Orlic. He pushed down the snooze alarm and rolled over, dragging the pillow with him. Just another moment, he thought, and she'd have said *yes*. He lay there for another five minutes, eyes shut, pillow wrapped tightly around his head, trying to recapture that final instant of bliss, but the woman of his dreams, all sweet enchantment, had vanished, replaced by the watchful staring eyes of his prime suspect.

The best part of the day is early morning, but not when you're chasing a Sagrantino hangover. Cenni got out of bed gingerly, afraid to wake the sleeping giant, and padded from bedroom to sitting room to bathroom, eyes averted from the early morning light that streamed into all the corners of the sitting room, illuminating the kitty litter that Rachel distributed into all the corners of his life. Maria Sotto, his cleaning lady of ten years and a former ally against his mother (who would rearrange his furniture any time she managed to get the key), had changed sides after the arrival of Rachel, claiming that the apartment now resembled a beach house in Sardinia. She hated cats, as did his mother, but for different reasons. Maria was allergic to cat dander and sniffed and sneezed her way through the apartment twice a week, but for an extra five euros she suffered the inconvenience. His mother was allergic to independence of any sort; cats, in particular, offended her sense of importance and control. Her current lapdog, a Pekinese named Cara Mia, had first gone to obedience school before joining his mother's household. Cenni smiled. Rachel might not fetch tennis balls on demand, but she sure as hell could take Cara Mia if push came to shove.

He put the coffee on to boil, kissed Rachel, who just happened to be sitting on the kitchen table, and reflected on the coming day. Piero, together with Sergeant Antolini, would walk the streets of Assisi (an impossible job on Easter Sunday, he was sure to hear later from Piero) to determine if any of the growing number of suspects had been seen going to or coming from the cemetery. As a bonus, perhaps the sergeant would take Piero's mind off his manifold sufferings; this week it was post-nasal drip. And Elena! In a moment of guilt he'd given her the day off. Piero was dogged, but Elena had flair. He needed them both on the case full-time. Half-holiday was a reasonable compromise, he decided; he'd give her a call, bring her in at noon. Dealing with Togni was the biggest problem of his day, but he'd already decided how to handle that Artful Dodger. His day had begun; the hangover could wait.

A man of fixed habit, Cenni emerged from his apartment building most mornings at five minutes after 7:00, into the Piazza IV November, the medieval heart of Perugia. On good days, he would take his time as he strolled southward toward Piazza Italia, often stopping at the Fontana Maggiore (the sublime work of Nicola and Giovanni Pisano) to view the allegory that extolled the virtues of punishment, a large lion thrashing a cub. Keeps me honest,

he'd told Piero when the inspector had asked why he liked
it so much. But on this particular Sunday he found himself
too distracted to give the great fountain or the little lion
more than a cursory glance.

At Piazza Italia, he began his steep descent into the bowels
of the medieval city, emerging finally into daylight and the
urban sprawl that surrounds Perugia. And then, by way of
another series of subterranean escalators and stairways, he
entered the largest underground car park in Umbria. A few
years back, a prominently placed bureaucrat (with a brother-
in-law in the building trade), had decided to move police
headquarters from Perugia Centro to the suburbs, a few hundred yards from the football stadium. Cenni had threatened to
quit, maybe get a transfer, join the caribinieri. "I like the uni-
forms—women love the red stripe," he'd told the questore. He
was kidding, of course, although not about the red stripe, but
Carlo had taken him seriously. He now received a handsome
stipend to pay his garage fees, large enough to lease a double-
wide space in the only section of the gigantic car park that
guaranteed twenty-four hour security.

He loved his car. His grandmother had given it to him on
his eighteenth birthday in 1980. It was already eight years old
then, a 1972 Alpine BMW with black leather seats and a lus-
trous silvery pearl finish. The interior still had its original seat
covers, worn to a buttery softness, but the exterior paint had
been renewed many times since. Every four years, on the car's
anniversary, he took a vacation to Germany and his car went to
the BMW factory in Bavaria for a new paint job and any other
work that Bruno, his German mechanic, deemed necessary to
keep it in its pristine condition. Chiara had once suggested that
he loved the car more than he did her. "You don't let anyone
smoke in your car," she'd said, "but you don't mind if they

smoke around me, and I have asthma." She'd particularly hated the engine's death rattle when they were stopped at red lights. Only his grandmother, who had her own issues with cars, had an appreciation of the delicate nature of a finely tuned instrument with a double-mouth Weber carburetor, differential pinion block, and oil radiator. She alone of women seemed to understand that the beauty of a car is how it performs on the open road.

Cenni knocked his shoes against the cement wall facing his car, then cleaned them on a pad that he kept in his trunk before getting behind the wheel. He now spent most of his days (and nights) in the suburban version of the fortified medieval tower, a two-story cement bunker surrounded by one-story concrete barriers. In the case of their particular bunker, its architect (the wife of the aforesaid bureaucrat) had given it a splash of personality: It was painted flamingo pink with pea green window frames.

On a normal day and in normal traffic, it took Cenni fifteen minutes to drive from his parking garage to this deconstructionist version of hell—when a football game was letting in or letting out it took a maddening two hours—but in neither case did the drive offer the pleasures of the open road or an opportunity to test Bruno's precision tuning. On Cenni's last birthday, his fortieth, he'd decided that it was time to act his age, to trade up for a more conservative model. The car dealer, one of the many along Ponte San Giovanni, and a strong advocate of automatic gearshifting ("Helps in traffic jams, Dottore"), had looked at him blankly when the subject of Weber carburetors was introduced. Differential pinion blocks and oil radiators never even came up. Cenni drove away somewhat relieved to discover that he and Bruno were joined together unto death.

2

HE SIGNED IN at the front desk, then started up the stairs, two steps at a time. He met no one. Those who pull duty on Easter Sunday always find ways to be with their families. The audacious get friends to sign them in; the timid come into the office, display themselves in the cafeteria, then disappear. He could easily do the same, leave after his conference with the questore, but this new case was a godsend, the perfect excuse not to appear at his mother's for dinner. Renato would be there. He hadn't seen his brother since Christmas and had yet to congratulate him on his recent appointment. He was now "His Excellency, the Bishop of Urbino," as his mother had mentioned three times yesterday, the second-youngest bishop in the Italian church, which generally preferred its bureaucrats seasoned and wrinkled.

They had been born sixty minutes apart, forty years ago, perhaps the only time they were that long apart until their eighteenth birthday. On that day, they had escaped the guests at one of their mother's drawing-room events: the count of this, the duchess of that, the inevitable principessa, who was invited to all his mother's parties, where she did her grocery shopping, slipping hors d'oeuvres into her extra-large pockets. The twins had a lot to celebrate that year. They'd both been accepted by the University of Bologna, to the law college. Alex had taken the lead in everything from the time they were children, even to selecting their university. He had planned and Renato had listened. They would get law degrees, fight corruption, perhaps run for public office.

Later that same night they were celebrating in a disco in Torgiano. He was drinking heavily, beer fortified by shots of whiskey from his friends, and was drunk. Renato was being particularly quiet. He had been sitting across from Alex, nursing

the same beer for over an hour, but now he was trying to tell
Alex something over the thundering music. It was a Bee Gee's
song. Alex thought he'd heard Renato say that he was not
going to Bologna, that he was going to Rome, to be a priest. He
had laughed out loud, and Renato had responded with an awkward smile. Then Renato said it again. They stared at each
other, Renato's face distorted through a haze of smoke and
alcohol. The beerglass that Alex was holding slipped from his
hand and shattered into tiny pieces. Slivers of glass and warm
beer sprayed them both, the avowed atheist and the future
bishop of Urbino. One of the slivers lodged in the fleshy part
of Alex's hand. It was still working its way out.

Cenni's office was on the top floor, a few doors down from
the questore's, a distinct disadvantage since Carlo Togni loved
to talk, and he particularly loved talking to his senior commissario, whom he regarded as his protégé when things were
going well and his nemesis when they were not. Either way, he
too frequently interrupted Cenni during working hours for
one of his general gossips. Fortunately or unfortunately,
depending on whether one was for or against crime, Togni also
had a small office in the city center, in the Palazzo dei Priori,
where he spent most days cultivating relationships, doing
lunch with his political brethren. His decision to visit the suburbs on Easter Sunday did not augur well for Cenni's day.

Two reports had come in during the night. Both were in
folders on his desk. From the handwritten labels, he could
see that one report was from Croatia and the other from
Rome. He was particularly surprised by the early report from
Rome, which normally treated Perugia the way the questore
treated Assisi, as a backwater town worthy of no special favors
and getting none. He assumed that the murder of an American, the niece of a friend of the PM, had sparked the prompt
response. What had been bothering him since yesterday

evening, though, was the identity of the person who had provided the questore with information on Sophie Orlic. The
previous night, Carlo had known that Orlic didn't have an alibi
for Friday evening. Only three people other than himself had
direct access to that information: Elena, Piero, and Fulvio
Russo. Italian pragmatism at work, Cenni concluded. Carlo
and Fulvio are sworn enemies, but when their interests collide,
they help each other out.

The report on Paola Casati contained nothing of interest,
just one short piece of paper listing her address in Rome and
the information that she was a student of art restoration,
currently working at the Borghese Gallery. No police record,
not even a parking ticket. The folder containing the Orlic
report was thicker than he'd expected. He thumbed through
it quickly and found it contained two documents. The origi-
nals of both were in Slavic but English translations were
included—a tribute to the power of the uni-lingual Americans, he thought with a sigh.

"*Buongiorno* Alex, may I interrupt?"

Cenni looked up in surprise. The questore was standing
directly over him. It was barely 9:00 and their appointment was
not until 10:00. The ear-to-ear smile that Carlo displayed, dazzling in its perfection of symmetry and whiteness, was always
good for a few laughs among his subordinates. The latest
rumor was that Togni and the PM shared the same dentist, a
man known for capping every tooth in his patients' heads,
whether they needed it or not, and even more celebrated for
squeezing in a few extra teeth for the cameras. The questore's
smile held no comfort for Cenni. He knew from past experience that the greater the display of porcelain, the more oner-
ous the meeting would prove. Ah well, he thought warily,
returning Carlo's smile with fewer teeth but with equal insin-
cerity, this is going to be more difficult than I'd thought.

He waved to the chair in front of his desk. "Carlo please! I'm still reviewing some of the reports on our cast of suspects, six so far and growing. I'd hoped to finish before our meeting at ten. Can you wait until I finish?"

"Oh Alex! Surely not six!" Togni added, dusting the seat with his handkerchief before sitting. "I understand this Croatian—the woman who found the body—had a number of run-ins with the American, actually threatened her in the street, *and in Assisi of all places*," he tacked on with emphasis. "City of peace and all that," he added, in case Cenni had missed his point. "Unless she has an unbreakable alibi—and I understand that she hasn't—she seems to be the likely suspect." His smile grew by two additional molars waiting for a response. A long silence ensued, broken only by the buzzing of two flies copulating on the windowsill.

The questore, the first to yield, as usual, spoke. "For Christ's sake. Alex, can't you swat those things? They're damn annoying!" And when Cenni didn't respond, "You know the PM's anxious for us to make a quick arrest. He wants as little yellow journalism as possible surrounding this case." He paused, confounded for the moment; perhaps he'd noticed the small dints on either side of Cenni's mouth, a signal to those who knew him well that the commissario was amused, or perhaps he was struck by the incongruity of his own words. "Well, the Leftist press, anyway. They're always out for the PM's blood, if you know what I mean. An early arrest and conviction would do a lot to keep the press quiet. What say you, Alex?" he asked, his tone now pleading. "Do we have enough evidence to arrest this woman?"

"She doesn't have an alibi for what we believe is the time of death," Cenni responded. "But neither do any of the other suspects. We're still waiting for the postmortem report. If what we've learned so far turns out to be fact, the uncle has the strongest motive for murder—money! Minelli left the bulk of her estate to him, if she didn't change her will. We'll talk to her lawyer in New York tomorrow. And from something the wife said, the family can use the money. What's more, if the rape were faked by a woman, as we discussed last night, the Casati women—all three of them—have as strong a motive as Orlic."

Cenni paused to let what he'd just said sink in, then leaning across the desk, he dropped his voice to a conspiratorial whisper. "Listen Carlo, I agree with you about the Leftist press. It's out for blood these days, ever since the PM's party recommended that we fingerprint all non-EC applicants for residence. *L'Unita* is particularly vicious in its denunciations, accusing everyone in the government, the police in particular, of being fascists."

He dropped his voice further. "Remember, Carlo, we still haven't lived down that incredible botch two years ago, when Russo arrested that retarded Albanian for the stiletto murders. Our friend in Assisi got a nice pat confession from the boy after some tender coaxing. We looked like fools, worse even, when two more Albanians were iced in the same way, and the killers turned out to be a members of a homegrown neo-Nazi group. The newspapers were delighted with that one, particularly when the Albanian's lawyer provided pictures of the kid's bruises to the press."

The questore's dapper little presence had noticeably deflated, his smile now a shadow of its former self. Satisfied that he was well along in achieving his purpose, Cenni leaned back in his chair and raised his voice, this time to an authoritative tone.

"Carlo, take my word for it. If we arrest this Orlic woman for murder, the press will scrutinize every move we make. God help us if it turns out she's innocent! Certainly we need to keep the PM pacified," he said, lowering his voice again, "although it's doubtful he'll survive all his scandals. But let's remember we're in Perugia. The PM had very little support here in the last election. If he goes down in the next election, why should we go with him? And we will if we're perceived as supporting him. At least, let's present the appearance of neutrality."

Cenni knew the questore very well and realized immediately from Carlo's now-puckered upper lip that he'd stepped over the line. Carlo Togni had yet to be neutral in anything if there might be something in it for him and, on principle, even if there wasn't, but God help the subordinate who remarked on it. The look of acquiescence on his face was gone, his displeasure now evident, and instead of capitulating on Orlic, he took a deep breath and reasserted his authority by standing. Even in elevator shoes, he was inches shorter than Cenni. Whenever he felt at a disadvantage in one of their discussions, he would manage, somehow, to stand while Cenni sat. This was a particularly difficult maneuver if they were in Cenni's office, and it was one that Cenni usually took pleasure in thwarting. But this wasn't a disagreement over assignments or promotions, and Cenni was more interested in winning his point than in annoying his boss.

But before he could attempt to salvage the situation, the questore, in that disconcerting way he had of changing moods in a moment, did it for him. He walked toward the door and looked outside, checking for eavesdroppers. "I see your point, Alex," he said as he walked back toward the desk. "But how can I explain to the PM that the Croatian is walking around free, particularly if she's murdered an American! You know how anxious he is to stay in with the Americans, the little sh . . . sycophant," he added, smiling to demonstrate his neutrality with respect to the PM. "What'd you say, Alex, anyone else we can arrest besides a member of the Casati family? Nothing permanent, you know, just to keep the PM happy for a few days."

He looked so pleased with himself, so charmed by his own tractability in coming up with a compromise—keeping the

PM off his back without aliening his favorite, and always intractable commissario—that Cenni knew he would have to agree to arrest someone, so long as it wasn't a Casati.

"There's always the boyfriend," Cenni acknowledged. "He has an alibi of sorts, but we haven't substantiated it yet. He's Canadian," he added as an apparent afterthought, knowing he'd get some objections from Togni on that point but prepared to counter them. "We can put him under house arrest and tell him it's for his own safety; then if his alibi is substantiated, he won't have any cause to complain to his embassy."

"For God's sake, Alex. How does that solve our problem with the press or with the PM? Canadian, American, they're all the same," Togni said querulously. "And a Canadian is non-EC, the same as a Croatian."

"True, but the Left won't see it that way. For them, the only people who are extra-community are Albanians, Eastern Europeans, and anyone from Africa. And the PM's even easier to please. The Americans and the Canadians are not getting along these days. The Americans won't object if we arrest a Canadian. The opposite, I expect."

"I trust your judgment, Alex," Togni replied, sounding pacified. "I always do. But do you really think he's the murderer?"

"No! Not the type, and for sure he's not the one who got her pregnant. I doubt he could," he added. "But if it keeps the PM and the press quiet, why not?"

"Well, if he's really not guilty, treat him nicely, Alex. Order in from one of the better restaurants, none of that Assisi tourist junk. Whatever he wants. And let's hope it turns out to be anyone but a Casati. I trust to your discretion, Alex," he added, as he started toward the door.

Cenni had just heaved a mental sigh of relief when Togni turned abruptly in the open doorway. "You know, Alex, it's because of me that *Il Lupino* is assigned to that backwater haven for religious nuts. Why should the press connect me with his past mistakes if we arrest Orlic for the murder?"

Cenni hesitated as though considering the questore's point. "Ah, but he wasn't transferred until a year after the stiletto murders. The Leftist press has a long memory, Carlo. Even worse, the American was murdered in Assisi which, unfortunately, is where we hid Fulvio. The press will make whatever connections suit its purposes. It's highly doubtful they'll say: *Carlo Togni got rid of Fulvio Russo*. More likely, it'll be: *Fulvio Russo was working for Carlo Togni when he beat a confession out of a retarded Albanian. Now he's working for Togni again*. Carlo, we've got to be very careful here. Don't worry about Orlic. I've got one of my men watching her." Dropping his voice again, with a nod toward the open door, he added, "We're no different from the PM, Carlo. We have our own careers to protect."

The questore was finally gone, and Cenni had gotten what he wanted, but at a cost. He'd have to put the Canadian under house arrest. I hope to God we can substantiate his alibi quickly, he thought to himself as he took a swig of his now tepid coffee. "Screw you Carlo!" he said *sotto voce* toward the still-open door. It was going to be another lousy day.

3

CENNI STARED AT the Orlic report with some trepidation. Sophie Orlic had the same type of Nordic good looks that Chiara had had, hair so blonde you could see the sun in it, translucent skin with just the faintest suggestion of the veins beneath. But the similarities ended there. Chiara's laughter had always been just beneath the surface. It would rise up for any occasion. She laughed heartily at everything, most of all at herself, and just as often at him. She'd had no pretensions, no secrets, and no intrigues. Orlic had smiled just once yesterday, and that only when Piero had tripped on his chair leg as he got up for his third piece of pizza. Yet he couldn't stop thinking about her.

He had decided last night, right before he fell asleep, that it was the mystery that bewitched him, and in a country built on mystery and steeped in intrigue, he had learned that most mysteries, the sacred and the profane, cease to exist when the structure beneath is revealed, or in her case, the facts of her life, the commonplace events. He'd establish the facts of her life, he decided, and then he'd forget her. He imagined her biography from the little he already knew of her: worked for a doctor, married the doctor, divorced the doctor, childless. Facts are what I need, he thought.

The top document was a brief dossier and contained what he was hoping would cure his malady, the simple data of her life: date and place of birth, family background, education. It was essentially the same information that Orlic had provided on her application for a *soggiorno*. What was not shown on the *soggiorno*, though, was that she was a widow with a twenty-year-old daughter. There was little about the dead husband and the daughter other than their names, Sergio and Christina, and a brief notation that the daughter was currently a patient in a state hospital in Zagreb.

The second document was a transcript from a war crimes hearing conducted by a group called "The Committee for Retribution." He didn't know the group, but assumed it was one of the many that had formed in the now-defunct Yugoslavia to ferret out war criminals. In this case, the committee was made up of Croats hunting Serbs. They wouldn't get very far, he thought, as anyone familiar with the Balkans debacle should know. The Orthodox Serbs would simply turn the tables and accuse the Catholic Croats of genocide, if not in the recent war, than in the previous one, which, if Cenni understood Serb reasoning correctly, was justification for the slaughter of tens of thousands of

Muslim Bosnians. Whole cities and villages had been destroyed; millions of lives disrupted; tens of thousands dead, maimed, tortured, raped, bayoneted; and he was a cynic. He didn't like himself for it, but it had all been so senselessly horrific, of absolutely no profit to any of the parties involved, that it was impossible for those on the outside looking in to understand or to grieve. He picked up the transcript and read:

Cases No 53, 54, 55: Sergio, Sophie, and Christina Orlic

In August 1995, Baranj, a village in western Bosnia, which at the time had a majority population of Croatians (52%) and minority populations of Serbians (23%) and Muslims (25%) was occupied by Serbian forces, and all Muslim and Croatian community leaders who were still in the village were brought to Serbian headquarters for questioning. In early September 1995, the village was reoccupied by Croatian forces. At that time, after investigation by the Croatian army, it was determined that 65 Croatian and Muslim men and three Muslim women, all from the same village, had been murdered and their bodies consigned to a gravesite outside the village. After the signing of the Dayton Accord, on December 14, 1995, and the disbursement of United Nations peacekeeping troops to the area, an investigation was begun into these same accusations by the newly formed Committee for Retribution. This report is made in support of the above allegations and is affirmed by the testimony, attached, of Sophie Orlic, who was deposed by this committee on the 15th day of April 1996.

Signed: Josip Nikic, Committee for Retribution

Testimony of Sophie Orlic, an Ethnic Croatian

April 15, 1996

The Serbs started to shell the village in mid-August. We talked about leaving, going to Zagreb to stay with cousins, but I was three months pregnant and had been ill for most of my pregnancy. Sergio was afraid the trip would be too much for me, and we were both sure that we had nothing to fear. In Baranj, the Croats, Serbs, and Muslims all get along together, we said. Christina's best friend was Serbian and at least a third of Sergio's patients were Serbs.

On the morning of August 20, two officers arrived at our home in a jeep. We knew one of them, Andjelko Visnar. He had owned a pharmacy in Baranj until 1991. There were some bad feelings between him and Sergio. Sergio had reported his suspicions to the local medical board that Visnar was adulterating certain cancer medications. The evidence was not sufficient to charge Visnar with a crime or to revoke his pharmacist's license, but the examining board issued a warning to him based on Sergio's testimony. He sold the pharmacy after that and left the village. I didn't know the other officer.

They took us to the Town Hall where they had set up their headquarters. We sat outside the mayor's office, on the wooden benches for petitioners, for more than an hour. We were the only ones there other than a guard who was posted at the front door. He had a gun but even if he hadn't, we wouldn't have tried to leave. Sometimes we heard laughter from inside and Sergio and I would look at each other and try to smile. Christina sat between us. She was holding my hand and she squeezed it very hard every time there was a noise from behind the doors. Sergio told her not to be afraid. Tell them what they want to hear, he said, and don't provoke them. "I'll take care of you, Kitten." That was the last thing he ever said to Christina. Visnar came out of the office. He stood in the doorway and motioned to

Sergio to come inside. That was the first time I felt really afraid. I knew when our eyes locked that he hated us.

That was at one o'clock. We hadn't eaten since early morning and the soldier who was standing guard offered Christina half of his sandwich. At times we would hear voices and laughter from behind the closed doors. I listened for Sergio's voice but I couldn't hear it. At two o'clock, Visnar came out again and motioned to us both to come inside. All of the blinds in the office were drawn. It took a moment for my eyes to adjust to the low light before I saw Sergio. He was seated in the center of the room, in a office swivel chair. His arms and legs were taped to the chair with black masking tape. A white towel was stuffed into his mouth. His eyes were shut, just slits of clotted blood, and he was bleeding from his nose. I don't think he saw us or even knew we were there. At first I thought he was unconscious, perhaps even dead, but I heard a loud gurgle and realized that he was choking, probably from the blood running down the back of his throat. Christina, who was behind me, screamed. I ran to Sergio before Visnar could stop me and started pulling on the towel. Visnar pulled me away, then slapped me hard across the face. I heard a squish and knew that he had broken my nose.

There were two of them there besides Visnar. One of them was the man who had come with Visnar to pick us up. I don't know what the third one looked like, but I remember his voice. The three of them took turns raping me, and then Christina. I didn't see them rape Christina. I kept my eyes shut, but I could hear noises and Christina crying and pleading, and then she stopped. I didn't resist and I didn't plead. When the three of them had finished, I heard one of them say to Visnar, tell Josip to come in if he wants some, and they all laughed. Josip was the soldier who had given Christina half of his sandwich. I think Josip also raped Christina, but I don't know for sure. I was still lying on the floor when I heard a gunshot. One of the men, the one in charge, started screaming. "You're a fuckin' fool, Andjelko. You've sprayed his bloody brains all over the fuckin' room. Get them all out of here," he yelled, "and clean up that fuckin' mess when you get back."

They took us to a large warehouse located behind the town hall. There were many women and children there, at least half of them Muslims. Some of them I knew by name, and others I recognized from seeing them in the streets. It was quiet; none of the women were talking or crying. A woman I knew, a patient of Sergio's, whispered to me that if you cried, or talked, they took you away and you didn't come back. We were there for two days. A guard brought in loaves of bread and olive oil twice while we were there. We got our water from a small bathroom and we took turns using the one toilet. We sat on the floor leaning against the walls and slept in the same spot. Some of the children played with each other, and so long as they didn't cry or make too much noise, the guards let them alone. That first night two guards came in and picked out four women in the dark who left with them. My nose was swollen to twice its size by then, and he passed us by, but then he returned and motioned to Christina. I tried to hold on to her, but he hit me across the face so hard I couldn't breathe for the pain.

Three of the women came back an hour later. Christina was among them. She wasn't crying and she didn't talk or look at me. She stared straight in front of her and didn't seem to know where she was. I knew from my medical training that she was suffering from post-traumatic stress. I was glad. I didn't want her to know or remember what had happened. I don't believe she even knew that her father was dead. The second day the guards brought us food once, and that night they didn't come for any women. We heard shelling all night, and the next day, about eleven in the morning, the Croatian army came. We were told to go to our homes, to stay off the streets, that someone would come to interview us there. A few of us who needed immediate medical attention were seen to by their army doctor. I miscarried the baby three weeks later. The doctor said it was the stress, but I also had gonorrhea. Sergio's body was found a few days after that, with the other villagers they had killed, in a lime pit outside the town. I buried him with my parents. Christina is in Zagreb, in a state hospital. Her doctor says her recovery will take time but that some day she may remember me.

Signed: Sophie Orlic

Cenni finished reading the report and picked up what was now left of his coffee—ice cold, he realized when he took a sip. It was all there, he thought, what he had wanted. The facts. He had plucked out the heart of her mystery. His hands were shaking. Later he couldn't explain to himself why he did it, but he poured the remaining black liquid over the second page of her testimony. He watched as a slow moving river of coffee ran down the center of the page, smearing the type. He took his clean white handkerchief and dried it, obliterating completely her last words and signature. He walked over to the window and looked down on the car park below. He could see his car, its gray metallic paint gleaming in the midmorning sun. It was parked between the guard's shed and the fence, the smallest space in the car park but the only one isolated from the other cars. No one could park next to him and ruin his paint job.

4

THE DAY HAD begun promising much, cloudless and warm when Renato Cenni left Urbino in the morning, but it was ending on a dark note. His unlined raincoat was too thin for the chill that had set in and the air was heavy with moisture. It was likely to snow again, and he had a two-hour trip back to Urbino if he ignored the speed limit. He got into his car, black and nondescript, purchased for its anonymity, and simultaneously started the engine and the heater, something Alex, who loved his car more than his comfort, would never do. Renato had an atavistic delight in speed and knew that this might be one of the last times he would enjoy the pleasures of solitary driving, of putting his foot down on the gas pedal as far it would go. Not that he risked much. The Church, unlike the police, purchased its cars for economy, not power. In another month he would be invested as the Bishop of Urbino. After that, he would have a driver and be expected to use him. The Church disliked idiosyncrasy and rarely tolerated it, excepting only those sons and daughters who had achieved religious notoriety, the ones who had refused to be shut up or shut in. Saint Francis of Assisi and Mother Theresa were the exceptions; he was the rule. His talents were for diplomacy and administration, as the cardinal had told him last week when he'd called Renato to Rome to announce his elevation to bishop. His successes, using those talents to carry out the work of God, had been many, just the one spectacular failure, his brother.

Alex was a good man, better than many of Renato's fellow priests and certainly better than most of those who worked at the Curia. They call themselves Christians and behave like the Medici, Renato thought, dividing up power and its spoils among themselves. They had no flocks and a good many of them had forgotten why they had come to Rome in the first place. He had no arguments to counter those that Alex set forth when he denounced the Church for its insistence on pomp and circumstance in the midst of poverty, or for its egregious silence on the evils of greed and corruption in post-war Italy. It was fruitless to point out the Church's counterargument, that men, even the holiest of them, are just men, that the Church is one, holy, and apostolic because of the grace of God, not the actions of men. Alex had studied law and theology at Bologna. He knew all the arguments and had all the answers. Renato often thought how very un-Italian Alex was in his notions of morality. Good or evil, black or white, nothing in between. "You're a bishop," Alex had thrown at him before they'd parted that evening. "You can find things out that I can't. An innocent woman may go to jail. Help me." Renato had agreed, of course. They were brothers.

He had arrived at his mother's house at 3:00, earlier than expected, so he wasn't surprised not to see Alex, but when five o'clock came and Alex still hadn't arrived, he knew his brother wasn't coming. Alex telephoned shortly after that. A new case, he had said hurriedly, an American, very political. It wasn't possible to get away. He'd visit Renato in Urbino. And then, right before he'd hung up. "Congratulations, Your Eminence." Renato had retorted that *Your Eminence* was a title used only for cardinals. "Soon," Alex had replied. Once they had finished each other's sentences, at times had even started them. Renato always knew when Alex was lying. Of course, he could get away, he was a commissario!

His decision to become a priest had not been easy. He had thought about it for years, almost from the time that his father had died. But he had not spoken about it to anyone at home. His mother, he knew, would be delighted but for the wrong reasons. To be a priest in Italy still conveyed prestige. His grandmother was an ebullient nonbeliever, and Alex would have scoffed. He had allowed Alex to sweep him along as he made plans for their future until the night of their eighteenth birthday. He told Alex that night.

Alex's reaction had been different from what he'd expected. He didn't try to talk him out of it, nor did he repeat any of the old shibboleths about the Church. Instead, he was distant and invariably polite. He had even helped him to pack the night before he was to leave for Rome. When Alex had rolled up Renato's favorite jeans, he had laughed. "Not for long," he'd said to his brother, making a sweeping motion with his hands. Most of his remarks that night were just as inane, the type you make to strangers with whom you're uncomfortable.

When they were ten, their parents had given them separate bedrooms. One of his mother's friends, a would-be psychologist, had told her that twins need to spend time alone if they're to develop healthy egos. They had hated sleeping apart then, and he would usually sneak into Alex's room after his parents had gone to bed. But that last night at home, he was glad to be alone. He had cried for hours and had fallen asleep just before dawn.

In time they became friends again. When Chiara was kidnapped, he had taken a leave of absence from the seminary. They had waited the weeks out together, hoping for her return. And when they knew she wasn't coming back, Renato had spent the next month with Alex. When the director of the seminary had balked at granting him a longer leave, he had proffered his resignation, which was rejected.

They were friends again, but not as before. With each new elevation, the last time to monsignor, now to bishop, Alex would resume the icy distance of formality, even use the occasional *Lei* when they were alone. This time I'm going to fight back, Renato decided shortly after six o'clock. His mother protested when he said he was leaving, but his grandmother smiled. She whispered in his ear when he bent down to kiss her goodbye. "Give him hell!"

This was his first visit to Alex's office in the suburbs, and he had some difficulty finding the building and then convincing the guard to admit him without an identity card. The priest's collar, visible after he had removed his scarf, worked its magic. "Second floor, third door on the right," he repeated out loud, as he ran up the stairs two steps at a time. At the top he stopped. Worried about his reception, he walked slowly down the corridor toward the only open door.

Alex was standing in front of his window looking out. The clocks had been set forward an hour, and he could still see the outline of Perugia framing the horizon. The last reflections of the setting sun streaked the sky with candied swirls of orange and purple and cast a soft tawny glow on the snow-capped mountains in the distance. He watched from his office as the lights of the football stadium began to go out, one by one, until they were all extinguished. He thought of the opening lines of Dante's invocation to the muses,

> *Lo giorno se n'andava, e l'aere bruno*
> *toglieva li animai che sono in terra*
> *da le fatiche loro[1]*

He felt oddly at peace for the first time that day. Perugia had won its third match in a row. It might even qualify for the European Cup. He laughed out loud at an irreverent thought: For the European Cup, even Renato would sell his soul! He looked at his watch, just a few minutes before 7:00. If he left now, he might catch Renato before he left for Urbino. He turned and saw his brother standing in the open doorway, framed in a halo of golden light.

---

[1] Day was departing, and the embrowned air
    Released the animals that are on earth
    From their fatigues

"Carissimo," Alex said softly, his eyes alight with pleasure. "For a moment I thought you were an apparition."

"One of the nicer ones, I hope!" Renato replied.

"Poeta che mi guidi," [2] Alex replied softly, then embraced his brother Italian style, kissing him on both cheeks. Just then the telephone rang. Alex checked the incoming number on the receiver. "Sorry, Renato, but I have to take this one."

Renato scrutinized his brother's face as he talked on the telephone. He's aging well, better than I am, Renato thought, recalling the gray hair that he'd plucked from his right temple that morning and the three pounds he'd gained since turning forty. They were not identical twins, but some strangers, the undiscerning ones, assumed that they were. Renato acknowledged with a small sigh but no real regrets that Alex was the better-looking twin, his hair thicker and darker, his eyes a deeper blue, his nose a bit less Roman.

Alex, who'd just replaced the receiver, noticed his brother studying him and smiled. Renato felt his heart jump. Whatever had been wrong between them was over, and then, with consternation, he thought, unless I'm elected pope. *That* Alex would never forgive!

---

[2]   Poet, you who are my guide.

Book Four

Little Rita

I

On Monday mornings traffic comes to a complete halt approximately two hundred yards before the turn-off to police headquarters. This was Elena's excuse every week for coming late and windswept to their Monday morning meetings. Cenni wondered if she'd offer up the same excuse today. He hoped for something new; otherwise it would be difficult to keep a straight face. Most of Italy was on holiday the Monday after Easter and those workers who weren't called in sick; the roads were virtually empty. He was pleasantly surprised, then, to find Rita Minelli's diaries sitting on the top of his desk, the relevant pages clearly marked with paper clips. For the first time in memory Elena had beaten him to the office. A report from the United States on John Williams had also come in during the night, but he decided to honor Elena's enterprise by reading Minelli's diary first. He flipped to the first page marked with a clip.

> **MAY 5, 2001**—Mamma was awake through the night, coughing and spitting up blood. I waited until seven to call Dr. Biscardi to be sure I wouldn't wake him. Call an ambulance, he said. I begged: Please come, Dr. Biscardi, just one more time, please! You know how Mamma hates the

hospital. And then, just before he hung up, he says spitefully, I suppose she's still smoking? Why did he have to say that?—he knows she's still smoking. It's the only pleasure I've had in life, Mamma says to anyone who'll listen.

Two weeks ago, I stood behind the door of her hospital room, waiting for the attendant to bring a wheelchair so I could take her home, and overhead a one-way conversation Mamma was having with her roommate, Mrs. Kreindler—an elderly Jewish lady who probably didn't understand a word of Mamma's fractured English. Mamma was telling Mrs. Kreindler what a wonderful life she'd had in Italy before the war and before Papa lured her away to Brooklyn with false promises. She blames Papa for everything bad that's happened to her.

My father, the count, Mamma said three times in so many minutes—carrying on about the beauties of Italy and the horrors of Brooklyn. And then she got carried away—forgetting Mrs. Kreindler's history, I guess—and started to praise Mussolini and describe the wonderful parties my grandfather gave to entertain him. She was in raptures over a gown that she'd worn to one of those parties, white handmade lace from Burano, and the diamonds she'd worn in her hair, and the general who'd sat next to her at dinner, so handsome and so young to be in such a high position—I'd heard it so many times before! I guess Mrs. Kreindler understood Mamma well enough. She hissed *Nazi* at her.

I don't know what came over me, but I stormed into the room yelling—We're in Brooklyn and Papa's dead. Can't you let him rest in peace! Mamma started crying and couldn't catch her breath. Sneaks never hear what they expect to hear, she said later, after I'd apologized.

But this time she was different, more subdued. As I was helping her button her cardigan, she looked up at me from under her brows. Very softly, almost as though she didn't want me to hear, she whispered, *You're a good girl, Rita.* Those are the only kind words Mamma's spoken to me since Papa died on June 10, 1974, a lifetime ago! The night they carried Papa out of the house, she was hysterical with fear. *Cara mia, non mi lasciare mai,* she begged over and over.

When we got home from the hospital, she told me to call her lawyer. I need to make a will, she said. No, Mamma! I cried. I didn't want her to know she's dying, but she knows! You'll be rich, Rita, she said. Mamma knows nothing about money. We've had so little all our lives that I suppose she thinks the money she inherited from Nonna is riches.

MAY 22, 2001 — Mamma is gone!—she died yesterday a little after five in the evening. She'd been in a high fever and delirious from early morning. Dr. Biscardi came in at noon and said she wouldn't last very long, maybe a few hours. He was very matter-of-fact and suggested that I call someone to sit and watch with me. There is no one, I said, and he nodded. At the door he turned. I'll drop by later in the evening, after she's gone, to sign the death certificate. Leave a message with my answering service. Cold bastard! He then asked if I had chosen a funeral home because, if not, he could suggest one. I told him that Mamma had always liked the Fossello Brothers. Of course, he said snidely, an Umbrian family, aren't they! Dr. Biscardi's family is from the Veneto and Mamma always said that he was a snob. He had often admired the Venetian candelabrum on Mamma's dresser, and I had

planned to give it to him after her death, but right then
and there, I changed my mind.

After he'd gone, I went back to Mamma's room to sit
with her. I took her hand in mine, and it was very hot,
hotter than it had been all day. She was mumbling inco-
herently, and sometimes she would cry out for her
mother or father, once even for her brother. She never
called out to Papa, and it was only the once that she
called my name. I'm here, Mamma, I whispered, kneeling by her bed, but she didn't recognize me. Doctor Biscardi had given her a shot of morphine to make her
comfortable. She'll be out of it until she's gone, he had
said, as though that were something wonderful.

I called St. Anthony's rectory to ask for a priest. The
parish secretary answered the telephone—a nasty
woman—and said that Mamma had had the last rites
twice in two weeks and that she wouldn't send a priest
over again, they had other things to do. I screamed at
her, threatened to call the bishop, even the Vatican, if my
mother died without receiving the last rites. I'll see what
I can do, she said, but I didn't believe her. Then at three
o'clock, a priest arrived at the door, someone I hadn't
seen before, young, in his late thirties, and very kind. Visiting from Italy, he said. He was surprised and pleased
that I spoke Italian, and he gave Mamma the last rites in
her native tongue—not the ten-minute version that the
other priests had performed, but the full rite.

We lit the candles together while he said a brief prayer.
Then he knelt down at the right side of her bed and taking
her hot hand in his, he spoke softly in Italian, so softly that
I had to strain to hear. Livia, I'm here to give you Extreme
Unction, to help you home to Jesus and Mary. Squeeze my
hand if you understand. And she did. He stood then and,

after gently removing his hand from hers, he dipped one of the cotton swabs that I had prepared into the vessel of holy oil that he'd brought with him. He rubbed the oil ever so gently on her closed eyelids and said the prayer for the dying: *Through this holy unction and His own tender mercy may the Lord pardon thee, Livia, whatever sins or faults thou hast committed by sight.* And then he did the same with her ears, her nostrils, her lips, her hands, her feet, reciting the same prayer with each separate anointment. When he finished, he pulled one of the chairs over to her bedside and sat down. He motioned for me to do the same. He then covered her right hand with his own and with his left hand he covered both of mine. We sat thus, in the darkened room, without once speaking, listening to her shallow breathing until she died. I came to understand during that vigil, in that labored last hour of Mamma's life, why she had loved Italy so much. I knew then that Italy was my home too, that we would return together.

MAY 27, 2001 — I met with John Costa today to go over Mamma's will. I knew that she'd inherited some money from Nonna three years ago, but she'd never told me the exact amount, although it turns out that the money from Nonna is the least of it. Two million at a conservative estimate! Mr. Costa said that Mamma had been a very clever woman—she had invested her money wisely. When I asked what money, he was surprised that I didn't know about Papa's insurance policy, two hundred thousand dollars, most of which Mamma had invested in the stock market, he said. She sold off all her stocks right before the market crash and, after paying capital gains, had invested the money in Treasury Notes. He told me all this with some awe, apparently very impressed with Mamma's investment assiduity. I think he was surprised at my silence, but how could he know that I had supported Mamma on my teacher's pay for twenty-three years, that I had lost my chance to go to Barnard because Papa died penniless, that I had grown old in the service of a lie. I felt the muscles tightening in my face and my throat constricting as he talked. I could only stare and knew he thought me ungrateful, but all I wanted to do was go home and cry.

MAY 28, 2001 — Today I put the house up for sale. The realtor thinks it will fetch quite a bit. The market is very strong right now. Two hundred twenty thousand at a minimum, she says, more if I'm not in a rush. Sell it to the first person who makes an offer, I said. Then right after I got home, John Costa called again, urging me to make a will before I leave for Italy. I don't want to think about money, I told him, and there's no one I want to enrich when I die. He suggested some charities, and I said I would think about it!

I had a strange dream last night, although I suppose Mamma would have called it a nightmare, but I woke up feeling at peace. I was standing in the middle of the Brooklyn Bridge with Papa, a schoolgirl again in my blue and gray uniform. We were surrounded by large brown grocery bags full to the brim with dollar bills and we started to throw the dollars into the air, like the bread-crumbs that we used to throw to the seagulls when Papa was still alive. We were laughing and happy and everyone who passed by smiled and waved. The dollars came float-ing down and lay all around us but we didn't pick them up. They were brightly colored streamers of worthless paper. Then Papa put his arm around my shoulders and we turned toward Brooklyn and started home.

MAY 30, 2001 — Mamma said often enough that I would come to a bad end if I didn't have her to look after me, and I suppose after yesterday she was right. But I don't feel like I've come to a bad end. All day, since I first opened my eyes, I've been smiling—grinning, Carol said when she came by in the early afternoon to ask if there was anything she or Mike could do. I was in the backyard picking the last of the tulips and singing. I was embarrassed that Carol caught me so happy so soon after Mamma's death. This morning, I stayed in bed until after ten, re-imagining every moment. There's so much to do before I leave for Italy in three days, and I don't seem to care. It's so strange that we met again yesterday. Foreordained, I told him. Although perhaps he's right, to say our meeting was foreordained may be a sacrilege, all things considered!

I've always liked going to confession. I still remember the first time, even after all these years. My best friend Diane and I practiced on each other for two weeks. Diane hated the thought of telling a stranger—a man!—her sins. She was embarrassed but I was excited. I liked the darkness, listening to the whispers of the other sinners while I waited my turn; I even liked telling the priest my sins. Sometimes, when I had no sins to confess, I'd make them up. Usually after reciting my sins, always venial, I'd tell Father Crespi other things, things that happened at home. He liked it that I spoke Italian. I told him how Mamma made Papa cry and that they didn't sleep in the same bedroom. He asked me lots of questions after that, and then gave me three *Hail Marys and* one *Our Father* for penance. After absolution, he would always say, God bless you, little Rita.

I felt lonely and guilty after buying the mink jacket at Macy's, and the Church of St. Francis was close by. So extravagant, I thought, but it *was* half price! I've always wanted clothes that would turn men's heads, and the saleswoman said three times that I was beautiful. It sets off your dark hair and eyes. It was flattery, just so I would buy the jacket, but I loved the feel of the soft fur around my neck, like a baby rabbit. I do look beautiful, I thought. Sexy, Gianni said later, when I tried it on for him at the restaurant. I saw a placard *Italian Spoken* on one of the confessionals and went inside. I knew his voice immediately. Even through the ornate grille I could trace the outline of his strong, beautiful face. I imagined we were sitting once again at my mother's bedside, his hand over mine, as we waited together for her to die. That we should meet again in Manhattan can't be a coincidence!

He laughed out loud when I confessed to buying a fur jacket with my mother dead only a week. And so many starving people in the world, he replied. I realized he was joking when he told me that the Pope had white ermine trimmings on some of his vestments. We talked for a little bit, and I told him how unhappy I was. He said that we should talk outside, later, as he had other penitents waiting in line. I sat in one of the pews for fifty minutes, waiting. Afterward we walked to a Spanish restaurant just a few steps down from the church. He wanted to pay for dinner. *Pago io e basta,* I said, and he agreed to let me pay, laughing at my accent. After we finished the first bottle of wine, a Rioja from Spain, a very special wine the waiter told us, I ordered a second. It was lovely, a polished mahogany color, soft and velvety at the back of my throat, not at all like the harsh Umbrian wines that we drank at home. I held my wineglass up to the light before each sip and talked and talked about what life had been like with Mamma. His eyes, so steady and kind, were a deep violet blue, the color of Mamma's sapphire ring. I drank far more than I should, and I was lightheaded when we left the restaurant. Twice I tripped as we walked toward Seventh Avenue. He caught me both times, finally hugging me about the shoulders. It was late by then, close to midnight. When a taxi stopped, he got in with me saying he would take me home. I protested but not seriously. In the taxi I told him about Mamma's money and began to cry. He kissed me on the mouth, a gentle kiss, like a pat on the head. I kissed him back, hard, and we kissed again. I think the taxi driver knew that he was a priest. I saw him observing us through the rearview mirror. He was surly when I handed him the tip, and he gunned the engine as he drove away.

We both knew what we would do as soon as we were inside the house although neither of us talked about it. I led him upstairs to my room where he undressed me. He fumbled once, with one of the hooks of my bra, so I undid it for him. When I was fully undressed, he kissed the inside of my breasts, then my nipples; and later, he eased me down onto the bed. I lost my virginity in my early twenties, at a New Jersey beach resort, a groping session that ended in pain and tears, and later, in my thirties, I had sex a few times in Manhattan, after picking up men in hotel bars. I only did the hotels five times, though, as I was afraid of getting AIDS. It had never been like this, first an exquisite melting and later like the tarantella that I had once danced with my father at a cousin's wedding, whirling and whirling,

faster and faster, until I'd almost fainted with the excitement. He spoke *sotto* voce and asked me often what I
wanted. *Mia dolce* Rita, he whispered as I fell asleep in
his arms.

At five I awoke to find him slipping on his clothes.
He said he must go, but I reached up and began to
unzip his trousers. We made love again, deliberately,
with great tenderness, until the first morning light
came through the bedroom window. Then he insisted
once more that he had to leave and placed his hands
over my mouth so I couldn't protest. I put on my pink
flannel robe and we went down the stairs together. At
the front door, just before he kissed me goodbye, he
opened my belt and slipped the robe off my shoulders. It fell to the floor. *Sei bellissima*, he said and called
me Little Rita, the same as Father Crespi had done. He
also said that we could never see each other again.

I studied him from behind the window curtains as he
walked toward the subway station. A train whistle pierced
the still air and he broke into a run. *We'll meet again*, I said
aloud to the empty house as I watched him climb the
stairs toward the elevated platform, two steps at a time,
and disappear from view.

JUNE 1, 2001 — Tried all day yesterday and most of today
to find his name and address. Called the rectory of St.
Francis twice and was told both times, by the same
woman, that they entertained many visiting priests from
all over the world, three of them last week from Italy
alone. Without a name she couldn't help (*wouldn't* was
more like it!). I called St. Anthony's and spoke again to
the parish secretary. She denies sending a priest to the
house to give my mother the last rites. Well, he didn't just

materialize out of thin air, I yelled in frustration. I wish I had asked his name the day that Mamma died, but I was too upset. When we were together at dinner he said to call him Gianni, but I don't think that's his name. I called him Gianni twice. The first time he didn't answer and the second time he laughed before replying. I don't blame him for lying. If his bishop finds out, he could be defrocked.

JUNE 2, 2001 — It's frightening to realize fully what I've done, even more so to realize that I have no regrets. I'm completely free, sitting in First Class, drinking Spumante, on my way to Rome. The second couple to view the house made an offer. The realtor thinks she can close the sale by the end of June. Another two hundred fifty thousand dollars, two and a half million dollars all told, not including my pension when I'm eligible. Whoever said money doesn't matter is a fool! John McIntyre accepted my resignation with more respect than he's ever shown me in the past, although at first he refused to believe that I had enough money to quit teaching before I was eligible for retirement. He's always patronized me, treated me like an old maid. He won't find anyone else in the department willing (or able) to run the Debating Society, the Scholars' Club, and organize two class outings a year, all without extra pay.

I bribed the secretary at St. Francis—two hundred dollars cash—to give me the names of the three priests who had been visiting from Italy last week (money for the poor box, I told her). She only agreed when I said that the priest had comforted my mother in her dying. I want to donate money to his parish in Italy, I said. Of course, none of the priests on the list are named Gianni.

The steward just came around to collect the dinner
trays and the man sitting next to me, an Italian film
director, ordered grappa for both of us. He reached over
and took the pen out of my hand. Stop writing and talk
to me! he said. And later, Let's meet in Rome for dinner.
He compared me to an Italian movie star, a young Anna
Mangani, only more beautiful!

JULY 6, 2001—Today I received my *soggiorno* and immediately applied for residency in Assisi. The woman who
took my application congratulated me, said my *soggiorno*
application came back from Perugia in record time. Ten
years is more than they ever give on a first application. But
then your family is Umbrian, she added. *You're really Italian!* Really Italian! I like that! *È vero, e scrivo adesso in ital-
iano per dimostrare la mia gratitudine.*

It's ironic that on the day I became an Italian resident, I started teaching a class in English, at Umberto's
school—Count Casati, as he likes to be addressed by
his staff! The woman who was supposed to teach the
class skipped out yesterday, back home to Liverpool.
She came to the house late last night, ten hours before
the class was due to begin, and handed in her resignation. I was in the sitting room when she arrived and
overheard her talking to Amelia in the hall. The school
didn't pay enough, she said. Amelia was very polite—she
always is—but in that top-drawer way she has of conde-
scending to those whom she believes are her inferiors. I
know the tone, she uses it often enough on me.

*But, my dear, you never did complete your degree, and you
have no formal teaching credentials.* And then, very sweetly,
Perhaps I can persuade the count to pay you a bit more. All to
no purpose, of course, as it was obvious the woman was

determined to quit, although I do think Amelia had some right on her side. Three times in five minutes the woman started a sentence with *between you and I*, a frequent gambit of the grammatically impaired. Amelia was on the verge of tears when she returned to the sitting room. I think she's afraid of my uncle's tyrannical tempers, and they have seven students signed up for the class. I can't do it myself, she said, her voice breaking. I have a class that conflicts with this one.

I can teach the course, I told her. Without pay, I added. She seemed skeptical but I reminded her that I was certified in New York State to teach English as a second language (of course, to my uncle an English accent—even a Liverpudlian one—carries more weight than a knowledge of grammar). She agreed but insisted on paying me—thirteen euros an hour. She'd just offered the woman from Liverpool fourteen euros, but I kept that to myself. I'm sure they're short on money. I overhead her telling Umberto they'd have to sell the Sisley.

Later Umberto came into the sitting room for his nightly cup of cocoa. Amelia told him about the class, in that breathless voice she uses when she's afraid of his reaction. She looked away from him, toward me, when she added that I'd very graciously offered to teach the course, probably to avoid the look of disgust that passed over his face. He didn't thank me, and instead told Amelia to instruct me in their teaching methods before I entered the classroom—in less than ten hours! I could have reminded him that I have a master's degree in English and twenty-three years teaching experience, but he intimidates me as he much as he does Amelia, and Paolo. Nobody intimidates Artemisia! Just before he went up to bed, he turned to me, *Rita dear, try not to pepper every other sentence with "you know." It will confuse the students.*

JANUARY 1, 2002 — Last night was wretched! John and I went out to dinner, to a small hotel-restaurant at the top of Assisi. I booked a room in the hotel and paid cash, even told them to put a bottle of chilled champagne in the room at midnight. I thought John liked me! He spends all of his time with me when he's not in the library working, so what else should I think. Lots of men like older women!

I ordered a five-course dinner and French champagne—not prosecco as the headwaiter suggested—and reserved a private table in the dining room alcove. The perfect New Year's! Not like those with my mother: Every year exactly at midnight two glasses each of spumante, in bed by twelve-thirty, mass in the morning, the last of the spumante with our New Year's dinner. Lies, and more lies, to the other teachers. *Party?* Of course. *With whom?* A friend. And the day after! *Good time?* Great! Got home at dawn. *Hangover?* Oh God, yes, slept until dinnertime I hated the lying, but I hated even more for them to know that I spent New Year's Eve with my mother.

When I could I avoided the teacher's lounge altogether from Christmas until mid-January. But it didn't matter. They knew I lied. I was in the last cubicle of the ladies' room and overheard Carol Stafford talking to one of the younger teachers about me. *She stays home every year with her mother. We could do something about it if she'd let us. Mike has lots of friends he could fix her up with (he thinks she's a knockout), but how do you get around the lies?* You don't, Carol, I said to myself after I heard the bathroom door slam shut. I went home early that day, told the school secretary I was coming down with a horrid cold to explain my red eyes.

Our evening was perfect until midnight. Before eleven we were high on a bottle of Moet and before midnight we were drunk, on the bottle of Rosso Montefalco that we'd ordered with the Florentine *tagliata*. We laughed at each other's jokes, silly ones, and made fun of the waiters and the other diners. At midnight, after we'd toasted in the New Year, I leaned across the table and kissed him on the lips. He kissed me back. It wasn't a passionate kiss, not the way Gianni had kissed me, but warm and friendly. I wanted desperately to make love, for someone to make it up to me for all those barren celebrations with my mother.

I can't do it Rita, I like men! John cried, after we'd undressed. Afterward we put our clothes back on and opened the chilled champagne that the hotel had sent up, and we cried together. It turns out that John has lots more to cry about than I do. His father physically abused him as a child and when John was twelve shipped him off to a Catholic orphanage in northern Canada, labeling him an incorrigible, which gave the friars at the orphanage the right to abuse him again, at first physically and then sexually. Later, as a young teacher at a small religious college in New England, John was accused of sexually abusing one of his own students. The student hanged himself from his dormitory window. John says he can't return to the United States or he'll go to prison. I urged him to go back. Prove your innocence. It's better that way! Oh dear God, what's wrong with me? First a priest and now a gay man!

JANUARY 3, 2002—With my uncle (and now my aunt) I'm always at fault! In August I found a woman sobbing

on the steps of the family mausoleum. She said in broken
Italian that her employer was blackmailing her, that the
woman wouldn't return her passport. Of course, I
informed the police. What decent person wouldn't?
Umberto and Amelia took the blackmailer's side. To be
expected! She's one of their darlings; she was Nonna's
caregiver in her last days and my uncle dotes on her.
Whenever she comes in to help with the cleaning he
manages to be underfoot.

Yesterday she followed me home, although she
claimed afterward that she was walking in the same direction and that I started the conversation. What conversation! She spat at me, called me a busybody, butting in
where I was not wanted—something like that, anyway. If
that had been all, as I explained to Amelia when she
rebuked me (now who's the busybody!), I wouldn't have
complained to the police. She threatened me! The
woman is mad, I think—and dangerous! I told Amelia
that and she scoffed. Don't be ridiculous, she said.

The policewoman—the one I spoke to in August
about the blackmail—wasn't concerned either. She
shrugged it off; said that the Croatian had just received
a bill from her lawyer for his services in August—a very
large bill, she said accusingly—more than she has. As
though this were my fault. Forget about it, she said. Don't
file a complaint or she'll be deported!

I was reluctant to agree with the sergeant at first. Of
course, I don't want any more grief from Umberto (or
Amelia). And God knows, I don't want the woman
deported. But she did threaten me.

Commissario Russo is the only one who showed any
proper concern. He'd noticed me talking to the sergeant at the front desk and suggested that we go into his

office for some privacy. We don't need every Albanian in Assisi listening in, he said to the sergeant. He recognized me at once for a Casati. You look like your cousin Artemisia, he said, only petite and prettier. Flattery, but I don't mind. Artemisia is always putting me down. Calls me *la Americana grottesca* behind my back, and sometimes even when she knows I'm listening.

At first the commissario disagreed with the sergeant. He urged me to press charges. Threats of this nature must be taken seriously, he said. But when I told him that my uncle wanted me to drop the charges, he changed his mind. You should listen to the count, of course, less trouble for the family. When I didn't immediately agree, he said he'd keep a watch on the Croatian for a while. I'll call you tomorrow, perhaps even the day after, just to be sure you're not bothered. He's very good looking!

MARCH 1, 2002—I hate Sundays! Ever since John met Matteo, he spends all day Sunday with him. And my family has no use for me, nor I for them, although they're so enamored of their darling selves, I doubt they'd even know that their opinion of me is reciprocated, in spades. Bugger them! So you see, dearest uncle, I too can speak the Queen's English.

And, of course, *he* can't leave his wife on Sunday, not even for a measly hour of lovemaking although it's his brother-in-law he's afraid of. Screws around on his wife Monday through Saturday, but never on Sunday. Mustn't miss the sacred family dinner! He's rather boring, not at all what I'd expected, but the sex is good!

I must be mad. I am mad! Every piece of my waking day is consumed by thoughts of sex. Today at early mass I wondered about the man sitting next to me and, later, at the communion rail, I imagined the priest in bed, and the man is a midget, shorter even than me! Oh, Gianni, where are you?

MARCH 2, 2002

> *Breathless, we flung us on the windy hill,*
> *Laughed in the sun, and kissed the lovely grass*

I memorized those lines of Rupert Brooke when I was in college. Perhaps I knew, even then, that one day they would belong to me. In June, in that little Spanish restaurant on Eighth Avenue, I was captivated by the color of the Rioja wine. Mahogany velvet, I said as I held my glass to the light. Not at all, Gianni rebutted. The crimson velvet of a Raphael painting! When I insisted on mahogany, Gianni said the gentleman's way to settle our dispute was for us to visit Raphael's portrait of Leo X in the Uffizi with a bottle of 904 Reserve and two glasses. We can toast a great Florentine patron of the arts, he said, and get drunk at the same time. Those words still resonate whenever I think of Gianni. Always in my imagination we meet in front of Leo's portrait. To the women who come and go, we're just two posturing strangers. We speak in code:

The lighting on the camauro and mozzetta is magnificent; it evokes the crimson-red of a fine wine, Gianni says.

Raphael is a magnificent colorist, but he's an even greater psychologist. Don't you think the strain on Leo's face foretells the Medici's failure to contain the Reformation? I respond.

He smiles at my allusion and I know that he remembers; I had called that night in June my *sexual reformation.*

So long as you're Teresa of Ávila, he'd responded,

mocking me. I draw the line at fucking Martin Luther, or, God forbid, John Knox!

I had protested his profanity, particularly its use with respect to St. Theresa.

Cara Mia, you're such a prude for someone who fucks so well, he had replied, before covering my shoulders with kisses.

It didn't happen that way at all. We didn't meet in the Uffizi. My train pulled into Santa Maria Novella on Sunday's schedule—an hour late—too late to stand outside the Uffizi for another two hours waiting for admittance. I had visited the Medici Pope many times before and Gianni had never appeared. Once in June, shortly after I'd arrived in Italy, I stayed so long in the Raphael room that the guard asked me to move on.

It was romantic silliness to moon around the Uffizi late on a winter's afternoon, and I had a four-hour wait before I could catch my train back to Assisi, so I decided to visit the cloisters of the Convento di Francesco in Fiesole, one of the places Gianni had spoken of with great affection. It was far too beautiful a day to waste sitting on a bus. The air had the moist, heady smell of winter turning to spring. Delicate cirrus clouds whipped across the eggshell-blue sky like the white sails in a regatta, and the afternoon sun beamed down on the tile rooftops and bounced off the Baptistery's bronze doors. A perfect day to walk. An hour up, an hour to see the cloisters, an hour back, and still time for coffee and a pastry in the station bar. I began the climb with energy and neglected to pace myself. In less than fifty minutes, I was short of breath and it was no longer possible to ignore the northeast wind that blew down from Fiesole. The massive cypress trees that lined the sides of the road and groped for the sky afforded little protection from the wind as it ricocheted through the great branches, seemingly gathering strength as it traveled downhill. As the road curved into an open bend right before Fiesole, a great gust of wind nearly blew me over and I looked about frantically for something to grab on to. I felt someone take hold of my elbow.

Signora, *prego*, a man said and pulled me along with him.

He didn't even know it was me!

When I spoke his name, *Gianni*—the name that wasn't really his—he could barely speak for the surprise.

Why, little Rita! You've grown up quite beautifully. Cut your hair and bobbed your eyebrows, he said and laughed. He had remembered my jetty eyebrows!

We walked against the wind, breathless, talking under and over each other the whole time until we reached the convent. Gianni was staying with an old friend in Florence, enjoying a day off from his duties, and had decided to visit the cloisters before returning home. He never did say where home was! At the end of our tour, he asked the caretaker to unlock the gates that open into the small wooded park that runs down from the convent to the main square in Fiesole. My guidebook said it was the pleasantest way to return to the Piazza, and we had decided that nothing less than the pleasantest way would do. When the caretaker said it was promising to rain, I scoffed. How could it? Those beautiful scudding clouds that I had admired in Florence. The sun on the rooftops. Impossible on such a perfect day!

We were ten minutes into our descent when the storm broke and the heavens opened. Great cold streams of water rained down through the trees and onto our faces and into our collars. It filled our shoes and soaked us to the skin. The rain blackened my eyes and ran down my cheeks in long smears of waterproof mascara. By the time we reached the top of the Piazza, I looked like a drowned rat in my wet mink, and Gianni, who was dressed in mufti—a thin windbreaker and jeans—shivered with cold. We sheltered in the doorway of a small hotel just outside the park's gates until I suggested that we go inside for a drink. The proprietor did the rest. He offered us a room where we could dry off and promised to send up towels and homemade grappa—to get the chill off, he said. He didn't seem to notice that we had no baggage. Perhaps he didn't care.

Cenni finished the diary pages that Elena had marked with paper clips and read the brief note appended to the last page:

The diary ends here—rather abruptly, almost like she dropped her pen in mid-sentence. Plenty here, though, to pin a few ears back: demon priest, married lover, gay boyfriend. All the makings of a Hollywood triangle (and let's not forget the movie director!!). If the motive was money, plenty here for someone!

Ottaviani.

He agreed with Elena that the diary ended abruptly. Minelli's last entry was dated March 2, fifteen days before her death. In a few places earlier there were no entries for two or three days, but never a two-week interval. Not another word about what had happened that night and not another word about Gianni. Rather convenient, he thought, that the last words *perhaps he didn't care* ended on the last line of the page, flush to the right-hand margin. He carried the diary to the window to examine it in a stronger light. To his inexpert eyes it seemed as though pages had been removed.

ANTONIO TURO was stamped on the inside cover. Turo, a well-known bookbinder in Perugia, would know immediately if any pages had been removed from one of his diaries. He'd send Elena around with it later in the day.

Nothing much in the diary to identify either of the lovers, the married man or the priest, although he had some thoughts about the married man. The priest was another matter altogether and probably easy enough to trace through the church in New York, although he'd be damned if he'd make a $200 contribution to its poor box. He'd put Elena on it, and he'd also have her check with the police in Fiesole. First hotel after exiting the park, Minelli had written. If the hotel proprietor followed Italy's antiquated registration laws, he'd have their names on file. And if not—which was just as likely—he could at least provide a better physical description of Gianni than violet eyes and a strong, beautiful face.

If Minelli were two months pregnant (and they'd know by the end of the day when Batori delivered the postmortem), then the circle of suspects may have narrowed rather than expanded as Elena suggested. The priest was not the father, not if they hadn't met since June. And, in Italy, a priest having a casual affair with an unmarried woman of legal age is hardly the stuff of scandal. Gianni—or whatever his name was—might get a reprimand from his bishop if he were indiscreet, but probably not even that. Minelli, with her New World notions of defrocking, took it all too seriously—but perhaps that's the way Gianni had wanted it.

Book Five

Disentanglements

I

PIERO CERTAINLY DIDN'T look Italian with his green eyes, ginger hair, and freckled skin, and with respect to punctuality, he didn't act it either. Cenni, who was himself a model of timeliness, wondered how, under the law of averages, two Italians who were punctual to a fault could have found themselves together in the same city, let alone the same police unit. At precisely eight o'clock every Monday they began their meeting with a discussion of the previous day's football scores and, on occasion, as on the Monday after Easter, with idle chitchat about their work. Cenni began, "How did the house-to-house go yesterday, Piero?"

"Some interesting developments, Alex. But, in general, it was a difficult day . . . you know . . . my mother . . . that I had to miss Easter dinner," he added in response to the confused look on Cenni's face.

"Murder takes precedence!" Cenni snapped. He was in no mood to hear about Piero's mother, an irritating woman, or one of the dinners her son had missed. It would do Piero a world of good to miss his dinner.

"Where's Elena?" Cenni asked, still snapping. "She knows we

start at eight. I thought she was already in the building. She can't blame traffic today."

It was fifteen minutes past the hour, and Elena never breezed into their meetings until twenty past. Besides, whenever he complained that Elena was late to a meeting, Alex would take the opposite view and remind him that Elena always brought the coffee. Piero unwrapped his apple tart and began to eat. "I hope she gets here soon," he said, after taking his second bite. "I need a coffee to wash this down."

Cenni's mood lightened considerably as he watched the door open slightly and Elena's hand come sliding round holding a white take-out bag. Coffee at last!

"May I come in?" she asked.

"*Basta*, Elena! Get in here. Now!"

The meeting had begun.

"You first, Piero," Cenni said, nodding at the report that the inspector was holding.

"A very long day, Alex!" Piero began lugubriously, giving it one last try. Cenni surveyed the objects on his desk. The ashtray? No, he might want to start smoking again. The coffee. Hardly! Piero's apple tart? Gone. He decided on the papiermâché paperweight that the questore had given him for Christmas. He missed Piero, who saw it coming and ducked, and hit Elena in the chest.

Elena thought it very funny, but she also wondered aloud if getting hit in the tits constituted sexual harassment.

"What tits?" Cenni responded, before conceding that he owed them both a holiday.

Piero began his report. "Sergeant Antolini and I visited every shop that sells that religious stuff, particularly the ones at the top of Assisi like you suggested. Not a single shopkeeper remembered selling that statue to Minelli. We also visited every restaurant and bar in lower Assisi with not a single identification of anyone connected to the victim. If we're to believe them, everyone in Assisi was either at confession, preparing for confession, or saying their prayers after confession. Our last stop of the day was at a little bar at the top of Assisi, the one right before Porta Perlici." He stopped and looked first at Elena and then at the Commissario to make sure that he had their undivided attention. "Paola Casati was in there on Good Friday—with a man! And not just any man—the son of the Minister of the Interior," he announced dramatically. He flipped open his notebook and began to read the bar owner's statement:

> The two of them came in close on to five. I'd just started cleaning the coffee machine and told them so. No more coffee, I said. I'd promised my wife I'd take her to the procession later in the evening, and I wanted to go to confession first. The boy, he's one of those punks, blond streak in his hair, earrings, one in his lip of all places! He got aggressive, said I'd lose my license if I didn't serve them coffee. I didn't like him, and what's more I recognized him from a picture in *L'Unità*. Son of that minister in the government, you know, Montoni! *L'Unità* claims he's involved with terrorists; you know the ones I mean. They blew up that McDonald's in Rome, where they killed that cleaning lady. *L'Unità* says the government's protecting Montoni because of his family. The girl—I'd recognize her anywhere—Luciana Stefanak's granddaughter. Poor woman died of a broken heart five years ago. Terrible what those people did to her!
>
> I've voted Socialist all my life, Inspector. Always with the people, if you know what I mean, but I don't hold with that muck. Blowing up working people in hamburger joints. Even I eat hamburgers! It's hardly the way to get rid of the *fascisti*, now is it? Too much money these

kids have nowadays. Playing around with what they don't
understand, is what I said to my wife.

Then with an added flourish, Piero told them about the bar
owner's wife. She'd been cleaning some glass shelves near
where the couple was seated and overhead bits and pieces of
their conversation. Paola Casati was upset, almost in tears, and
said very little. Montoni spoke in undertones, but every now
and then he'd raise his voice in anger. Piero quoted what the
wife overheard: "Stuff it, Paola . . . not a single thing your
cousin can do! Can't prove a thing, but why couldn't you keep
your trap shut? Or if you had to blab, why involve me?"

Piero stopped reading to interject, "It was Sergeant Antolini
who interviewed the wife. 'Are you absolutely sure he said
cousin?' she asked the wife. Get this, Alex, and I'm quoting
exactly: '*Si, certo,* I'm sure he said *cousin,* but the girl, she used
a name, she said *Rita.*' "

Cenni interrupted. "The woman may have read about the
murder in the papers. Maybe, unconsciously, she substituted
the name *Rita.*"

"Sergeant Antolini thought of that too," Piero responded
smugly. "She's pretty smart, you know." He flipped the page of
his notebook and read, "Question: Do you remember seeing
the American's name in the newspapers. Perhaps you heard it
on TV? Or from your husband?"

Cenni prompted, "And her answer?"

Piero read again from the notebook. "My husband, he told
me about that dreadful murder. Said the dead woman was an
American, but he didn't say her name, leastwise I don't remember him saying it. And I don't read the newspapers or watch the
news on TV either. All that violence makes me nervous. I know
the name *Rita* when I hear it; she's my favorite saint. The girl
said *Rita.*"

Piero's news was hot, and it made the commissario hot under the collar. The report from Rome on Paola Casati, delivered yesterday and in record time, had been totally innocuous. Just a few easily ascertainable facts: where she lived and worked in Rome. Not a word about any political activities. If what Piero had discovered yesterday was verified by other sources, Paola Casati may have done far more than just vote Communist in local elections; she may have acted on her beliefs. If she and the boyfriend were involved in the McDonald's bombing and she'd told this to Rita, possibly on the day that they'd met in Cascia, then Paola Casati had a motive for murder, particularly if Minelli were threatening to talk. And from what he knew of Rita Minelli, the chances of that were high. Passages in her diary suggested that she viewed herself as a self-appointed vigilante. And if Paola Casati had implicated Montoni to Rita, as it seemed she had, then he also had a motive for murder.

Elena observed the commissario pacing up and down in front of the window. He's furious at Rome, she reflected. It's more than just the count's influence with the current government; it's the whole kit and caboodle. The pecking order could as easily be reversed, and then the count would be pacing the floor. An ancient game and a well-practiced one. Most of her fellow officers learned quickly, adjusting on a dime to each new administration and each new set of unwritten rules. Fifteen years on the force. He should be used to it by now, Elena thought, but with some sympathy.

Saturday was a case in point. She had succumbed to the power of the aristocracy, just like that *stronzo* Staccioli. So much for abolishing titles, when they still tell us what to do, and we do it! She should have insisted on securing Minelli's room but instead had permitted herself to be overruled by the count, and by Staccioli, who'd pulled rank. That might have been excused if she hadn't joined the others in the kitchen for coffee. The memory of the commissario reminding her of what she was always reminding everyone else was humiliating. Well, maybe her news would make up for it.

She cleared her throat to attract his attention.

Cenni looked up, puzzled. He'd forgotten in his anger that Piero and Elena were still in the room.

"Do you want my report, *capo*?" Elena asked, clearing her throat again as though something were stuck. And then, because he looked so troubled, she smiled, hoping he'd smile back.

Cenni struggled to clear the image from his head of the count roasting on a spit. "Sorry Elena, I was thinking of something else. Nice job that, reading Minelli's diaries. Do the follow-up today; locate the demon priest, as you call him, and the big-time Hollywood director. And pay a visit to Turo, the bookbinder. Find out if any diary pages are missing. And both of you revisit every shop in Assisi that sells religious articles. I want to know where Minelli purchased that statue, and when. Assisi's full of that junk, so check everywhere, even the grocery stores. The maid says she wasn't carrying a package when she left the house. Williams doesn't remember a package either." He finished giving orders and saw the relief so expressively written on Elena's face. She can barely contain herself, he realized. Probably struck gold yesterday.

"Okay, Elena, you're on, but before you report on yesterday's activities, tell Piero what you found in the American's diaries," he said mischievously.

"He already knows; he knew before you did," Elena responded, grinning. "Screw the diaries. What I learned yesterday is a lot more interesting!" Without waiting for his nod, she began.

2

NEITHER THE COMMISSARIO nor Piero had been particularly excited about her news. The junior officers had gone across the street for a coffee at the end of their meeting, and Piero was completely unimpressed. "Big deal, the count was at home on Friday. He told us that. Only now you've handed him an airtight alibi, and we still don't know who murdered his niece."

Piero was right; she had given her news more importance than it deserved, Elena concluded. Well, the commissario ought to be grateful anyhow. One less suspect to worry about. And it was still possible that the count was involved. Maybe he used an accomplice to do the dirty work: the wife, the daughter, even the granddaughter. With all that money as a motive, the whole family could be in it together. An animating thought! Send them all away for ten years. Actually, though (she mentally backtracked), the wife and granddaughter weren't so bad; at least they'd been civil . . . but the daughter. Piero had that one right. A bitch on wheels. When Elena and the senior forensic officer tried to take Artemisia's prints on Saturday, she'd given them the deep freeze, refusing to cooperate. And later, she deliberately messed up the first set of prints and laughed.

Elena had stumbled upon the count's alibi purely by chance. Piero and Sergeant Antolini were the ones sent out to verify the family's whereabouts at the time of the murder by talking to bus-boys, waiters, neighbors, and shop assistants. But the woman who provided the count with an alibi turned out to be an Irish journalist. It was the journalist who made the approach, in the Bar Sensi, where Elena had stopped for a coffee late Sunday afternoon on the off chance that she'd find Piero there, wolfing down one of his ubiquitous apple tarts.

Elena had taken her coffee to the back to avoid talking to any of the press who were hanging around the bar. She'd first noticed the woman when she became aware that the woman was noticing her. A snappy-looking redhead in her late thirties, she was sitting on a barstool in the front, talking on and off to Orlando, and drinking white wine as though it were water. Whenever she had anything to say to Orlando, she'd lean across the bar in a conspiratorial manner. At one point, Orlando nodded toward Elena. That was when the woman downed her wine in a single draught, dropped a few coins on the bar, and got up to leave. But instead of walking out the front door, she came down the stairs and plunked herself onto a chair opposite Elena, without so much as a by-your-leave, and began asking questions. Pushy, Elena thought at the time, but it turned out okay in the end. Better than okay!

"Parla inglese?" the journalist began. As soon as Elena nodded yes, the woman bombarded her with questions concerning Giorgio Zangarelli. "Is Zangarelli a suspect? What's the connection between the American's murder and the Albanian problem? What's the count's involvement with Zangarelli?"

"Whoa!" Elena had finally interrupted, not understanding a thing the woman was talking about. She knew Zangarelli's name all right. Anyone who'd worked with Fulvio Russo in Perugia knew about his rich—ridiculously rich—brother-in-law. *Il Lupino* never stopped talking about him, and neither did the Umbrian press, particularly after Zangarelli and Russo were caught trying to buy land that the government had seized. That's when Russo got sent down to Assisi. It turned out that the woman was investigating another of Zangarelli's dubious ventures, ferrying illegal workers in from Albania to work in his fish-packing factories in the south of Italy and the north of

Ireland. The journalist had nothing to add concerning Rita Minelli's murder. She was strictly interested in Zangarelli. "Something smells here," she'd said, laughing at her own pun. On Good Friday, a few minutes after 4:30, she'd followed him to the Casati home and watched as the count greeted Zangarelli at the front door. She'd waited until the count let him out again, shortly after 6:00.

"Did you really hang out there, in front of the house, for an hour and a half?" Elena had asked, wondering how she could be so sure that Zangarelli had been inside the whole time.

"Sure, in that little hole-in-the wall café across the street. What else is there to do in this burg but drink coffee or go to church! Doesn't much matter where you drink it, although the coffee in the Bar Sensi is better than most. I had a perfect view of the house from the café. I even saw the maid leave by the side alley a few minutes after Zangarelli went in."

Cenni's mind worked in strange ways. That was a conclusion Elena had come to some time ago. He'd shrugged off her news that the count was involved with Zangarelli, and possibly with the *Camorra*. "Who isn't?" he'd asked sarcastically. But he'd really perked up when he heard about the maid leaving the house shortly after 4:30 and made Elena repeat it twice. Did he think Lucia was involved in Minelli murder?

3

"VOI SIETE AMERICANO! Sono qui per la vostra sicurezza!" the fat policeman said slowly and very loudly three times before miming the words—pointing first to John, then to the front door, as he turned an imaginary key, then staging a garroting with himself as dummy. Williams ascertained from the dumb show that he was being held in custody for his own safety. In reply, he stammered out, *"Sono Canada, non sono American!"* in pidgin

Italian, also three times, but the man didn't seem to understand. Finally, the policeman dialed Commissario Cenni and handed the telephone to Williams. The commissario was very understanding, returning an "of course" to each of Williams's objections, but he wouldn't budge. "Sorry, Signor Williams, it's for your own safety. I know you're Canadian; you know you're Canadian; but it's what other people think that worries me. We've had one murder and I don't want any more, of Americans or pseudo-Americans."

The commissario was lying! They were holding him in custody because he was their prime suspect! He should call the Canadian embassy to complain that the Italian police had imprisoned him in his own apartment. But if he did that, the commissario might get angry with him, perhaps deport him! Bad things happened to him whenever he made people angry. He'd learned that before he'd reached his fifth birthday. He had wound the little knob on the top of his father's wristwatch as he'd seen his father do every morning, and for his help, his father had beaten him black and blue.

He was twelve when his father, the son of dour Presbyterian Scots, had sent him away to a Catholic charity school run by the Irish Christian Brothers. "You'll be among your own kind," his father had declared in front of his Irish Catholic mother, who had immigrated to Canada from the north of Ireland when she was eighteen. "They'll know what to do with an incorrigible!"

Incorrigible was the word his father always used when he referred to his youngest son. At the age of seven, when John had visited his oldest sister's house, he had looked it up. *One who cannot be corrected or reformed,* the dictionary said. It was a safe word. It branded the son but not the father. Any family could have an incorrigible: an unruly, disobedient, willful son. You read about them all the time in the Bible, and in the Newfoundland papers, boys who stole and lied, who left home and were never heard of again. But a gay son was a different matter altogether. The Presbyters of the church might look at the youngest son and question the manliness of the older brothers, or, God forbid, that of the father. John was the last of six children. The two eldest were boys, then three girls, and finally John, born ten years after the youngest girl. His father was delighted. Another son to help on the farm. His mother was forty years old and worn out.

John never saw his mother again after he was shipped off to school. She died of breast cancer a year later, but he had thought of her every day since. In his memories she always looked as she had that last morning at home. They were to leave early, just after sunrise, and his mother shook him awake at 4:00, whispering to him to get up and come into the kitchen. His father was still asleep in the other room. "Will you have a boiled egg?" she had asked. He hated eggs in the morning; they upset his stomach, but it was the one thing that she could offer that wouldn't smell up the kitchen and wake his father.

They'd sat together at the worn pine table, at the end where his oldest brother had carved his initials, while he ate his egg and drank his strong boiled tea with extra milk, just the way he liked it. His mother had farmed with his father for thirty-two years, run a tractor, cut down trees, milked cows, raised chickens and six children, kept a spotless house, and she still had gentle manners and a soft loveliness that even his father couldn't beat out of her. She had protected her youngest child from his father's belt as best she could, often taking the blows for him.

She held her tea mug cradled in her long, tapered leathery fingers, the nails cut straight across like a farmer's, and John had thought that her hands were beautiful. "It's best this way, John," she sighed, her lilting brogue more pronounced than usual, her eyes rimmed with unshed tears. "He had a brother like you who drowned himself when he was seventeen! He

can't seem to help himself, John. You'll be happier at school."
She took his right hand in hers and turned it over, palm
upward, and placed a medal in it. "Our Lady of Knock. It
belonged to your grandmother," she said proudly. "Your father
doesn't know I kept it. Our Lady will watch over you, my poor,
wee John." When he drove away with his father in the pickup
truck at 6:00, she stood dry-eyed at the front door. They didn't
wave to one another. It was easier that way, but John secretly fingered the gold medal all the way to the railway station.

The fat policeman sat in the corner by the door and read his
newspaper. Occasionally, he would laugh to himself and look
up for a moment as though hoping to share the joke, and then
he'd look away, a scowl on his face. He reminded John of
Brother Jerome. Jerome had been a tremendous size, larger
even than the fat policeman, with black wavy hair and swarthy
pockmarked skin. Some of the boys had called Jerome "black
Irish" behind his back, and once one of the boys had said it to
his face. Jerome had been in a good mood that morning, and
the cheeky boy was the hurling captain—he favored the athletic boys. Jerome had laughed heartily and slapped the boy
with an open hand on his back. "Good one, lad, but don't try
it on too often." They had just undressed for their showers, and
the print of Jerome's hand glistened through the steaming
waters like a huge red birthmark.

Brother Jerome had transferred to St. Andrew's from
another college two years after John had arrived at the school.
From the moment Jerome had learned that John was a Scots
Campbell, not an Irish one, and had been baptized into the
Church of Scotland, he'd had it in for him, although John
admitted to himself years later that he might have helped his
animosity along. John had always been a great student of history, and in one of Jerome's classes, he had challenged the lay

brother's assertion that the Scots had turned Protestant because of Henry the Eighth's lust for Anne Boleyn.

But his mother had been right, school was better than home. Some of the older boys were bullies, but if you kept out of their way, you could manage. He liked to learn, and he was first in his class every year. Even after the arrival of Brother Jerome, school was better than home. And then came a rash of robberies in the dormitories. One of the boys lost a wristwatch and another a ring. Jerome was their dormitory monitor and he searched all the lockers. In John's he found the medal. "This is Our Lady of Knock, something a devout Catholic wears around his neck," Jerome said with clenched teeth, "not something a dirty Scot hides in his locker, not unless it's stolen." And then he put it into his mouth and bit down hard. "Gold," he announced to the dormitory at large. Until that moment, John had always accepted Jerome's insults, banking his anger, but when Jerome put his mother's medal into his foul mouth, anger filled him up so fast he couldn't push it down. "Don't call me a dirty Scot, you filthy bugger!" he'd cried, his normally pallid skin flushed a blood red.

Jerome slammed him down onto his bed, then grabbed him by the shoulders and swung him round, pushing his face into the mattress and his knees to the floor. "Drop your pants, you little queer," he raged. "We'll find out who's the bugger around here. Thieving, murdering Protestants," he exploded, slashing out at John's bare buttocks with his belt buckle, twenty-four strokes in all. John could hear someone crying in the background. It was little Matty, his upper bunkmate, he realized. "I've read your file," Jerome bellowed. "Stole from your own Da! Even his own people, the dirty Protestants, don't want his kind around," Jerome announced to the other boys who'd been made to look on.

The next day the medal was returned to him, by gentle Brother Luke, with greatest sorrow. "We know it's yours, John; it's listed with the possessions you brought with you when you first came to us. Brother Jerome neglected to read that part of your file. But not to worry, John. Brother Jerome is being transferred to another school." When John saw the medal in Brother Luke's outstretched hand, he tried to mouth "my mother," but he couldn't form the words. He was choked with tears. Luke cradled John in his arms, wiping away his tears. "Poor, wee John," he'd said ever so softly, stroking his head. A year later, they were lovers.

John graduated from St. Andrew's at seventeen with highest honors and went on to McGill, on full scholarship. When the investigation into abuses at the Irish colleges first surfaced, he was in his third year at McGill. Many of the accusations of physical abuse were lodged against Brother Jerome, who had been transferred from college to college, until he finally left the order. Some of Jerome's former students had provided John's name to the prosecuting attorney. John agreed to testify, but he never told about Luke; they had been friends as well as lovers. It was because of Luke that he converted to Catholicism. It wasn't until later that he'd learned of the other boys. "Luke's boys," the newspapers called them. Apart from the money that John received every year in compensation for Jerome's beating, that was the only part of the scandal that affected him. He wept when he learned of the other boys. Luke had told John that he was special.

After Luke, he had remained celibate for five years. When it happened again, he was the seducer. He was teaching geography at a small religious college in Maine and met a boy very much like his younger self at St. Andrew's—lonely, diffident, different—only this boy was older, eighteen on the day that they made love. To celebrate the boy's birthday, his roommates had dragged him out of his dormitory room and forced him on a woman at one of the strip joints just outside the town. "Prove your manhood," they had demanded. Jeff had walked away from the woman and from them, returning to the university on foot, a good five-mile walk, crying the whole way. John recognized Jeff as the two of them entered the elevator in their dormitory building. Jeff was a clever student, one of his best. He invited him to his room for a drink. He told Rita the whole unlovely story on New Year's Eve, the only person he ever disclosed it to.

"Jeff hanged himself by tying a belt to the hook on his windowsill. After placing the noose around his neck, he let himself out the window by holding onto the ledge. He must have known that when he dropped down from the ledge it would be impossible to climb back up. His room faced the chapel, and he was seen dangling against the building by some students as they walked to early service. It was too late to do anything, of course. He had been dead for hours.

"Jeff was eighteen and obviously gay. Anyone could see that after talking to him for five minutes—the same as anyone can see it about me—but it was with me that he first acted on it. He was religious, and he couldn't live with having broken God's commandment or the knowledge that he would do it again, and again. He left a note in his room. It didn't even mention me. It was addressed to his parents. *'Mommy and Daddy, Forgive me and pray for my soul. Your Loving Son, Jeff.'*

"The police listed Jeff as a suicide but Jeff's parents refused to accept the verdict. The father hired a private detective, who learned that we'd been together that night. Another teacher had seen Jeff enter my apartment. The detective turned his findings over to Jeff's parents, who insisted that the college and the police prosecute me. The college terminated my contract and the police asked me in for questioning. Jeff was seventeen when he first enrolled at the university, and on absolutely no evidence, they decided that we'd been lovers before he turned eighteen. I was accused of corrupting the morals of a minor. I left the United States, and I won't go back."

4

PIERO AND ELENA left the commissario's office with a mile-high list of tasks to complete before the three of them would meet again later that day. And while they were meeting, Cenni had received another two reports, both concerning Williams.

The first, from Newfoundland, Canada, was interesting but not directly related to Minelli's murder. Williams had been one of a large number of young men in a class action suit filed against the Irish Christian Brothers for the systematic abuse of boys, and he had been compensated by the religious order to the tune of $15,000 Canadian a year, for ten years. The way Williams lived, he was not hard up for money.

The second, from the United States, disclosed that Williams had a motive for murder. The State of Maine had an outstanding warrant for the arrest of Williams, who was charged with endangering the morals of a minor. Williams had denied the allegation and fled the country.

Minelli had written in her diary that she had urged Williams to turn himself in. Had she goaded Williams, pushing him relentlessly to do so? Williams struck Cenni as a passive, fearful man, and he also struck Cenni as a liar, at least in some of his responses regarding Minelli. Cenni felt sure from observing Williams's giveaway tic that he had known about Rita's pregnancy, and also that they had discussed it on the last day of her life.

But from what Elena had reported, Williams's alibi appeared to hold up. The priest at San Stefano's had confirmed Williams's attendance at five o'clock mass—"He sat in the front pew, received communion, stayed to the end, left about twenty to six." The priest had refused to confirm that Williams had gone to confession before mass, considering this privileged information. But Elena was sure that Williams was home free there as well. "The priest's body language was loud and clear," Elena insisted. "He wanted to tell me he'd heard Williams's confession; he just couldn't say it directly. Afraid of *Il Papa!*" she added irreverently.

Further, the waitress at Il Duomo confirmed that Williams had come in early Friday evening. "Came in a few minutes after we'd opened, about ten minutes to six. I told him we wouldn't be ready to serve pizza for at least another twenty minutes. I brought him a bottle of water—no bubbles—and his pizza twenty minutes later. Spinach and ricotta, always the same. After he finished his pizza, he waited a short while for his friend. When she didn't show, he left at a little before seven."

There was plenty of time for Williams to have killed Minelli if he hadn't gone to confession at 4:30. Even so, Cenni was confident that Elena was right, that Williams had gone to confession, which would have cut considerably into the time he needed to get to and from the cemetery. Also in support of Williams's innocence was his demeanor in offering an alibi. Perfectly natural, not a tic in sight. Cenni had no doubts that given the right circumstances anyone could kill, but it didn't seem likely that Williams had killed Minelli. Still, he was pleased. He had enough on the Canadian now to keep him in custody for at least another two days. If the questore pressed him, again, to arrest Orlic, he'd counter with Williams. And tomorrow he'd bring Williams to Perugia for questioning. He wanted to know what he was hiding. If Williams balked, he could always hint at extradition.

5

HIS HEAD ACHED. The two aspirin hadn't helped. Now he had a pain in his stomach and a sore head. Batori had called shortly after two with a feeble excuse for not delivering the postmortem as promised. "Tuesday morning, first thing," he said, adding the perfunctory, *"di sicuro!"* Cenni was sorry now that he hadn't signed the petition to remove him. "Useless old fart," he murmured aloud.

"*Scusi*, Commissario."

He looked up from the report he was reading, shielding his eyes from the light, and tried to smile. The senior forensic on the Minelli case stood in the open doorway, three hours ahead of schedule! What excuse would he give?

Instead, the man brandished a manila envelope. But before handing it over and departing, he asked if they could talk privately.

"*Certo*, Dottor uh . . . Greci," Cenni said, hoping he'd gotten it right. *"Per favore,"* he said, waving to a seat and nodding to him to close the open door.

"Crime scene photographs, analyses of trace evidence, print comparisons," Greci stammered out in a rush of words.

"Standard stuff. Why the need for privacy?" Cenni asked, puzzled.

"Unexpected prints in unexpected places," Greci announced mysteriously, using his right pinky to slide a pair of thick wire-rimmed spectacles up the bridge of his nose.

Cenni frowned, thinking of Sophie Orlic. "Go on."

"On Saturday before you arrived, we scanned the entire vault for prints, not just the altar and the area around the body, but the walls, floors, everything except the ceiling," he added, conscientiously. "Oddly enough, this made Russo very nervous. He said we were wasting our time and the lab's resources. He walked off in a huff when I refused to stop."

"Were you . . . wasting time, that is?" Cenni asked in an effort to appear interested, concluding from the contempt in Greci's voice that the technician had worked with *Il Lupino* before.

Ignoring Cenni's question, Greci droned on, "We've recently started using new techniques for finding and collecting latent prints from difficult surfaces: lasers, iodine fuming, digital photography, among others. On porous surfaces, like rough stone, laser scans work faster and are more reliable for finding hidden prints than the old dust and lift methods, and we can check bigger areas in a shorter time. I found a large number of prints, mainly partials, on the left side of the Casati vault. A few of the prints were on the bottom sarcophagus, *but most were on the floor.*" He emphasized the last bit of information before stopping to catch his breath.

Cenni smiled encouragingly, letting his thoughts race ahead. *Russo was doing it in the cemetery!*

"Then I used a technique I learned from our British colleagues to highlight the prints. They turn a dark, highly visible blue, easy to capture in digital photographs. Some of our investigating judges don't think these techniques are trustworthy, but they do work."

Cenni smiled politely. "Interesting."

"What surprised us all was the violence of Russo's objections. When we left the area around the altar and moved out toward the periphery, he was in a panic. Batori commented on it as well. It wasn't Russo's investigation, but if it were, he would have stopped me."

Cenni looked at his watch longingly. *The man moves in his own time.*

Greci continued, "Everything in the vicinity of the victim is part of the crime scene. Russo knows that! Besides, it's not his case. Russo threw his weight around when he was in Perugia, but he's not in Perugia now." Through the thick lenses, his eyes flashed with malice.

Cenni interrupted. "It would appear, Dottore, that you and Russo have worked together in the past."

This proved to be the invitation he had been waiting for.

"We had a run-in a few years back, before he got sent down to Assisi. Russo contaminated evidence at a crime scene involving some syndicate thugs. Deliberately, I thought. I reported the incident to my department chief. I didn't know then that Georgio Zangarelli was Russo's brother-in-law. *I do now!* I've just returned to Perugia after three years in Foligno, and I intend to stay." The visible tightening of Greci's neck and jaw muscles confirmed this intention.

Cenni slipped in quickly before Greci could continue, "Let *me* get to the point, Dottore! You're suggesting that Russo is involved in some way with the crime under investigation. No doubt you've included all this in your report." He nodded to the manila envelope that Greci was still clutching. "I'll forward your report to Antonio Priuli, the investigating judge in this case. It's standard procedure, as you know."

Greci sat up straighter before replying. "As I said earlier, I'm not returning to Foligno! None of this is in my report."

"Why not?"

"Russo's prints are not in the national database. The ones I used for comparison are from internal police files." Greci swallowed hard twice.

Cenni took a moment to respond. "You mean, I suppose, without consent!"

"*Certo*. And none of the prints I found in the vault, including Russo's, permit identification using the standard twelve-point comparison rule. They're all partials. I made enlargements on transparency paper and then placed one partial on top of the other, to come up with a complete print. They're Russo's all right—palm prints and fingerprints—but don't tell that to Priuli once he hears how I generated the complete image. He's no different from the rest of them—suspicious of modern technology!" he added, with the righteous indignation of the true technocrat.

"So why tell me all this if you can't provide me with the evidence? I need to assert probable cause. I can't pull rabbits out of a hat!"

"You've a reputation for dealing on the square. More to the point, everyone knows that you, not Carlo Togni, run the Perugia Questura, and that it was you who got Russo sent down to Assisi." He looked at his watch. "Half an hour ago—less even— I got a call from Rome: *Stop wasting government money!*" His eyes glittered. "Russo's been working his magic again. But I'm not going back to Foligno!"

Cenni smiled. *My mother was born in Foligno. Not that she ever admits to it!*

Greci smiled back. Cenni had taken his point.

"As I was saying, Commissario! I did the same with all the partial prints that I found in the area by the sarcophagi, creating complete images using transparencies. The obvious areas to look for prints were the altar, the statue, the vases, the steps, and the immediate area around the body. I found complete matches for the countess and the Croatian on the altar and some matches around the gates, but nothing on the statue or the vases. Someone had wiped them clean. There were no matches anywhere in the vault for the granddaughter or the Albanian helper."

He paused for effect before dropping his bombshell. "I found partials for Rita Minelli and Artemisia Casati in the same area where I found Russo's prints, in front of the sarcophagi."

Cenni nodded. *Whatever happened to hotel rooms?*

"The Canadian and Umberto Casati, you compared their prints?" he asked, knowing the answer.

"I did, for completeness. No matches. But I think you know why I focused on the women, Commissario. Here, look at this." He pulled a sketch from his breast pocket and laid it on the desk. It was a drawing of the left side of the vault. There were numerous sets of overlapping fingerprints and palm prints on the floor and a smaller number of prints on the lower sarcophagus.

"The prints in red are Russo's, the ones in green are the dead woman's, and the ones in blue belong to Artemisia Casati. You'll notice all three prints are on the floor—red, green, and blue—with the red prints facing the sarcophagus, the green and blue prints facing the outer wall. The prints on the lower sarcophagus, the red and blue (no green) all face the same direction, upward. . . ."

"Red, green, yellow . . ." Cenni groaned out loud. His headache was turning psychedelic.

"Blue, not yellow," Greci corrected, smugly.

"*Madonna Santa!* What difference does it make? Say what you have to say. Russo was fucking the two women in the vault. Sometimes up the ass!"

6

THE SILENCE IN the room was palpable. Greci, who had naturally dark skin, had turned a blackish red after Cenni's outburst. Greci finally responded, after clearing his throat. "Actually the latter—you know, what you just said—was true of Artemisia

Casati only, not the American." He avoided Cenni's eyes. "The American was straight missionary."

Straight missionary. The man's a throwback!

"Sorry, Dottor Greci. Headache," Cenni offered in apology and rubbed his temples in proof. "Did you find anything else to support this inference," he asked politely. "Semen stains, for example?"

"No, regretfully. On Saturday, I took only two samples of a number of dried stains in that area. I assumed they were pigeon droppings, which they were. On Sunday, when I realized the implication of the partial prints by the sarcophagi, I went back to the vault with a knife and some swabs. The vault floor had been cleaned. I thought I detected a whiff of carbolic. The vault was still cordoned off, but there were no officers in sight!" Greci went on for another twenty minutes before he was finally induced to leave, after Cenni inquired if he knew of any good restaurants in Foligno.

Greci was maddeningly long-winded, but he had been thorough, and he had given Cenni a lot to think about, not all of it pointing to Fulvio Russo. The bindings on Minelli's diaries were clean of prints. The only prints on the inside pages were smudges, and in Greci's view, all were Minelli's. On a more discordant note, he insisted that Minelli's wallet had also been wiped clean of prints, by Sophie Orlic.

When Cenni challenged this, Greci was adamant. "*Ascolta*, Commissario, Minelli's purse and wallet had Russo's prints all over them, which Russo can justify since he checked their contents after the body was found on Saturday. But Minelli's prints are missing on both; someone wiped them after the murder. The only other prints I found were the Croatian's, which is okay on the purse since she admits to handling it. But we also found a partial thumbprint of hers inside the billfold. She missed it when wiping the wallet. Amateur!" he commented snidely. "It's a partial and doesn't conform to the twelve-point rule, but mark my words, it's hers."

Cenni was flummoxed. Too many suspects and now, too many clues. Someone in the house had wiped the diary, unless Minelli had done it herself, which made no sense. Earlier in the day, while reading the diary, it had crossed Cenni's mind that Russo might be the American's married lover. Now he had proof. And it would seem that *Il Lupino* was also Artemisia's lover.

Had the ice queen known that Fulvio was fucking her older cousin? And if she had, how had she reacted? Or, were Fulvio and Artemisia working together, to get Minelli's money? Artemisia had access to her cousin's room and could easily have removed pages from the diary. But why? Had they contained accusations against Fulvio as the father of her child, a declaration that she was planning to change her will, or other secrets not yet revealed? Secrets to die for? Cenni acknowledged with reluctance that Sophie also had access to the diary. According to Amelia Casati, Sophie had been in the house all day on Thursday to help with the rough cleaning.

The real conundrum was how to explain Orlic's print on the inside of the billfold. Theft after she'd found the body? Supposedly, she and her helper had been together from the moment they'd entered the vault, so how had Orlic's print gotten on the billfold if not on the evening before, when the American was murdered? Not such a conundrum after all, Cenni decided. Orlic could have rifled through Rita's wallet another time, perhaps on Thursday when she was helping in the house. He'd talk to Lucia; she might know if Minelli had complained about missing money. There had to be an innocent explanation for Sophie's print on the billfold.

Distracted by thoughts of the blonde Croatian, he opened the manila envelope that Greci had handed him and thumbed through the report absentmindedly. Appended to the back were photographs of the crime scene, including a striking photograph of the altar and the matching stone vases. What was it Greci had said about the vases? No prints! Of course, that was it, what had been nagging at him for two days. No prints and no flowers. The vases were empty!

7

CENNI HIT THE redial button for the fifth time. Again, the same anonymous voice. *Please try again later.* Why did he continue to pay for Piero's cellphone when he never turned the damned thing on? He could call Elena, but she was overextended. Sergeant Antolini? Just the person. The supremely bored male voice at the Assisi end said the sergeant was away from her desk, "Probably out for a coffee."

When Cenni first reviewed the pictures that the forensic team had taken of the vault, he'd experienced the exhilaration of discovery. But when the significance of the empty vases dawned on him, he came crashing down. On Saturday, Sophie Orlic had described her weekly routine to him in very precise Italian. "I remove the dead flowers from the vault, replace the water, and arrange the new flowers." He'd been so sure that Sophie was not Minelli's killer, even surer that she was not capable of murder—although he was not as precipitate as Elena, who just that morning had staked her professional reputation of two years and three months against Piero's five years and his fifteen, that Williams was not the murderer. Women's intuition! Well, he might have to adjust his own intuition. Someone had removed the flowers before Minelli's body was discovered. If the action had nothing to do with Minelli's murder, why were there no prints on the vases? And if Orlic was not involved, why hadn't she mentioned the missing flowers? Flowers were her business. She had to have noticed!

He began calling Piero, for the sixth time, as soon as he exited the building. He wanted to order a search of all the cemetery's dumpsters, the closest to the Casati vault first, but not until he knew exactly which flowers they were looking for. Luckily, today was a holiday of sorts—what days weren't?—which meant the dumpsters hadn't yet been emptied of Friday's trash. He also needed to talk to Sophie Orlic again, but department rules were clear: He needed another officer with him during the interrogation. Sergeant Antolini. He leaned over and tapped his driver's shoulder. "Assisi, Mario. *Subito!*"

8

THE REAR EXIT of the Assisi police station is located behind the file cabinets, hidden from general view unless you happen to be on a stepladder, filing, which is where Sergeant Antolini happened to be when she saw Russo rounding the corner and leaving through the back door. She froze and crouched low on the third step of the ladder, until he returned a few minutes later. He was empty-handed both coming and going. She stayed where she was another few minutes, waiting to see if he would return, lost in thought, remembering yesterday: Easter Sunday with Piero.

She had dressed in street clothes at Piero's request. "Better not to attract too much attention. Too many journalists about." They had gone into every bar and restaurant in Assisi, or so it had seemed, questioning every busboy, waitress, and proprietor who might have seen something or someone on Good Friday. By 2:30, her feet were killing her—she was wearing the latest in needle-point toes—and Piero suggested that they stop and rest.

"We deserve a break, and besides I have something for you. It's in my car." After he retrieved the package, they sat together on the wooden bench outside Porta San Giacomo, and Piero watched, deadpan, as she unwrapped the oddly shaped package. When she saw the marzipan bunny's ears, she gasped in delight and he broke into a huge grin.

"Oh Piero, how grand! But it's way too big. I'll never finish it by myself. Help me," she said, breaking off the bunny's right ear. "Here," she said and laughed at the expression of horror on his face. "Of course, now I remember, you hate marzipan. Well there's got to be something here you do like," she said, ripping off the rest of the wrapping.

"Look Piero, chocolate feet—dark chocolate too, your favorite. Oh dear, the bunny is missing a toe. Poor crippled bunny," she said, making him laugh.

After eating the chocolate, the discomfort of the previous two days vanished. They were friends again. Well, not quite friends. Piero flirted with her outrageously. At one point, he noticed some marzipan on her cheek and leaned over to clean it with his handkerchief. She could smell the chocolate on his breath and closed her eyes, waiting for the kiss.

"Shit, that's done it," he exclaimed.

"Well, that's rude!" she said, opening her eyes.

He pointed to the back of a blonde walking away from them toward the cemetery. "Sophie Orlic," he said, despondently.

"Is that all? What does it matter to Sophie Orlic if you kiss me? And if it did matter to her, why does she matter to you?"

"It's not Orlic I'm worried about," Piero replied. He pointed to a man walking a short distance behind Orlic. "That man who just passed, the one who bowed to us, he's a detective, Antonio Martini. Alex assigned him to watch Orlic. The biggest gossip in Perugia. Tomorrow it'll be all over the building that he caught me kissing you, and on duty, too. Alex'll have my head!

Oh well, never mind." He laughed, his good humor returning when he saw how concerned she looked. "They'll all be jealous. Even Alex!"

His last remark reminded him of what he had been stewing over for most of the day, and he turned serious. "I'm worried, Genine. Yesterday, Alex couldn't take his eyes off Orlic. I've never seen him go so easy on a suspect. During the interrogation, he let her get away with murder, no pun intended," he added, noting Genine's raised eyebrows. "Orlic managed to avoid answering most of his questions. She's the obvious suspect: she found the body, she threatened the American, and even Alex thinks that a woman staged the rape. What more does he want? And late last night, the questore called me to ask what's going on. He quizzed me about Orlic. Wanted to know if she had an alibi. I said no, and now he wants Alex to arrest her."

"So how come she's still free to walk around Assisi?"

"Because Alex refuses to arrest her. And I'm caught in between. The questore wants me to spy on Alex and report back to him."

"Will you do it?" She hesitated before speaking further. "I suppose it could be good for your career . . . you know, to have the questore's confidence," she said flatly, pulling away from him ever so slightly.

"What do you take me for? It was because of Alex that I got promoted—a full year ahead of time too. He's the only brass above the rank of inspector who isn't solely concerned with his own career. Of course I won't do it. I talked to Elena about it, and she thinks we should tell Alex, but I'm not so sure. Alex can be damned stubborn when he gets his back up. If he finds out the questore is going behind his back, he might do something really stupid, like quitting. I told Elena we should manage this on our own. I'm just not sure how."

"I don't know, Piero. Elena could be right. Does she agree with you, that Orlic is the killer?"

"Elena, the feminist? Not a chance! Not after Alex told her that Minelli was two months pregnant. She's been reading the diary. She says there's plenty of evidence that the American was having an affair with a married man." He lowered his voice. "And with a priest! Elena says whoever got Minelli pregnant is the killer. For Alex's sake, I hope she's right."

"Piero, do you remember what I told you about *Il Lupino*? How he's always hitting on me? Well it's not just me, you know. He does it with every woman who comes into the station if she's halfway good-looking. You never saw Rita Minelli when she was alive. Dark and exotic, big black eyes, and petite, the type men like to protect. Built, too," she added and colored.

"After the New Year, she came into the station twice while I was there and asked if she could see the commissario privately. He rarely agrees to see anyone in his office, but he saw her, and very willingly, even came out to escort her into his office. I think they were having an affair. So does Franco." They stared at each other, dumbstruck for the moment.

"Oh my God, Piero, what if he's the killer!"

9

ANYTHING THAT PUT *Il Lupino* in a bad light seemed perfectly plausible to the sergeant whereas anything positive, such as his coming into the office to do some work on a holiday, was highly suspect. There was nothing at the back of the station of interest to anyone, just a weed-filled dirt track and a large green dumpster. The dumpster was emptied of its discarded food wrappers, plastic bottles, soiled bathroom towels, and crumpled office papers every Tuesday, Thursday, and Saturday,

unless a public holiday or a general strike intervened. Sergeant
Antolini might have concluded that *Il Lupino* was garbage
picking had there been anything in the dumpster worth picking, but she decided instead that he had gone to the dumpster
to rid himself of something that he wouldn't want found in his
own trash, something small enough to conceal on his person.
Perhaps something connected to Rita Minelli's murder.

The garbagemen would empty the dumpster the following
morning, shortly after 7:00, and deposit the contents in the
huge landfill outside Città di Castello. Impossible once that
happened to find anything, although at the moment she had
no idea what "anything" might be. Sergeant Antolini put nothing beyond *Il Lupino*, not since he had blocked her promotion
a year ago, shortly after he had groped her and she had threatened to report him for sexual harassment. She knew that if he
caught her going through the dumpster without a reasonable
explanation her promotion would be blocked again. "Screw
him!" she murmured to herself, absentmindedly massaging a
cramp in her right thigh, "he'll probably block it anyway."

At the end of five minutes when Russo hadn't reappeared,
she decided that it was safe to search the dumpster. A few
minutes earlier, she'd heard his office door open and shut
again, so he might have already left the building. He had been
in the building since half two and it was now half four, a holiday record for him, but it seemed safer not to walk by his
office to check, just in case he was still around. No point in
drawing attention to herself.

Boxes of latex gloves were kept in the bottom drawer of
the right-hand file cabinet. She opened one of the boxes and
removed a pair, just in case. She took the stepladder, too; she
would need it if whatever it was had slipped to the bottom
of the dumpster. Please God, I hope there's nothing too

disagreeable in there, she thought, remembering the elaborate mayonnaise lunches that Franco's mother prepared and which he rarely finished. Her uniform was fresh from the dry cleaners.

The dumpster was full. She wasn't sure what she was looking for, but decided to ignore all the papers and envelopes that were stamped with the imprimatur of the Polizia di Stato. She could check those later if she found nothing incriminating first.

Three-quarters of the way down and still nothing! She was now surrounded with the debris of three days of police work: mistyped *soggiorno* applications, mistyped envelopes, mistyped letters, empty water and coke bottles, grease-stained pizza boxes, even a depleted perfume vial that had once held a cheap rose-smelling scent. Lucille! The new typist doused herself with the stuff. Better she should learn how to type, Antolini thought dispiritedly, as she plowed through another pile of mistyped letters. *Niente!*

Nothing for it! She couldn't reach any further into the dumpster without tumbling in headfirst; either she'd have to abandon her search or climb in. She looked around and decided quickly. Russo would have left by now; the only other person in the building was Sergeant DeGiulio, the duty officer. No worries there; it would take a direct hit by a howitzer to get him off his rear.

Seven euros to clean her uniform and that with a twenty percent police discount. She removed her uniform pants and folded them neatly over one of the ladder rungs. It was a mildly cool day in late March yet she was flushed, warm, even stripped down to panty hose. Nerves, she concluded. She climbed into the dumpster backward, feeling her way carefully, groping with her right leg for a secure footing. Once she reached bottom, she worked quickly, pushing the office papers to one side. She still had no idea what she was looking for. And then she saw the plain manila envelope stuck to the side of the dumpster, three-quarters of the way down—about as far as an arm could reach—and was sure she'd found it. She slipped on the gloves that she'd shoved into her pocket and, after prying the envelope loose, opened the flap gingerly, heart pounding. Perhaps it contained Minelli's love letters or, better yet, an accusation of paternity!

Ugh! Of course, he'd be into porn, hard-core too. Easier for him to discard it with the police trash then get rid of it at home. Her disappointment was acute, and she dropped the envelope in disgust, then quickly changed her mind. The girls were young, all of them easily under sixteen; one of them, with tight black ringlets and tragic eyes, looked no more than ten. *Il Lupino* was a commissario of the state police after all! The photos could be useful, particularly if they were covered with his fingerprints. She knelt down to retrieve the envelope and that's when she saw the black scarf, coiled under a pizza box. She pushed the box aside and lifted the scarf with great care. Cashmere! A crumpled paper was lying beneath the scarf, and she retrieved that as well, smoothing it out. Another of Lucille's mistyped letters. It had Good Friday's date at the top, an indicator of when the scarf had been thrown into the dumpster. Late Friday evening after the cleaning woman emptied the trash baskets into the dumpster.

A few weeks back, *Il Lupino* had accused just about everyone in the station of stealing his cashmere scarf, finally settling on the Polish cleaning woman, a migrant worker who was frantic with worry that she'd lose her job. Sergeant Antolini had felt sorry for the woman and the two of them had searched everywhere, even in the dumpster, but it hadn't been found. And now here it was, possibly the murder weapon. Piero had told her only yesterday that a black fiber had been found on the

American's body, a particularly long one, caught in an earring. Sergeant Antolini straightened up, pumped her fist in jubilation, then wrapped the scarf around her neck and turned to climb out of the dumpster. That's when she saw him. He was holding her pants.

"Cold in there, I should think. You'll want these."

10

SOPHIE ORLIC LIVED right before the San Giacomo gate, which opened out into two country lanes, one leading directly to the cemetery and the other to a small, deconsecrated church in the valley below. There was little about Via Metastasio to distinguish it from any of the other secondary streets in Assisi other than its precipitous incline. The building in which Orlic lived was undistinguished. Like most stone residences in Assisi, it had been sandblasted to pink and white perfection with money donated after Umbria's last killing earthquake. Orlic lived alone, above a small shop that sold trinkets: postcards, plaques, statues, keyrings, embossed napkin rings, coffee mugs, tablecloths, ceramic cutlery, almost all decorated with pictures of St. Francis feeding the pigeons, a bird now roasted to pink and white perfection over open fires and served as a delicacy in the best Assisi restaurants.

Across the street from Orlic's apartment was a restaurant, and against its door leaned the officer Cenni had assigned to watch his designated chief suspect. Antonio Martini was working at one of his front teeth with a toothpick while watching with some interest a young backpacker dressed in hiking shorts as she walked up the steep incline headed toward Assisi's main square. Observing Martini, while Martini observed the fräulein, Cenni reflected that he too frequently forgot that Elena and Piero were the best to be had at the Perugia Questura. He excused himself to Sergeant Antolini and walked across the street to confirm with Martini that Orlic was still inside her apartment. Martini, who had the grace to remove the toothpick while speaking to his superior, informed Cenni that Orlic had not stepped out of her apartment since late afternoon when she had returned carrying a bag of groceries. He also assured Cenni that she had no idea she was being watched.

The bell was answered immediately by a return buzz and a muffled shout of *avanti*. When the commissario and the sergeant rounded the corner at the top of the stairs, it was evident by the expression on Orlic's face that she had not been expecting the police. She and Cenni exchanged looks for a moment, neither of them speaking, although it was obvious to the commissario that the woman was not sure if she should ask them in. Then, decision made, she moved to one side and pushed the door partly open, indicating by this grudging gesture that they might enter.

Cenni was momentarily surprised by the apartment's lack of warmth and comfort, mainly, he admitted to himself, because it was difficult to accept that a woman of such beauty would live in such squalor. It was a bed-sitter of sorts, with an unmade single bed in one corner and little in the way of furniture to suggest its sitting room function: summer leavings of two white outdoor chairs; a green plastic table covered with gardening implements; a battered wooden dresser with four large drawers; and attached to the back of the front door, a clothing rack with six pegs, from which hung a motley collection of cotton print dresses, oversized cardigans, one good wool dress carefully placed on a hanger, a black winter cape, and a tan windbreaker. In a corner opposite the bed was a large cardboard box containing a jumble of shoes and boots. The single mirror in the room was turned to the wall. An upholstered chintz chair, its cotton insides protruding from both the arms and the back, was the premier piece of furniture in the room, and Orlic offered this to the sergeant before seating herself on the edge of one of the plastic chairs. Cenni seated himself on the remaining chair, not waiting for an invitation.

He'd had a quick look around while Orlic was clearing the seat for Sergeant Antolini and was disheartened though not surprised to see a large flower arrangement of exquisite color and form in the center of the dresser: Chinese red blossoms with yellow centers. Fallen petals on the dresser and the floor suggested that the blossoms were no longer fresh. If anything, Cenni thought, the beauty of the flowers diminished the room even further.

He launched immediately into the interview. Subtlety was wasted on Sophie Orlic.

"Signora, the flowers on your dresser, tell me about them."

"They're peonies."

Cenni sighed. How quickly he forgot. No open-ended questions. "Why are they here, Signora, in your apartment," he emphasized. "When did you buy them, where, how many, why?"

"On Friday, in Rivotorto . . . I like flowers."

Her breathing had grown shallow, changing the timbre of her voice, but she continued to hold his gaze.

"Signora, how many?" he asked again.

"I really don't know, as many as the florist would sell. You can count them for yourself," she added, nodding to the arrangement on the dresser.

Cenni indicated to Sergeant Antolini to count the flowers and waited patiently, not taking his eyes off Sophie Orlic, who continued to sit, motionless.

"Twenty, Commissario, although two of them are without petals, just bare stems," the sergeant reported after she had finished counting.

Sophie responded to this unintended criticism with vigor. "It's hot in here and they weren't fresh on Friday when I purchased them. The florist in Rivotorto takes flowers from another shop in Perugia when that florist can't sell them. Italians aren't terribly fond of peonies. They prefer traditional flowers—roses, carnations, mums. He still asks top price, though," she added at the end of her surprisingly long speech, shrugging as though to say, *What would you expect!*

Cenni observed that the only time Sophie Orlic was roused to animation—and that was seldom—was when she spoke about her flower business. He knew from Elena's research that Orlic was doing reasonably well, with an ever-increasing list of clients. What does she spent her money on? he wondered, looking around again, this time openly, at the barren apartment. Certainly not on herself, and the report from Croatia stated that the daughter was in a public hospital.

Cenni held Orlic's gaze, making it difficult for her to look away. He said, "One of my officers spoke to the florist in Rivotorto. You purchased eight peonies on Friday. The remaining lot, twelve to be exact, was delivered to the Casati home shortly after noon on Friday. The florist also said that there were no other peonies to be had from any of the other florists around here, that these were a special order from Turkey. How is it that you now have twenty?"

Cenni wondered if he'd been too quick to reveal what he knew about the peonies, but his doubt disappeared as he watched her hands clench. The only chance of obtaining the truth from Orlic was to confront her.

"The countess brought me twelve peonies on Friday afternoon. Only eight of those are mine," she said, nodding to the arrangement on the dresser. "I forgot to mention it. The countess asked that I use her peonies in the Easter arrangement that I was preparing for the family vault. I had them with me on

Saturday, in one of my flower baskets, as you may remember," she said boldly. "Since then the vault's been sealed, so I put the countess's peonies in a vase with my own flowers. Simple enough," she said smugly.

"Not simple at all, Signora," Cenni replied. "The countess gave a sworn statement to me on Saturday that she didn't leave the house until seven, and then only when she went with her husband to view the procession in the Piazza del Comune."

The Croatian returned his gaze steadily. How was it possible that he'd ever imagined, even briefly, that she might be dull-witted? She had the intelligence and instincts of a world-class midfielder.

"Signora, again! How did you come to possess twenty peonies?"

"As I just told you! The countess brought them to me on Friday—at about four or five o'clock—I can't say for sure." She hesitated before speaking again. "Perhaps she's forgotten. More likely, though, she's afraid of the police, the way we all are. Or should be. Ask her again!" she said.

II

IT WAS NOW 5:15 and Cenni was standing outside the San Giacomo gate waiting for his driver to pick him up. The inter-rogation of Sophie Orlic had not gone well, and Cenni was embarrassed that it had taken place in front of Sergeant Antolini. He had permitted a woman—even worse, one not suckled on Dante—to best him, and not just about the peonies. He had tackled Orlic on a number of inconsistencies:

Question: "The previous week's flowers, what happened to them? The vases in the Casati vault were empty when Minelli's body was found."

Answer: "How should I know? Lots of people have keys to the vault. Anyone could have removed them, even the American."

Question: "Why didn't you mention the missing flowers during your interview on Saturday?"

Answer: "You didn't ask, and I had other things to think about."

Question: "You deposited eight hundred euros in cash in your bank account on Friday evening. That's a lot of cash. Where did you get it?"

Answer: "Most of my clients pay me in cash. I hold the money in my apartment until I have enough to make one large deposit. The banks charge each time you use the ATM."

Question: "We've had two men with metal detectors comb-ing the cemetery looking for the key you lost. They found nothing. Again, where did you drop the key?"

Answer: "I found it earlier today. It slipped through a small hole in the lining of my pocket. Would you like to see it?"

Question: "Our forensic team found your fingerprint inside Minelli's billfold. You said on Saturday that you didn't touch anything inside her purse." This final accusation caused a slight, barely perceptible change in her affect. She swallowed before responding. But, as always, she offered the best possible answer. "They're mistaken. I never touched her wallet." She refused to budge from this last assertion.

He could have browbeaten Sophie Orlic into a confession, if not for murder then for something: theft, accessory, inter-ference, lying (that would really give the Italian press a hoot—*Arrested for lying to the police!*). There were far too many inconsistencies in her story—stories! But he hadn't the heart to bully a woman with her tragic history. And he still believed that she was innocent of Minelli's murder. Covering up for the countess perhaps, or someone else in the family. Someone had given her the peonies. Just that morning, Carlo had accused him of being soft on criminals. Perhaps there was some truth in that, although he still had the best conviction record in the questura. Grilling suspects into making confessions was more in Fulvio Russo's line. His convictions came from painstaking detective work.

The car pulled up and he slid into the back seat. He leaned back warily, closing his eyes. His headache was back. Tomorrow he'd have to decide how to handle the problem of Orlic's print on Minelli's wallet. Right now, he was due back at the questura for two more interviews—Paola Casati and her well-connected boyfriend. Montoni, now there's someone I'd enjoy grilling into a confession, he thought, as the car moved silently down the country lane on its way to Perugia.

12

"WHY DID YOU buy the peonies?" the commissario had asked her, looking around the shabby room in amazement, as if she could have no appreciation of flowers beyond the money they brought in. What did he know of her life before Assisi? What did any of them know? Her beautiful home with its highly polished furniture and sage green wall-to-wall carpeting, a woman to help her with the cooking and cleaning, a wildflower garden that had been featured in two magazines. A lifetime, destroyed in a few hours.

Even the countess, who referred to her as *My dear friend,* treated Sophie like a servant. *Sophie, be a dear, carry this upstairs. Sophie, hand me my glasses, there, dear, right next to the sofa. Sophie, you ironed a crease in that sleeve. Would you mind re-ironing it, dear? The count is so particular about his shirts. Sophie, dear, what would we ever do without you?* The countess had discovered very quickly, not even two weeks after her mother-in-law's death, that she (and her husband) did very well without Sophie.

On Friday morning, at the wholesale florist in Rivotorto, Sophie had met two women from Assisi, friends of the countess. They had addressed her with great respect—*Signora Orlic this, Signora Orlic that*—which Sophie knew was not usual from women in their position toward women in hers, women from Eastern Europe who cleaned their houses. Sophie was confident from the way they had praised her flower arrangements that they would soon become clients. A good sign! Sophie was always on the lookout for signs.

And then she caught sight of the peonies, blossoms of true red that shaded softly at the tips to a delicate strawberry color. The single row of wide cup-shaped petals appeared exquisitely fragile against the flower's green foliage. She couldn't see the centers but she knew they were the deep yellow of Sicilian lemons. They were behind the back counter, in the small refrigerator where the florist stored his special orders, out-of-season blossoms that he imported from Turkey for his wealthier patrons. Sophie had never purchased any flowers from that refrigerator. The cost of even one flower was dearer than six of most other varieties. But as soon as she had spied the peonies, she knew that she had to have them. It was the very flower that Sergio had picked when he'd made love to her for the first time.

The florist said he was very sorry but that Countess Casati had a standing order for any peonies that came his way. "I rarely get peonies of this quality, Signora, and the countess would be gravely offended if I sold them to you." But after Sophie had offered double the asking price, he agreed to sell her eight of the twenty that he had in stock. "You're one of my best customers," he added, as he wrapped the flowers in tissue paper and handed her a receipt for forty-eight euros, her food allowance for two weeks.

The first time that she and Sergio had picked a *peony pereg-rina*, her grandmother had warned her that it was a flower sacred to the wood gods. And now there were twenty of them wilting on her dresser. What could she expect!

13

THE INTERVIEW WITH Paola Casati had gone exceedingly well. Piero had found her at a little after 4:00 PM sitting in the Bar Sensi, at one of the back tables by herself, smoking, drinking coffee, and staring off into space. She hadn't protested in the least when Piero told her that the commissario would like to have a word with her. "Came along like a little lamb," Piero said. And no members of her family had been around to protest on the lamb's behalf. Cenni knew he'd have another morning visit from the questore if her grandfather found out, but he trusted Paola. From what she'd told him, she and her grandfather did not get on. Cenni had asked her not to talk to anyone, particularly not to her grandfather about their little talk. "Forget about it," he'd cautioned her, "I know I will." Paola was the only Casati he liked; he hoped it could stay that way.

Cenni almost always felt guilty when suspects, even the ones he didn't like, were too easy to manipulate, perhaps because he hated taking unfair advantage. The police always went into the game with a two-goal lead. He disliked even more the inevitable role of bully, despite knowing that a good part of the job required exactly that, bullying the public into behaving itself. But with Paola Casati none of the usual tactics had been required: no promises, no threats, no charm. "Tell me about McDonald's," he had led off, and she had followed with a full confession.

"I swear, Dottore, I had no idea that anyone was inside. I asked Guilio repeatedly what time the last of the staff left. He swore to me—to all of us—that there was never anyone inside after midnight. I don't think he even checked!" she cried, weeping down the front of her jacket. He gave her his hand-kerchief, which she had used to wipe her eyes and nose before conscientiously returning it to him, holding it out by its dry hem. He dropped it into the trash when she wasn't looking and handed her a roll of paper towels that the cleaning people had left on top of the file cabinet.

"She was younger than me, by a whole year," she cried. "She must have suffered horribly! Burns over ninety percent of her body. It'll haunt me forever." Cenni knew she'd forget soon enough, but he didn't tell her that.

"Seven brothers and sisters. She sent money home every month. I wanted to send them money, but my grandfather wouldn't let me. He says I must forget that it happened. *You mustn't talk about it, ever, to anyone! You're worse than your mother!* He yelled at me my first night at home." She looked up at Cenni with soulful eyes. "My parents killed themselves and an old woman who lived below them, while making a bomb. I was only two at the time. My grandfather still blames my mother."

Cenni had agreed with her—reparation must be made and the best reparation was to send money to the girl's family—but anonymously, he had urged. "Spending five or ten years in prison won't help the seven brothers and sisters, and it won't bring her back. Atonement is better than punishment." He had been rather amazed at his capacity for sopping up tears and casting forth aphorisms. She had insisted on making a statement, even if he would never use it. *It would soothe her bat-tered soul,* she'd said. The little lamb had a distinct flair for the melodramatic.

Concerning the murder of Rita, Paola insisted that what she'd told the police on Saturday was the truth, except that she wasn't alone during her walk, she was with Giulio Montoni. At the end of their walk, close to five, they had stopped for a coffee at a café at the top of Assisi and, afterward, they'd gone in his car to the top of Mount Subasio, where he'd wanted to have sex and she'd wanted to talk. They had a huge blow-up, which ended with her returning his ring. Maybe because they were making so much noise, a family of wild boar had attacked the car. Giulio had never seen *cinghiale* before. He'd been scared to death and furious at the same time—they broke the radiator of his Porsche. A park ranger heard the noise and helped Paola to chase them off. "Three of them were babies, still spotted," she said, smiling through her tears. After they'd made a statement to the ranger, they drove back to Assisi and Giulio took his car to the garage below Santa Chiara for repair. It was already five minutes to 7:00, and she went directly to the Piazza to wait for her grandparents.

She added that Giulio had called her the following day—Saturday about noon—when he'd heard about Rita's murder. He wanted to see her but she had refused. She never wanted to see him again! She had no idea where Giulio was between 7:00 and 8:00 on Good Friday, but she very much doubted that he'd visited the cemetery or that he could have killed Rita. "Wouldn't have the nerve," she said scornfully. "Besides he didn't even know what she looked like."

Candy from a baby, Cenni said to himself after Paola Casati had signed her statement and left. Not even that. He doubted that a robust one-year-old would let go of a sweet as quickly as Paola Casati had stammered out a full confession. Guilt is a policeman's best friend, he reminded himself, and smiled at his own banality. He patted the signed statement that he had in his pocket with some satisfaction.

Obtained illegally, and not for use against the impetuous Paola, but it might have its uses!

And now to the boyfriend (*scusi*, Paola, ex-boyfriend), Cenni said to himself as he walked down the deserted hallway toward the interrogation room. Giulio Montoni had bragged, yelled, threatened, bleated, whined, and wept, catalogued in that order in the report that Elena had handed to him over an hour ago, shortly after she had delivered Montoni to the police station in Perugia. He'd had an hour alone in the interrogation room to think and sweat. With any luck, he was scared shitless by now.

He wouldn't lead off with McDonald's. Montoni would know that a commissario stationed in the Perugia Questura would have nothing to do with the Rome investigation. Cenni was strongly inclined to agree with Paola that Montoni was not involved in Minelli's death. He was certain that Minelli had been killed before seven o'clock, and probably before sunset, which on Good Friday was at 6:32. According to Paola, Montoni had been with her between 4:00 and 7:00.

Guilio Montoni might walk away from this one, as he had in Rome, but the least Cenni could do was send a message to the Minister of the Interior that Perugia was not now and never would be the PM's territory. It appeared from what Montoni had told Paola on Good Friday that he had planned the McDonald's bombing to shock his parents into noticing him and not in support of any political belief, although bombing a McDonald's for political belief was beyond Cenni's comprehension. If McDonald's and fast food had become the symbol of a world going to hell, then the world had better get on with it as there was little chance at this point of changing direction.

The young man sitting in the interrogation room bore no resemblance to the punk described by the café owner to Piero. The blonde swathe of hair was gone, dyed back to its natural

color, over the weekend no doubt, after Montoni had heard
about the American's murder. He had gotten rid of the lip ring
as well, which was a good thing as he was chewing rather vigorously on his bottom lip when Cenni entered the room. The
boy's nerves were shot. It would have served him better to let
Cenni begin, but his arrogance, which seemed to be his telling
characteristic, took over.

"Do you know who I am?" he started off, as he had with
Elena, his rich and very important parents his first and last
defense, and offense.

"*Certo.* You're the son of the Minister of the Interior. Now
let's get down to this business of murder and where you were
on Good Friday."

14

A COLD BEER would go a long way to improving his foul
mood, Alex decided as he rummaged through the refrigerator.
But his mother had been visiting again. Nothing but yogurt,
orange juice—the red kind that he hated—and *aqua gassata*.
Damn Maria! He'd have to speak to her again about hiding the
key from his mother.

A long day! And for lunch, a disgustingly stale panino from
one of the vending machines in the basement. It was a wonder
that any of the machines were still vending. All five of them
had large dents in their fronts and sides, from violent kicks,
some of them his. And then, one begging telephone call after
another, calling in favors, sitting on friends, two calls to
Renato to remind him of his promise to use his contacts. He
hated begging and understood why Minelli had despised her
mother's doctor. *Cold bastard!* was mild to what he would have
called him.

None of the calls had panned out as he had hoped. The archives in Rome had no record of the Gentileschi document that he'd found in the Casati library. Artemisia was off the hook, for now! Umberto Casati's finances had taken a leap into the black a few weeks back. Wildcatting in oil futures. Renato had gotten nowhere in his inquiries, blocked at every step, although he did confirm that Umberto Casati was Opus Dei. *Be very careful, Alex,* his brother had warned before hanging up.

John Costa, Minelli's New York lawyer, had provided some interesting information. Rita had called him a week before her death asking that he draw up a new will in John Williams's favor, disinheriting the uncle. The lawyer was sure that she had called from her uncle's house, as he'd returned the call immediately afterward to confirm the mailing address. Anyone in the house could have listened in on the extension, Cenni reasoned. Her money was to go to Williams, unconditionally, with the request that he care for her child should anything happen to her. Alex was liking Rita more each day.

Whether Williams would ever see the money was another question. The lawyer had mailed the will to Minelli for execution but it hadn't yet arrived, or if it had, someone had disposed of it. The lawyers would now have a go at it. It was no longer a police matter.

Of course, this gave the Canadian an additional motive for murder, but the priest who'd heard Williams's confession on Good Friday had called Elena just that afternoon (after speaking to his superior) to acknowledge having second thoughts about what he could or could not reveal. Nothing of what Williams had confessed, he stated emphatically, but he could verify that Williams had been to confession. First in line on Good Friday, at 4:30, he had assured Elena.

The few thousands that Rita had left to a cousin in New Jersey were hardly worth killing over, not that it mattered anyway, as the cousin had never left New Jersey. And the Italian director that she'd met on the plane, the longest shot of all, had been in the hospital recovering from surgery for piles. Hardly a director anyway, just an over-the-hill film editor trying to score. *Anna Magnani.* Hard to believe that little Rita would have fallen for that one!

Still no signs of Rita's "Gianni." The parish in New York had provided a list of visiting priests over a period of three months, nine in all. Elena was still checking them out. And then the interviews. Paola Casati crying down his front. Nice kid! And that shit Montoni, playing at politics to get attention. The girl that he'd murdered was worth a thousand of his kind. Montoni would walk on that one, and from all the other mishaps in his life, so long as his family had power and money. Not a thing Alex could do about it, other than to give him an uncomfortable hour or two.

He lay down on his bed fully dressed. Rest his head for a minute . . . then boil some water for pasta. Too tired to eat and too hungry to sleep. Sophie! Something wrong there. Maybe Carlo is right! No! Has to be Fulvio, proven twice over, first by Greci with his reds, greens, and yellows—Christ, the man's a bore!—and then by the sergeant. Great find that . . . the scarf in the dumpster . . . knot of fringe missing on one end! Send it off to Rome for comparison. Get the thread back from Batori. Questore . . . Batori? He settled his head deeper into the pillow.

Sergeant Antolini . . . good legs . . . lace panties . . . nervy little thing, taking chances like that! Lucky Piero! Always complaining! His eyelids fluttered . . . five more minutes . . . a black snake coiled around her neck . . . looking out a window. Sun-bright hair tied back with a striped ribbon.

He reaches out and recoils. The right hand is a fingerless stump . . . the index finger hanging off by a threaded clot of

blood. She turns, and he stares into the face of a child, a delicate oval of perfection with bright glass blue eyes, veined in
red. He watches in horror as the veins elongate and become
red watery streaks running down the porcelain face onto a
white party dress. The child is in his arms—he's running down
a dark cobbled alleyway, his lungs on fire. He hears the wild
thumping of her heart and the pounding footfalls behind.
Trapped! The child begins to cry, a whimper at first, then
louder, insistently—a loud ringing in his ears. It stops, and he
sinks back into the soft folds of sleep. It begins again.

He opens his eyes, half-awake, half-asleep, and sees the
reflection of the moon against the glass. The time is projected
in large red numbers on the ceiling. He shivers in a cold sweat
and wipes his brow. It's after 11:00 and the heat's gone off. He
reaches for the still-ringing phone. *"Pronto, si . . . si . . . si, Carlo.
Ho capito, domani alle otto."*

15

SERGEANT ANTOLINI WATCHED, half-asleep, as the early
morning light played with the shadows on the walls, glinting
warmly upon the moss-green coverlet on her bed. She wanted
to bask in the warmth and contentment of this state before fully
waking but a rising current of excitement quarreled with her
languor, urging her to open her eyes fully, to put substance to
the half-formed objects of her dreams. And then she remembered yesterday and sat up with a start. The commissario
(Alessandro, she murmured) had come out of nowhere to find
her rooting through the police dumpster! Half-dressed, too!

The evening before she had arrived home late and gone
immediately to her room, refusing the *pappardelle con la lepre*
that her mother insisted on warming up. "I feel a cold coming
on," she had lied, ignoring her mother's nagging concern. For

some fifteen minutes, she struck various poses in front of the closet mirror, her uniform jacket buttoned up to her chin as it had been when *he* had discovered her in the dumpster. Front, profile, and finally, from the rear. Were the lace edges of her panties discernible through her hose? "Short legs," she sighed wistfully, but they appeared longer when contrasted against the dark blue police jacket. She colored when she remembered Easter Sunday. Was it only two days ago that she had seriously considered Piero's proposal that they see each other exclusively? Genine is too particular, she frequently overheard her mother tell friends. Maybe her mother was right. Most of her high school friends were married, or engaged. Twenty-four on her last birthday. She peered anxiously in the mirror looking for lines.

It's true that she'd been ticked off when Piero didn't call again after their first date but that was nothing more than wounded pride. With most of the men she dated, she was the one who cried off. She took a small piece of the Easter bunny that was sitting on her dresser and sucked on it. Piero is sweet! Good-looking too, although in a pallid, freckled sort of way. And they had laughed a lot on their first date. She did so love a good laugh. But he talked too much, and always about food or football. On Sunday, she had wanted to pinch him, just to get a word in edgewise. He could stand to lose twenty pounds, and he complains too much. But they did have police work in common, and their nagging mothers. Ugh, two nagging mothers.

She dawdled getting ready for work. In the shower she let the warm needles of spray sooth her body and massage her skin, while she lathered herself gently and relived again the events of the previous day. She repeated every word the commissario had said to her, parsing each phrase for subtle shifts in meaning. She squinted her eyes and could see ever so clearly the half-smile on his face when he'd helped her out of the dumpster. He hadn't commented when he'd handed over her trousers, and he'd turned his back while she put them on, without being asked. Not many men around who would do that, not Italian men anyway. He was delighted when she had handed him Russo's scarf. "But please don't do anything like this again, sergeant," he'd said gruffly. "We don't want anything happening to you, now do we?"

In her bedroom, Genine found herself still dawdling. Instead of hastily throwing on her clothes, she paused to look at herself in the mirror again. She seized a hairbrush, pulling it through the tangles of her hair, and began to wonder if instead of pulling it into a simple French braid while she was at work, she should let it hang loose. She ran her fingers through the tangles, releasing the strands, shaking her head to encourage the natural wave. In a sudden burst of self-knowledge, she spoke aloud. "I'm in love," she cried to the half-eaten marzipan bunny on her dresser, "absurdly, hopelessly in love, and we both know who with."

But being a practical woman, Genine immediately amended her last thought. Not that she looked practical, not even when dressed in police blue. Fragile—ethereal, some might say, seeing the white gold hair, porcelain complexion, and wide-set blue eyes. Not even her parents, who had watched in horror when she swung from the tops of trees with the best of the neighborhood boys, credited her essential toughness. Genine's last thought as she double wrapped the gunbelt around her twenty-four-inch waist was that nothing is hopeless, not if you want it badly enough.

16

AN ALARM RANG in Cenni's head as soon as the call came from reception—*Package here for Commissario Cenni from Dottor Batori.*

Batori loved to talk—to taxi drivers, waiters, strangers on park benches, and particularly to colleagues. He always delivered postmortem reports himself. Cenni practically had to lift him out of his visitor's chair to get rid of him. He grinned, remembering the time that Batori had hand-delivered the Ronchitti postmortem. Not even the gastric attack Cenni had faked to get rid of the doctor had worked. Batori had insisted on examining him; "professional courtesy," he had said. Cenni was registering far too many deviations from the norm to ignore. Yesterday, the delayed postmortem report. Today, a premature burial service—at noon—with the news personally delivered to him by the questore at 8:00 this morning. Two trips in one week to the burbs. Carlo should consider asking for a raise.

The envelope was the usual size, with the usual number of typed sheets inside, but there was one significant difference. The medical examiner normally listed the cause of death at the top, in bold type, followed by the details. For the first time in Cenni's memory, Batori's postmortem report began with the details.

A healthy specimen, albeit a dead one. All the major organs had been in good working order; Minelli had taken care of herself. The stomach contents revealed nothing beyond a penchant for eating right: a partially digested apple, suggesting that she had eaten it shortly before her death. Nothing else.

Batori had been right about the child, a fetus of some eight weeks, a girl, blood type AB, and normal to all appearance. Cenni sat back for a minute, stopped reading and looked off into space, but quickly shook off his melancholy. He had two deaths to contend with now, and possibly two murders. But the decision to prosecute for two murders was not his to make. It would be made by Antonio Piruli, the investigating judge.

No bruising to the genitalia or the pelvic area; no foreign body fluids present in or on the victim's body; no foreign pubic or head hairs present in or on the body; no trace evidence (soil, fibers, grass) inconsistent with the environment in which the victim had died. Conclusion: no evidence of rape beyond the outward displacement of her clothing. The Great Equivocator stated *unequivocally* that it was *unlikely* that the dead woman had had sex within the past seventy-two hours.

The report then discussed the head wound, which Batori had originally described for public consumption and with great assurance as the probable cause of death. Not any longer! A slight contusion only, causing very little internal bleeding. The victim might have been knocked out for a minute or two, but the blow didn't kill her. In other words, there was no extensive inter-cranial injury as Batori had claimed on Saturday. The report also stated that the bruising was consistent with her being struck by the statue of the virgin, as evidenced by the paint chips found embedded in her hair. Nothing new there, Cenni thought.

And finally—cause of death—asphyxiation by suffocation, evidenced by petechial hemorrhages in the victim's eyes, face, lungs, and neck area.

Instrument of Suffocation—unknown.

Time of death—Friday, March 29, between 4:00 PM and 8:00 PM, with a footnote that rigor mortis was fully developed at 9:00 AM on Saturday, March 30.

Cenni flung the report across the room in disgust, as much with himself as with Batori. Petechiae, or tiny purple or red spots on the surface of the skin, are caused by small areas of bleeding underneath it and are often evident to the naked eye. Batori couldn't have examined the inner surface of Minelli's eyelids at the cemetery, or he would have noticed the pinlike hemorrhages immediately. And, of course, Cenni hadn't been there to observe or direct the examination thanks to Russo's late notification to the questore of Minelli's murder.

Batori's rather notorious habit of jumping to premature conclusions had surfaced again. But Cenni had to acknowledge that he was partly at fault. He had noticed two pinlike red spots immediately under Rita's right eye during his examination and had passed them off as age spots, similar to those his grandmother had on her cheeks. But Minelli had been forty-five, not eighty-eight. He cursed his own carelessness.

The medical examiner's postmortem findings, assuming they were correct, complicated the investigation considerably. The possibilities were many. Someone might have struck Minelli on the head and then suffocated her. Or, just as possible, the head wound and the suffocation were unrelated. There was no proof that Minelli had been knocked unconscious by the blow to her head. And if she had been knocked unconscious, the blow might have occurred an hour before her death, or thirty minutes, or even one minute. There was no indication in the postmortem report one way or the other.

Three full days had now passed since Minelli's murder, and Cenni was further from arresting her killer today than he had been on Saturday morning. He had foolishly accepted Batori's assertion that the statue was the weapon, and he now had to begin again.

Cenni reflected on what he knew of suffocation. Cross transfer of fibers can occur when there's person-to-person contact; when the fiber is easily shed; and when the pressure and duration of contact are sufficient and the receiving surface is susceptible to transfer. In Minelli's murder, he knew only that person-to-person contact had occurred. The time it takes to smother a person, particularly if the person doesn't struggle, is short, no more than a few minutes. As Batori had noted at the end of his report, there was no bruising around the nose or mouth or to Minelli's hands or arms to indicate a struggle or prolonged contact, which suggested that the deceased might have been knocked out from the blow to the head and then suffocated while she was unconscious or just regaining consciousness. Batori had also noted that he'd found no fibers in the nasal passages or in the lungs, and then annotated his statement by indicating that only the very shortest fiber fragments are easily drawn into the nasal passages or lungs.

Cenni read the remainder of the report aloud, emphasizing, for his own displeasure, each of Batori's equivocations concerning the black fiber that had been attached to Minelli's earring, the only obviously foreign fiber found on her body. *Probably* animal hair, *possibly* cashmere, based on a *cursory examination*. And to confuse things even further, Batori went on to state that cashmere is a lengthy fiber, usually loosely woven, concluding, through some inner logic that escaped Cenni, that since no short fibers were found in the victim's nasal passages or lungs, the weapon of suffocation *may have been* a fabric made of cashmere (or anything else under the sun, Cenni said to himself). The black fiber, *probably* animal hair and *possibly* cashmere, had been sent on to the Forensic Police Lab in Rome for further analysis. Well, that was a godsend anyway. He wouldn't have to involve Batori in his request for a comparison with the black scarf found by Sergeant Antolini.

Even the time of death was an equivocation; to list the time of death as between 4:00 and 8:00 was sheer cowardice on Batori's part. The evidence, empirical as well as physical, suggested that Minelli had been killed no earlier than 4:30, when she was last seen in Assisi, and no later than 6:30, when she had agreed to meet John Williams at Il Duomo. Sunset on Good Friday had been at 6:30; she would hardly have stayed in the pitch-black cemetery after that if she were still alive. Batori had made a colossal blunder in deciding prematurely that the cause of death was the blow to Minelli's head; he was now covering himself by invoking the classic four-hour window for time of death.

Unlikely! May! Might! Probably! Possibly! The medical examiner had given the police nothing concrete. Cenni was angry but he refused to expend energy on what couldn't be changed. Minelli had been suffocated, in a manner unknown, between the hours of 4:00 and 8:00 on Good Friday. That was what the postmortem concluded and that was what he'd work from, of course, making some necessary amendments of his own. And now, he had a funeral to go to. He grabbed his jacket from the top of the file cabinet where he had tossed it that morning and headed out the door.

17

THE DECISION TO bury Rita on the same day that the autopsy report was delivered had been made without Cenni's knowledge. According to the questore, Amelia Casati had handled the burial arrangements: the priest and church, the black-edged cards, flowers, death notice, even the bribes. Cenni had no doubt about the bribes. The English violet exuded the perfume of privilege and beneath her litanies of softly spoken *my dears*, Cenni had detected a will of iron and a self-righteous snobbery. Three times on Saturday, she had referred to her husband as *count*, and once to herself as *countess*, although in a clever, self-deprecating way. He wondered if the red-rimmed eyes were a sham. She'd left him with the impression that she thought her American niece a bit common as well as a nuisance.

The excuse offered by the questore for hurrying Minelli into her grave was that Assisi's mayor (Umberto Casati's dear friend) wanted to avoid further unpleasantness, which scares

away the tourists! Rita's funeral would be held in the cemetery
chapel, which was still officially closed for renovation, and not
in her beloved St. Stefano's. The final insult: She was to be
buried among the war veterans and paupers in the lower
section of the cemetery. "Not forever," the questore explained
when Cenni had protested. "Just until people forget. The
countess is afraid the family vault will become a sideshow."

"More sideshow, more money!" Cenni had countered. The
countess was becoming a thorn in his side.

The tolling of the bells began, and Cenni watched as
Amelia and Umberto hurriedly approached the chapel, followed by a beggarly procession of relatives and one friend,
John Williams. He trailed after the family, escorted by Inspector Staccioli; Assisi's mayor and its commissario, Fulvio Russo,
walked last. Sophie Orlic was not among the mourners and
neither were any of the Casati servants. He presumed they
were at the house preparing the funeral-baked meats. Cenni
followed the procession into the church and seated himself in
the front pew of the side aisle for a clear view of the mourners,
which, as he acknowledged warily, gave the mourners an
equally clear view of him.

The coffin, a heavily polished mahogany affair (no money
spared!), was covered with a large spray of yellow roses.
Some fifteen or more wreaths on tall wire stands crowded the
altar, and one heart-shaped bouquet of tiny white bell-
shaped flowers (for the child, he assumed), was placed for-
lornly to the side, adjacent to his pew. He found himself
inching away from the bouquet's overwhelming fragrance,
and when he next looked over at the Casati family, Artemesia, sitting alone in the second pew, was smiling at him. She
covered her nose with a lace handkerchief and nodded
toward the flowers, suggesting through body language that
he should do the same.

Paola Casati, seated with her grandparents in the front pew, was dressed simply in a leather jacket and black beret. For most of the mass and funeral service, she stared straight ahead, oblivious to what was happening on the altar. Her grandfather also stared straight ahead, but Cenni saw his lips moving to the *Pater Noster.* Amelia Casati, her emotions safely hidden behind a lace mantilla, held herself erect throughout the mass, until the very end when the priest stood before the altar and recited the final prayer for the dead.

O God, Whose attribute it is always to have mercy and to spare, we humbly present our prayers to Thee for the soul of Thy servant Rita which Thou has this day called out of this world, beseeching Thee not to deliver it into the hands of the enemy. . . .

She gave a loud moan and swayed, grabbing her husband's arm for support. Umberto, after stealing a look in Cenni's direction, whispered what must have been a warning, as she immediately straightened up, although she continued to hold onto his arm until they had exited the chapel. John Williams, in the fourth pew with Staccioli and Fulvio Russo, was the only one to display emotion, weeping intermittently, but softly, throughout the service. Staccioli and Russo eyed him with visible contempt when during the *Absolute*, he blew his nose openly and heaved a loud sigh.

Cenni was not sure why he was wasting a half-day attending Rita's funeral, beyond a direct order from the questore. He had no expectation that one of the mourners would suddenly confess as the body was interred, although he did note with some interest Amelia Casati's near collapse in the church. The best murderers always give the best performances. Even first-time killers often managed their guilt through self-justification: *She brought it on herself!*

As they exited the chapel, he looked around for signs of last night's furious police activities, but saw none. Even the dumpster had disappeared. Two of his officers had spent two hours examining the five days worth of debris it contained, and as Piero had complained afterward, it was not all wilted flowers. Elena had determined after speaking to the florist in Rivotorto that Orlic had a weekly order for two dozen long-stemmed yellow roses for the Casati vault. They'd found the yellow roses in the dumpster. And Sergeant Antolini had finally located Giuseppe Guido, Assisi's village drunk, in a detox tank in Foligno. He had been in his usual begging position on Good Friday, right outside the San Giacomo gate and was eager to express his outrage:

"Passed me right by, the countess did, carrying a bunch of flowers, headed for the cemetery. I watched her walk down the road until she disappeared around the bend. "Four-thirty, exactly," Guido claimed, displaying his wristwatch. "Not even a nod for an old friend," he complained. It seemed that Amelia Casati was one of Guido's patrons. He could forgive those who never gave, but not a lapsed regular. He had abandoned his begging immediately after that. "No point in my waiting for her return. I guess her money's too good now for the likes of me," he'd added in disgust.

So Cenni had two witnesses to confirm that the countess had not been at home all Friday afternoon. But contrary to what Sophie Orlic had insisted the evening before, Amelia Casati had not left her sitting room in order to deliver a few peonies to the flower lady. She had been in the cemetery at the time of the murder. It was starting to come together.

18

"DIMMI!" CENNI SAID, joining Elena and Piero at their table in the rear of the Bar Sensi. He'd just returned from the burial

service, and he now had two hours to kill before he could re-interview the Casati family. The count had insisted that his family and guests be permitted to have their funeral lunch in peace before talking, *again*, to the police, and the questore had agreed.

"Guests! What guests!" Cenni had replied caustically. "The only people attending the funeral were immediate members of the family and four outsiders. Of those, Williams and Staccioli are lunching in Williams's bed sitter, courtesy of the police, which leaves that asshole of an ass-kissing mayor, and Fulvio—no comment there!" But Cenni knew there were no rewards in fighting the system.

He could have returned to Perugia to finish up some paperwork, but at this time of day that trip could take two hours, back and forth. He decided to hang out at the Bar Sensi and see whom the regulars had picked as the murderer.

As soon as he sat down, he realized that Elena and Piero were in the middle of a fight. Elena was fuming quietly to herself and Piero was looking uncomfortably flushed. Cenni wondered why, but didn't ask. Nor did he have to. Elena blurted it out before he had time to order a coffee.

"How's *your* blonde today, Commissario?" she asked recklessly, standing at attention. She nodded at Piero, "His is acting up. She's told him to lose twenty pounds, and he's starving himself, and me! I have a flash for the two of you. The worse thing that can happen to a man is to fall for a blonde with tits. You lose all your marbles!" On that inelegant note, she walked to the front of the bar, sat down on one of the stools, and turned her back on them.

"What brought that on, Piero? She wouldn't get that way without some provocation. What did you say to her?"

"We had a pizza while we were waiting, and Elena offered me the last piece, you know, like she always does. I said I was on a diet, that I had to lose twenty pounds." He hesitated before adding, "And that she could stand to lose a few pounds herself."

"You've forgotten to mention that you threw Sergeant Antolini at her! I'd have thought you had more sense!"

"Don't, Alex! I think Elena's really mad! Normally she laughs when I tease her, but I've noticed that whenever I mention Genine, she gets huffy. Should I apologize, tell her I was kidding? She's not really fat, you know. Come on, Alex, help me out here."

Cenni could see that Piero was upset, and he was beginning to get the picture concerning Elena. Lately, Piero's name cropped up in Elena's conversations to an outrageous degree.

"My only advice, Piero: Never quote a platinum blonde with big breasts to an underendowed brunette, particularly about weight. For the rest, you're on your own." As he watched Piero walk toward the front of the bar, Cenni reflected that his two junior officers worked extremely well together and that they had become close personal friends in the last year. He hoped that Elena's crush on him—and that it was no more than a crush—would wear off quickly, or he might have to transfer her. But he'd worry about that later. Right now, he had more immediate concerns.

The postmortem gave the cause of death as suffocation, but Cenni had decided to keep this information from the family. He'd gotten the questore to agree, in exchange for a promise to be "nice." Being nice apparently meant dressing according to a code. Umberto Casati had found Cenni's jeans and leather jacket *disrespectful*. He was also miffed that Cenni had *conspicuously* not addressed him or his wife by their titles, but there was nothing official that he or his wife could do about that and nothing that Cenni would agree to do.

The questore, who wanted to be all things to all people, had tried to soften the blow. "I know Saturday was your day off,

Alex. I told that to the count, and that you went straight to the cemetery from a football match, the reason for the jeans. But tone it down, Alex, *per favore*. I've got too many people on my back right now." Of course, when Cenni had asked for names, the questore had fobbed him off.

Cenni mused that approaching Umberto Casati about Giorgio Zangarelli's visit on Good Friday would be awkward. He'd lied when he said he was alone in his library Friday afternoon, but since the information provided by the Irish reporter substantiated that he had, in fact, been at home, he was within his rights to refuse to answer questions about the reason for Zangarelli's visit.

The wife was a bigger problem. She'd been caught in a lie, and not a white lie either. By two accounts, she'd been out of the house that afternoon. But Sophie would hold to her story that Amelia Casati had been delivering flowers to her apartment. And the other witness was the town drunk. Cenni had some thoughts about how to move Amelia Casati to a confession. Laying on guilt might do it. She appeared to have a conscience. He'd say that he was planning to arrest Sophie Orlic, who Cenni now suspected was protecting Amelia Casati. Someone had struck Rita on the head, and for him the wife was the likely suspect. But she knew nothing of the faked rape and, therefore, of the actual cause of death. Telling her that Rita had been suffocated might have the effect of getting her to talk about what had happened, but it might also cause her to shut down completely, in an effort to protect Sophie or someone in her family.

And then there was Lucia. According to the Irish journalist, the maid had left the house a minute or two after 4:30. If Lucia were not outside the kitchen door hanging up clothes as she'd sworn on Saturday, then anyone in the house could have gone out the kitchen door and down those treacherous steps to the *vicolo*, exiting at via Fontebella without being seen. Umberto Casati had been seen saying goodbye to Giorgio Zangarelli at 6:00, so he was an unlikely candidate. In addition, Cenni had strong doubts that with his arthritis Casati could have maneuvered that dangerous stairway. Amelia Casati and Paola were both out of the house by 4:30. That left Artemisia, and she was still a dark horse so far as Cenni was concerned. The bookbinder had confirmed that four pages had been torn from Minelli's diary. That pointed to someone in the house, perhaps Artemisia acting as Fulvio's accomplice. On Saturday, he'd noticed that Artemisia had an ace bandage wrapped around her right ankle. She could easily have twisted an ankle if she had used the garden steps.

"Commissario, *scusi.*" Cenni looked up to see Elena standing over him, with a hangdog look on her face.

"*Si*, Elena," he said, smiling.

"Sorry about before . . . you know . . . what I said! But I've got some information for you, from our door-to-door inquiries earlier today and from that man over there." She pointed to the bus driver who had been sitting on the bar stool next to hers.

"*Dimmi,*" Cenni repeated. "Talk to me."

19

THE COMMISSARIO AND Elena traveled back to headquarters in separate cars, at his request. He wanted to review the day's events with Piero. At first Elena was glad of it; she needed an hour alone to forego being the cheerful, companionable, never-takes-offense Elena. A lot like a friendly beagle, she thought. When they get bored throwing sticks at you, they push you away. Amazed at her own contrariness, she laughed. Now you resent the commissario because he doesn't pine for your company. And who would, after that nasty crack you made today? You're lucky he's still talking to you, she told herself. The commissario's obsession with Sophie Orlic was not something one aired in a public bar, yet there had not been a single word in retaliation from him. He'd even taken her along to the count's house to take notes, a job he usually reserved for Piero.

Back in the office, she removed her jacket and settled down to write her report with regard to the inquiries that she and Piero had conducted in the morning and the four interviews that the commissario had conducted in the afternoon. Piero had gone off to visit the Canadian, who had called the commissario to say he wanted out of his bed sitter and was willing to talk. "Four days alone in a room with Staccioli works better than the rack," Elena had wisecracked. But he had nothing new to reveal, not a hint of Minelli's lover's name, so they decided to leave him with Staccioli for another day.

She couldn't settle to work, not yet. She was antsy, still thinking about the fool she'd made of herself earlier in the day. Basically shy where women were concerned, Piero was very slow on the uptake. Elena doubted he even knew what had sparked her tantrum. But the commissario knew! She could tell from the way he'd treated her later in the day: mournfully gentle whenever he spoke to her, and that disconcerting way he had of searching her face, then quickly looking away when she caught him at it. Fortunately, she had regained her equilibrium after deflecting the advances made by the bus driver before he'd learned who she was.

The bus driver had initially seemed genuinely surprised when Elena told him to back off, which he didn't. This caused Piero, who hadn't taken his eyes off Elena after her outburst, to move nearer. Orlando, the bartender, finally got the bus driver to chill out, with the rather startling news that the cute brunette he was hitting on was actually a cop. Then the bus driver was eager to discuss Rita Minelli's murder. He insisted that he'd seen Minelli walking on Via Fontebello on Good Friday, shortly after he had discharged his passengers and parked his bus. "Near as I can guess, about a quarter to five. She passed me walking in the direction of the Basilica. Sexy lady, hard not to notice. Damn shame to kill the good-looking ones," he added, winking at Orlando. "And then on Monday I seen her picture in all the papers. Knew her straight off. You can ask my wife." A wife, yet he's hitting on me, Elena had thought, grimacing at Piero.

She'd immediately informed the commissario of the bus driver's claim but Cenni was skeptical, particularly after he'd learned that Elena and Piero had finally located the store where Rita had purchased the statue, a hardware store in Piazza Mattioti. The owner was certain that Minelli had visited the store on Good Friday, "at four-thirty, maybe a few minutes later." He'd wanted to close early and tried to rush her out. "She bought the same statue she always does. I sold her half a dozen of them in the last few months, asked if she was starting a new religious order," he'd said, amused at his own wit.

The commissario had latched on to that right away, telling Piero to get on to the people who emptied the dumpsters near the Casati vault to learn if they'd found any statues like it in the last two months. "It starts to make sense," the commissario said, thinking out loud. "The statue was her excuse for visiting the vault if anyone saw her. No doubt, she threw it into the dumpster when she left. I can't imagine what she'd be doing on Via Fontebello if she had purchased the statue on her way to the cemetery. From the hardware store in Piazza Mattioti to the cemetery is no more than a ten-minute walk, fifteen at the outside. A detour by way of Via Fontebello would take her at least thirty minutes and only if she were trotting. Ask him if the woman on Via Fontebello carried a package?"

The answer Piero brought back was "No, not that he saw any-way." Cenni sat quietly, thinking. He'd then asked Piero to show the bus driver Artemisia Casati's picture. The driver was a bit sheepish, particularly when Orlando, looking over his shoulder, blurted out that the woman in the picture was Count Casati's daughter. He insisted, stubbornly, that Artemisia Casati might look like the woman, but he was a hundred per-cent sure that it was the murdered American he'd seen on Via Fontebello. When the commissario approached him directly and asked if the woman had walked with a limp, he looked around nervously, answering *Maybe*, then quickly changing it to *Maybe not* before flying out the front door as though pursued by the devil.

"Didn't even pick up his change! Who says cops are bad for business," Orlando had quipped.

Elena didn't dwell on Piero while she was at the Casati house; she was too busy taking notes. The interviews had begun with the count. As soon as the subject of Giorgio Zan-garelli came up, the count insisted that Elena leave the room. It didn't matter in the end, because the commissario told her everything anyway, probably more than he would have told her under ordinary circumstances. Sometimes having people feel sorry for you pays off, she thought.

Apparently, the count was helping Zangarelli to become a Knight of Malta, which Cenni thought extremely funny. "Zan-garelli could buy and sell the Vatican twice over, and he's down on his knees begging to be a Knight of Malta! The biggest fools in Italy parade around in those moth-eaten cos-tumes. They'd be pathetic if they weren't so dangerous. Casati's helping Zangarelli to 'resurrect' his family's three hundred-year-old coat-of-arms; creating one is more like it. Is there anyone in this country with a little money who doesn't claim at least one duke in the family tree? Or a pope?" he added, thinking of

Umberto Casati. "What's your guess, Elena? How much is a Knight of Malta worth on the open market?"

Elena had stayed in the room the full time during the interview with the countess and had been surprised to hear the commissario announce, deadpan, that he intended to arrest Sophie Orlic for the American's murder. The countess's eyes teared up a bit at that. Elena was surprised that she could still see out of them, they were so pink and puffed up, but she held steadfast to her story that she'd been out of the house no more than fifteen minutes, twenty at the outside, just long enough to bring the peonies to Sophie. "It was foolish of me to say that I had been home all afternoon, Dottore. I certainly see that now, but you made me quite nervous on Saturday. I'm not used to being interrogated," she added, throwing the blame back onto the police.

The first real slip in her attitude of *noblesse oblige* came when the commissario quoted the beggar, Guiseppe Guido, to her. "Why, that nasty, ungrateful drunk! When I think of the money I've thrown into his lap over the years! He's lying," she said flatly and refused to discuss it further.

The interview with Lucia was all nervous giggles and excuses. "But if I'd told you I left the house at four-thirty the countess would have docked me four euros. What difference can thirty minutes make to the police?"

The interview with Artemisia was the strangest of all. She was supremely unruffled, even more so than she'd been on Saturday. Artemisia was even polite to Elena, although on Saturday she had looked right through her. The most bizarre moment in the interview was when Artemisia openly flirted with the commissario, suggesting that he was using Rita's murder as a pretext to see her. The commissario had laughed good-naturedly in response, but Elena sensed his extreme discomfort in the subtle shift of his body away from Artemisia and toward her, and his asking a question to which he'd already had the answer.

Then Cenni told Artemisia that she'd been seen late on Good Friday on via Fontebello. She denied it immediately. "Oh, I don't think so, Dottore. Surely that was my cousin. Some people say . . . said," she amended, smiling in recollection, "that we looked alike—never could see it myself. What do you think?" she asked him sweetly. And when the commissario asked Artemisia how her ankle was healing, she beamed with pleasure. "You noticed," she said. "*Sei molto gentile!* It's fine now," and she held it up for him to admire. "I twisted it on a loose stone walking up to the Piazza del Comune on Good Friday."

Later, on their walk back to the Piazza del Comune, the commissario had been very quiet. Elena spoke to him twice before getting a response.

Elena got up from her desk and walked over to the small mirror that hung over the file cabinet that she shared with Piero. Her cousin Fausto had nicknamed her *The Tractor* when they were children, referring to her short, muscular stature. But Elena knew that he also meant the way that she ploughed through life, never looking sideways. It's not easy for a tractor to compete with a skinny platinum blonde. Elena had dark curly hair, cut very short so she didn't have to worry about it, and decent enough features, nothing out of the ordinary, although she was rather vain about her short, slightly uptilted nose. If she wasn't in competition with Miss Congeniality of the spectacular breasts, she'd do fine, though she had to admit that she was a bit lacking in the cleavage department.

Well, no matter. She still thought Piero a fool. He'll never lose a pound, let alone twenty, and she didn't care. But with Sergeant Antolini, he'd always be thinking about his paunch, worrying if it offended her blonde sensibilities. Elena didn't mind his complaining, either. Most of the time she thought it

rather funny, that he always had something to moan about
and, really, it was mostly about his mother. More important than
any of that, he was kindhearted and gentle, and even good-looking in a non-Italian sort of way, like a misplaced Irishman.
Tourists were always stopping him on the street, asking him
questions in English. When she'd first joined the force, he had
covered up most of her mistakes, teasing her about them afterward. And he'd kept the woman-haters in the department—and
there were plenty of those—off her back, particularly after the
commissario had given her a coveted spot on his team. They
would have been good together—she knew that—but if Antolini
is what he wants, well too bad for him. She brushed her hair
back from her face and stuck out her tongue. "Idiot, don't embarrass yourself like that again," she said to the woman in the mirror,
and went back to work.

20

"DO YOU THINK Italians are liars?"

Alex looked up quizzically. He was eating a shrimp and egg
tramezzino. "Why?"

"There's a survey here in the paper. It says fifty percent of
Italians are liars."

"Does this question have a philosophical or a personal
basis?"

"Both, I guess. Genine said on Easter Sunday that she liked
me a lot. She said she was going to introduce me to her
mother. And today when I asked her out for Saturday night,
she said it's impossible, that she has a family birthday to go to.
It says right here in *La Repubblica* that sixty-five percent of Italians think it's okay, even necessary, to lie to family and friends,
and particularly to lovers."

"Must be true. Says so right there in *La Repubblica*!" Cenni responded.

Piero said with extreme irritation, "I don't like to think we're a nation of liars."

"Would you rather be English or German? And tell people to their faces when they look terrible. Or French? And tell people to their faces when you don't like them? You worry too much about such things. All people are liars. Italians are just better at it than most. Consider it a sign of superiority." He pushed his half-eaten sandwich away from him. "I think they're trying to poison me. We'd better go," he said, making a face.

Their waitress stopped them as they were walking out the door. "Commissario, you didn't finish your tramezzino. Was it okay?" she asked.

"Better than okay. Absolutely delicious! Watching my weight," he said.

21

AFTERNOON TEA WAS beautifully arrayed on the rosewood pie crust table. Dainty little triangles of white bread spread with smoked salmon, almond thins, and ginger snaps—the last from the Christmas tins that her great nephew Erik had sent from Stockholm—and on the top tier of the lazy Susan, three different chocolate desserts from Pasticceria Sandri. As a special treat, at the end, they would have wild strawberries with dollops of whipped fresh cream. The berries, delicately sweet and deep red, looked quite wonderful piled high in the Chinese blue-and-white porcelain bowl. She and Renato had always served berries in that bowl; their favorites were lingonberries, which they'd loved for their tart sweetness.

Renato had often compared them to her, and every year at Christmas Hanna would find a jar at the bottom of her Christmas stocking. Hanna didn't believe in God, or an after-life, but she wished she could; she wanted so much to see Renato again. She was so lonely. Lately, she seemed to miss him even more than she had immediately after his death some forty years earlier.

Madeleine, her housekeeper, was very secretive about her sources and wouldn't tell Hanna where she'd found wild straw-berries at the beginning of April. She had never been talkative and hated to gossip, saying it was a sin. She had become even more reticent in the last year, insisted on addressing Hanna as *Signora Cenni* and keeping a proper distance. She was very religious, praying even while she dusted. Hanna wondered if Madeleine felt prayers were necessary to ward off the evil of working for a woman who had lived in sin for thirty years. Hanna's daughter-in-law also had concerns in that respect, but more for what her friends might think—or say behind her back—than any fears that her mother-in-law might burn in the fires of eternal damnation. Hanna doubted if anyone even remembered any more that she and Renato had never mar-ried. Everyone referred to her as Signora Cenni. Protesting against conventions is such a bore if no one notices, Hanna thought, and then laughed at herself.

She drummed her fingers on the tea table, then finally picked up one of the ginger snaps and bit into it. She con-sulted her watch. Of course the silly woman would be late. It was ten after 4:00. Italians are always late, so she probably won't arrive until 4:30 or worse, and Hanna was hungry. And then she heard the peal of the bell. She counted slowly to see how many seconds would pass before it rang again. Five seconds, then two more peals. Anxiety or hunger? she wondered.

"Signora Russo, *madame*," Madeleine announced lapsing into her native French, which she always thought more appropriate for social occasions.

The woman rushed across the room before Hanna could get up. "Please, Signora Cenni," she said, "please don't get up," and almost fell into Hanna's lap in her anxiety to please.

"Hanna," she corrected her, with her brightest smile. Signora Russo was a silly woman, but she might like her anyway. Alex had asserted that Grazia Russo would do anything for her husband, who was a fool and a murderer, but Hanna had always preferred people who had wild passions, so much more interesting than those who wrote their lives on ruled tablets, keeping within the lines. But she had promised Alex to use her charm—"your greatest gift," he had said with outrageous flattery—to find out where Russo was on the night of the American's murder.

Grazia Russo was new money, and lots of it. Her family owned the largest fish-packing business in Italy, and that was only what they told the tax collector. Her brother, now head of the family, was a member of parliament and had once been a close advisor of the PM's. Grazia was Giorgio Zangarelli's baby sister for whom nothing was too good. Grazia, who was neither beautiful nor ugly, tall nor short, skinny nor fat, witty nor dull, could have had her choice of husbands because of the money, might have chosen someone who liked her or even loved her. Instead, she had fallen for blond good looks and arrogant pretensions, for a northerner who looked down on Grazia's good southern roots. "He cheats on her with every attractive woman who comes his way, laughs at her to every man who'll listen, and she continues to protect him," Alex had said in amazement. "I'm sure she'll give him an alibi for the time of the murder if she thinks he's implicated, but see what you can find out."

Hanna and Grazia had finished the salmon canapés—and their discussion of Grazia's proposed gift to the Galleria Nazionale—eaten all but one each of the ginger snaps and almond thins, so as not to appear greedy, and shared the chocolate desserts, one and a half each, when Hanna finally got around to talking about the murder. She began with the usual exclamations of horror, and glee! Gruesome, frightening, terrible to be alone with murderers on the loose, rape, no woman safe in her own bed. Hanna was eighty-eight and wondered if perhaps she had gone too far on the last one. And then she did go too far. She told Grazia that it was just by sheer luck that she'd not visited the Assisi cemetery on Good Friday, where she had wanted to copy some tombstone legends for a new book she was writing on the Etruscans, forgetting for the moment that her frailties alone would give the lie to her last statement.

"That's strange!" Grazia said puzzled, helping herself to another dollop of cream. "I always thought the Etruscans hadn't ventured any farther east than Perugia and that the Assisi cemetery is relatively recent, dating from the seventeen hundreds!"

How embarrassing! Grazia seemed to know things, Hanna realized.

"*È vero*, Grazia. But some scholars contend that the cemetery is built over an older burial site, and the Etruscans were a very difficult people, you know. They never could stay put!"

Grazia looked at Hanna, blinked, and attempted to swallow the last mouthful of whipped cream that she'd been savoring, but couldn't quite contain it. She burst out laughing and some of the cream landed in Hanna's lap. It cemented their burgeoning friendship.

After the cream cleanup, Grazia looked at her watch. "Oh I really must go, Hanna. It's nearly six."

Hanna asked if she had to be at home to get her husband's dinner, and Grazia responded sheepishly that he was working on a murder case and wouldn't be home until late. She lowered her eyes for a moment, gulped, and then proceeded to tell Hanna very straightforwardly, without any beating of the breast—Hanna hated breast-beaters—that her husband rarely came home to eat: only on Sundays, when her brother Giorgio came to dinner.

Hanna interrupted her for a moment to ring for Madeleine, using the little silver bell that Madeleine insisted was the only proper way to get her attention.

"*Madame*, shall I bring the Signora's coat?" Madeleine asked. Signora Russo was still comfortably settled in her chair and it was well past teatime.

"A bottle of Prosecco, Madeleine, and two flute glasses, the red ones from Murano, I think."

"But *madame*, the dottore said. . . ."

"We have a guest, Madeleine," Hanna interrupted. "Signora Russo would like some Prosecco!"

22

THE COLD CUT into her exposed flesh and she thought longingly of the sitting room fire below. Umberto hated high heating bills. Even on frigid days, he insisted that she set the temperature no higher than sixty-eight. She sat on the edge of the bed, staring transfixed at the thermostat. Just this once, she thought, getting up. Perched once again on the bed, she smoothed the chenille counterpane, poured herself another glass of wine, and waited for the sounds of water guzzling in the pipes, and the warmth to follow. Seventy-five degrees; he'd have a conniption! She picked up the pillbox that Camillo had given her, his last gift, and fingered its delicate ornamentation, a filigree of silver snowflakes. She opened it again and closed it immediately. The number of sleeping pills would be the same as before: twelve.

Her throat tightened. O God, let me cry, she prayed, but the tears wouldn't come. Just an overwhelming ache of sadness. God had been merciful to Rita, more merciful than to her. Her niece had died happy, looking forward to motherhood. She'd had all of the joy and none of the sorrow. Imagine a woman of Rita's age trying to raise a child alone in Italy. What could she have been thinking? It would have been dreadful. Unforgiving stares, repressed snickers, open snubs! Italians don't like non-conformity. Rita was saved from all that and worse. The child might have died before its mother, as her Camillo had done. Rita was better off now.

Her niece's furious rage had come upon Amelia without warning. Month after month, Rita had placidly accepted Umberto's harsh sarcasm, Artemisia's cruel mockeries, never responding. She could have stopped them, Amelia admitted to herself. But if she had, Artemisia would have turned on her, so she had let them be. After several months of viewing such torture, Amelia had concluded that Rita was morbidly dull, that she didn't understand or even care how much she was despised. But she had been wrong. Rita had cared.

What caused her to strike out at Rita? She had tried repeatedly since Good Friday to remember the exact sequence of events, to record the day's happenings in some order, to write it all down for Umberto, and the police. Her head ached with trying, but it was still just a jumble of words and accusations. It had begun years ago, this wreckage of her brain, this piling up of detritus, and ended on Good Friday when Dottor Saldelli confirmed what she already knew.

The burned soufflé was what finally pushed her to consult the doctor. The dinner had been so important to Umberto.

Giorgio Zangarelli, multimillionaire many times over, member of parliament, former adviser to the PM, was their guest. Umberto was helping the swarthy Calabrian to research his history, to *discover* his family's patrician roots. Zangarelli was determined to become a Knight of Malta and was willing to pay—or do—whatever was necessary to make it happen. And in return, Zangarelli was helping Umberto with his investments. Amelia had begged Umberto not to intercede on Zangarelli's behalf, not to dishonor their name by supporting Zangarelli in his ridiculous pretensions. "Just because he's rich, he acts like our equal. We can sell the Sisley if we need money that badly. It's worth at least a million," she had proposed.

"Money is what counts and a million is pocket change. Next to money, all the rest—name, titles, honors—are just trimmings," he had responded, ignoring her advice as he always did.

The night of the dinner, of Zangarelli's introduction to the Hospitallers of Umbria, Umberto had bragged, rather ostentatiously Amelia thought, about her skill in the kitchen. Always the aristocrat, he had laughed it off when Lucia had served supermarket ice cream instead of chocolate soufflé, but for days afterward Amelia had endured his biting comments. He had even accused her of being slovenly. That had hurt more than anything. "House proud," was how her mother had once described Amelia.

Ten long years her mother had cared for her father, ten torturous years after the first whispers of Alzheimer's, as a brilliant, witty mathematician turned into a garrulous child. And now it was the daughter's turn. Dottor Saldelli had offered Amelia hope, explaining carefully and slowly—too slowly, already speaking as though to a child—about fetal research, new drugs. But what could he know of the torment in store for her family, for Paola . . . for Umberto? Dearest Umberto, who had absolutely no patience. And Artemisia, how would she treat a mother with Alzheimer's? The thought of her daughter's reaction terrified her.

Friday, after lunch in the sitting room, thinking about the future—unbearable to contemplate—she had decided at a little after 4:00 to take the peonies that the florist had delivered earlier in the day to the cemetery. Camillo had so loved valerian pink peonies. "More English than the rose, more English even than my mother," he had said of them laughingly. Don't think about Camillo, not yet, she told herself. Concentrate, think of what I should write in the letter first. She closed the filigreed box. It must be perfect, no mistakes.

> I walked quickly through the deserted streets, out Porta San Giacomo and down the cemetery road, through the iron gates that were still unlocked. I removed the roses and threw them into the nearest dumpster before refilling the vases with water from the chapel fountain. When I returned, I found Rita inside, placing a statue of the Virgin—a horrid cheap thing—on Camillo's altar. I snatched it up and we traded insults, two grown women! Then out of nowhere, Rita said she was pregnant, that she was planning to marry John Williams. She made outrageous claims. The house, our house—seven hundred years in the family—belonged to her; we would have to leave. She had a will that proved her claim. I laughed. It was one of those apocryphal wills that Anna scribbled whenever she was angry at one of us. Remember how we laughed when we found seven of them hidden throughout the house after her death.

She put down her pen and took another sip of wine. I shouldn't have laughed, she thought. Rita had had a screaming fit and accused Artemisia of plagiarizing the ideas in her book from a manuscript in the library. And then she accused Paola of being a terrorist, a murderer. Paola would go to prison, she threatened.

After the humiliations that they had endured, catering to that upstart Zangarelli to save Paola. No, she mustn't write any of that about Paola . . . or Artemisia. That's not for the police to know. Mentioning the will is okay though. Thanks to Lucia, everyone in Assisi knew about Anna's wills. She continued writing.

> I must have struck Rita with the statue. I was holding it in my right hand and Rita was lying face-down on the vault floor. I dropped it and tried to turn her over but I couldn't. My hands shook so. There was just one tiny drop of blood on the step. I ran for help to the front gates but they were locked. I cried out, but no one came. I let myself out the side gate with my key and walked back to Assisi as quickly as I could. When I came through Porta San Giacomo, I rang Sophie's bell. I told Sophie everything, even that Rita was pregnant. Sophie insisted that Rita couldn't be dead; she said she was probably just stunned. She insisted on going back by herself. Stay in the flat, she said. Don't talk to anyone until I return! Umberto, I couldn't stop shaking.
>
> But Rita wasn't stunned, she was dead. When Sophie told me, I wanted to call you immediately, but Sophie said I mustn't, that I would go to prison. She had taken care of everything; the police would never know. She even returned with the peonies. They were my excuse for being outside the house. Tell the police you left home to bring the peonies to me, Sophie said. But it all went horribly wrong, and it was my fault. I didn't see anyone, coming or

going, so I thought it would be safer to tell the police that
I had been home all afternoon. It all became so complicated, Umberto. Dottor Cenni told me yesterday that he
will arrest Sophie, and this morning I heard Fulvio tell you
the same thing. I listened at the door, just like Lucia!

Amelia read through what she had written. It rambled on
so. Suicide notes were short and to the point. *Forgive me, darling. I love you. Remember me always*—something like that, but
how else were the police to know what had happened? She
owed it to Sophie to tell them, but not those things about
Paola and Artemisia. Those she would keep to herself.

The room had grown quite warm. She hoped Umberto could-
n't hear the water gurgling in the pipes. It was just the sort of
thing that would attract his attention. He might even come up to
check on her. She lifted her glass to drink and saw that it was
empty. She poured the last of the bottle into her glass and slowly
counted the pills, one by one, as she swallowed. She thought of
a tradition they had in Spain of eating twelve grapes to welcome
in the New Year. But this was hardly like that!

Her missal, the one Anna had given to her on her wedding
day, lay on the night table. She searched through its pages until
she found the funeral prayer that the priest had intoned that
morning. She read it aloud: *O God, Whose attribute it is always to
have mercy and to spare, we humbly present our prayers to Thee for the
soul of Thy servant Amelia which Thou has this day called out of this
world, beseeching Thee not to deliver it into the hands of the enemy. . . .*

23

THAT SAME AFTERNOON, Artemisia stood at the attic window looking out at the distant outline of Spello—*Hispellum*, in
Roman times, when the town had served as a retirement home

for pensioned-off legionaries. "Retired Roman soldiers!—That's a good one," her nanny, Marie, had said thirty years earlier looking out the same small window. "Tourist crap! Roman soldiers didn't live long enough to retire. Imagine it, tomato gardens in the day, Roman orgies at night, and for the meat course, feeding their holier-than-thou neighbors to the lions."

The attic room in which Artemisia was now standing had been Marie's bedroom. Here, late at night, lying in the creaky iron bed with its straw-filled mattress and mended flannel sheets, Artemisa had learned to love Marie and hate her mother. They would lie together like two stacked teaspoons, Marie hugging Artemisia around the middle to keep her from falling out of the narrow single bed, and Marie would talk about Sicily, and witchcraft. Everyone in Sicily believed in black magic but only special people like her grandmother practiced it. Casting spells was her grandmother's trade. "The only way to keep others from beating you down," Marie said. "Make them afraid of you!"

Artemisia had never thought about it when she was a child (it had seemed perfectly natural at the time), but the maidservant who dusted her father's law library, ironed his socks, scrubbed pots and pans, and toilets—maliciously at times, using the pots and pans brush—who said *Si, contessa*, twenty, maybe thirty, times in a day with a sweet smile, was the same woman who spat on the rough bleached floorboards of her attic room at night. "English *putana*," Marie had recited like a mantra when Artemisia's mother had once made her re-iron a white linen tablecloth, twelve feet long and five feet wide. "Look," her mother had said, pointing to a slight yellowing on the edge, "it's scorched. Wash it again please, Marie, and re-iron it."

Marie said other things, too—delicious, terrible things. One hot summer's evening, after she had returned from a beach outing to the Adriatic, she'd found Artemisia in her room, lying on top of the counterpane, kicking her heels and sobbing in a white rage. The countess had gone to open a ▓▓▓▓▓ir at Costa di Trex and had taken Camillo with her. Ar▓▓▓ d been left at home—punished for striking her br▓▓▓ t same night Marie told Artemisia that the countess ha▓ ▓ Italy because she couldn't get a man in England. "Blo▓ sow," she had called her, "dried up, like the parche▓ Puglia, eyes the watery blue of the dirty Adriatic." Ma▓ fixation about the dirty Adriatic.

When Marie was homesick, she would talk to Art▓ the Sicilian indigo sea that raged below her grandm▓ house in Cefalù. Whitecaps and seabirds riding high▓ pristine blue-violet waters, huge crashes of white flecke▓ smashing against the rocky coastline, spraying the prom▓▓▓▓ above with the damp bouquet of brine and crushed sea shells. Marie said the Adriatic, which belonged to the mainland, was a warm cesspool of slime, devoid of strength or beauty. She worshipped strength and beauty. The men of Cefalù were dark and wiry, the strength of panthers in their limbs, and the small-boned women were dark beauties, with wild hair frizzed by the sea air and coal black eyes, descendants of the original Sicanians and Greeks. The others were imposters, Normans who had come to Cefalù nine hundred years earlier to steal and had forgotten their way home.

Artemisia was jealous of her brother, who had silky yellow hair and blue eyes. Camillo was her mother's favorite. But Marie mocked Camillo's pale hair and pale eyes. "Mommy's little fairy," she had called him in the guttural language of Sicily, which only she and Artemisia could understand.

On her eighth birthday, Artemisia's parents moved her bedroom from the attic to a room on the second floor, to sleep with the adults. She didn't want to leave her little room and begged to stay in the attic with Marie, who helped her to dress

and bathe, and who took her for long walks to the top of La
Rocca, where they could almost see Sicily in the distance. At
night in her attic room, Artemisia could hear Marie through
the open door, moving around, talking to herself, and the
hall light, a bare bulb that hung from a looped wire, cast a soft
tawny glow into her room until the early morning hours when
Marie rose to begin her day's work. Her room was a square box,
with a small iron bedstead, a bureau with three ill-fitting drawers, and hooks on the wall for her dresses, but Artemisia could
see into all the corners of the room at night, and if she stood
on the bed, she could almost touch the ceiling.

Her new room on the second floor had a twelve-foot-high ceiling, and there was no hall light to cast a friendly glow into the
dark spaces surrounding her bed; her mother insisted that she
sleep with the door closed. That first night, after her birthday celebration, she lay in the suffocating darkness. *Hail Mary, full of
grace, the Lord is with thee, blessed are thou among women and blessed
is the fruit of thy womb, Jesus,* she prayed out loud. If she chanted the
Hail Mary until early morning light, she would ward off the dead
who hovered in the vast spaces above her head, vampires who
would suck her blood if she slept! She knew about vampires
because Marie had seen them in Sicily.

The next morning, when Marie came to dress Artemisia for
school, she found her charge huddled by the doorjamb, stiff
with cold. "I fell asleep and the vampires came for me," she
told Marie, the tear tracks visible on her soft cheeks. When
Marie told the count that Artemisia was afraid of the dark, he
said she should have a nightlight but her mother disagreed.
She reminded the count that Camillo had also been afraid of
the dark and that it had lasted less than a week. She'll get over
it, she told the count, and he concurred.

That afternoon, when Marie picked her up at school, she
gave Artemisia a ring with a tiny star ruby in its center. She'd

found it in one of the trinket shops on via San Paolo. "It cost me a week's wages, but it'll protect you from the vampires." That night, when the count and countess were out to a concert, Marie taught Artemisia how to execute the banishing ritual of the star ruby. It was very like the Sign of the Cross that Artemisia's grandmother had taught her when she was little more than a baby, only the words were different, "Sicilian words that drive away the evil spirits and bestow strength." Marie had learned the ritual from her grandmother, who had learned it from her grandmother. It was as old as Sicily itself. Artemisia still executed the ritual that Marie had taught her all those years ago while she recited the banishing words: *Do What Thou Wilt Shall Be the Whole of the Law. Love Is the Law, Love Under Will.*

At nineteen, Artemisia had visited Sicily, stopping in Cefalù to visit the Abbey of Thelema, now a shrine to Aleister Crowley, the English-born genius of the occult, who had practiced black magic in the Abbey until banished by the Italian authorities for undisclosed acts that hinted of human sacrifice. Marie had introduced the eight-year-old Artemisia to the occult, but Aleister Crowley, who was still referred to as *The Beast* fifty years after his death, had made Artemisia a disciple. She had read all the master's books before she was sixteen.

That same year she had also stopped to visit Marie, who had gone to live only a few hundred yards from the Abbey with a younger sister, in their grandmother's house. From the sister, Artemisia learned that Marie was in prison on the mainland for stabbing and killing her lover in a jealous rage. She also learned that the grandmother had been a disciple of Crowley's, and it was from him that the grandmother had actually learned the star ruby ritual. Another of Marie's lies. Two months ago, the sister had written to Artemisia to ask for money, for masses, she said. Marie had died in prison in a fight with another inmate. Mad, malevolent Marie, who had once loved Artemisia.

This was what Artemisia was thinking as she clutched the small ring in her right hand and perused the letter from Marie's sister once again. Artemisia had tucked the ring away at the bottom of her jewelry case when she had returned from school in England. It was a cheap manmade stone, costing no more than a few hundred lira, hardly a week's wages as Maria had claimed some thirty years before. But it had served its purpose; it had protected a frightened eight-year-old from vampires and, later, a lonely adolescent from more dangerous fiends, the girls at Artemisia's English boarding school, who had tormented her because of her heavy accent and coal-black hair. One of them probably still had prong marks in her right breast. Artemisia smiled at the thought. She had stabbed the girl in dining hall with her fork, stopped only by its hilt from piercing an artery. The girl, whose name Artemisia had long forgotten but whose blonde hair and blue eyes she still remembered, had referred to her as "that dark Sicilian."

24

AMELIA CASATI DIED in the early evening hours, on the Wednesday following Easter Sunday, and on the same day that Commissario Cenni had struck her name from his list of suspects. The body was found by her husband shortly after 6:00, and the call to Commissario Cenni from Sergeant Antolini came at exactly 6:30. The thirty minutes it took for the commissario to drive from Perugia to Assisi were the most remorseful of his life. In his fifteen years as a policeman he had viewed many suicides, but Amelia Casati was the first to take her own life on his watch. Whatever reasons she may have had for killing herself, Alex knew that he alone was to blame. *May God in His forgiveness have mercy on her soul—and on mine,* he prayed as he maneuvered his BMW through the crooked, crowded streets of Assisi. From time to time Alex forgot to remember that he was an avowed atheist.

The Casati maid answered the front door after two rings. She was crying and her dark eyes were barely visible behind reddened, swollen lids. After a brief, whispered good evening, further muffled by the handkerchief she was holding to her face, she showed the commissario into the family sitting room where father and daughter were seated together on the chintz-covered couch. Artemisia looked around when he came in, smiled charmingly, and took a long drag on her cigarette. Umberto Casati, unaware of the commissario's entrance, was staring off into space. His rounded shoulders, no longer rigid with pride, sagged forward toward the warmth of the sitting room fire, and his hair, combed meticulously on Cenni's previous visits, stood on end, giving him the rumbled, unkempt appearance of an old man who had stopped caring. Umberto Casati had lost his aristocratic bearings.

Cenni took a seat directly across from the couple, in the wing chair that Umberto Casati usually reserved for himself, and out of respect waited for the family to begin. A dazed look was all that the widower could manage. He struggled hopelessly to speak and then, with shaking hands, thrust an envelope at the commissario. It contained a suicide note. Cenni recognized that as soon as he read the salutation, *Forgive me, my darling.* Four words, six syllables, but they were enough to lessen some of the guilt he had assumed after learning of Amelia Casati's suicide. He had investigated thirteen suicides in his years as a policeman and had found justification for only one, a man of fifty-five with terminal cancer. The pain was unbearable, he'd told his wife before jumping to his death. He left no suicide letter for his family to weep over in the years to come.

The reprieve Cenni gave himself enabled him to read the letter with some objectivity. Sad, foolish woman, he thought, as he returned the letter to its envelope. Amelia Casati had lived in Italy for more than forty years. She should have known that the circumstances—the niece's provocation, her own illness, her husband's influence—would have kept her from prison.

"It's your wife's handwriting?" Cenni asked, pocketing the letter.

"Yes, but you can see for yourself. Her checkbook is in the top drawer." The count pointed to the refectory table. "Amelia . . . my wife always paid the household bills."

"I'll take a sample of her handwriting when I leave . . . for our records," Cenni responded, hoping to hurry it along. He was anxious to curtail his visit and return the family to its mourning. Just at that moment, Lucia returned, carrying a tray of cups and a pot of coffee. Perhaps the sight of the family maid stiffened Umberto Casati's pride. He straightened up when she entered the room, and when he again addressed Cenni, it was in the supercilious tones of the seventeenth Count Casati. Equilibrium was returning.

"I suppose now you can terminate this intrusive murder investigation, at the very least stop harassing Signora Orlic. My wife was very concerned that you had threatened to arrest Sophie. . . ." He looked sheepish. "I called Sophie, to thank her. I read her Amelia's letter."

Artemisia, who'd sat quietly next to her father until then, touched her father's arm to interrupt. "Oh, but Papa, I'm afraid it's just the opposite. Mamma's letter gives the police even more reason to arrest Sophie. Don't you agree, Dottore?" she asked, flashing Cenni a second charming smile. "Rita caused all that trouble for Sophie last summer, and then again over the New Year. Surely you remember, Papa. It must have been such a temptation when Sophie found Rita lying there, primed and ready, so to speak." She looked first at Cenni and then at her father with an expectant smile.

"Please don't say such things, *cara*. Your mother's letter exonerates Sophie, you know that! Dottor Cenni will think you . . . us . . . vindictive," the father responded anxiously. Cenni noticed that he had avoided looking into his daughter's eyes.

"But Papa, Mamma didn't kill Rita. Didn't the commissario tell you that?" she asked slyly, looking at Cenni sideways through a ring of smoke. "She was suffocated, Papa. The police found a fragment of the cloth used to smother her caught in her left earring. And despite how it looked, she wasn't really raped . . . so her murderer must have been a woman!"

The count looked daggers at his daughter.

"Well, that's what Fulvio says, anyway," she added.

HIS SESSION WITH father and daughter had given Cenni quite a bit to think about on the return trip to Perugia. He had expected Umberto Casati to tear into him for not informing the family that Rita had died by asphyxiation, at the very least to insist that Cenni remove himself from the investigation. He had also expected the father to support the daughter's demand that the police arrest Sophie Orlic. Instead, he had retreated into a brown study after hearing Artemisia's startling accusation. Afterward, as Cenni was leaving to return to Perugia, Umberto Casati had asked him quietly, out of hearing of Artemisia, if he agreed with Fulvio's assessment that the murderer was a woman. He also asked, seemingly as an afterthought, if Sophie were still a suspect.

The commissario had been direct and evasive at the same time. "Signora Orlic is a suspect, certainly, but there's still investigative work to be done and tests to come back from Rome. We still don't know who impregnated your niece."

Umberto Casati had jumped on Cenni's last words. "Of course, the lover. The obvious suspect. No doubt he faked my niece's rape to make it appear as though a vagrant had killed her." The relief in his voice was palpable.

Umberto Casati was surprisingly supportive of Sophie, too supportive. He was hardly an egalitarian, yet for a servant who cleaned his house, and a *straniera*, he had shown true concern. Cenni reminded himself that Sophie and Umberto Casati had a history together that preceded her recent services as cleaning woman and flower lady. Sophie had lived in close intimacy with the Casati family for two years as caregiver to the grandmother. A stunningly beautiful woman in the role of Florence Nightingale! No way around it, Cenni concluded: Umberto Casati was in love with Sophie.

25

THURSDAY DAWNED WARM and sunny, a beautiful spring day, until another early-morning call put quit to that pleasure. "We're meeting at the questura with Fulvio Russo at nine. Be there!" Togni had ordered before hanging up. With no one else to complain to, Alex bent Rachel's ear, figuratively and literally, scratching behind her right ear vigorously, as he exploded. Rachel wondered if *cazzo* were a new endearment, not that it mattered as she preferred ear scratching to all else.

At the questura, Cenni held his anger, just barely, until Fulvio Russo was out of the room, but the instant the door slammed, he let loose. "Screw Rome and its threats. We're the police, for Christ's sake, sworn to serve the law, not knuckle under to a bunch of ass-kissers in Rome. If you want Sophie Orlic in jail, Carlo, you arrest her, but if you do, you'll have my resignation and a media frenzy to boot. I have good friends at *L'Unita*, and I'll use them. God damn it, Carlo, we're supposed to be on the same side."

Cenni no longer had any doubts about Fulvio's guilt. The little shit had finally revealed himself, delivering a series of threats that, so far as Cenni was concerned, were not credible. He doubted that Fulvio had come to Perugia on Umberto Casati's behalf as he claimed, or that Umberto Casati was talking to Rome threatening legal action against the Perugia Questura, or against him. Men in Casati's position rarely displayed their antagonisms publicly for the world to feast on, and they didn't send the second rate to deliver their threats. The final giveaway that Fulvio was acting on his own was when he cautioned that his visit was confidential, that the count preferred to keep his concerns unofficial, *for now*. If Umberto Casati were planning revenge against Cenni for his wife's suicide, he'd find another way—one far more deadly than public exposure.

One nasty fact kept intruding on Cenni's conviction: Artemisia's seemingly offhanded remark that Fulvio had told her about the fringe caught in Rita's earring—*the left earring*. It had him tossing and turning most of the night. Batori had a genetic inability to keep his mouth shut, and he probably did tell Fulvio about the fringe, but Cenni was the only one who knew *where* it was found. He had searched his memory and was sure he hadn't mentioned the left earring to anyone, and definitely not to Batori. Fulvio could only have known it was the left earring if he had placed it there purposely, and why do that? The fringe was from his own scarf! Cenni had some thoughts on the matter, but first things first!

"What the hell do you mean, Alex? Of course, we're on the same side," the questore replied to Cenni's earlier outburst. A thin film of perspiration stood out on the questore's brow.

"You're taking this personally. Some of us think you've lost perspective. This woman, the Croatian, it all points to her, particularly now that we have this." He picked up the suicide note that Amelia Casati had written to her husband and waved it under his senior commissario's nose. "Remember, Alex, it was your decision *not* to tell the family that the niece was suffocated. Maybe that was a good thing and maybe not, but I gave in to you. Now I'm in the hot seat! We've just been handed a chance to bail out and you're balking!" He stopped, pulled out a handkerchief to wipe a drop of sweat from the tip of his nose, and continued. "It's because of this"—he waved the letter again—"that we know the Croatian was the last person to see Minelli alive. So who else could have smothered her? Assisi cemetery is hardly the Rome railway terminal!"

Cenni stopped drumming his fingers on the questore's desk and responded. "*She* has a name, Carlo, and it's not *the Croatian*. The name is Sophie Orlic, and she didn't murder Rita Minelli. Or if she did, it's not yet proven. Consider this. If Sophie Orlic did smother Rita Minelli, why the hullabaloo to abort the investigation? Some tests are not even in yet. What's another week matter, unless someone's worried about what I'll learn in that week? And who's that someone? It's *not* Umberto Casati."

The questore interrupted. "How'd you come by that, Alex? It's his niece who was murdered. Now, the wife's a suicide. It makes sense that he'd want the murderer caught. And he's got the connections to make it happen. Who else but the count?"

Cenni considered the question and the questore. How closely tied was Carlo to the attempted cover-up? He claimed that the pressure was coming directly from headquarters in Rome, that he had no idea who was pulling the actual strings. Why risk it? Cenni decided. He'd keep his own counsel.

"Can't say for sure, Carlo, other than that Casati appeared genuinely touched that Sophie Orlic had risked her own safety to help his wife. It's just a hunch; I'm probably wrong."

The latter was the first of two concessions that Cenni made to the questore. The questore made two concessions as well, both under the threat of blackmail.

"You've got five days to prove her innocence, Alex. Five days—not a second longer. After that, the evidence goes to Priuli. We'll let him decide if there's enough there to bring the . . . that woman to trial."

The questore had also agreed to stop talking to Fulvio Russo, also at Cenni's insistence. "I mean it, Carlo. I don't want that shit to know anything that's happening in this investigation. And keep Batori in line as well. If you or he talks to Fulvio again, I'll—"

"*Si, si, si*, I heard you perfectly—you'll resign! I'll keep my word, Alex, but you'd better keep yours. Resign if you have to, but no newspapers."

Cenni exited the questore's office in a concentrated rage. He'd bought himself five days, but at a cost. If he should act on his threat to resign, he'd to do it without involving *L'Unita*. Five days to prove Sophie innocent and Fulvio guilty.

Carlo had seemed sincere in his belief that it was Umberto Casati making the calls to Rome, and Cenni hadn't argued the point. For the next five days, he'd work alone. Carlo was far too ambitious to risk anything for one of his men, even his favorite commissario. Cenni was convinced that Fulvio Russo was trading on his brother-in-law's clout, that Giorgio Zangarelli was the one in Rome pulling the strings.

Returning to his office, two down from the questore's, he slammed the door, rocking it on its hinges. Two could play at that game! He sat down at his desk and swiveled his chair to look out the window. Fulvio was standing next to the guard's shack, probably waiting for a driver to bring his Ferrari around. Pretentious prick!

The government in Rome fed itself on corruption: money, power, *raccomandazioni*. How else could an incompetent like Fulvio become a commissario di polizia? The so-called Second Republic was no different from the first, the deep pockets were just deeper. Alex was heartsick at the absurdity of it all and at his own presumption. Alessandro Cenni, lone ranger, fighting the power brokers, and for a *straniera*. *Fool* is more like it, he thought. He opened his bottom drawer, rifling it for the pack of smokes he kept for emergencies, and spied his crumpled handkerchief, still in the wastebasket. The cleaning staff was on holiday. Italy isn't such a bad place to live after all, he reflected. He patted his breast pocket where he'd filed Paola Casati's confession. Corruption comes in many flavors, as Fulvio would soon find out.

26

As THOUGH HIS day were not wholly ruined by Fulvio's visit to the questura, his mother took her shot at it when she telephoned him shortly after 10:00. "Madeleine called me early this morning to complain about your grandmother. Hanna was drinking again yesterday, a full bottle of champagne for afternoon tea. And later she forced Madeleine to open a bottle of Brunello Reserve, from your grandfather's special collection, two hundred euros, at least! Drinking with some woman that Madeleine's never even heard of, a Grazia Russo! That's not an Umbrian name, darling, not one of our crowd.

"Madeleine says the woman is a friend of yours," his mother continued, the tone now gone from warmly concerned to coldly accusing. "This is serious, darling! (Back to warmly concerned). Madeleine's threatening to leave, to

return to Marseilles. She says your grandmother's too old and
too weak to live by herself and too eccentric for her to stay with.
È Vero, Alex, Madeleine said *crazy*, not eccentric. I've tried to be
a good daughter. You know I have. I've invited your grandmother numerous times to live with me, and even before your
father died, to live with us. Perhaps it's time to consider one of
those nursing homes."

His mother's last remark was meant to annoy him; she
blamed her sons for indulging their grandmother's whims.
Hanna Falkenberg would never live in a nursing home and
absolutely never with her daughter-in-law. She would leave
Italy first, perhaps return to Sweden to live with one of her
equally eccentric great-nephews. But his mother wouldn't want
that either. Hanna was still the largest shareholder in the family's chocolate business. She had contributed half the capital
for the startup in 1935 and a good part of the labor for nearly
sixty years. She was still listed as titular head on the company's
letterhead. She would cut his mother out of her will, and anyone else, even her adored grandsons, who tried to force her
into a nursing home. Fourteen years ago his grandmother
had given up a full professorship in Etruscan studies at the University of Perugia—forced out because of politics, not age—
and she was bored. She did not wear old age gracefully. She
refused to sit still and collect knitting patterns.

His mother was right in one respect. He had asked his
grandmother to invite Grazia Russo to afternoon tea. He
needed to know where Russo had been on Good Friday.
According to Sergeant Antolini, Russo had left the Assisi station well before four o'clock. Cenni couldn't ask his colleague
directly if he had an alibi, and his suspicions alone were not
enough to have Russo declared a murder suspect. His grandmother had a wonderful manner with other women when she
tried, although she didn't try very hard with *our crowd* as his

mother referred to the society women of Perugia. Cenni had counted on Hanna using her charm and advanced years to disarm Grazia into dangerous confidences.

The second call came from his grandmother ten minutes later. "Sorry, darling, I have a huge hangover and Madeleine's not talking to me. She let me sleep in and I asked her very specifically to call me at nine. Bitch!" Alex told his grandmother that he already knew about the hangover.

"A bitch and a snitch!" Hanna responded, and laughed dolefully. "I suppose she deserves some sympathy. She hired on as French maid to a docile old lady, a *Signora Cenni* with white curls and crocheted collars on your mother's say-so, and got herself a Swedish termagant. She handed in her notice this morning. Well, I'll miss the wild strawberries! Perhaps I should hire a Swedish masseur, someone willing to wrestle me for the champagne bottle. But no matter, love. I got the information you asked for, although I don't think it's exactly what you were hoping for. Russo was with his wife at the time the American was killed."

His grandmother was besotted with Grazia Russo, Cenni realized after hanging up the telephone. Hanna insisted that Grazia was telling the truth, that Fulvio Russo had been with his wife most of Friday afternoon, and definitely between the hours of 4:30 and 6:30, the hours that Cenni considered crucial.

"But how is it possible, Hanna?" her grandson had exclaimed. "He rarely goes home in the evening, certainly not on a Friday evening." It was a standing joke in police circles that Russo wouldn't recognize his own wife without an Identikit.

But Hanna insisted that Grazia was telling the truth, that Grazia and Fulvio had been at home Friday evening during those two hours. "They were expecting a visit from Grazia's brother, who had telephoned a little before four. He said he had something very important to discuss with both of them and he wanted Fulvio there when he arrived. Fulvio had another appointment but he canceled it after the brother-in-law called. Grazia overheard him; she had the idea that he was talking to a woman. Grazia was so happy. She planned to cook dinner herself, for the three of them. White sole! She loves to cook, something that beast rarely lets her do. He prefers their French chef. And then the brother never showed up. Shortly after six he called to say he wasn't coming, that he was late for another meeting. Fulvio left the house twenty minutes later, didn't even wait to taste her dinner. Told Grazia he was having dinner with the count and wouldn't be home until very late. The beast!"

Perhaps his grandmother *should* get a Swedish masseuse, someone with a strong Nordic will, Cenni reflected, after hanging up the telephone. French maids were too timid. After two bottles, even he would have trouble separating fact from fiction.

27

CENNI FELT ODDLY nervous as he pulled into the parking lot directly behind the church of St. Xavier in San Benedetto. He had telephoned Rita's "Gianni," now identified as Father Sebastian Breci, immediately after his meeting with Fulvio and the questore. Their conversation had been brief, friendly, and cryptic. Much had been left unsaid that needed saying, and he was genuinely surprised at his reluctance to say it. He'd been so sure that he'd conquered the tendency, ingrained in early childhood, to cower before the fathers of the Church. But apparently not. He had to remind himself again, as he had that morning, that Rita's priest was just another witness in a murder investigation, worthy of no greater regard than any of the other witnesses and, recollecting the disapproval registered by the Brooklyn taxi driver toward the wayward priest, of no lesser regard either.

The door of the rectory opened wide before he reached the porch, and Cenni knew instinctively that the man standing in the open doorway was Rita's Gianni. He was quite tall—two or three inches taller than himself—with long graceless limbs. Even from a distance, Cenni could see the priest's bony wrists hanging down a few inches below the cuffs of his black robe. If Cenni were inclined to judge the looks of other men, he would have said that the man in the open doorway was ugly, fantastically ugly even, with thinning lank hair of a nondescript brown, an amazingly hooked nose that a kinder person might call aquiline, a sharp longish chin, and an Adam's apple of a size clearly visible above the Roman collar. The priest's only attractive feature was a pair of wide-set blue eyes, startling in their intensity of color. But then Father Breci smiled, extending his hand in welcome, and his gross features were transformed into a radiance of warmth that Cenni imagined would encompass the whole of humanity. He decided at once that he liked Rita's Gianni.

Father Breci spoke first. "*Buongiorno*, Dottor Cenni. I asked our housekeeper to hold back lunch so you could join us. Father Mario, our curate, will join us as well. Afterward we can retire to my study for a private conversation."

Cenni had no wish to be disarmed by wine, food, and fine talk and later find himself needlessly gentle in his questioning, and he declined.

"Thank you, Father, that's good of you. Unfortunately, I have less than an hour to spare; another appointment," he explained politely. "I'm sorry to keep you even longer from your food, but if you don't mind . . ." He hoped his smile conveyed his intent, *No hard feelings, but I've a job to do.*

Father Breci indicated his acceptance of the commissario's agenda by leading him straight off to his study. As soon as they were behind closed doors and seated, Cenni began, *in medias res.*

"As you already know from the newspapers and our telephone conversation earlier today, Rita Minelli, a forty-five-year-old American from Brooklyn, was murdered on Good Friday in the Assisi cemetery at some time between the hours of four and eight in the evening." Cenni reached into his jacket pocket and pulled out a folded paper, a fax by its appearance, which he opened and read aloud.

"On Good Friday, between the hours of four and six, Father Sebastian Breci was hearing confessions in the Church of St. Xavier. Between six and seven on the same evening, he was in the rectory of St. Xavier preparing to say mass, his presence verified by his housekeeper and his curate. Between seven and eight, also on the same evening, he said high mass in St. Xavier, witnessed by a few hundred of his parishioners." Cenni refolded the paper and shoved it back into his pocket.

"An incontrovertible alibi, Father, particularly as it was provided by the San Benedetto Municipal Police. But I'm not here to establish your whereabouts on Good Friday. I need your help to find Rita Minelli's murderer. And I regret that in doing so, I may cause you some small embarrassment." He paused a moment and observed the priest with anxious attention.

Father Breci looked grave, and with a slight inclination of the head indicated that he understood the significance of Cenni's last statement.

He exhaled in relief. The priest was not going to dispute his relationship with Rita Minelli.

Cenni continued, "We found two diaries in Signora Minelli's room. From the first, we know that she'd had a brief affair in Brooklyn with a priest, whom she'd first met when he visited her mother to administer the last rites. From the second diary, we know that she'd met this same priest, by accident, in Florence just a few weeks ago, on March third, to be exact. From further information, obtained from a hotel proprietor in Fiesole, it appears that she and the priest stayed overnight in the hotel, in the same room," he added, and realized that his cheeks were burning. "We have reason to believe, Father, that you're the priest described in Rita Minelli's diaries." Cenni stopped and looked to the priest for confirmation.

"Yes, that's right, Dottore. But to counter your directness with some of my own, I'm puzzled as to how knowledge of my friendship with Signora Minelli will aid the police in finding her murderer. Our time together was very private, and I'm reluctant to violate that privacy, for her sake as well as my own, unless you can convince me that it serves a need beyond satisfying the voyeurism of the police or, just as likely, an obsessive need to tie up loose ends to no purpose. I am not a suspect in Signora Minelli's murder, as the fax you just quoted from clearly indicates, and which, I gather, was provided by one of our local police officials, a parishioner of mine no doubt, perhaps someone whose confession I hear, or one of the officers I take coffee with. . . ."

Cenni felt his cheeks color again as he listened to the priest. He knew at once the reason for the priest's bitter words and interrupted.

"I'm sorry, Father, I should have made it clear that the investigation by the San Benedetto police with respect to your whereabouts on Good Friday was based on a request by the questura in Perugia for the name of a local priest with a disposition to Formula One racing. We requested the name of any local priest who may have been away from San Benedetto between the evening hours of four and eight on Good Friday. I believe the wording of the request was something to the effect that we had a speeding ticket to deliver and two very angry officers who wanted to make the delivery. There was no mention in our request of a murder investigation or of you in particular."

Cenni watched as the priest readjusted his attitude. Again, the radiant smile!

"I see, of course. Very considerate of you, dottore. I don't read the dailies very often, you know, but Father Mario left his copy of Monday's *La Repubblica* on the sitting room table and I happened to see Signora Minelli's picture. It wasn't until then that I even knew of her murder. Rita was a friend, dottore, and I feel her loss to an extraordinary degree," he said sadly.

"I called my bishop immediately after seeing Rita's picture to inform him that I would be calling the police and why, but unfortunately he was away for most of yesterday and didn't return my call until a short while ago. In the meantime, you called me." Then he digressed. "I'm rather curious. How did you find me? I never gave Rita my name or my address, so that information wouldn't have been in her diaries."

"We had two sources, Father. The first was the Church of St. Francis in New York City, which was mentioned in her diary. The parish gave us the names of priests who had visited in June; your name was among them. But we actually found you by contacting the Etrusca Detective Agency in Perugia. A receipt from the agency for three hundred euros was found in Signora Minelli's purse."

"Four hundred euros from Rita to find me! Another two hundred euros from me to them, not to find me! What was *your* donation, Commissario Cenni?"

"A promise not to charge them with blackmail. Does your bishop know that you've agreed to talk to us?"

"The bishop and I always agree in theory, although not always in practice," Father Breci responded. "His Excellency is concerned that I not bring scandal on the Church and suggested that so long as there's no question of an involvement in Rita's murder that I decline to answer your questions."

"And you, Father, you don't agree?" Cenni queried.

"I prefer not to embarrass the Church, my parishioners, or myself without good cause, dottore, as I'm sure you'll understand. But in the matter of finding Rita's murderer, I have some responsibility. She was my friend. But perhaps you'll explain how by delving into my friendship with Rita you expect to find her murderer?"

Cenni stopped shilly-shallying. "Rita spent the night with you a little more than two weeks ago. We know from the autopsy report that she was about eight weeks pregnant when she died, and we also believe, from a receipt that we found in her purse for a home pregnancy kit, that she knew about the baby. She'd been having an affair with a married man in Assisi. Perhaps she'd threatened to file a paternity suit or tell his wife. I believe I know who the man is, but I have no proof. I also believe that he's the murderer." The expression in the priest's eyes was deeply sympathetic—or perhaps Cenni just wanted to tell someone about Sophie Orlic.

He continued. "There's a great deal of pressure on me from Rome to arrest a Croatian woman for Minelli's murder, a *straniera* without money or influence. This woman had a few disagreements with Rita Minelli before Good Friday; unfortunately, she's also the one who found the body. I've managed thus far not to arrest the woman despite the pressure, but I'm running out of time. I need to have identification of this married man very soon, and I'm hoping that when you met Signora Minelli in Fiesole, she may have told you about the child and talked about the father, anything concrete, perhaps even a name!"

The priest seemed for a moment scarcely to have heard Cenni's request. He stared off into space, and Cenni could see that he was thinking about something far away, and then he spoke. "It's difficult to believe that little Rita was a middle-aged woman expecting a child. Forty-five, you said! I thought she was years younger. She seemed such a child herself, desperate for love and incredibly persistent in seeking it out, even from an ugly creature like me." A less perceptive listener might have contradicted the priest's last statement, but Cenni knew that Father Breci wasn't seeking contradiction, that he was simply making a statement of fact.

The priest continued. "In this country we lock up mothers who physically abuse their children or we remove the children from their care, dottore. But we do nothing about the mothers who emotionally abuse their children, those who can't love anyone but themselves. God knows why these women have children. To satisfy some desire to reproduce themselves, I suppose, or because the Church tells them it's their duty, or because they want someone to care for them in their old age. They don't love their children; they never caress them, laugh with them, praise them, and they never let them leave. Rita's mother seemed so average to me as she lay dying in that dark ugly room, just another old woman in need of God's mercy. But God forgive her, she was a monster!"

He stopped and nodded apologetically. "I'm sorry, Dottor Cenni, you're here to inquire about a murder in Assisi on Good Friday, and I'm going on about another murder that began forty-five years ago in Brooklyn.

"In answer to your earlier question, Rita knew about the child when we met in Fiesole. She cried and laughed for most of the evening after she'd told me. She glowed when she spoke about the wonderful life they'd have together—travel, the-atre, books, music, all the things that Rita had never shared with her own mother. 'I know it's a girl, a blonde with green eyes, like her father,' she asserted at one moment. And in the next moment, she was weeping, fearful of raising the child by herself, afraid of being alone and also, I think, afraid of turning into her mother. When I asked about her family in Assisi, she cried, 'Oh them, they all hate me!'

"I offered her money, to help with the child. 'Money's not the problem,' she replied. 'I have plenty.' She didn't want to talk about the child's father, the logical person to help, I should have thought, and I didn't push her. From the little she did let out about the father, it was apparent that the romance was over; no love lost there, was my guess. What I do know about the man are a few tidbits she dropped in the course of the evening. Married; a rich wife; lives in Assisi. But no name. I'm sorry, Dottore, but those are the few sorry facts I have to offer."

It was not what Cenni had hoped for, and his disappointment was extreme. He had wanted to hear Fulvio Russo's name from an unimpeachable source, a Catholic priest, a confidante of the murdered woman, someone with a strong alibi for the evening of the murder and no axe to grind. But it was more than he'd had before and it still added up to Russo: married man, blonde with green eyes, rich wife, lives in Assisi. Further confirmation for Cenni, but nothing concrete with which to oppose the questore or any of the others who were agitating for the arrest of Sophie Orlic. He thanked the priest and was rising from his seat when Father Breci spoke again, barely audible this time. "I knew Rita had plenty of money, that she didn't need financial help. She'd told me so that night in Brooklyn. I offered money when she told me about the child because I wasn't able to offer anything else. I wanted the appearance of caring without actually caring. Perhaps if I had done more, if I had been a better Christian, she'd still be alive!"

"What more could you have done, Father? From Rita's diaries and from our interview with the Etrusca detective agency, we know that she pursued you relentlessly. You did your best—" Cenni stopped in mid-sentence, surprised at how matter of fact he sounded. He'd just glossed over the priest's guilt and pain with a rather silly, stock response. Even worse, he had joined the ranks of those who had betrayed Rita. He tried again.

"I'm truly sorry about Rita, Father. You're right, a good many people let her down, but I don't think you were one of them and I don't believe Rita thought so either. In her diary she writes with great joy of the hours that she'd spent with you; they were the happiest in her life. On the afternoon of her death, a friend—a man that she'd met in Assisi—offered to marry her, to help raise the child. On the last day of her life she was happy."

The priest had escorted Cenni to the door and stood in the doorway, watching the commissario depart, when Cenni turned abruptly and walked back.

"The day that her mother was dying, where did you come from? You appeared out of nowhere!"

"Confused you, did it? Rita asked me the same question in Fiesole, only she was under the impression that God had sent me—a Brooklyn miracle! It was through one of the curates, a classmate of mine from seminary days. We were sitting together in his study when the parish secretary handed him a request for someone to administer the last rites to Rita's mother. My friend had confessions to hear that afternoon, so I volunteered. Even after I told that to Rita, she insisted that God had sent me, that I was her own special miracle. I certainly hope not," he said, grimly, and closed the door.

28

IT WAS JUST before 2:00 when Cenni left the rectory. He still hadn't eaten and he had an appointment with the Minister of the Interior in Rimini at three. That appointment he'd also made in the morning, but with the fervent expectation that he could cancel it after his meeting with Father Breci. Counting his chickens! The few bits of information that the priest had provided, although pointing to Russo, were hardly sufficient to get Carlo off his back, and to give Carlo his due, to get the PM and his powerful friends off the questore's back. There was nothing for it; he'd have to fall back on his last resort, blackmail. But not on an empty stomach.

In summer, San Benedetto del Tronto is packed shoulder-to-shoulder with tourists. In August, the cars are double-parked, bumper-to-bumper, for miles along the Adriatic coast road, directly across from the miles of side-by-side seafood restaurants, cafés, wine bars, pizza stands, gelaterie, and pasticcerie. For a quick lunch, he needed only one to be open. But aside from a lone umbrella blocking the horizon and a few intrepid souls wading in the foamy brine—northern Europeans, he supposed, as no self-respecting Italian would be seen in a bathing suit before June—the beachfront was forlorn and most of the shops were shuttered. Finally, he spied an open café, advertised by two flying standards: the blue-and-white pennant of the San Benedetto third division team (not doing particularly well this year) and the red-and-black pennant of first division Milan (also not doing well, upon which Cenni reflected with some pleasure). He particularly disliked Milan, and when Perugia was finally out of the running for the league cup, which was almost always, he rooted for whatever team was likely to rout the red and black. He hoped the food was better than the proprietor's taste in football.

The place was overrun with Milan paraphernalia: various-sized red-and-black pennants, team pictures, team shirts, and in the place of honor, an autographed blow-up of Paolo Maldini. Even the man behind the counter was dressed in red and black. Cenni was starved and the food in the display case looked surprisingly good: at least five different types of seafood tramezzini, including shrimp and egg, his favorite. He ordered two and a short coffee.

"Nice picture of Maldini," he commented to the rather sour-looking proprietor who served him his coffee and sandwiches. "Great defender! Beautiful play he made last week against Inter, moving the ball behind Vieri to pass off to Rivaldo."

The sour look immediately disappeared and the smile that the proprietor gave the commissario could have lighted the heavens. "*Certo*, signore. If the refereeing weren't so biased, we would have won that game. But for sure, this Sunday we'll be back. Perugia is a cakewalk." Cenni smiled and asked for his bill and a "shrimp and egg" to go. Just as he reached the door, the proprietor called him back. "Signore, for you—on the house—for luck this Sunday!" He handed Cenni the largest of the red-and-black pennants that he had for sale.

29

RIMINI CAME ON him all too soon. It was already 3:00, the hour of his appointment, and he had yet to decide on a strategy. It wasn't that he hadn't been thinking about it since leaving San Benedetto, but his mind had refused to settle. He had the weapons to win but the stakes were high, too high for a single strategy. He'd have to stay loose, listen, feel, digest the silences He was no longer playing children's games with the questore. Montoni was the most influential of the PM's ministers, and rumored to be the most dangerous.

The Rimini of beaches and bars he knew very well. He had spent two summers there when he was at university, much to the distress of his mother, who thought it demeaning to have a son who managed a video arcade. Chiara had worked as a waitress in one of the posh hotels, and on the nights when they were off together, they would cruise the seedy bars and nightclubs that lay between the railroad tracks and the beach, drinking beer with tequila chasers. They told themselves they were living *la dolce vita.* Later, when the bars had closed, they would make their way to the beach, retching and reeling with drink, and after making love would wash off the sand and the sex in the warm Adriatic waters. Chiara had once proposed that they visit the old town for history's sake—but they never quite made it.

Montoni's house was in the historic part of town, a stone two-story building a few steps from the Piazza Malatesta. He rang the bell exactly five minutes after 3:00, not at all surprised that the door had not opened wide as he approached. He hadn't been explicit on the telephone, but the minister knew why he was coming and would use psychological advantage, for sure make him wait. No matter, he was good at games.

A maid answered the door finally, took his name and his coat, and led him into a large entrance hall. He looked around, wondering what manner of lifestyle suited the PM's most ruthless minister. Cenni imagined that Montoni would be quite good at chess, having managed to hold the PM's shaky coalition together through five assaults in the previous year alone. He couldn't tell much about the minister from lurking in the hallway. The furnishings were about what one would expect: all in meticulous taste, nothing bold or original, antiques or knock-offs that one sees in the better furniture stores and decorating magazines, nothing that revealed the personality of the owner—with a single exception. A pair of elephants with their trunks entwined was carved into a massive stone plaque set high above the entranceway. It was the armorial bearing of the Malatesta family.

"Buona Sera!" The voice was deep and throaty, and Cenni recognized it at once. He turned to find the minister standing directly behind him. Isotta Montoni was one of those rare

women about whom the word handsome could be used without it sounding foolish or old fashioned. She was a large
woman and unusually tall, just an inch or so shorter than he
was, and in very high heels, they stood shoulder-to-shoulder.
Her hair was black, a dyed, glossy raven black, and combed
conservatively, straight down and pushed behind her ears. He
knew she was in her mid-fifties, yet the skin of her face was taut.
She showed none of the softening lines of age. Whether this
was accidental—a woman too busy in pursuit of a prominent
career to lie in the sun—or planned vanity, it suited her image
well. Her eyes were also dark, almost black, almond-flecked
and slanted in shape, giving her a Eurasian appearance,
although he was aware that she claimed a long lineage in
Emilia-Romagna—a direct descent from Sigismondo Malatesta
and Isotta degli Atti, she had written in her recently published
memoir. The experts in Italian heraldry said otherwise, but in
considering Isotta Montoni's lust for power and the infamous
lusts of her ancestors in attribution, Cenni was inclined to
give Montoni the edge. She offered her hand and he took it,
not at all surprised by the strong grip. A consummate politi-
cian, she knew the value of a bruising handshake.

"*Buona Sera,*" Cenni replied. "I hope I'm not too late."
Might as well assert that he'd kept her waiting. Gain the upper
hand. She smiled, recognizing the gambit.

"Traffic, Dottore," she said. "Well no matter, you're here
now. Please come into the sitting room."

After they were seated across from one another, in matching
white leather chairs—the perfect foil for her all-black per-
sona—he waited for her to begin. Actually, they both waited.
But finally, perhaps to establish her senior position, she started.
"You said on the telephone that you wished to talk about my
son and that you hoped he would join us at this meeting. My
son is in the house, of course, but I think we should proceed

without him, at least until I understand what this is about. I'm
sure you'll agree, Dottor Cenni." Her tight smile said clearly,
We'll do it my way.

Cenni had begun badly with Father Breci. It had taken him
too long to get to the point. He took a more direct course with
the minister.

"I'm investigating the murder of an American in Assisi, the
cousin of your son's girlfriend Paola Casati. During the course of
my investigation, I've learned that your son and Paola were
involved in the December bombing of McDonald's. The murdered American was also aware of their involvement. She'd
threatened to expose them, to go to the newspapers if they
didn't acknowledge responsibility for what they'd done. On
the afternoon of the murder, your son and the Casati girl were
seen together in Assisi. We have witnesses who heard them
arguing in a bar about the American less than a ten minute
walk from the scene of the murder. Neither of them have adequate alib—"

She interrupted. "Dottore, if you're here to declare that my
son is an accomplice to murder, I don't know why you're discussing it with his mother, although I certainly appreciate your
attention to my . . . how shall we say? . . . my maternal concerns.
Shouldn't you be talking to Giulio? Perhaps I should call him—
now?" The smile she directed at him was deadly venomous.

"Oh-h, but before I do that, perhaps you would clarify one
thing. After you'd telephoned this morning, I spoke to my son
about your visit. Giulio tells me that you interviewed him and
Paola in Perugia on Monday and that he and Paola provided
alibis for the time of the murder, with a very reliable witness, a
ranger from the National Park Service. Paola and my son were
having it on, as my son terms it, in his car at the top of Mount
Subasio when a family of wild boar attacked his car. This officer heard the noise and came to investigate. I wonder, Dottore,

why one officer of the law is making assertions that can so easily be countered by another officer's testimony? Policing alla the provinces, I can only suppose."

Her enemies referred to Montoni as the black widow. It suits her, Cenni thought.

"*Onorevole*, let me clarify," he replied. "Together they've offered an alibi for the time between five and seven, and Paola Casati can account for her time, with witnesses, between seven and eight when she was attending the Good Friday procession. But we have unfortunately been unable to place your son between seven and eight, and both of them between four and five—two blocks of unsubstantiated time, giving them each the opportunity to have murdered the American, singly or together. The motive we've already discussed. I reviewed these lapses in your son's alibi with him at length on Monday; apparently, *onorevole*, he's forgotten to mention the lapses to mamma," he added with unnecessary sarcasm. Giulio Montoni brought out the worst in him.

He continued. "Let's stop sparring. I can charge your son and the Casati girl with Minelli's murder but I doubt that I'll convince the investigating judge to jail them. I'm not even sure the questore will permit me to bring them before the investigating judge, but if I make the charge and a fuss, and I'll do both, it'll be in all the newspapers. And I mean all the dailies. This is way too hot for any of them to pass up, even those who don't like offending the PM. What's more, Paola Casati provided me with a written statement of her involvement in the McDonald's bombing and it incriminates your son as the leader. Your son, *onorevole*, walked away and let others in the group take the blame!" No reason at this point to hold back, he'd decided.

"I want something from you and I'm willing to give something in return. But if I don't get my something, Paola Casati's statement goes to the papers along with my statement implicating your son in Minelli's murder. I'm not naive enough to believe that the son of the Minister of the Interior will actually be charged with a crime, but I'm absolutely certain that the political furor will shake the PM's coalition to its very shaky foundations."

She responded without a flicker of emotion. "Put it on the table, Dottore. Let's see what we're fighting over. That is, if we're fighting over anything."

He said, "Someone close to the PM is applying pressure, daily, on the questore. I've been told twice already to arrest the woman who found the body, a Croatian, for Minelli's murder."

"So why don't you arrest her, Dottore? Don't tell me all this fuss is over a *straniera*. Is she perhaps very beautiful?" she asked, her eyes locked to his, a slight twist to her full mouth. She's mocking me, he thought.

"She's innocent, and I want the pressure off, today. I also want a name. Who's applying the pressure!"

"Two somethings, Dottore! You said one! Do I get two in return?" she asked, her tone bordering on the flirtatious.

He pulled a folded white paper from his jacket pocket. "Paola Casati's statement, the only copy in existence!" She leaned forward as though to take it, and he drew back.

"It would seem, Dottor Cenni, that you're quite comfortable in your present position, with no ambitions to move on. I find that regrettable. You seem to have some remarkable gifts." She smiled. "I'll give you your beautiful Croatian, Dottore. Don't look for anything more," she added, extending her hand for the paper.

Cenni still held back. He wanted to know where the pressure was coming from. If from Giorgio Zangarelli, it was one more proof of Russo's guilt. Two years ago, Zangarelli, then an

active member of the PM's coalition, had tried to take Isotta
Montoni out in a violent disagreement over immigration quo-
tas. Zangarelli used cheap immigrant labor in his fish-packing
business, mainly Albanians who came into Italy through Brin-
disi. Montoni had won and the Albanian quota was cut, but
even in victory she was not one to forgive. If the pressure were
coming from Zangarelli, she'd give him up readily.

"Two somethings? I think that's doable for someone I like,
Dottore. The paper, please."

30

UNTIL RIMINI, ALEX had planned to eat a solitary meal
later that evening at La Cantina, where he ate his dinner three
or four times a week. It was a trattoria of no account, a local
food critic had written, but he liked the food and the prices.
Scratch that, he decided, on the drive back. It was the first time
in six days that he could stop worrying about Sophie Orlic. He
needed an outlet for his relief.

Isotta Montoni had left him alone in her sitting room for
ten minutes while she'd gone to make a telephone call. In the
end, she came through with exactly what he wanted. The pressure would be removed and, as a bonus, Giorgio Zangarelli's
name was printed in childlike letters on a scrap of paper. "I
hope she's worth it, Dottore, your beautiful Croatian. You shot
yourself in the foot today. But not to worry. Giorgio may not
like you, but I do."

When he was leaving, she shooed away the maid and helped
him with his overcoat, brushing against him seductively. He
could feel the pressure of her knee against the back of his and
he blushed like a schoolboy. She laughed when she saw his confusion. "I never let politics interfere with my pleasures, Dottore.
Call my office the next time you're in Rome," she said and

slipped her card into his breast pocket. No chance of that, he thought as he exited the super strata at Gubbio, but he had figured out on the return trip what it was that he needed.

It seemed to him most of the time that everything in Italy is illegal. Fines are imposed for putting doors in places where windows had been, for putting windows in places where doors had been, and for anything else nonsensical that the legislators could legislate. Unlike the laws on windows and doors, however, which shone clear in the cold light of day, the laws on prostitution were nebulous, perhaps because it was chiefly a nighttime activity. Even the commissario, who was now in his sixteenth year as a police officer and a graduate of the finest law school in Italy, had trouble distinguishing between what was and what was not legal. For Sonila, the woman in Gubbio that he was on his way to visit, it was crystal clear. "What I do in my place is my business, and what I charge in my place is my business." Cenni tended to agree. He'd been visiting Sonila for fifteen years, beginning the year after Chiara had been kidnapped. They were close in age, although Sonila might be a few years older. Not that she admitted to it. In her record book, she had lost a few years in their time together while Cenni had found a few.

Five years ago, at about the same time that he'd visited Sandro, his Freudian friend, he'd had long discussions with himself about his reluctance to accept the loss of Chiara, to marry and have children, to stop visiting Sonila. This internal debate had raged on for six months. In the end, he'd even told Sonila about it. She'd stopped the debate in its tracks. "*Caro,* when the time comes you'll know." He was beginning to wonder if the time had come. Four nights in a row, he'd had the same nightmare. A young woman, always with flaxen hair, turns into a crying, terrified child. He and the child are pursued by an unknown enemy, whose faces he cannot see and whose footsteps are always gaining on him. Last night he'd awoken twice in a cold sweat; twice he'd tried to drop the child to save himself and both times he had failed. She had wrapped her legs so tightly around his torso that he couldn't let go.

Daytime was not much better. He was fixated on Sophie Orlic. He had just risked his job to blackmail a minister of state, and he was not sure of his motive. Was he fighting to save Sophie because she was innocent or was he bewitched by her blonde beauty, by her resemblance to Chiara? The similarities were outward only, not even that. Sophie, at thirty-seven, was far more beautiful than Chiara had been at twenty, but the Croatian's beauty was a frozen dead thing and her temperament was brooding and contemptuous; she was detached from everything and everyone around her.

She was nothing like Chiara, who had loved to laugh, or like Sergeant Antolini for that matter. The sergeant had a dazzling smile. Renato had once accused him of being contrary. "You always take the opposing view purely for the pleasure of disagreement," his brother had yelled in frustration during one of their heated discussions on football. What if Renato were on to something? With the exception of Elena and Sergeant Antolini, everyone else concerned in the case was convinced that Sophie was the murderer. Sonila has a Freudian bent; she'll sort me out, Cenni decided. Besides he needed her tonight. He was horny.

Book Six

Things are what they are.

I

THREE TIMES IN five minutes tourists looking up at the message boards rather than in front of them had collided with the commissario and then excused themselves in languages other than Italian. *Sorry mate, perdone, oops* (the last was not even an apology). The coffee at the station bar was barely drinkable. He had two short ones after getting off the train. And the cornetti would shame even an Irishman, or was it an Englishman? Both, he decided. He had two cornetti as well. And yet, Rome Termini was still one of the more exciting, exasperating, and Italian of places to be in the capital—a bit like Naples, he often thought, but with a purpose.

Zangarelli's secretary had given him an appointment for eleven when he had called the previous evening. *L'onorevole* is having breakfast with the Prime Minister, she had told him, showing off. It sounded like *l'onorevole* was coming back into his own, which was hardly good news. Isotta Montoni, Cenni's other *l'onorevole*, had been quite specific that Giorgio Zangarelli was his nemesis in Rome. Cenni was way out of line coming to see the man, but he had a policeman's hunch. His grandmother's drunken evening with Grazia Russo had yielded

more than just misinformation about Fulvio's whereabouts on
Good Friday. The bottle of Brunello Reserve that the two
women had shared led to secrets being exchanged, marital
secrets in Grazia's case. *Giorgio hates Fulvio*, she'd had told
Hanna. Every time we're alone together, he yells at me to get
a divorce. So if *Giorgio hates Fulvio*, why is Giorgio making my
life a hell by pulling strings for Fulvio? One way to find out,
Cenni decided. Ask Giorgio.

At precisely one minute to 11:00 *l'onorevole*'s secretary
escorted the commissario into the great man's office. "He'll
be with you shortly," she said, and left him to look around at
the oak-paneled walls and elaborately carved ceiling mold-
ings with some irony. Democracy is a wonderful thing, he
thought. We should try it some time. His own office, with
matching wooden desk and chair and an antique file cabinet
(no separators though), was considered something of a perk by
his colleagues, but it paled in comparison to what was considered appropriate for a member of parliament. The paintings
and sculpture and Persian rugs were no doubt personal
items—one of the paintings was an early de Chirico—but the
highly polished marble floors were the same in all the offices
he had passed. That his entire detective squad would fit comfortably in Zangarelli's inner office was just too irritating for
comment, Cenni decided.

"Do you like abstract art, Dottore?" a voice asked, startling
Cenni, who had just slipped on his glasses (for reading only)
to check the signature on a painting of red, green, and yellow
swirls (or was it blue?) that was hanging next to the de Chirico.

"This one, not particularly," Cenni responded, turning
around to greet his interlocutor. "But mostly, yes, I do."

"I agree with you about that one—childish. I'm trading it
and one other for a Jackson Pollack," Zangarelli replied with
a generous smile. He walked over to Cenni to shake hands, and

the two of them stood together for a quiet moment, observing the interlocking swirls.

Cenni had heard *Il Lupino* speak of his brother-in-law more times than he cared to remember, but he'd never met him in person. He had always imagined him as a smarmy, menacing type, laced in gold jewelry. Seeing Zangarelli for the first time today, Cenni realized that he had prejudged the man, but he had some excuse: any brother-in-law of *Il Lupino*'s, etc., etc.

The senator was in his mid-forties, of medium height and slight build, had dark olive skin, intense green eyes, a full mouth, straight nose, and by most standards of pulchritude (Italy set the gold standard), he was quite good looking. He was dressed impeccably in a business suit and displayed no flourishes of gold, not even on his wrist, which sported a leather watchband. Equally surprising, his speech had none of the Calabrian slide of r's and t's. In fact, he had no discernible regional accent whatsoever. The Zangarelli fortune had been accumulating for two generations now, but it generally took more than two generations to mold an Italian gentleman. *L'onorevole* was a fast learner.

"Dottor Cenni, you neglected to give my secretary a reason for this meeting, other than saying it's highly confidential. I agreed to see you because of my sister. Grazia tells me you have a very nice grandmother." He smiled graciously.

Their meeting was brief, under thirty minutes, with only a few of them focused on the Minelli case. Cenni put out a few feelers with no response from Zangarelli. The remainder of the meeting was devoted to Fulvio. Zangarelli had turned into a human Vesuvius, spewing out epithets in Calabrian that left nothing to the imagination, even to an uninitiated Umbrian. Cenni left the Piazza Madama very sure that Zangarelli was not acting on Fulvio's behalf. He'd actually found himself apologizing to Zangarelli for his part in Fulvio's reassignment to peaceful Assisi, and not to some remote and dangerous outpost in Sardinia or Sicily.

"I'm insulted, Dottore," Zangarelli had snapped. "You thought I'd let a fool like Fulvio represent me in a scheme to buy up half of Umbria. I kept quiet for Grazia's sake; she loves the bastard." He grinned outrageously before his next comment. "It's difficult to arrange an accident in Assisi and have it look natural."

Alex had more than an hour to kill before his train left for Chiusi, and he walked slowly through the twisting narrow streets of Rome, stopping twice for a coffee to help him think. Zangarelli had listened politely to him and he to Zangarelli, but neither of them had revealed much beyond their absolute contempt for Fulvio until just as he was leaving. "Dottore, your family's well established in Umbrian society, at least that's what Grazia tells me. Don't you people stick together? Signora Casati . . . Artemisia; it's a damned shame what you . . . what the police have put her through this week, and all because of a *straniera*. What are you going to do about it?" And then. "Surprising, isn't it, that she's still unmarried, a woman like that? So beautiful and the daughter of a count—a real catch!"

Cenni didn't say anything in defense of the police, just shrugged. Yes, he thought—a real catch!

2

"BUGGER ALL! HOW MANY times do I have to tell you? No calls, particularly from my wife." Fulvio Russo's high-pitched voice came screeching across the transom into the interrogation room where Sergeant Antolini was hiding out, pretending to file.

Why does she put up with him? Genine wondered. With her money she could have him whacked. Cheaper than divorce! And then she grinned, remembering Grazia's brother. Wouldn't even cost.

Ever since finding his cashmere scarf in the dumpster, Genine had been paying close attention to *Il Lupino*, hoping he'd screw up again, say or do something incriminating that she could pass on to Alex. She had certainly noticed a difference in his temper in the last few days and in his habits. Everyone had, particularly after the countess had killed herself. He never left his office now; it was close to 5:00, and yesterday and today he had been impossible, driving Lucille to tears three times. He was at it again.

Worse, all of a sudden he was her best buddy, stopping by her desk umpteen times to ask her umpteen questions about the Minelli investigation. Did Cenni have any new clues? Had Cenni given her a copy of the forensics report? What specifically did Cenni have her working on? Cenni, Cenni, Cenni! And always at the end, why hasn't Cenni arrested the Croatian? And today, out of the blue, "I hear Cenni has another suspect—a priest, the father of Minelli's child. What's that about?"

"What new suspect?" she'd replied. How did he know about the priest? Piero had sworn her to secrecy; the stuff in Minelli's diaries was strictly *need to know*, on Alex's orders. For self-protection, she was now hiding out in the interrogation room. It was next to his office but he never came near it: too close to the women's toilet, which on most days smelled of sewer gas—something to do with a faulty return the janitor said. Funny enough, the men's toilet smelled fine.

She heard his office phone ring again. He picked it up after three rings with his usual impatience, his tone loud and aggressive, but his voice dropped a few notches almost immediately. She strained to hear but all she caught at the end were a few muffled words. *Call back* and some random numbers.

She looked across the room at the transom, which was wide

open. Why not? Slipping off her shoes, she carried her chair over to the connecting door and climbed up. Just in time too, as his *telefonino* rang almost immediately. He spoke softly so she couldn't hear everything, but she heard enough. "*Sì, ho capito* . . . the cemetery."

And then, loud and clear, "At seven—I'll be there!"

3

THE ONLY MIRROR in her tiny apartment was an ugly unframed piece of glass indiscriminately covered with black spots where the silver lining had worn off. Sophie generally kept it turned to the wall, having no use for it. She wore no makeup, not even lipstick and on most mornings she combed her hair by rote. It was strange that she cared so little now about how she looked. She had once been quite vain. Her grandmother, who knew much of Shakespeare by heart, had often quoted Lear's fool to Sophie when she'd catch her only grandchild preening in front of the mirror, "There was never yet fair woman but she made mouths in a glass," her grandmother would say, and then nullify the effect of her scolding, by hugging and kissing her beautiful Sophie. Before she was five years old, even before she began school, Sophie knew that she was beautiful. Friends of her grandfather who visited the house would slip her a few coins, for sweets they said, and then ask for a kiss in reward. She would stand on tiptoe, put her arms around their necks, and kiss them on their cheeks, even the ones who came direct from the fields smelling of sweat. She liked the power that she had over them. She also liked the chocolates that she would buy with their coins.

Sergio had liked her vanity. He was pleased when other men admired his wife. Even at the very beginning of their marriage, when there was little for extras, there was always money for a strapless evening dress or a pair of dangling earrings. She always knew when men desired her, and in Baranj she had applied her makeup with care whenever she had visited the pharmacy, where she would flirt with Visnar, a harmless diversion. Once he had tried to kiss her, and she had laughed and pushed him away.

Sophie wished that her grandmother had quoted the poet who'd said *Vanity is a snare*. Visnar had raped Christina and then killed Sergio, the two people she loved most in the world. Once the knowledge that she was admired had excited her, but that was in another lifetime. Two years ago, when she was caretaker for Anna Casati, the count had tried to kiss her in his mother's bathroom. She had been washing out a pair of his mother's soiled panties. He had apologized afterward, after she had pushed him away. That same evening she had cut off her hair, "almost to the roots," the countess had remarked in horror when she saw Sophie the next day. Even if the countess had played dumb, Sophie was sure that Artemisia knew why; she had been jealous of her for years. Whenever Sophie and the count were in the same room together, Artemisia would follow her father possessively with her eyes.

A film of dust had accumulated on the surface of the glass and she wiped it off with the bottom of her dress. The lipstick that she'd borrowed from Alba was saturated in cheap perfume, and she retched as she lavishly applied the opaque red color to her pursed lips. She peered intently at her face in the mirror, trying to see herself as he would see her. The diffused late-afternoon light filtered through the dirt-encrusted window of her apartment, revealing deep shadows under her eyes, soft bluish bruises that came after nights of restless sleep. She should have borrowed some face power from Alba. Talcum might help, she thought, and tried some, but the chalky powder only made the shadows more pronounced. She hadn't slept deeply in months, other than in the early morning hours when, physically exhausted, she would lose consciousness, falling into dreamless death. Christina's doctor had given her forty sleeping pills when she had visited Zagreb two months earlier. They're very powerful, he had warned, and at first she had used them sparingly. In the beginning she broke the pills in half, but when the dreams returned she took them whole.

It began one morning when she'd found a small yellow caterpillar on her bed. She'd killed it and dropped it into the trash. The next morning she'd found a second caterpillar, an even larger one. It was on her pillow, lying next to her right ear. It hadn't come through the window. The window in her apartment had been painted shut, the frame welded to the sash, and couldn't be opened. She'd tried chipping away the paint with a screwdriver, but the sash was covered by many layers of old paint, and she was afraid that if she continued chipping, she would break the sash or even the window. The rent was only two hundred and fifty euros a month, and she didn't want to lose the apartment, so she'd left the window alone. And there was no way for even an ant to come through the front door after she had installed rubber liners around the wooden frame to keep out the cold. She checked the drains—the sink and the bathtub—but there was no way the caterpillars could have come through either opening. When she wasn't running water, she left rubber stoppers over the outlets and she always kept the toilet seat down. The commune was working to repair the earthquake damage all over Assisi, and she'd seen large gray rats balanced like tightrope walkers on the drainpipes that lay exposed in the open ditches. Rats come into the house through the drains and the toilet, her grandmother had told her. She wasn't stupid, either, as Christina's doctor had implied when he'd asked about her flower arrangements. She checked the flowers for bugs and insects before she left the florist and then afterward, again, when she reached home, and she always tightly wrapped the discarded greens in newspaper before throwing them away.

When she was ten, her best friend had told her about an insect that could climb into an elephant's ear and devour its brain. For months afterward, Sophie had awakened in the night from bad dreams, only to have her grandmother lull her back to sleep. In the dreams that had begun eight months ago, the caterpillars were feeding on her—the small intestines, then the large, her organs, and finally her face. The dream always ended before they reached her eyes. The caterpillars would exit from her mouth and nose, carrying little bits of red flesh, and she would awake and find that her bedclothes were soaked with sweat, and sometimes with urine. She knew that she cried out in the night because her landlord had asked twice in the last two days if she'd had a visitor in her room. The screaming would have to stop, he'd said.

Sophie refused to believe Dr. Bocic when he told her that the dreams were a delayed effect of the trauma that she had suffered six years before. Always he said the same thing: "Sophie, you must grieve. Weep, for Christina's sake, for Sergio, but most of all for yourself. Catharsis will come if you release the pain. The pain grows and hardens every day that you refuse to acknowledge it. Christina will get better, I promise you, and when she does she'll need a mother who can feel, not a machine to make money."

Then on Holy Thursday Dr. Bocic had called her, very excited. Christina had mentioned her father for the first time; she'd said very little, asked only where he was buried, but still it was a beginning. At the suggestion of an old friend, an eminent clinician, he had tried a new drug regime—divalproex, a mood stabilizer, with the usual dosage of paroxetine—and Christina had responded well. And he had other news. This same friend ran a clinic in Switzerland for patients with post-traumatic stress disorder. Acknowledged as one of the best in Europe, the clinic had had great successes with victims of war crimes, and as a kindness to him his friend had agreed to accept Christina now that she was beginning to respond to treatment. The cost would be minimal, a thousand euros a month to cover food and her bed and another thousand euros for travel expenses. And Christina would have to be accompanied to Switzerland by at least one medical attendant.

On Good Friday Sophie had asked the countess if she would lend her the money. She had agreed immediately and then five days later she was dead. Sophie thought briefly about asking the count for the money, particularly after he'd read her Amelia's suicide letter. "Please help Sophie as she's helped me," Amelia had written, almost her very last words. But Sophie was afraid that the count might ask for more in return than she was willing to give. And she would need money every month, maybe for years, if she were to pay a thousand euros a month for Christina's keep.

The truth was in that letter. The American had been lying face-up when Sophie had found her in the Casati vault. In her letter, Amelia had written that she'd left Minelli lying face-down. And then Lucia had confirmed Sophie's suspicions. She'd stopped Sophie yesterday, on Corso Mazzini dying for a gossip. "Rita Minelli was suffocated," Lucia told Sophie, not waiting for the prefatory chitchat before launching into her explosive news. "The countess didn't kill her. Someone else did!" she added, without trying to lower her voice. "I just happened to overhear Commissario Russo talking to the count," she added in explanation. If Amelia were not the killer, then Sophie knew who was. It all made sense, finally. Everything that had happened on Good Friday fell into place. Anything that had seemed strange or oddly distorted had an explanation.

On Good Friday, midway through creating bouquets for Easter, with flowers and greens everywhere, on the kitchen table, in the sink, the tub, on the floor, even on the bed, Sophie's bell rang. It was the countess. Sophie buzzed her in and watched silently as she stumbled up the steps, holding on to the hand railing, her legs almost too weak to support her shaking body. She was completely distraught, out of breath, sobbing, yet trying to talk at the same time. Sophie had tried to calm her, urged her to sit on the bed and drink some water, but the countess shook her head, and instead grabbed Sophie's hands for support. She wouldn't let go. Sophie still had faint thumb marks on the insides of her wrists where the countess had squeezed too hard. It took the countess a few seconds before she could summon breath to speak. When she finally could talk, it was in hoarse whispers.

"I killed her," she said twice and began to cry, but quietly this time, not sobbing wildly as before.

"Who did you kill?" Sophie asked insistently, but the countess didn't seem to hear. She stared blindly in front of her and then her eyes widened in horror.

"The baby, Sophie. I killed Rita and she's having a baby."

Finally she sat—on the edge of the bed—and made a conscious effort to calm herself. She inhaled deeply, drank a few sips of the water that Sophie had offered earlier, and recounted what had happened. At first she asserted that Rita was dead and the baby was dead. "I'm a murderer!" she cried. "They'll send me to prison!" And the next moment she was begging Sophie to return with her to the cemetery. "Remember that night when the count's mother almost died, Sophie, when she'd stopped breathing. You saved her life! You can save the baby's life, too!" she pleaded.

Sophie was sure that the countess was mistaken and she told her so. "A little whack on the head never killed anyone. Your niece is still alive. Perhaps she was unconscious for a minute or two, but she's fine now. She's probably back at the house looking for you." They agreed finally that Sophie should go to the cemetery. "You stay here," she told the countess. "I can walk faster if I'm alone."

She grabbed her cloak from the peg and the keys that were hanging underneath. She remembered Sergio's words the time that Christina had tumbled from her bicycle and knocked herself out. "Heads are designed to take blows, Sophie; otherwise most of us wouldn't enjoy life past the age of five." Sophie was certain that Minelli was all right, and that the countess was needlessly hysterical. She reasoned that when Minelli came around and found herself alone, she'd have left the cemetery, probably locking the vault and the side gate behind her. Sophie knew that the American had keys to both.

A few weeks earlier, a potential client had asked Sophie to visit her family's mausoleum to give her a quote for a flower arrangement. Sophie had visited in early evening after the front gates were locked and had seen Fulvio Russo leave the Casati vault, followed minutes later by Rita Minelli. She watched from behind one of the larger mausoleums as Rita locked the vault gate. Sophie wasn't surprised. It was no secret—at least not to her—that Russo used the cemetery for sexual liaisons. During his interrogation of her the previous summer, over the question of Irene Rapaic's passport, he'd suggested that she might meet him in one of the vaults. "A little charge of blackmail can easily be dropped," he'd hinted with a smirk.

That was probably the reason for Minelli's visit to the vault on Good Friday, a liaison with Russo! Why else would she be there, with it so close to dark? If Minelli had locked the gates after her, Sophie would need her keys to get in, the larger one to the side gate and the smaller one to the vault. It was already ten to 6:00 and would be dark very soon, no point fumbling around looking for the right key among twenty-odd ones, she reasoned. She removed the two keys from the ring. "I'll be back in less than twenty minutes. Stop worrying," she'd said to the countess. "Your niece is fine."

When Sophie got to the side gate, she found it unlocked and for just a moment she panicked. What if it were true? What if the countess had killed her niece? She thought of turning back, of calling the police, but she didn't trust the police; she was a *straniera*. Even before she reached the vault, she saw the gate swinging in the wind and from the porch, in the waning light, she saw the body stretched out on the stone floor, the head resting on the first altar step. She knelt beside the body and felt for a pulse but she knew it was useless. The eyes were open, staring up at her but without sight. The countess was right. She had killed Rita and her baby!

It was the baby that put the idea into Sophie's head to create a diversion, something to draw attention to Minelli's pregnancy and to direct the police to look at the men in her life. She knelt beside the body and gently closed the dead woman's eyes, and then she crossed herself. Sophie hadn't liked Rita Minelli, but they were both devout Catholics, and even one's enemies deserved reverence in death. When Sophie lifted the dead woman's hips to unhook her stockings, she spied the pen with its silver pinstriped cap lying under the body. Sophie had seen the countess write checks many times using the same pen. It must have fallen out of her pocket when she'd struck her niece with the statue. She slipped it into her own pocket. Then, catching hold of the bottom of her cloak, she used it to hold the statue of the Virgin while she wiped it clean of prints using the bottom of her dress. Minelli's purse was lying partially open on one of the altar steps. Holding the purse with her cloak, she removed the billfold. Eight hundred euros were inside. If she took the money, it would create another diversion. Who would accuse the countess of murdering someone for a measly eight hundred euros? And it would almost pay for Christina's trip to Zurich. She slipped the bills into her pocket and wiped the billfold before returning it to Minelli's purse. The peonies, still wrapped in their florist paper, were on the altar, the perfect alibi for the countess if someone had seen her outside the house. *I took them to Sophie to put in the Easter arrangement,* the countess would tell the police. She dumped the water from the vases and wiped their surfaces with her dress.

Sophie was exhilarated when she locked the vault gate. She'd thought of everything: the diversion, the flowers, the fingerprints, even the money. It was sheer luck that she'd found the pen! But she wouldn't have found it if she hadn't thought of the diversion. It wasn't until she reached the side gate that she stopped congratulating herself. She'd locked the vault out of habit. Only someone with a key could have locked the vault.

She stayed calm. She reached into her cloak pocket for the key, but it wasn't there, just the larger key to the side gate. After five minutes of searching along the path, she gave up. It was now dark, and she could barely see her feet in front of her. She had to get back to the countess. She'd said twenty minutes and it was now closer to thirty. She'd figure something out later.

Amelia was eerily calm when Sophie told her that Rita was dead. "I knew it," she said. Sophie also told her that she had worked everything out. "The police will never suspect you." Amelia accepted this, too, without question but she denied that the pen was hers.

"Mine is a fountain pen, Sophie. This is a ballpoint. Isn't it just like Rita to buy a Mont Blanc ballpoint?" They reasoned together that it must have fallen out of Rita's purse.

Sophie didn't find the key, so she borrowed her assistant's the next morning and pretended when she inserted the key that the gate was unlocked. There was no way that the police could disprove her story, that she'd lost the key on Saturday morning. She'd slipped the pen back into the American's purse before they reached the police station, while Alba was distracted. It had disappeared after that! Commissario Cenni had shown her the list of items found in Rita's handbag and it was not on the list. But it was clear now.

The pen was Fulvio Russo's. He must have dropped it when he'd smothered the American. When Russo signed her release papers on Saturday he'd used a pen very like it, but she'd thought nothing of it at the time. As the countess had said on Friday, *Lots of people own Mont Blanc pens.* Fulvio Russo was the father of Minelli's child; he'd pay to keep his wife from finding out.

A thousand euros a month would mean nothing to him; he was rich. But she wasn't stupid like the American; she knew how to protect herself. She'd write a letter and address it to Commissario Cenni. She'd give one copy to Lucia and swear her to secrecy; the other copy she'd leave in her room. She'd tell Russo about the letter even before she asked him for the money. She had it all worked out. She wouldn't become a victim like the American.

Russo was to meet her behind the Casati vault at seven o'clock. There would still be some light. She looked at the hands of the small desk clock that Sergio had given her for her twenty-fifth birthday. Six forty-three. The plainclothes detective was still slouched against the restaurant door. He observed everyone who walked by, mainly the young girls, but he rarely looked up at her window. She had watched him now for five days and knew his habits, probably better than he knew hers. At precisely 6:45, he would go inside the restaurant for a coffee, more likely a grappa, and would stay inside for ten minutes. She could walk from her door to the cemetery gates in less than ten minutes. She'd worry later about how to get back into her apartment without being seen.

4

Artemisia watched as the workmen removed the painting from the wall. They worked slowly and with great care, aware that she stood within two feet of them, paying jealous attention to their every move. She was the curator of the Gentileschi show and had labored for more than a year to get the Uffizi to agree to lend *Judith Slaying Holofernes*. She wouldn't breath freely until the painting was in the hands of the shippers, at which point her responsibility toward it was over. The director of the Galleria had insisted that she not return to work, that she take time off to be with her father, to mourn her mother's passing. She knew what he was thinking when she'd arrived at work mid-afternoon, that she was cold-blooded. Not that she cared much what he thought. She never cared what other people thought of her, which in Italy put one on the outside looking in, but which also gave one a great deal of freedom. It was wonderfully liberating not to be always seeking approval.

She walked alongside the painting as they carried it down the corridor toward the museum's packing room, observing again the look of great deliberation on Judith's face, the furrowed brow, the lips set firmly together. She had spent hours looking at the painting in the Uffizi when she was writing her critical biography of Gentileschi and knew every splatter of blood as the bright red liquid flew up to cover the hands and the arms of Judith and her maidservant, Abra. "The true genius of Gentileschi," she had written, "is not reflected in the look of horror on Holofernes' face as the cavalry sword slices through his jugular or in the blood that permeates the painting, but in the mood that Gentileschi conveys, of intense concentration, distaste, and of sisterhood on the faces of Judith and Abra as they go about their work." It could easily be a mistress and her maid performing a particularly burdensome household task, Artemisia had often thought, rather than two women slitting the throat of a common enemy. Her fascination with the painting, something she had not discussed with anyone, lay in her wish to be Judith. Judith had had the courage to kill without pity or hesitation. Artemisia had always feared that when her time came, she might slip into cowardice.

Two evenings ago she had watched as they carried her mother's body out the back door and through the garden that she had tended so lovingly for forty years, to the Assisi hospital for the requisite autopsy. There had been no blood when her mother had died. She had slid quietly into a coma and then to her death after swallowing a pillbox of Seconals, but there would be blood when they cut into her flesh to examine each of her organs. Not even her father's title and influence would exempt her mother from that final violation.

Their last day together had followed its usual routine. She had spent the morning at the museum and returned home early, as she did every Wednesday, for lunch. Artemisia couldn't remember anything unusual about lunch that day. Her mother rarely joined in the conversations about art that she and her father carried on, and she didn't like to gossip, so she didn't join in those conversations either. When they'd finished lunch, her mother told them that she had a headache and would take a nap. Her father had remarked caustically, "Three glasses of wine and I'd have a headache, too." Artemisia never drank at lunch, and when her mother bent down to kiss her before retiring to her room, she'd turned her head aside, away from the sour smell of wine on her mother's breath and away from her last words: "I love you, darling."

She had spent the afternoon in her room, writing. Had she gone next door to check on her mother, Amelia might still be alive. But she hadn't gone next door, not even when she realized that her small stock of sleeping pills was missing. Artemisia had decided when she was a child to punish her mother for loving her brother more than she loved Artemisia. When she was older, she understood that her mother couldn't help it, that it was just the way things were, but Artemisia had continued to punish her anyway, to push her away whenever she'd tried to get close. She'd even been glad for her mother's pain after Camillo's death; somehow she knew that her mother would not have felt the same intense pain if her only daughter had died, and for that Artemisia had no forgiveness.

She left the museum at 5:00, after signing the packing receipt, and returned to Assisi. She pulled in across from the taxi stand in Santa Chiara, put the car into neutral, and settled in to wait. She could see his Ferrari parked next to the newsstand. Not even an unconscious tourist, she thought, would have the nerve to park there. But no one in the municipal police would dare give a commissario di poliza a traffic ticket. The pecking order in Italy is very clear, and only fools challenge it. Of one thing she was sure, he wouldn't see her car when he got into his own. He was far too solipsistic to notice anything that didn't immediately concern him. And even if he did look about, her car was partially hidden by scaffolding. The wooden structures that bounded the buildings across from the Church of Santa Chiara had been erected years earlier, after the earthquake of 97, for some purpose no longer evident to any but earthquake historians. Soon, she thought mockingly, they'll cover it with Assisi pink stone and charge admission!

Three times in twenty minutes she reread the letter she had wrestled from Lucia. Finally, she opened her handbag to gaze at the dagger before lifting it out of her bag. A shaft of light pierced the windshield and caught the star ruby straight on, exploding it with light and color. She said the banishing words that she had memorized when she was only ten, away at boarding school for the first time, and that she had recited every day since: *Do what you will shall be the whole of the law. Love is the law, love under will.* She felt a scorching blood fire emanating from the ruby. *Do what you will shall be the whole of the law,* she repeated again as she covered the gemstone with her right hand. Its power entered her soul, investing her with the will to destroy her enemies. She laughed out loud, throwing her head straight back. She pictured the misericorde sinking into his veined neck, the blood flying upward. She knew her *Judith* well. Misericorde, an oxymoron, she thought. There is no mercy in death; death was the last enemy, and the cruelest one.

She looked around, amazed as always at the size of the crowds that had invaded Assisi over Easter Week. A taxi driver was observing her through the car window. He's looking at me strangely, she thought, puzzled. I've probably parked in his spot. Very possessive about what doesn't belong to him. Doesn't he know who I am? Seventeenth Countess Casati, old Assisi family, Fourth Crusade. She shrugged and indicated with a time-out sign that she was leaving shortly. Very shortly she realized, as just then she caught sight of the red Ferrari pulling in front of the newsstand. He was already in the middle of the crowded square, moving toward Corso Mazzini. He'd just missed hitting a woman with a baby stroller. How like him, Artemisia thought, women and children first!

Artemisia changed gears but waited a few seconds before pulling out. She had time to catch up. He skirted the barrier that had been erected for the holiday week to prevent tourists from driving their cars into the Piazza del Comune. She followed behind, but at a safe distance. Not that it mattered, because even if she tailgated, it was doubtful he'd notice her.

Driving on the main streets of Assisi in Easter Week requires all
of one's concentration. It was after 6:30, and tourists were
streaming down the center of the street on their way back to
the train station or to their hotels. They moved to the right or
left only when a car was directly upon them, and then with
stares of resentment. The Ferrari, still a hundred yards in
front of her, had reached the entrance to the Piazza del
Comune. But this time he didn't drive across the Piazza and up
via San Paolo as he usually did. Instead he circled the fountain
and turned up via San Gabriele. Normally, he would have
driven directly across the Piazza, taking the shortest route to
the cemetery, however many barriers had been erected by
the Assisi police. He relished the exercise of power, and he
regarded the local police as his errand boys. But the policewoman who was stationed in the Piazza would notice his car
immediately. He doesn't want anyone to see him driving in the
direction of the cemetery, she realized; since Rita's death he'd
grown more circumspect.

She took her time driving to the cemetery, overly cautious
perhaps, but he might look back. The sun had begun its
leisurely descent, and the sky was a deep showy pink, streaked
with scarlet red, like the color of blood in oxygenated arteries,
she thought, remembering her research for the chapter on
Judith Slaying Holofernes. Once, when they were having rough
sex, she had bitten him with such ferocity that she'd drawn
blood. It was faintly sweet with a not-unpleasant metallic taste
in the front of her mouth, but when she swallowed, it was
thick and viscous, like mucus, and she gagged, spoiling his
final moment. He had slapped her hard across the cheek-
bone, slamming the back of her head against the stone altar.
She'd left a small white scar on his neck, directly below the left
ear. Later, he had apologized for hitting her, telling her at the
same time how stupid his wife was. "The cow thinks I was cut

by a knife while trying to break up a fight between two Albanians. She actually called Giorgio to insist that he do something about the Albanian problem!" he'd said with a laughing sneer. Artemisia had laughed with him, but inside she was seething. He shouldn't have hit her.

They always met in her family's vault, and although she'd given him that key, he had his own key to the cemetery gates. He had a fetish about having sex in the cemetery. All his women did it there at least once, he'd told her. Only Grazia had refused. He liked having sex on the top of the tombstones and had pleaded with her to do it on one of the exposed flat stones in the older section of the cemetery, on the grave of a soldier who had died in the First World War, Maurizio Rossi. Just nineteen when he was killed at Caporetto. BELOVED SON AND BROTHER was the inscription on the stone. "Too risky," she'd said, refusing. "The caretaker might see us." In fact, he had begun to bore her. That was his second mistake.

Rita was a slut! Had Fulvio fucked her cousin on Maurizio's grave? Perhaps it was to meet Rita that he'd stood her up on King's Day. It certainly wasn't to have dinner with Giorgio as he later claimed. Giorgio had been with her. His final mistake!

5

"CALL PIERO. DO nothing on your own!" the commissario had ordered when Genine finally reached him by telephone. Autocratic, like my father, she decided, then quickly erased that thought. No, more like an older brother. He's just forty, a fifteen-year difference, not so old, really, was what she was thinking as she pressed the redial button on her cell phone. "Sorry, sorry, and sorry, the line is unavailable," she mimicked. She had hidden herself and her Vespa in the passageway between the cemetery wall and the wooden flower stand at the front gate while waiting for Russo and his mysterious caller to appear. On the fifth redial, she saw a red Ferrari flash by, unexpectedly traveling along the back road, followed in short order by a black Mercedes. Both cars were headed toward the side gate. Alex had insisted that she wait at the front gate.

She wheeled her Vespa out from the narrow alleyway and mounted it with the intention of following when she saw a dark figure in a pilgrim's robe approaching on the cemetery road. She quickly leaned the Vespa against the front wall and hid herself again.

ARTEMISIA WAS HEADY with exhilaration and walked with a bounce as she made her way down the hill after parking her car at the side of the road. His car was parked at the bottom, partially hidden under a canopy of cypress trees, just a few steps from the cemetery's side gate. It was dusk and soon the waning rays of the moon would be the only light in the Assisi night sky. He liked it dark but so did she—Artemis, goddess of the hunt and of the moon, and of all the creatures of the night. But tonight the Greek goddess would give way to the Israelite warrior—the virgin to the avenging widow. Judith of Bethulia had also been a night hunter and a far more dangerous one than Artemis with her puny arrows. Artemisia hummed softly to herself as she gently eased the iron latch back into its place and started upward on the dirt track toward her destiny, her bounty bag slung over her left shoulder, the misericorde razor-sharp within.

SOPHIE'S WOOLEN CAPE and hood were a bit too warm for the evening. The weather had changed and she remembered how much Sergio had loved the first days of spring, when the hard brown earth turned soft and green. But the hood covered her blonde hair and hid her face. She didn't notice the Vespa until she was on top of it. She glanced nervously around. The caretaker's, probably. He often left it in the cemetery overnight, but not outside the gates. Getting old and careless. That's when she saw the black cat slide through the iron bars. It crossed directly in front of her and sat for a moment to rub its sore eye. The cat had recently been in a fight, probably with a larger animal; the fur around its face was caked with dried blood. It finished its ablutions, looked up at her sideways, and approached, meowing softly as though ready to make a friend. She hissed at it and slammed the gate, almost on its tail. It growled and took off running down the cemetery road toward Porta San Giacomo. She hated cats.

A dark cloud drifted across the setting sun, shaking her out of her reverie. The cat had been a distraction. She looked at her watch and walked faster, skirting the main gravel-lined path and instead taking the narrow dirt track that zigzagged behind the mausoleums. A few feet before she reached the Casati vault, she could see the policeman leaning against the back wall, his blond hair luminous against the darkening pink stone. She could see his leer suggestive of things to come. And then she felt herself falling, drifting slowly down to the dark lovely green earth.

FULVIO WAS A man's man and he hated the wincing softness of women. Grazia was always whining. "Please Fulvio, I didn't mean it. Please Fulvio, you're hurting me. Honest Fulvio, I won't tell Giorgio." She would tell, though, if she found out about Rita. She had wept for hours when she'd read in *La Repubblica* that the murdered American was pregnant. "The poor baby," she'd cried, without a single concern for the dead woman, he'd thought with contempt. Giorgio had nearly killed him three years ago when he saw bruises on his sister's arm, even after Grazia swore they were the result of a fall down some stairs. "Fall, my fucking ass," Giorgio had shouted, punching him in the face. "You hurt my sister again, and you're fucking dead. And next time I won't dirty my hands on pretty-boy scrum like you, I'll leave it to my associates." Giorgio never made idle threats.

First it was Rita, and now the Croatian. At least Italian women knew the score and kept their mouths shut. Maybe he should have told Artemisia about this meeting. She'd know what to do, but he didn't trust her. Artemisia wasn't afraid of anyone, but she didn't care about anyone either. She'd turn on him in an instant if he became a threat.

The air was warm and heavy, too warm for the season, and he could feel the wool of his jacket rubbing against his skin; he was wet through. The dread and shame had returned, gnawing at his insides, devouring everything within. His mother had whipped him with a leather strap whenever his father had crossed her or whenever she'd had too much to drink, which was always. But he was no longer a child; he could fight back. He struck a match to re-light his cigarette, and that's when he saw the dark triangular shapes moving toward him. The Croatian was in the lead. He recognized her immediately from her purposeful stride. And then she was gone.

THE SCREAMING WAIL of the police car competed with the loud whirring in her ears. Sophie was bleeding, but not as badly as the policewoman. She moved her fingers gingerly along her head wound to check its depth and length and though she winced at the pain, she decided it was not so serious. It would need stitches but not that many. She looked down at her red-stained hands, sticky with blood. Most of it belonged to the policewoman. She tore off the bottom of her dress to make a tourniquet for Sergeant Antolini. She even remembered her name. So much had happened and in such a short time that she barely had time to think. Fulvio Russo was dead and with him her scheme to get money for Christina. She saw the men in uniform approaching, their white chest bands iridescent in the lowering light. She had to plan quickly.

6

THE ROAD FROM Gubbio to Assisi is a tarted-up one-lane mountain pass of some forty kilometers, mainly curves but with a sufficiency of straights for it to pose as a super strata in Italy. It took Cenni a treacherous fifty minutes, passing on the right, the left, and sometimes through the center, to arrive at the cemetery at precisely 7:35 in response to Sergeant Antolini's frantic call for help.

His instructions to her had been clear. "Call Piero *now!* If you don't reach him, call Elena. Do nothing on your own, Sergeant; that's an order. Wait for me at the front gate and stay out of sight. Russo is dangerous!" And just before he hung up, "Nice work, Genine . . . thanks." But he didn't trust her to follow orders. She's too nervy by half, he decided, remembering her foray into the dumpster, so when he wasn't passing cars, and even when he was, he dialed Piero, then Elena, and in desperation Antonio Martini, but an electrical storm over Gubbio was blocking transmission.

The scene-of-crime was immediately behind the Casati vault. It was a nightmare of noise, lights, and confusion, a replay of the thunderstorm he'd just left behind. Blinding strobe lights were focused on the body of Russo, who was lying uncovered in a halo of coagulated blood, his body cordoned off by a bright band of yellow tape. A battalion of police officers—municipal, carabinieri, and state—were milling around the edges of the scene, joined by a complement of unidentified bystanders. Only the finance police seemed to be missing.

The commander of the Assisi carabinieri and Dr. Batori—who'd happened to be in Assisi presiding at the autopsy of Amelia Casati—were center stage. As Cenni also noted to his distress, they were the only officers appropriately garbed for a blood-soaked crime scene; at least they had covered their street shoes with plastic. The forensic team had not yet arrived, and without the constraint of their silent, ordered profession-alism, chaos reigned.

As soon as he saw Cenni, Batori excused himself and approached the commissario. "It's all over but the cheering," Batori said, a disquieting smile lighting his face. "It would appear that we have Minelli's murderer right there," he said, pointing to Russo's horribly savaged body almost with glee.

Cenni reminded himself that Russo had once threatened to have the medical examiner fired. Batori had been on the scene when Sophie Orlic had made a brief statement to the carabinieri before being removed to the Assisi Hospital, and he proceeded, without invitation, to give Cenni a description of the events that had led to Russo's death.

"The other one, the pretty blonde, she was gutsy, bleeding like a stuck pig, yet she insisted on making a statement before they took her off to the hospital. These head wounds bleed like the dickens, you know. But she'll be all right, a few stitches, a few days rest. *Il Lupino* hit her with a brick," he added. "He would have killed her if the young countess hadn't intervened. She saved the blonde's life. He can tell you more about it," he added as an afterthought, pointing to the carabinieri com-mander. "He took her statement." Batori then pointed to one of the bystanders, a little man, not five feet tall, who looked over at Cenni with an air of expectation. "He's the caretaker here; he found the three of them together behind the Casati vault and called the carabinieri."

"And him?" Cenni interrupted, pointing to the blood-soaked body of Fulvio Russo. "It would appear that his throat was slashed. By whom?"

"Slashed right enough," Batori responded in awe. "Right through the thyroid ligament. Couldn't have done a better job myself," he nodded. "Not that the service provides us with such elegant tools. A huge ruby on its handle and as sharp as any of my surgical instruments. Worth a fortune, too, I'm told. According to the blonde. . . ."

"Her name is Sophie Orlic, Signora Orlic," Cenni interjected.

"Signora Orlic, then," Batori conceded before continuing. "She said that the countess was carrying the dagger to protect herself from Russo. The countess and the blon . . . Signora Orlic—she worked for the family, you know—they'd both suspected Russo of murdering Minelli. They joined together to accost him in the cemetery. They're damned lucky it's not one or both of them lying there." It seemed to Cenni that Batori was caught between admiring the women for their courage and reproaching them for their foolishness. "Damned fine women," he opted for finally, and excused himself to join the forensic science policemen who'd just appeared on the scene.

Marshal Stefano Sbarretti had waited for Batori to leave before approaching Cenni. They had met only once and that on a somber occasion where social exchanges were out of order—at the funeral in Perugia of two officers who had lost their lives in a gun battle with car thieves—but Cenni knew of Sbarretti's reputation. The caribiniere was some years younger than Cenni and highly ambitious for honors and advancement, but he was also punctilious in observing the rules of engagement. He avoided stepping on toes, at least where the outcome was in doubt.

Sbarretti spoke first, "Commissario Cenni, we meet again and again under disastrous circumstances. One of your own, too!" he said, nodding with distaste toward Russo's body. "I apologize for the circus," he said, looking around at the large group of police and bystanders who now attended the scene, "but it couldn't be helped. The caretaker was the first person on the scene. He found the three of them just a few feet from the Casati vault and called us immediately. We had a police car in the vicinity and when my officers saw who was down and learned who was involved, they called me. One of Russo's junior officers, a sergeant, was also on the scene. She got here just after the caretaker called us. She notified your people in Assisi, and four of them came trooping up, with Batori in tow. A medical doctor would have been more helpful," he added.

"And now I see that someone's tipped off the press," he said, looking over toward the caretaker. "If I'm not mistaken that's a reporter from *Telegiornale Umbria*." He pointed to a tall, dark-haired man holding a camera and talking avidly to the caretaker. "I'd better nip that in the bud right now. And you'll want to talk to the caretaker yourself. He's the most reliable witness we have to what happened here." He hesitated for a second. "There's Russo's officer, of course, but she's probably not reliable. One of *Il Lupino*'s babes is what I've been told by some of my men; he had them standing in line," he added with a sly grin. "She's back at the hospital with the Croatian."

Carabiniere vaffanculo! Cenni said to himself. And aloud to Sbarretti, "*D'accordo*, you mean Sergeant Antolini."

Sbarretti was a filthy-minded chauvinist, Cenni concluded, but he had his uses. He overheard snatches of what Sbarretti was saying to the reporter—*national security, best not to offend, Prime Minister, clearance,* and again, *national security. National security* was the most powerful equivocation used by the PM since 9/11 to restrict freedom of the press, but reflecting on the potential for scandal to the Perugia Questura, Cenni was not unhappy to have Sbarretti do his dirty work.

The caretaker, an elderly man well beyond official retirement age, peered up at Cenni, open-faced, anxiously waiting for the commissario to initiate the conversation. Cenni recognized the fusion of apprehension and ebullience that often overtakes witnesses to murder. He imagined that for a caretaker in a provincial cemetery there was little to relieve the daily tedium of a life spent shooing children off the gravestones of their ancestors.

"I'm sorry but I don't know your name," Cenni said with a smile. The smile was all that was needed.

"Vittorio Scapaccino, commissario. I know you, from the American's funeral. I knew the other commissario too." He nodded toward Russo. "He used to bring his women into the cemetery in the evenings, when he thought no one was here. Ghoul!" he added, spitting in the direction of the body to show his contempt. "The *straniera,* the flower lady. I knew her, too. Very beautiful, but she never smiled. Didn't say hello if she could help it."

Cenni interrupted. "And the other one, you knew her?"

"The dark one? The young countess? I saw her a few times in the cemetery but I didn't know who she was, not until now," he added conscientiously. "She's one of the women he brought here. Not at all like her mother, that one; she never smiled neither, anyways not at people like me."

Cenni interrupted again, aware that the only disinterested witness he had to the events of that evening had difficulty

staying on subject. He didn't mind when a witness rambled—
ramblings often yielded more than direct questions—but he
was determined to get to the hospital.

"Marshal Sbarretti tells me that you telephoned the police,
that it was you who found the body. When? How? Just those few
questions and we can get you home to your dinner."

"No problem at all about my dinner, commissario. I already
rang my Marinella," he replied, holding up the ubiquitous
cell phone. "I told her to hold dinner."

"What time did you find the body, Signor Scapaccino?"
Cenni asked.

Looking somewhat abashed, Scapaccino replied at once, "A
little past seven, commissario, two, three minutes at most."

"You're very exact. I don't see a wristwatch."

"Oh, that's easy, commissario. I heard the seven bells of
San Ruffino. I always stop to say a prayer," he said and blessed
himself. "As soon as the bells stopped ringing, I heard the
scream. Horrible it was, like the squeal of a pig having its
throat cut! I slaughter a pig every year for Pasqua. Forty years
now, and I still hate the sound," he said with a shiver. "I thought
it was two male boars fighting. It's been a very hard winter, and
the *cinghiale* are foraging closer and closer to the town. Ate a
quarter of our shrubs this year. The direttore says—"

Cenni cut him short, again, wondering how he could gracefully get the hell out of there. He glanced at his watch; 7:40
already. Where was Piero? Or Elena? He looked over to Sbarretti for relief, but he was still talking to the reporter. He
sighed deeply.

"Where were you when you heard the scream?"

"In the rear, next to the little church there." He pointed to
the cemetery chapel, still visible in the diminished light.
"They're renovating it, and the workmen left bricks and other
materials lying along the path, in the public area. The direttore

asked me to move the materials to a safer place before I left for the evening. I was almost finished. Just one more load, I said to myself and I can go home, so I ignored the scream and kept working. And then I heard a woman's voice."

Cenni nodded encouragingly, to keep him going.

"I found them over there," he said, nodding toward the crime scene. "The young countess, she was sitting on the ground soaked in blood. It was everywhere, on her clothes, shoes, even in her hair!" He paused, and looked over at the forensic police who were now photographing the body. Avoiding Cenni's eyes, he swallowed hard. "The commissario's head was in her lap, lolling, twisted like, and then I saw what she was doing. She had a knife in her right hand and she was sawing away at his neck like you would at a chicken bone. And talking to him! I didn't know what to do," he said in a whisper. Even in the low light, Cenni could see the dark flush of shame.

"Where was the flower lady?" Cenni cut in, almost afraid to ask.

"A foot or so away. She was sitting on the ground, the same as the young countess. I could see blood running down the side of her face. And then, just like that, another woman comes out from behind the vault. A ghost, I thought." He giggled nervously. "It was a police officer. I watched as she walked over to the young countess. She knelt down to speak to her, so I couldn't hear what she said, but she must have asked her for the knife."

"Did she give her the knife!" Cenni asked, hurrying him along."

"Gave it to her all right; the blade right across the palm. Then the young countess she just ups and walks away, soaked in blood, as though nothing had happened." He shuddered.

It was right then that Cenni lost control. He stormed over to Sbaretti, who had just walked away from the reporter. "We need to talk, Sbarretti! What happened to Sergeant Antolini?"

"Sorry, Cenni. I thought you knew. Didn't any of your people tell you? There're enough of them here. While she was disarming the countess, she cut her hand. She's back in Assisi, at the hospital, having it looked at. Can't be too serious, though, as she was the one who telephoned your people to get them up here."

"Artemisia Casati is not a countess, Sbarretti. You should know that even if the rest of these jokers don't. And where *is* her highness? I *assumed* one of your officers took charge of her. Or don't the carabinieri arrest murderers anymore?"

Sbarretti turned a dark red. "Listen Cenni, you're the wonder boy here. The carabinieri are not involved in this fiasco and we're not getting involved. Your witness—he pointed to the caretaker—said she up and left after handing over the knife to your sergeant. I assume she went home. You want her arrested, do it yourself. One of your officers wants to talk to you," he said sharply, ending the exchange by turning on his heels and walking away.

Cenni turned to find Piero standing at his elbow gasping for air.

"Che cosa?" Cenni said.

"Hospital with Genine . . ." Piero responded in a stammered half-sentence.

"Catch your breath! Then tell me where you've been, you and Elena. The carabinieri seem to be in charge here."

Piero took two deep breaths and continued. "Elena's on her way to Perugia, with Genine, to see a specialist. That Casati bitch almost sliced her hand in two. It's a deep cut, Alex, and the doctors in Assisi were worried about permanent nerve damage."

"I heard. You can tell me about it in a minute." He pointed to the chaotic crime scene with contempt. "Where were you when all this was going on?"

"Sorry Alex. Our cell phones were down during the storm; I didn't get any of Genine's messages or yours until shortly before seven. Neither did Elena. We got here a few minutes after the carabinieri arrived." He lowered his voice. "Too late. She was gone. She actually stole Genine's Vespa. Jesus, but I hate that bitch!"

7

LUCIA OPENED the door, took one look at the two policemen, and stepped aside, not uttering a word.

"Where is she?"

"In the sitting room."

For a moment Lucia stood silent and watched as they strode down the hall. Just before they reached the sitting room door, she called out, "*Mi dispiace*, Commissario. I didn't give her Sophie's letter, she took it from me. *È vero.*"

Cenni nodded. "We'll talk later."

Three people turned to stare at the two policemen who burst into the sitting room. The faces of two of the three registered an uneasy anxiety. Umberto Casati and Giorgio Zangarelli were standing together by the fireplace with their drinks placed on the mantelpiece above them. From their somber expressions they appeared to have been in deep discussion. Artemisia Casati was sitting in a high-backed wing chair, unbloodied, wearing a white silk evening dress. Her thick short hair was wet and unruly, drying naturally into soft ringlets around her angular face, and except for a light smear of lip-gloss, her face was scrubbed clean, like that of a child just ready for bed. She looked surprisingly unghoulish for a woman who fewer than forty minutes earlier had slashed a man's throat to shreds. She looked over at Cenni, smiled, and ever so subtly raised the hem of her dress to display a pair of very shapely ankles.

The bitch actually showered and is relaxing with a drink, was Piero's outraged thought.

Umberto Casati rushed to speak first. "Dottor Cenni, thank heavens you've arrived. My daughter's just told us how that beast—" Before he could say anything further, Zangarelli lightly touched his arm, stopping him in midsentence. "Umberto, let's hear what the commissario has to say."

Cenni ignored them both. He walked over to the wing chair and stood directly over Artemisia Casati. "Please stand, signorina," he said, so softly that Piero, on the other side of the room, nearly missed it. What Piero didn't miss was the look that Artemisia shot Zangarelli. Not a pleading look exactly, but more like a request for advice, was how he later described it to Elena.

With a slight nod, Zangarelli signaled *yes* and Artemisia stood immediately, almost as though she were a puppet, Piero thought as he watched the scene unfold from across the room.

"Artemisia Casati, you're under arrest for the murder of Fulvio Russo," Cenni enunciated slowly and with force, placing equal emphasis on each word. His voice carried into the hallway, and Lucia, who was hidden from view behind the sitting room door, gasped audibly, causing everyone in the room to turn that way.

Cenni added loudly, "Signorina Stampoli, please bring the signorina her coat." He turned and addressed Umberto Casati. "You'll want to put some of her things into a bag and bring them to the station house within the hour. We'll be moving her to Perugia after I complete the paperwork."

The tension was oppressive and Piero, who had a head cold, had trouble breathing. He felt as though the air were being sucked from the room. He looked first at the count, then at Zangarelli, and finally at Artemisia, waiting for one of them to speak. It was Zangarelli who broke the silence. "Where's your warrant, Cenni?"

"I don't need a warrant to hold her in protective custody. I'll get the warrant tomorrow. I have eyewitnesses to what happened. One of them is a police officer."

"She acted in self-defense. You can't arrest someone who acted in self-defense."

"L'onorevole!" Piero knew from the tone that no respect was intended. "Self-defense is yet to be proven. What's not in dispute is that she assaulted a police officer, causing her serious bodily injury. Sergeant Antolini's in Perugia right now, seeing a hand surgeon." He looked at Artemisia. "She almost sliced my officer's hand in two."

This last accusation seemed to surprise Zangarelli, who turned to Artemisia. "Is it true what he says?"

Artemisia looked away from him and at her father, who'd heard the news about Sergeant Antolini's injury without visible surprise. "The policewoman, she came out of nowhere, *Papa*. She asked me for the knife and I gave it to her. I think I handed it to her by the hilt, but I was completely distraught. Perhaps I didn't," she said, wrinkling her brow and closing her eyes tightly as though trying to recreate the scene. "I don't think I did what he says, but I don't remember. *È vero, Papa*," she said desolately, and turned to Zangarelli. "Help me, Giorgio, I don't want to go to jail!" she pleaded, reaching out for his hand. One lone tear rolled down her cheek.

Lucia and the count went off together to fetch Artemisia's coat. "The fur one, *Papa*," Artemisia called out as they mounted the stairs. Giorgio Zangarelli disappeared into the count's study, presumably to use the telephone to call in favors, and Piero, still in the sitting room, was talking to the questore on his cell phone, explaining in hushed tones why Rome might be calling him shortly.

Cenni was alone in the vestibule with Artemisia.

Cenni said, "You killed Rita, didn't you? Fulvio was just your lackey."

"I don't know what you're talking about," Artemisia replied, looking around to see if anyone else were listening.

"You know exactly what I'm talking about," Cenni snapped.

Artemisia smiled serenely. "Prove it!"

8

CENNI LEFT THE Assisi Hospital at nine o'clock with nothing left to do but wait for morning. Artemisia Casati was in restraints, on suicide watch, her strong aristocratic wrists tied with white linen straps to an iron bed, locked securely in the only quarters that the hospital staff deemed worthy of a countess, a private room with a view of La Rocca. Sergeant Antonio Martini was standing guard outside.

Sophie Orlic was asleep, filled with Demerol, her shapely head swathed in bandages. "A superficial wound," the doctor told him, "She'll recover quickly." Cenni looked in on Sophie before leaving the hospital. Her right arm was flung above her head like a restless child, and like a child she had been crying in her sleep. Her cheeks were wet with tears when he tiptoed out of the tiny cubicle.

Fulvio Russo was also at rest, in a four-by-eight cold storage bin in the hospital's basement, his mutilated body awaiting the medical examiner's knife, his head still attached to his torso, but just barely. And Sergeant Antolini was spending the night with Elena's family, her wound reasonably lashed together by the best (and only) hand surgeon in Perugia. She reassured the commissario repeatedly—he called three times in an hour—that she'd be fine, a little nerve damage perhaps, but nothing for him to worry about.

He spent the last few hours of that tangled day at the home of the questore explaining and re-explaining the events of the previous week. Three brutal deaths in seven days, two of them coming in the midst of an active police investigation, *his* investigation. He accepted Carlo's dressing-down silently.

After vigorously debating for an hour how much of the night's events they would report to the prime minister, how much to the press, and how much to the investigating judge, they arrived at an uneasy compromise. As close to the truth as possible, Cenni insisted, given Sbarretti's quick eye and the number of local police and medical personnel who had been at the crime scene that night. "Not to mention seeing justice done," he added and watched as Carlo winced.

"Not the full story, Alex, not your version anyway," Carlo had immediately retorted. "Did you really have to take her out in handcuffs and then perp walk her all the way to Piazza Santa Chiara!"

"It's not my rule, *No cars on via San Francesco.* The count is responsible for that one—protecting his peace and quiet is what I'm told." He sounded childish even to his own ears.

"But straight across the Piazza, Alex! With a few thousand tourists in town for the weekend and nothing for them to do at night but hang out in the Piazza. Did you have to humiliate the woman? The count will never forgive you—or me."

"You tell me how I could get her to the station without going through the Piazza. Stop feeling sorry for her, Carlo; she's a pathological killer. She murdered her cousin and tonight she killed again, almost twice. Fulvio's in cold storage with his head attached by a bloody thread, Sophie Orlic has twenty stitches in her skull, and Genine's lucky to have her hand still attached— her right hand, too!" The questore noticed for the first time the manic gleam in his favorite commissario's eyes. "If I had my way, the bitch would be sleeping in a cell tonight, in Perugia, and not in luxury in the Assisi hospital, on suicide watch of all things." He laughed derisively. "Who got you to agree to that? The father? Zangarelli? Or did it take a call from the PM?"

"Never you mind! This whole story of yours, that the Casati woman murdered her cousin—where's your proof, Alex? I'm not saying you're wrong . . ."

"No, but you're hoping it!"

"You have nothing to back it up, other than a stray comment by Artemisia Casati that the piece of thread you found on the victim was attached to her left earring. You insist that only you and the murderer could have know this, but this Croatian woman has an entirely different story. She gave a sworn statement to the carabinieri tonight that it was Fulvio who tried to kill her. And the reason she gave makes perfect sense. In her statement she claims that Fulvio murdered Minelli, and that he tried to kill her to keep her quiet. She even wrote a letter to this effect for her protection before leaving for the cemetery— addressed to you, I might add."

Jesus wept; Voltaire smiled, Cenni muttered to himself. "Now you're taking the Croatian's word over mine. Yesterday, you wanted me to lock her up and throw away the key. Think on it, Carlo! Fulvio goes to the cemetery with the intent to murder Sophie Orlic, but he's not carrying a weapon. *If I'm lucky, he thinks, I'll find a stray brick along the roadside, or perhaps I can smother her with my coat sleeve.* Even Fulvio wasn't that much of a fucking fool!"

"Language, Alex. The wife may be listening."

"I hope she is. She usually agrees with me," Cenni added caustically.

"No doubt, but I run the questura, not Romina and not you. There *is* another point of view, Alex. The count concedes that his daughter acted irrationally tonight. He apologizes profusely

for Sergeant Antolini's injury; he's even volunteered to pay her
medical expenses and a nice sum in compensation. His story
is that Artemisia is having a nervous breakdown and even
threatened to commit suicide. Who can argue with that? The
cousin is murdered, the mother takes her own life, and her
married lover tries to kill her, all this in the same week. Listen,
Alex. You've been fighting to keep this Croatian woman out of
jail. You've succeeded and that's all you're going to get. And
don't forget to release Williams. All we need now is the Canadian Embassy breathing down our necks."

Finally, and with great reluctance, Cenni had agreed to
adopt Sophie's version, that Artemisia Casati had attacked Fulvio Russo in defense of her own life. He doubted that the
police would ever learn the full truth about tonight, but most
of what he knew, or suspected, he had promised Carlo to keep
to himself, for now. "Forget *for now*," Carlo shot back in anger.
You wanted *Il Lupino*. You got him, and without lifting a finger.
Case closed."

9

DO WHAT YOU *will shall be the whole of the law!* Artemisia said
the banishing words to herself repeatedly as she looked out the
hospital window. The parking lot was directly below, and she
could see the last of the visitors returning to their cars. Visiting
hours ended at 9:00 and her father had stayed until the final
warning bell sounded before kissing her on the cheek. In the
five days that she had been in Assisi hospital, it was the first
time that he'd stayed so late. He usually arrived at 6:30 and left
promptly at 8:00, for his dinner. His habits were set in stone,
Assisi stone, Artemisia thought to herself. Even her mother
hadn't been able to budge him: breakfast at 7:00, lunch at 1:00,
drinks at 7:00, dinner at 8:00. But this visit he had waited until

the very last minute to leave. The first warning bell had sounded before he broached the subject on his mind. He began tentatively, reminding Artemisia of their obligations to Sophie. "We owe Sophie a great deal. Think of all that she did for your mother." And then, after a slight pause, he added, "And for you, Artemisia. A great deal!" he emphasized, observing his daughter carefully to see her reaction. She said nothing, sitting silent and watchful, waiting for him to continue.

"Sophie needs financial help for her daughter. She's transferring Christina from the public hospital in Croatia to a private clinic in Switzerland in three days, and I've promised to accompany her on the trip, and to help with the expenses," he added, sheepishly. "After the trauma that Sophie's been through—that we've all been through as a family," he amended, "she needs our support."

Sophie's not family—she's not even Italian, Artemisia thought without change of expression.

He hesitated again, walking over to the nighttable where Artemisia kept a framed picture of her mother and brother. He nervously fingered the frame, avoiding her eyes. "That apartment she lives in near Porta San Giacomo, it's a disgrace. I had no idea that anyone in Assisi still lived that way. It has no central heating, just one of those portable gas heaters to use in the winter. You know how dangerous they are. We should outlaw them. Now that I think of it, that apartment may be the very one that Paola lived in with her grandmother before she came to us." He was still gazing at the picture of his wife and son; then he placed it face downward on the table. Artemisia knew what was coming.

"Paola is going back to Rome in a few days time to continue her studies. We'll need someone to act as housekeeper. Sophie has agreed to work for the family again, but more as a member of the family than as a servant." He added, "I thought I would give her your grandmother's room." The final bell had sounded. "Of course, when you come home, we'll have to make other arrangements."

When she failed to respond, he continued, "You'll need time to heal and to forget, and you can do that better in the hospital." He turned to look at her directly, and for a moment Artemisia thought he was going to say something else, something profound, but instead he bent and kissed her briefly on one cheek, English fashion. At the door, he paused for a last look. *"Ciao bella,"* he said, and left.

His anxiety to let her know what was on his mind without stating it directly had been apparent. He hadn't mentioned marriage, but she knew her father too well to assume he intended anything else; he was far too conventional to live with Sophie without the blessings of church and law. And Sophie? She certainly understood Sophie, perhaps even better than she understood her father. A clever woman, Sophie! Too clever to agree to any arrangement other than marriage to the seventeenth Count Casati. Her mother's title, *countess*, would pass to Sophie when her father remarried, and she, Artemisia, would be a mere signorina again, a signorina at thirty-seven! Artemisia was well versed in the rituals of Italian nobility and knew that her mother's title had not actually passed to her, but she had enjoyed being called *countess* by those who didn't know. Sophie was still young enough to have more children. Her father would be pleased to have another son, a son to whom he could pass his title, another Camillo! Artemisia had seen the way her father's eyes had followed Sophie through a room when the Croatian had been her grandmother's caretaker. Sophie must have been aware of his interest. Women were always aware of such things. With the wife dead and the daughter safely tucked away in hospital, Sophie had played her hand just right. Clever Sophie!

She saw her father by the streetlights' illumination as he emerged from the portico. He had osteoporosis and his tall slim figure with rounded shoulders was unmistakable. A woman walked next to him, and she recognized Sophie's blonde hair. She must have been waiting for him in the lobby, Artemisia thought. Sophie wore a sweater lightly thrown over her shoulders, and as they walked it slipped down one arm. Artemisia watched as her father helped his housekeeper to secure it again, and then with his arm still around her shoulders they walked toward the parking lot.

"Domestica!" she exhaled softly. A cleaning woman! And not even the equal of Lucia, who was at least Italian. Not to despair, Artemisia thought. Her father was very conventional. He would never marry Sophie before a year of mourning had passed. Plenty of time. Of course, she would have to be careful. Sophie must have realized who had attacked her. Fulvio had been at least five feet in front of the Croatian when Artemisia had hit her from behind with the brick that she'd found lying along the dirt track. Sophie had to have seen Fulvio before she went down; she had to know that he couldn't have been the one who hit her. Clever Sophie, lying like that! She wondered if her father knew, if Sophie had confided in him? But even Sophie couldn't know for sure who had killed Rita Minelli. Not even Cenni knew for sure, no matter what he said.

Good Friday, that fateful day! She had waited at the top of the stairway until she heard Lucia slam the kitchen door, and then crept down the back stairs. It was just after 4:30, plenty of time to get to the cemetery. To avoid meeting anyone in the street, she left by the garden steps, turning her ankle in the process. At her urging, Fulvio had called Rita in the morning to demand that she meet him one last time to talk about the baby's future, at five o'clock in the cemetery. But he'd lost his nerve. Shortly after 4:00 he called Artemisia, insisting that he had to be at home with his wife to meet with Giorgio. Giorgio terrified him and now with Rita pregnant, he had a terminal case of paralysis. "If he finds out about the baby, he'll have me killed," he'd said repeatedly. "Grazia wants to have a child and Giorgio would consider it a double insult if I got another woman pregnant and not his sister." Giorgio was an excuse. Fulvio was a coward. He was leaving it to her to solve his problem.

She had chosen the day with care, waiting for Good Friday when the streets and cemetery were sure to be empty in the late afternoon. "If we put it off we'll lose the moment. Once she tells one person about the baby, it'll be all over Assisi," she'd responded, hoping to buck him up. It would also give Rita time to execute a new will. Her cousin's lawyer had called from New York on Holy Thursday and left a message with Lucia that the will was in the mail and Rita had written in her diary that she was planning to disinherit the family. That item she had kept to herself. Fulvio didn't know about the will and wouldn't care. Money was the one thing he didn't need—and was the only thing Artemisia could think about since she had seen the figure of two and a half million scribbled in Rita's diary.

After their trysts, Fulvio always left first. Artemisia would wait five minutes, giving him time to get away. His arrangement was the same with Rita and it was in those five minutes that Artemisia would kill her cousin. What Fulvio didn't know was that the weapon of her choice was his cashmere scarf. She would leave traces of it on Rita's person and then hide the scarf where it was likely to be found. After Rita's death, rumors of her unborn child would spread like wildfire and just as quickly her name would be linked to Fulvio's. The incomparable Lucia would see to that. Giorgio would move heaven and earth to shield his sister from public shame: no police, no courts, and no trial, just an execution. She relished the irony of using the scarf that Rita had given Fulvio for

King's Day. He had taunted her with it, asking her to feel its softness, a reminder that he and Rita were lovers. As though she would care who he fucked.

He didn't know that she had his scarf. He never wore his coat when he went out to lunch, even in the coldest weather. It appeared macho to walk around Assisi in shirtsleeves in the middle of winter. She had stopped at the station during his lunch break and asked to leave a note in the commissario's office. She walked away with the scarf tucked under her coat, and no one the wiser. The pen was a stroke of luck. It had fallen out of his pocket on to the floor of her car the last time they were together. She had handled it carefully, wrapping it in her handkerchief to preserve his prints. If the scarf didn't work, the pen would. She'd leave it lying under her cousin's body. The caribinieri would be first on the scene when the body was found; they were only a few minutes from the cemetery and they all hated Fulvio, who liked to throw his weight around. They'd find the pen and think it had been dropped, unnoticed, by the killer. Each Mont Blanc pen had its own serial number; it would be traced to Fulvio. At Rita's funeral, he had taken her aside and whined about that, too. He couldn't understand how his pen had gotten into her purse. The fool thought Rita had stolen it from him.

In the end it worked even better than she could have hoped. She had taken the dirt track behind the mausoleums to avoid being seen and came upon her mother and Rita quarreling. Their voices were raised to an agitated pitch of accusation and denial and twice she heard her own name. She hid in the shadows of the towering cypress and watched as her mother, her arms swinging wildly, rushed toward the front gate and then returned almost immediately, out of breath and talking to herself. She re-entered the vault for just a moment and rushed off again, passing so close to Artemisia she could have touched her daughter's hand.

Artemisia had waited outside the vault but heard no sound. She entered and found Rita lying face-down at the bottom of the altar steps. She knelt on one knee and covered her cousin's right hand with hers; she felt it tremble with life. She rolled her over and watched as Rita slowly opened her eyes. She smiled up at Artemisia and Artemisia smiled back.

It proved strangely easy to kill. She'd pressed the scarf down over her cousin's mouth and nose and held it there until Rita stopped breathing. Rita's eyes were huge pools of fear and pleading, but she didn't struggle, probably because she was still weak from the blow to her head. Artemisia watched as the light left her cousin's eyes and wondered if there were any truth to the tale that a murder victim imprinted the killer's image on his retina. It was an old wives' tale and Artemisia doubted that there was any truth to it, but the thought fascinated her. Was her likeness permanently etched on Rita's retina? It gave the cousins a special bond—almost like sisters, she thought.

Artemisia had hated Rita while she was alive—hated that Rita was rich and independent, hated when people said they looked alike—but now that Rita was dead, Artemisia remembered that her cousin had been kind to her when she was a child, kinder to her than her own mother. She had hated her mother, too, but now that she was dead, she had begun to miss her. Strange that she should miss her mother when she hadn't even liked her. Perhaps, later, she would miss Sophie in the same way. *Ciao bella.*

10

THE SUN, HIGH above the Medieval city, cast a radiant light on the massive stone buildings that dominate the great central street of Perugia. Even the soft shadows in front of the majestic Piazza dei Priori were luminous with light. Some children were playing hide and seek, skipping in and out of shop doorways, touching the shining windows as they passed, leaving fingerprints as mementos. Yet no one shooed them away or looked upon them unkindly, not the shop owners who came out afterward with spritzer bottles of ammonia water nor the ample pedestrians whose bulk served as hiding places for the smaller children. The adult world was benevolent, even when a child forgot to say *scusi*. It was that sort of a day.

Alex could not support spending the whole day sitting in his office in Foligno and was taking an afternoon off. In addition, he had a *lettera raccomandata* to collect at the central post office. The notice in his mailbox was clear, he must sign for the letter himself. The police, he recalled, were always sending out *lettere raccomandate*, and until today he'd had no idea how annoying they could be. The return address was unknown to him, some place in Valle d'Aosta. He decided not to open it until he was seated with a coffee in front of him.

A waiter standing outside the Pasticceria Sandri recognized Cenni as he approached and pointed to a desirable table to the right of the front door, although there were plenty of tables to be had without undue influence. The city of chocolate was not yet one of the great tourist attractions of Italy, which for Cenni was clearly to its advantage. He could still enjoy a quiet stroll down Corso Vannucci and find an empty table in his favorite café, where he would read his letter at his leisure without encountering the icy stare of an impatient tourist waiting for his seat. He nodded *yes* to the waiter and ordered his coffee with an extra kick, a *doppio corretto*.

The contents of the *lettera raccomandata* were two sheets of fine linen bond, written on one side only, an extravagant use of paper for an Italian, he reflected. He didn't recognize the handwriting, but he admired it immediately. The letters were beautifully formed, long and slanting to the right, without any display of squiggles, flourishes, or smiley faces. He settled down to read, curious to know who had wasted four euros to send a letter that might easily have been posted for fifty cents. It was written in English.

My dear Dottore,

How deeply disappointing for you when they sent me to a sanatorium and not to a prison for the criminally insane, as I hear from my father you had urged. It's a very nice sanatorium too, with lovely views of the surrounding mountains. An excess of fresh air, I find, but then northerners have such a fetish for the outdoors, even to bringing it inside. The food is a bit excessive as well, very heavy in the use of cream and butter. You'd hardly know me. I've gained five pounds in the five short weeks I've been here. But, thank God, it won't be very long before I return home and resume a healthy Mediterranean diet. The Board of Governors met yesterday about my case, at the insistence of my father and with the intercession of Giorgio and the PM. Giorgio's political fortunes have changed for the better, Italian politics being what they are.

My psychiatrist agrees with my father that my mental state has improved dramatically. Dr. Missani attributes my confusion after Fulvio's death to the stress of my mother's suicide and to the knowledge that Fulvio was responsible for the murder of my dear cousin. The board agreed, and I will be home again in a few short weeks.

I wanted to be the one to give you my good news and to suggest that we let bygones be bygones, as the English might say. We Italians are too much driven to vengeance,

but perhaps the two of us can break that cycle. I forgive
you, Alex (may I call you Alex?)—I forgive you, even
now when I hear from my dear father that you are still
working to have me imprisoned, and from Foligno of all
places. How very impolitic of you, Alex, and how very
unkind! We're all better off without Fulvio, particularly
his wife. He was a coward and a bully. Giorgio tells me
that he not only beat Grazia, he enjoyed it! He was also a
murderer, as the magistratura clearly ruled, but then I
don't suppose I need remind you of that.

Giorgio has asked me to marry him and I've accepted,
so we'll be spending much of our time in Rome, but
we'll often visit Perugia, where, no doubt, we will meet
from time to time. (The position of director of the Galleria Nazionale is still vacant. Giorgio and I expect to add
considerably to its collection of old masters. I thought
acquisition of Judith Slaying Holofernes, the one currently in the Naples museum, would be a good beginning.) I certainly hope we do meet again, Alex, and that
when we do, we'll greet one another as friends or, at the
very least, friendly enemies.

Lest I forget, please offer once again my sincerest
apologies to Sergeant Antolini. I don't know what got
into me! A bientot,

                                          Artemisia.

Two sheets of finely scripted bitchiness, Alex concluded, as
he folded the pages and put them back into the envelope, the
writing of a calculating, manipulative psychopath, rubbing in
his demotion to Foligno under the cover of extending the
olive branch. Translation: Fuck you.

Genine had advised him just last week that the count was
hoping Artemisia would be home soon. At least that was what

Sophie Orlic had told the sergeant when she'd appeared at the Assisi station to apply for a *soggiorno* for her daughter. It was exactly what he would have expected of Umberto Casati, an arranged marriage for his psychopath daughter with the very rich Zangarelli. After marrying a count's daughter—a beautiful one at that—Zangarelli would finally become a Knight of Malta, and Umberto Casati would benefit in countless ways, money being his first object.

His grandmother had been right; Fulvio was at home on Good Friday. Cenni had visited Grazia a few days after Fulvio's funeral, unofficially, with Hanna tagging along, and Grazia had sworn that Fulvio had been at home until well after six o'clock. But by then, Fulvio had been positively identified through his DNA as the father of Rita's child, and there was nothing Cenni could do to convince Grazia that her husband had *not* murdered Rita. He had reported his conclusion to the questore and to Antonio Priuli and was overruled by both. Since Artemisia had feigned madness, if she were tried for one murder, or for both, she would never be convicted. Carlo had emphasized that point repeatedly, adding, "I can think of far worse assignments than Foligno. I called in a whole lot of favors to keep you in Umbria, Alex. Show a little gratitude!"

Alex's own reasoning had followed suit. Artemisia's mother, about whom he still felt remorse, would have preferred it this way; it was obvious now that she had protected her daughter throughout her life, and afterward. And Grazia. What would she have wanted? Cenni thought for only a moment. It didn't matter what she would have wanted. Artemisia was right, Grazia was better off without Fulvio. Yet, despite Carlo's arguments and his own reasoning, he couldn't let it go. He had filed a protest with Priuli. He wasn't surprised that Priuli had rejected it or that Umberto Casati knew of it, Italian politics being what they are! Perhaps he should have listened to Greci and kept quiet.

In the future, he would stick to the bare essentials of policing, keeping terrorists at bay and young children safe from pedophiles. It was a chaotic world, and he had no hope of imposing order where it was not wanted. What in this world made sense anyway? Four weeks ago, Sergeant Antolini had given Piero the brush-off, and Piero had stopped talking to him. This morning, Piero had called to chat, ostensibly to discuss Perugia's disastrous relegation to the Second Division, but after hemming and hawing, he'd mentioned offhandedly that he had taken Elena home to meet his mother. And Lucia, fired by Umberto Casati as a gossip, was now working for Alex's grandmother, for whom gossip was meat and drink. Rita's money was to be split between the Canadian and her uncle—a million each, after lawyers' fees. According to Genine, the Canadian had gone off with a waiter from Assisi to map the Medieval world.

Artemisia was the winner. She'd marry Zangarelli and reign supreme over the Galleria Nazionale. If she could convince Naples to sell its *Judith*, Alex had no doubt she'd send him a special invitation to its unveiling. And he'd go, too. This was not the end, not by a long shot. Sophie was now living with Umberto Casati, perhaps even sleeping in his bed, and he no longer cared. He had another blonde to contend with.

Sunday was Renato's investiture as bishop of Urbino, and Alex was still grappling with the question of whether to take Genine to the ceremony. If he did, it would be tantamount to a formal declaration. Just then, in the middle of his musings, a young boy, flying low as a dive-bomber, banged into his table, knocking over his third *doppio corretto*. Alex concluded that it was time to head for Gubbio. He handed the torn pieces of the *lettera raccomandata* to the waiter—"for the trash, *per favore*"— dropped a few coins on the table, and got up to leave. It was that sort of a day.

Bread of Angels

THE SUNDAY OF Renato's investiture as Bishop of Urbino had arrived warm and heavily perfumed after two days of downpouring rain. Spring floated through the partially open car windows, carrying with it the loamy effluence of freshly plowed earth and the occasional whiffs of apple and peach blossoms. His mother and grandmother had declared a truce for the day, his mother taking the front passenger seat and his grandmother sitting in the back. He would have preferred it the other way around as his mother had a habit of squealing every time he passed another car, but that morning she was busy talking about Renato's new home, an eighteenth-century palace full to the brim with gold plate, and had failed to notice that he was passing four cars in a row. The blood rushed to his head when he swung back to his side of the road just a few feet ahead of an oncoming truck. He looked back in his rearview mirror at the flash of high beams from the Fiat Punto that now trailed behind and caught his grandmother's eye. She smiled, he hoped in complicity. But at other times when he looked back, he could see her staring out the car window, a look of solemnity on her face. He wondered what she was thinking. She was proud of her grandsons—they both knew that—and he had always marveled at the ease with which she had accepted

Renato's decision to give his life to a God whose existence she had always denied. But even today, twenty years later, Alex still struggled against his brother's decision.

A few kilometers before the exit for Urbino, he could see the tall round towers of the Palazzo Ducale, shining golden in the morning sun. Alex loved Perugia, but he also had the sensibility of an aesthetician and so had to acknowledge the superior beauty of Urbino, a city he had decided in self-confident brashness at the age of eighteen was the most beautiful in Italy. He had yet to change his mind. He loved the elegance and harmony of its rose-colored brick buildings, its lofty seat high above rolling hills of vines and olive trees, the pellucid light that bathed the city in a voluptuous pink even in the darkest days of winter. His fondness for Urbino came at least in part from his great admiration of its most famous son. The gentle confluence of harmony and sheer luminosity that marked the works of Raphael were, he reflected, simply a manifestation of the painter's birthplace.

After dropping his mother and grandmother in front of the cathedral, an accomplishment achieved only by identifying himself as a policeman five times in five minutes, he parked below the city and began the long climb back up. He had time before the ceremonies would begin, and he walked slowly, pacing himself, enjoying the warm sun on his face and the chattering of the new communicants, their parents, grandparents, siblings, aunts, uncles, cousins, friends, as they wound their way upward toward the cathedral. The little girls, preening in their flowered coronets and white bridal communion dresses—silks, tulles, organzas, poplins—skipped and danced, twisted and turned, to their own delight and that of their admirers. The boys, somber-faced, embarrassed, hair slicked back, dark Sunday serge suits, white armbands, dawdled behind until pushed forward by gentle nudges. He remembered the day that he and Renato had received the Eucharist for the first time; he had been as awkward and as reticent as the boys he watched today. Renato had been different, though, eager and very serious. He had even warned Alex that morning not to brush his teeth in case he might swallow some toothpaste.

A woman and a young girl walked directly in front of him. The girl, slight for her seven years, was always a few steps ahead of the woman, but never too far ahead. Every few minutes she would turn around to reassure herself that the woman was still following behind. The girl had an anxious, pinched expression, as though she were holding in her happiness. Her dress was more simply cut and shorter than those of the other girls, of a lawn material, gossamer in its fineness. She carried a prayerbook in her right hand. He couldn't see the woman's face but her carriage was severe and unbending. Another communicant from across the road called out the girl's name. "Rita!" Alex gave a start, but it was a common enough name for girls in Umbria. Rita waved back and, distracted for just that moment, she tripped on a loose stone and dropped her prayerbook. It narrowly missed falling into one of the many puddles that lined the side of the road. The girl quickly bent and retrieved the book, then looked around to see if the woman had noticed. The woman, now alongside the girl, grabbed her roughly and shook her, before taking the prayerbook into her own hands.

It was one of those small moments of parental harshness that we witness every day without paying close attention, but Rita Minelli's diary had made Alex aware of the impact of the smallest gesture, whether good or bad, on the human heart. He didn't know if the woman were even the girl's mother; perhaps she was just a friend or a distant relative, but he was sure that when the girl remembered her First Holy Communion later in life, the scene that had just taken place would recur.

And then, as sometimes happens in our quiet moments of reflection, he realized that less than an hour ago he had acted just as harshly to his mother. She had been talkative and happy in the car ride from Perugia to Urbino, thrilled that one of her sons was soon to be a bishop. She had prattled on endlessly about Renato's new residence with its forty rooms, its fifty gold dinner plates, its renowned centerpiece, Raphael's *Madonna of Urbino*.

He had taken pleasure in puncturing each of his mother's assertions. The rooms were unheated, the gold plates were unsanitary and unpleasant to eat from, the Raphael was a false attribution, so that even his grandmother had jumped to her defense. It was true that his mother was a snob but she loved her sons, and not once could Alex remember her shaking him or his brother as the woman in gray silk had just shaken the young Rita—certainly not for an infraction as minor as dropping a prayerbook. Well, just once, he remembered, and then until his teeth hurt, but that was on the day he had dared his twin to jump from the roof of the hay barn in the back of his grandparents' farmhouse. Renato had broken his tibia in the fall!

Every seat in the cathedral was filled. People were standing in the back and along the side aisles when Alex walked up the center aisle to take his seat next to his grandmother in the right front pew. The bishop-elect's family were the honored guests of the diocese along with a contingent of priests, monsignors, and bishops, the latter dressed in purple cassocks and birettas, all waiting for Renato to make his entrance. The Apostolic Nuncio walked first onto the altar, splendid in white and gold brocade, his slender neck weighed down by a jeweled miter. When he bent his head, Alex could see that the miter was lined in scarlet silk. He was followed by two bishops, also dressed in heavily embroidered vestments, their white miters banded in gold. Renato came last, a humble contrast in unadorned white linen and crimson skullcap. Earlier that day when his mother had sung her praises of Renato, she had done so with a measure of grievance; the future bishop had refused her offer of a chasuble and stole in silk damask with symbols of the cross, sheaves of wheat, and tongues of fire, all hand-stitched in brilliant threads of red and gold. His miter, she told them, would be plain white, no decoration at all, his crosier a simple shepherd's staff, and the pectoral cross that he had chosen was silver rather than gold. Even worse, he had refused to assemble the usual court of archbishops and bishops on the altar to assist in his Episcopal ordination. The altar would be empty, she complained, just the three anointing bishops, a deacon, and two acolytes to assist at the mass. Alex could only be grateful that Renato had spared them a ceremony of many hours in length; he wondered, though, how he had pulled it off. The Church loved its pomp and circumstance.

The ceremony of investiture harmonized gracefully with the celebration of high mass. After the gospel, the Apostolic Nuncio and, in turn, the two assisting bishops, laid hands on Renato and intoned the words of ordination: *So now pour out upon this chosen one that power which is from you, the governing Spirit whom you gave to your beloved Son, Jesus Christ, the Spirit given by him to the holy apostles, who founded the Church in every place to be your temple for the unceasing glory and praise of your name.* As Alex watched the remaining rituals—the anointing with holy chrism, the bestowal of the symbols of episcopacy: the miter, the crosier, the ring, the pectoral cross, and, finally, Renato's enthronement in the bishop's chair—he shared his brother's joy. But joy is ephemeral, and as the congregation rose in one body to cheer their new bishop and the bells rang out over the city, another less dignified image of his brother sprang to mind, of that day years ago when Renato, in cassock, had jumped over the fence and onto the football field to celebrate Perugia's defining win over Lazio. Renato had returned in triumph holding aloft Vannini's left boot. Alex doubted that the Bishop of Urbino would have time to attend football matches, and a lump rose in his throat as he resumed his seat with the rest of the congregation to await the homily.

The Cenni twins had certain characteristics in common. A talent for diplomacy was one, a tendency to intractability, another. How these dissimilar traits met in harmony in the same person was a mystery to all who knew the twins, but they did. Renato, who delighted the archbishop with charm and tact, also tempted his wrath on many occasions. When Renato had first come to Urbino, he had begun the practice of letting girls serve at mass. A girl was serving today, in fact. He had also adopted the habit of delivering very short and very pointed homilies from the communion rail. "A priest is of the people, not above them," he had said to the archbishop when asked to explain why he eschewed the pulpit. Apparently, he was not going to change his habits as bishop, Alex thought, as he watched his brother descend from the altar and approach the communion rail. He stood directly across from his family. As the Bishop of Urbino he acknowledged their presence with a shy smile and an unobtrusive wave, and his mother, who had finally managed to contain her weeping, began again.

After thanking those in attendance, Renato spoke directly and simply to the new communicants:

> My dear girls and boys, today is an important day for me and a far more important day for you. Some of you may think that the grandeur of the ceremony that you just witnessed—and which gave me great joy—means that the ordination of a bishop is a more important event to God than the sacrament of Communion. It is not. The most

important event in your Christian lives is the one that you will partake of today, as it was for me more than thirty-two years ago. When you were infants, your parents brought you into the Church through the sacrament of Baptism, but they did this without your knowledge or consent. Today you embrace Christianity with full knowledge and an open heart. Today you give yourselves fully to Jesus Christ. In the last month you learned from the *suore* that when you take the host into your hands, you hold the living body and blood of Christ, that when you ingest the host, you become one with Christ in love. And this is true and important and sacred, but there is another and an ever greater lesson that you must take into your hearts today and remember always. Each time that you receive the body and blood of Christ—and I hope you will do it often—you are bidden by Christ to become one in love, one in tolerance, one in kindness with all women and all men, wherever they may live, whatever language they may speak, whatever religion they may practice, whatever the color of their skin. My children, there are no exceptions. To receive Christ in love, you must love all humanity. Today I ask that each of you, each boy and girl who is about to receive the Holy Eucharist for the first time, choose another from the congregation—a stranger—to come forward with you to the altar, to share the gift of Jesus, so you may always remember that your commitment to love God carries with it the equally joyous commitment to love all of his children. God bless you.

The intense whispering that Alex could hear behind him, lasting throughout the Liturgy of the Eucharist, suggested that Renato's invocation to the new communicants to join with a stranger at the altar was neither expected nor planned for. He remembered how carefully the *suore* had drilled his Communion class, incessantly, for weeks before the event. The boys were to march down the aisle on the left and the girls on the right, each positioned according to height. That year he had grown faster than Renato, and the sisters, in rigorous application of their self-made rules, had placed him at the back and Renato in the middle. Despite the twins' vociferous complaints, they had received the Eucharist separated from each other. Alex was confident that in the three decades which had since passed, the communion drill hadn't changed. Perhaps, he thought, Renato is indulging his wicked sense of humor while finally getting back at the *suore*. Whatever the case, his brother was certainly flexing his newly acquired Episcopal muscles in disturbing the good sisters' time-honored routine.

As Renato and the Apostolic Nuncio descended from the altar, each holding a ciborium of communion wafers, the chords of *Panis Angelicus* swelled the Cathedral and the children started down the aisle. The girl in the gossamer lawn dress, little Rita, led on the right. Even down the length of the cathedral, Alex could sense her distress as she moved slowly and hesitantly up the aisle. The boy on the left was well ahead. As soon as the boys stopped, each one positioning himself next to a pew, Alex realized what the *suore* intended the new communicants to do. Each child would go forward to the communion rail with the person at the end of the pew. He could step aside, he thought, but then his grandmother would have to step aside as well. As Rita drew closer, she looked up at him with a timid, expectant smile. He remembered clearly Renato's words—*You are bidden by Christ to become one in love, one in tolerance, one in kindness*. Alex smiled back, stepped out of the pew, and took her small hand in his.

THE END

Acknowledgments

My editor, Laura Hruska.

My siblings, Margaret, John, Helen, and Patrick, and my thirteen nieces and nephews, for being there.

My dear friend Laury Magnus, who said when I began searching for character names, "I'm thinking Artemisia," and who suggested that I read Mary Garrard's excellent biography, *Artemisia Gentileschi*, to put flesh on my thoughts of plagiarism, but mostly for her day-to-day encouragement when I first began to write.

My good friends, Cathy Costa, Barbara Fisher, and Kathleen McCann, for their enthusiastic manuscript readings, and Ann Schwartz for her continuing support and advice.

In Assisi, Orland Tanci and Anne Robichaud for introducing us to the real Umbria; Angelo Maccabei, Lani Irwin, and Alan Feltus for the cover photograph; and all of our good friends and neighbors who made us most welcome in the years that we lived in Italy.

The very helpful state, carabinieri, and municipal police, who tirelessly answered my many questions on the workings of the Italian justice system. Any errors, procedural or otherwise, are my own.

And always, Miguel, who asked the questions (and answered many of them) while I struggled with Italian, and who serves as the model for the best parts of Alessandro Cenni.